"Trouble, Colonel."

"How big?"

"Fifty-point-nine kilos. You want her stunned or stone cold?"

"Neither, right away. Will she startle badly if we walk in?"

"Yeah. Pulse and respiration say she's on the edge of something pretty crude. So we'll tippy-toe. Casual like we own the place. Just let me lead. Unless you're wearing body armor."

"By all means, lead." She could feel his eyes appraising her singlesuit and the shape of her flesh beneath it.

Patty drew her repulsor, checked the charge and the load. After forty-five seconds, she told him: "Key the door."

He hit the latch.

She struck the heavy oak panel with her shoulder and ricocheted diagonally across the foyer, flying horizontally about a foot above the simulated flagstones. Landing on her hip, one knee, and an elbow, partly concealed by the foot of the archway into the lounge room, she swept a sixty-degree field of fire.

At the center of which was a blonde. She was trying to stand erect, but one hand was clawed into her flat belly. The other held a Schlicter rail gun.

"Friends-no-fire," Patty called. She clacked her own gun flat down on the flagstones—but kept a hand on it. That left her face, spine, and shooting hand exposed.

The woman spent ten seconds trying to raise the Schlicter above the level of her own hips, then gave up. The weapon thudded on the carpeting. She sagged onto the cue-form sofa and hugged her knees.

"Turn it ... off!" she cried.

DAVID DRAKE
THOMAS T. THOMAS

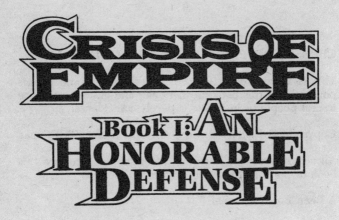

CRISIS OF EMPIRE
Book I: AN HONORABLE DEFENSE

BAEN BOOKS

CRISIS OF EMPIRE: AN HONORABLE DEFENSE

Copyright © 1988 by David Drake and Thomas T. Thomas

A Baen Books Original

Baen Publishing Enterprises
260 Fifth Avenue
New York, N.Y. 10001

First printing, November 1988

ISBN: 0-671-69789-7

Cover art by Paul Alexander

Printed in the United States of America

Distributed by
SIMON & SCHUSTER
1230 Avenue of the Americas
New York, N.Y. 10020

*The populace cannot understand the bureaucracy;
it can only worship national idols.*

*—George Bernard Shaw,
"Maxims for Revolutionists"*

Chapter 1

Taddeuz Bertingas: CHANGING THE GUARD

"FLASHPAD AURCLUSTGOV EYESONLY SUPRACODE010101 HANDBREAK."

"Oh, Chrysostom!" groaned Taddeuz Bertingas, Deputy Director of Communications for Aurora Cluster, honoring the patron saint of preachers and political speechwriters.

Saint John Golden-Mouth—"Chrysostom," in the ancient vernacular—had been ecumenical patriarch of Constantinople, 3407-3347 B.P. The saint had gone to dust before, probably, the first artificial intelligences were awakened on Earth. And long before, certainly, the titled muffinheads of Central Center, with the wax still soft on their patents of nobility, had learned to break into the military code circuits for sending Anniversary greetings to their boozing buddies in the hinterlands.

To deal with messages like this, the Palace poodles routinely beepered out the entire Communications section and put them on midnight alert. This coded message would be as stupid and inconsequential as every other they'd received. The Plalace staff had even tracked down Bertingas himself—who had made a point, in past weeks, of keeping his sleeping arrangements particularly vague, as a privilege of his rank. Bertingas's aide, Gina Rinaldi, could have handled this "crisis" one-handed, or at least kept its electrons jelled in the in-bin until the duty staff came to work after breakfast.

"Gina?" he called through the open door, toward the cubicularium nearest his corner office. "Could you give me a hand with this? The autoscribe seems to be defective. . . ."

The hum of the bullpen out there, the click of keyboards, the clink of crockery, and the buzz of barely subdued mutiny—brought on by being rousted before dawn—hushed immediately.

"Sure thing, Tad," his assistant replied.

"No, she can't," snapped the artificial intelligence device on his desk. "I'm holding a top-secret message and she's not—"

"Shut up. You're broken," Bertingas said, disconnecting the AID from the message pad. There were times when dumb circuitry had its attractions.

Gina Rinaldi stepped briskly through the doorway and came around to his side of the desk. Without asking, she drew up a chair, smoothed her tight skirt over her hips and under her thighs, and sat beside him. She pulled her chair up to the message pad, rubbing one slender, nylon-sheathed knee against his, tucking her slim shoulder under his arm, pushing her long black hair and the scent of it into his face. Gina pretended not to notice his reaction, but she was smiling to herself.

"That's impressive," she said, nodding at the message heading.

With quick finger strokes, she called up Bertingas' logon code and authority access as D.D.ofC. Then she began breaking the number groups.

Gina was a Deoorti haploid female. Bertingas had never met a haploid male nor any of the diploids, but she definitely had the Human phenotype. One who did not know the signs would hardly guess, in passing her on the street, that Gina had a totally alien genotype. But the signs were there: The ratio of her body mass to its volume was too small, indicating a stabilized-sodium metabolism. Her skin color was too coppery, although in some artificial lights it shone a bright carotene yellow. Her skin was too cool to the touch and dry, like supple leather, although she was smooth, warm, and Humanly damp in the right places.

The real giveaway was Gina's face: too broad, slightly triangular, with the eyes too widely set, and too large. Her supraorbital ridges and the eyebrows masking them were too prominent and curved too far down at the sides, tracking almost vertically across her temples. The eyes themselves were black buttons, depthless, opaque, like pieces of heavily leaded radglass.

Gina had an intuitive psychotype. She was a pattern reader and a flex builder. Her talent was cutting through the evasions, distractions, and false distinctions of Human speech, winnowing out the absolute meanings and acting on them. She was an optimizer, not a maximizer, and felt at home in multi-valued systems. Given a problem, she could always find a workable solution—and for that talent alone Bertingas valued her highly.

As a tribute to her skills, Gina Rinaldi had risen in the Human-dominated Communications Department, earning her own cubicularium and the right to use at least a piece of her own last name, not just a number, as a personal logon code.

Now, under her hands, the flashpad message from Central Center came clear:

"To the Honorable Deirdre Sallee,
Senator, Governor of Aurora,
Chair to the Subcommittee on
Trade and Commodity Transports,
Natatrix and Electrix Supremator,

*Holder in Fief of Ombud, Gareth, and
Galilee Green,*

"Greetings:

*"Regret to inform you that this date,
Earth reference 12 November 5341 post Pacte, at
ten-hundred hours, His Excellency Stephen VI ten
Holcomb, Hereditary High Secretary to the Pact Council in Absentia, was assassinated in chambers. Surviving members of his Gentlemen of the Bath are now
under extradition orders, per Kona Tatsu directive
12/11/41-328AAA.*

*"Roderick, Heir to the Chair, is now reported safe
at Bartleby House. Regent nominateurs are assem-
bling to form the new government in his minority.
Proto Council requires your confirming nomination
to be registered immediately.*

*"Proto Council further requires that additional
signals of loyalty from all administrative and military
officers and significant representatives of trade in
Aurora Cluster shall be transmitted to Central Center no later than 20 November 5341.*

"Seriously suggest you comply soonest, Dee-Dee.

> *"Cordially,*
> *"Avalon Boobur,*
> *Chamberlain and Chief,*
> *Kona Tatsu"*

Bertingas let out a low whistle. Gina turned her
head, putting her lips only centimeters from his. She
raised one incredible eyebrow at him.

"Killed the High Secretary, have they?" he said.

That was just to make conversation. What was
really going through his head was a fading vision of
his next planned walking tour, a summertime, ram-
bling hike through the high country beyond the Palisades. For the last nine years this had been his vacation
from the arid details of Department work: to get
among the pathless trees and rocks and breathe clean,
unfiltered air again. Like a landscape dissolving in

heat haze, he saw that vision dissipate. The shockwaves from this assassination would tie him up for weeks—and he had been due to go on leave in two days. Damn all fools!

Gina kept a respectful silence in the presence of an EYESONLY AURCLUSTGOV. She may not technically have been a full Pact citizen, as few aliens—and none that Bertingas knew personally—were, but she was still a contract/casual in the Department and had some official standing.

"Killed the High Secretary," he repeated, still thinking about green grass. "And now they're pressuring our new lady governor to take sides. Her and everyone else . . . So far just you and I and our little clockwork friend here"—he tapped the silenced AID—"know about it. Until, that is, we send this up to the Puzzle Palace. . . ."

Levering himself with a hand upon Gina's slight but preternaturally strong shoulder, he rose out of his chair and moved toward the window. Before he got there, something from the message tugged at Bertingas's attention. He turned, bent down, and peered at the crystal display tube.

" 'Dee-Dee'! From the chief spook and secret busybody? That's *too* delicious!"

Smiling wickedly, Bertingas turned back to the dark glass of the window, which looked out from the ninety-ninth floor of Government Block. Below him, the patterned lights of Meyerbeer twinkled and dimmed under a sky that was turning silver-gray. Beyond them lay the deeply shadowed grounds of the Cluster Governor's official residence and picnic park, the Palace.

Meyerbeer. Named for Giacomo Meyerbeer, a German composer of French operas with an Italian first name. Someone out of the eighteenth century—old-style reference, of course—when differences among people were measured by the languages they spoke and the gods they worshipped. Sometimes, but not always, by the color of their skins. And not, as now, by the atomic structure of their tissues or other pseudoplasm and the number of their fingers or pseudopods. The irony of it—hanging such a cosmopolitan name on a backwater town in a small administrative cluster of only thirty planets—seldom failed to amuse, and embitter, Taddeuz Bertingas.

He folded his hands behind his back. Gina folded her hands on the desk. The AID burbled over an injunctive DO-loop.

If Deirdre Sallee and her pack of Central Center playmates had had the good grace to get here a few months, instead of just a few days, before the High Secretary, Stephen the unlamented VIth, had the bad grace to get himself dead, then Taddeuz Bertingas might have been able to *make* something of this situation. As her official Director of Cluster Communications, Sallee would undoubtedly have appointed some adenoidal, senatorial, hereditarily useless son of a twitch. If she had done that sooner rather than later, Bertingas would by now have placed his collection of ingratiatingly useful little strings and hooks in the man. Together, with himself directing, they certainly would have figured a way to profit from the secret, EYESONLY knowledge that had come in on the flashpad.

Now, however, with no dummy to front for him, Bertingas could think of nothing better than to reseal and rescramble the message, then send it over to the receptor AID at the Palace. Except, of course, he would bump his holdings in Haiken Maru to the limit of his credit line, as soon as the translite market opened this morning. . . . Oh, yes, the little fish would be schooling now.

Politics is the art of timing. Bertingas had missed his opportunities—through no fault of his own!—by a few months. Maybe only a few weeks. Galling!

"Well, Gina," he said from the window. "Zip up the codes on that and transfer it to the Palace. Let's see how long their new TaskMaster AID takes to break it and work out the implications, hey?"

"Yes, sir." Her fingers went to work on the pad, but her face and those incredible eyes remained turned toward Bertingas.

"Now, to do what we're paid for . . . How much do we have in the biobanks on H.E. Stephen VI? Any recent holopix?"

"We have those cibatint separations from the last Birthday Romp. Archive quality, not presentation quality, but we can enhance them. They all show that endearing but lopsided grin. Not right for the obits. Can be touched up. We also have about forty megabits of synthesized quotes from his various speeches and encyclicals."

"What are those good for?"

"Insomnia."

"Well. See if you can weave them into some kind of life statement. You know the thing. 'Shining star of a 1,200-year dynasty leading Humanity—and the other races—in an unbroken dynamism of this and that, blip and blah.' Just let it roll."

"Yes, sir."

"And tell the lab techs not to emphasize that lower lip of his when they resurrect the holos. You remember the flak we got, during the Fourth Investiture, about that 'visible dribble' in the close-ups? The boys have to keep everything fuzzy, sentimental, gooey. They know the drill. Can't let our sense of realism and historical perspective get the better of ourselves."

"No, sir, I mean, yes, sir."

"Good then. Well . . . Where's my coffee?"

"Right away, sir." Gina swiveled in the chair, exposing a deep flash of well-remembered thigh for him, and slipped out of the room. A good girl. Smart, efficient, respectful, almost Human. But not quite, thank God.

Four minutes and counting.

In his mind's eye, Bertingas could see the serial processors of the Palace AID doing a collective hiccup over the news in that flashpad message. He was a realist and understood that the number of taps and holds and gimmes hooked into that multiphase brain probably equaled the number of politically active interests in the cluster plus ten percent. That made the Palace brain and its grapevine a serious competitor with Bertingas's own Department as an information resource. Leaky but effective.

That's why he had long ago arranged for all important messages from the Hyperwave Satellite Network to be channeled through his office first.

Bertingas and his soon-to-be named boss, the official D.ofC., were in charge of both the medium and the message. Their specialty was basic macloohanism: a mixture of psychology and technology. They were charged with interpreting the wishes of the Cluster Governor and presenting them as dicta, perceptions, and personal messages that would be seen, heard, and read correctly by the public. Bertingas and the D.ofC. also maintained the flashpad and other comm links of the government, internal and external, public and private, confidential and cooperative. The Department operated on many levels.

Of course Bertingas, his colleagues, and his various superiors debated themes and techniques within the discipline of communications. The major division was between those who thought of the public as a passive audience, credulous sheep, content to accept any perception the medium chose to push. They believed people basically wanted to be entertained. On the other side were those communications practitioners who believed the public was an active force, aware, making perceptual choices, questioning any gap between words and actions. They believed people basically wanted to be informed.

These two camps, deeply polarized with time, had become known as the Imageurs and the Veracitors.

Bertingas prided himself on being a member of the Veracitor school. Every appointed D.ofC. he'd ever had—it seemed to be a requirement of the job—had been an Imageur.

"Equals amateur," as the old maxim said.

Imageurs were always weak on the theory, fuzzy about budgets and schedules, and unconcerned with the long-term futurely effect. They were quite definite, however, on the effect they wanted to create—any effect that would please the Cluster Governor.

However, the technology that the Department had to work with was complex, and that required a steady head in the D.D.ofC.'s slot. A Veracitor like Taddeuz Bertingas.

For example, the Shadow Box, an advanced form of datalog repeater was a cantankerous system to operate and maintain. It had to be, inevitably, to contain at any one instant a few hundred terawords of Human and alien conversation, trade and trysting, spying and skullduggery, gossip and knowledge. Not to mention the megabit blocks, in picform, of Human and alien faces smiling, frowning, smooching, schnoodling, and mugging that went along with the conversation.

The Hyperwave Satellite Network, however, was beyond even a Veracitor's understanding. It took an imaginative theoretical physicist to deal with a device which sent message-carrying laser beams among specific spatial points in the Aurora Cluster and the 4,000 other worlds of the Pact. The network delivered those beams through hyperspace by firing them into the ring described by a rotating micro black hole.

The messages followed the same wormholes through which all of Pact civilization had grown outward from the Human focus of planet Earth, in Sol System. The civilization and its political/cultural web had expanded, not through the lightyears of realspace, but through the sinusoidal adjacencies of hyperspace. A traveler's mass was compressed, collapsed and popped out of existence in this spacetime, and where it first reappeared—that was the "nearest neighbor." The Pact's clusters were, physically and administratively, star groups reached through the mass-jump of hypertravel.

Messages modulated on a photon beam and shot through the center of a rotating singularity could follow those adjacencies in space. Sometimes, however, when the beam bent back on itself, the messages traveled in time as well as space. Then the wonk would hit the widget, and technicians would be called in to align the beams to a little more than Normal Government Tolerances.

Each black hole, also, had to be mass-tuned to its distant counterparts, and that required a numbers-cruncher extraordinaire. As Bertingas understood it, you had to bleed the hole with antimatter, keeping it just hungry enough that the photon spread from the message beam wasn't constantly filling it. Otherwise it flipped over and detuned. Or whatever . . . More tricky work.

Compared to the problems of nursing and feeding the Hyperwave Satellite Network, maintaining the Freevid planetary cable medium was idiot's play. After all, the 'Vid was just a null-cyber network of optic fibers and linosite lasers. The Department used it mostly for entertainment, anyway.

Ten minutes and counting.

Bertingas double-checked his timetick against the AID's mindless quartz clock circuit. He considered plugging its voice loops back in and snooping on how the news of Stephen's assassination was progressing throughout the capital. First he would have to put up with the AID's electronic tongue-lashing about the rituals of secrecy. He was definitely not in the mood for that. He began to drum his fingers on the table.

Gina brought his coffee without a word and left. From the bullpen, the normal drone of working bodies—some carbon based, most not—had risen to an audible level. Everyone out there was still waiting to be told what the midnight alarm was all about. Meanwhile they chatted, groused, and fiddled with old busywork.

Twelve minutes. Two minutes later than the last time he looked.

Bertingas's own professional expertise had been with the Baseform Scatter Platter. That was the cluster's optical, encyclopedic data base, accessed by fiber cables, taking feeds from the HSN. Physically, the Platter was located in Meyerbeer—down in the basement of this Block, to be exact. Bertingas had started there, ten years ago, as a record assistant with a shiny new badge in informational sets from the Central Center Universalis Organum. A squeaky little read/write datahead. From that job, he had progressed through coordinator for a whole sector of knowledge, vector chief, and finally director of the Platter Base, before becoming the D.D.ofC. Ten long years to rise one hundred floors in the same building. The careers of Veracitors moved slowly.

Ping!

The comm circuits in the AID made that special sound when the call came from the Palace. Twelve minutes and twenty-three seconds. So much for the superiority of the multipath brain.

"Bertingas speaking."

"This is the major-domo. Her Excellency has called an emergency extended staff meeting for seven o'clock. Can you make it?" It was the voice of Multiple Mind itself, and for once no drawl demodulated its synthetic demeanor. What a strain that must be!

"Of course," Bertingas answered. "Morning or evening?"

"Umm." Tick-tock. "Morning, of course."

"Thank you. Usual place?"

"The Golden Pavilion, of course."

"Thank you. Please tell Milady Sallee that, as Deputy Director of Communications, I shall be honored to attend for the Department. Unless, of course, she wishes to take this opportunity to name her Director . . . ?"

"Umm. Noted." Click.

Damn! The meeting was in half an hour. No time to get back to his apartment and freshen up. Did he have a clean shirt in the lower drawer? Was there a charge on his shaver?

Bertingas did the best he could, even using spit and a towlette to worry a scuff on the toe of one uniform boot. The limp collar of his tunic and that bit of frayed silver braid, he would would just have to cover with panache and, in a pinch, an artful turn of his head. Such was the life of a career bureaucrat.

He took the electrostatic drop tube, signaled it to repulse mode, and lifted to the level of the airlip. The charge in the tube had the expected effect of beating a few grams of residual dust out of his clothes. Bertingas arrived in a small cloud of smokelike particles, which he fanned away with his hands.

Government Block was an equilateral pentahedron, modeled on a famous series of tombs in Old Egypt, an obscure Earth reference. Bertingas often thought it served the same purpose in Aurora Cluster politics. Because the building had no true roof—the 150th floor was a single room, the office of the Planetary Administrator, with a fantastic view from four sides—aircars had to land on a narrow shelf jutting out from the east face at Floor 123.

The morning glare was already strong on the white syncrete of the airlip. Bertingas found himself in an impatient queue of officials from several different departments. Evidently it was going to be a big meeting, with lots of aides and sideboys. He noted tunics in the excitant orange of General Services, the aquamarine blue of Water Supply, the brown and red of Energy Supply. His own tunic, the black with gray flashes of Communications, was of course absorbing most of the sunlight. He could feel the sweat working its way down his sides and from his hairline. He imagined his collar tabs wilting even further.

The staff cars hummed up out of the nearby parking complex, lowered onto the lip with a blast of warm air from their ducts—more heat!—loaded and lifted off. It was a mechanical ballet that would not be hurried.

Bertingas should have beeped for his car from the office. Then it might have arrived, on remote, out of turn. Now it was going to come in order behind the —let's see . . . six, seven, nine—true heads of department here on the lip. Deputies who were merely acting head didn't have the same clout.

While he was counting the minutes, multiplying by the sweat trickles he could feel, and dividing by the number of bureaucrats ahead of him in line, a sleek two-seater slid onto the platform under the nose of a seven-place wagon. The bigger car honked imperiously at the smaller one. Evidently the driver couldn't see the unobtrusive pair of gold zigzags, mark of the Kona Tatsu, on the fenders.

The little car popped its offside hatch and a hand pointed back in line, straight at Bertingas.

"Tad! Get in!"

Heads and eyes in the queue turned to look at

him. Bertingas looked at the anonymous white hand. It could only belong to one person.

Straightening his tunic, he ran forward and swung a leg over the airskirting. The interior was chilled and dark, a blessed relief from the glare of the airlip. Before he could pull the hatch down, his friend—maybe his friend this week—Halan Follard was feeding power to the high-side fans and sliding the car off the lip.

Chapter 2

Halan Follard: TRUSTWORTHLESS

Twisting the control yoke through a partial figure-eight, Halan Follard shifted the car's airflow from the high portside fans to the low starboard ones, rocking the body across its center of gravity. The same move also boosted the bow thirty degrees, then dropped it off to the left.

The little aircar made a rolling turn that reversed direction and slid it 500 feet under the pattern of other cars coming onto the Government Block's airlip.

Follard gave himself a tight smile, proud of his mechanical kinesthesia. Then he focused attention on his passenger.

Bertingas was splayed across the seat, panting. His tunic collar was loosened to catch the stream of cool air from the dash. His fingers plucked at the stiff material of the uniform pants, trying to lift it from his perspiring thighs. Follard helped by turning down the air conditioning two more notches and stepping up the blower. The cabin dropped ten degrees in ten seconds and a grin spread slowly across Bertingas's face.

"There are fresh collar tabs in the map box," Follard said. "They should cover for your rank and department."

"Why, thank you," Bertingas said, popping the lid. "But how did you—?"

"Intuition," Follard replied, smiling. A Kona Tatsu Inspector General sometimes had to pass for a member of the middle ranks in the halls of Government Block. Let Bertingas think what he might.

Most of the people in Follard's circle, the outer circle, thought of Taddeuz Bertingas as a harmless fool. Pedantic, foppish, self-centered, soft-centered. A career climber who never would reach the top rung. An innocenti, not a cognoscenti.

The inner circle didn't think of Bertingas at all.

Follard himself thought he detected some steel in the man. Not a lot. A sliver, not a shard. And it was well padded by the attitudes and affectations that anyone would acquire after ten years in Aurora Cluster's Government Block. That sliver was doubly padded, because Bertingas was in the mind-manipulation business. Deluding and self-deluded. He slithered around with the kind of people who make a word mean exactly what they choose it to mean . . . the last Director of Communications, for instance.

Bertingas *was* soft, like this planet.

Of the 4,000 or so Pact worlds, Palaccio was the strangest—but Humans had to luck out just once.

It was a severely oblate globe, squashed like a pumpkin grown on one of the high-gee worlds. In addition to that, Palaccio's axial inclination was nil: the north and south poles were a true ninety degrees from the plane of orbit around the primary. Consequently, there was almost no climatic variation: eternal winter and darkness at the two poles; eternal summer in the broad band around the equator; spring and fall passing through 50 to 70 degrees of latitude north and south.

The planet had a strong magnetosphere, with its magnetic poles coinciding precisely with the rotational axis. So radiation from the local solar wind hardly affected the climate.

Palaccio was larger than Earth—by several diameters. The internal structure, however, was much less dense: silicon and potassium at the core instead of nickel and iron. So the surface gravity was 0.92 gee, making everyone feel good and strong, if a little light-headed.

It was the only planet where the natural ground cover was a mass of tightly packed tendrils which never grew above 4 cm, was invariably an emerald green, and was called "grass." Where every tree was either a stately *Sequoia sempervirens*—perfect for roofbeams and ship's keels—or a spreading, leafy apple tree, complete with ruddy, edible fruit. Where every cliff was columniated marble, topped with your choice of Ionic scrollwork or the Corinthian acanthus-lead pattern. Where the air was as pure as oxygen and nitrogen mixed from cylinders. Where the water was as sweet and flat as fresh-burned hydrogen.

For the Humans, who had discovered this planet—there were no indigenous intelligences—it was a Mediterranean paradise. Hence the name "Palaccio."

For the Pact aliens who had immigrated, it was a hell world.

The sunlight was too bright and the wrong color for delicate alien eyes raised under red giant primaries. The light was too dim for eyes grown in the blue-white actinic glare of brighter stars. Tree pollens irritated delicate membranes or grated in delicate joints. Chlorophyll from the "grass" burned under delicate alien feet. The gee-pull was too strong for spidery alien frames from the moonlets or for gliding membranes from the heavy-gas worlds. The gravity was too weak for robust alien circulatory systems and molecular bonds developed on high-gee worlds. The water lacked essential trace elements necessary to delicate alien metabolisms—or water itself was an alien poison. The microbes that Human settlement had brought attacked everything.

The non-Humans suffered from sores and burns, allergies, aches, falls, sniffles, and fits of homesickness. Quietly, interspecially, the multiple races that congregated with Pact Humans called the planet Porifera, the smelly sponge. Or just "Stinkworld."

However, it was inevitable that Palaccio, being equidistant from the other Aurora worlds, would become a center for government and communications. It was, after all, perfect for Humans.

And so Taddeuz Bertingas—after ten years in a desk job, in a Human-dominated government, on a paradise world, in a cluster with almost no dissidents, not even commercial pirates—was bound to be well-insulated, self-centered, self-deluding, soft-centered, and all the rest.

Well, it was time to wake him up.

"This isn't the way to the Palace," Bertingas said, lifting his head and pushing himself up in the seat.

"No, it isn't. I thought we'd take a little detour. Enjoy some scenery."

"Those are the Palisades. I've seen them—and beyond. Nice car you've got here. Fast. Now, shouldn't we be getting on to that all-hands meeting?"

"Look at the cliff structure," Follard prompted. He tipped the aircar and pointed down through Tad's window. "Huge blocks at the base there, supporting those strong white columns, which in turn support the Uplands Plains . . .

"Or that's the way it seems. But if you look hard, and if you know anything about geology, it's just illusion. The blocks at the bottom support nothing. They've simply broken off from above and landed at the foot of the cliff. The real strength, the native rock of the planet, is hidden by those crumbs of white stone.

"Those columns that we can see," Follard continued, "they support nothing either. They only stand out because the background rock is weathering away. They're simply what's left.

"No, the strength to support the Uplands is not on the face of the cliff, but deep inside, with the native rock and the web of the planet, which we can't see."

"You're trying to tell me something, aren't you?" Bertingas teased. He wore a soft, superior smile which occasionally made Follard want to strike him.

"Call it a parable of the stones," Follard said. "You know the High Secretary's been assassinated?"

"Ahhh . . . No, I didn't. That's terrible. Who did it?"

"Doesn't matter. His friends, retainers, or next of kin. All of the above. None of the above. He had no enemies, so it must have been his friends who did it. As I said, it does not matter. Stephen ten Holcomb is like those white blocks out there. He seems to be the foundation of the Pact. He has told us, in his usual flood of words, that he is the 'binding link' of our political structure—but he binds nothing, supports nothing. He's just a piece of stone that fell down long ago, when his family line happened upon the Secretaryship."

"I see. That explains a lot. Can we go to the Palace now?"

"Listen well, little man," Follard said, intentionally putting a hiss and a rasp into what he called his Inquisitor's voice. "There are others who would like to take the throne at Central Center. They would say they were 'ascending' to the Secretaryship. But you and I know that, from our parable here, they are only pieces of stone, falling where gravity takes them."

"What others? Who are you talking about?" Bertingas sounded petulant, as he would after that "little man" jibe.

"The pillars, the forces that seem to support the Pact. The heads of the commercial conglomerates. The loosely allied cluster commanders. The cluster governors who have been in place too long and are years removed from the give-and-take of any real political arena. Every one of them has a plan, a plot, a daydream that, with luck and help and the right conjunction of forces, he—or she—can step up to the throne. And what would that be? In the context of our parable?"

"Another block of marble, falling off the cliff to land in the rubble heap at the bottom," Bertingas said sullenly. "That heap *does* have a lot to say about who we'll salute, what we'll be doing, how we live, what we believe—"

"Salute, maybe. But when was the last time you changed your socks, let alone your mind, because of something Stephen VI said? He's a peacock on display. A figurehead."

"Possibly. However, he does select the cluster governors and all the rest. They have the real power in our lives."

"Nonsense, Tad. They select themselves. The High Secretary makes about three key appointments a day, just by nodding his head. They merely put themselves in the way of that nod and they're in. That's all."

"You have microphones in this car," Bertingas said loudly. "You're trying to trap me into sedition. Well, it won't work. I'm loyal to the Pact. I'm loyal to the High Secretary, whoever he will be. To Governor Sallee. To the Director of Communications, if and when he's appointed. To the—"

"Why don't you just say you're loyal to the Pact and be done with it?"

"I *am* loyal."

"You can be loyal to our society, can't you, to the ancient forms that make this interspatial empire *work*, without wasting your time or tears on the fools who appear to hold power."

"Eh?"

"The fabric of our society. The daily agreements and transactions that put food on the table, water in the pipes, power in the overhead, and jingle in the pocket. Those are the things that support our lives—the things to remember when the rocks start falling on the cliff face. Put your trust, your loyalty, in the people around you."

"Why is the Inspector General of the Kona Tatsu telling me this? I would have thought it was your business to, ahh, inspire loyalty to the High Secretary. At least here in Aurora. And to his chosen governor."

"That's my field of duty, of course—when the High Secretary is alive and fulfilling his obligations, however competently, to govern. But His Excellency is by now formally couched under marble in the Hall of Ages. The safety of the Heir is in doubt, and strong forces are at work to determine Roderick's affairs once and for all."

"Which forces?" Bertingas sounded genuinely curious.

"Ask yourself who owns or controls half of Aurora Cluster and even more in her nearer neighbors."

"Haiken Maru?"

"Yes, our dominant conglomerate. With a charter for trade only—not to farm freeholds, not to provide banking or other contract services, not to hold administrative office. . . . We all know how closely those charters are monitored."

"You think they will try to influence the succession?"

"Do stones roll downhill? We of the Kona Tatsu believe they will try to *buy* the succession. The only question is, with what coin?"

"Not with money, you mean?"

"Will Haiken Maru influence the political side? Will they maneuver to install an overt innocent—but one of their own choosing and purchase? Or will they support another candidate, one whom they can influence indirectly? Or will they simply launch a war, funded with their considerable resources, to take the throne for their Centrist chairman, Villem Borking?"

"Well, what are they going to do?"

"We don't know yet."

"Oh. So, again, why are you telling me all this?"

"We do know a thing or two," Follard said, maneuvering the aircar away from the cliff and turning toward the Palace precincts. "For instance, who the next Director of Communications will be. His name is Selwin Praise."

"I've heard of him," Bertingas said. "He's part of the entourage that Deirdre Sallee brought from Central Center. On the face of it, he's a Playmate: wealthy family, subsenatorial, no distinction for about five generations. Educated at New Harvard. Took his degree in time-lapse financing. Graduated in the class following Roderick's. Did some freelance banking with the family inheritances until those blew away. Then he went to the Forum and became a drinking buddy, presumably an Old acquaintance. All of that's in the public knowledge."

"Clearly," Bertingas said, "this Praise is the choice to head a sophisticated technological department. Like mine. Thank you."

"What isn't public is that Selwin Praise is a Kona Tatsu light operative. Under direct report to Avalon Boobur."

"I see."

"Normally that would be none of your business. None of mine, either. Trouble is, Boobur is *supposed* to share such details with his cluster chiefs. Just as a courtesy. I found out about Praise from my own contacts in Central Center, people I tend to trust. They have nothing good to say of your new boss. No definitives, just a lot of circumstantials that suggest a cabal within a cabal. The implication is that Boobur isn't running his man with too close a rein, either. So Selwin Praise, who on inspection is a just jolly boy and a no-count, wears a very big question mark on his back."

"What do you want me to do?" Bertingas asked. Too eagerly, for Follard's taste.

"Nothing overt. Follow his orders. Treat him at face value—or better. But keep your eyes and ears open. And share with me, on a secure line, anything that looks suspicious."

"And, in return . . . ?"

"I'm treating you as a friend, Tad. You may need one soon."

Follard brought the car in high over the Palace perimeter. Below them was a stretch of parkland, dotted with low, porticoed buildings; silvery reflecting ponds; a few deeper, bluer lakes; white-graveled walkways and carriage drives; and small, square formal gardens, some of them buried in hedge mazes.

Halan knew from personal inspection that some of those hedges concealed radar transponders. The pools covered automatic missile/anti missile defenses.

At the center of all this idyllic beauty, like a black thunderhead over green pastures, was the Dome. It was the Palace's electromagnetic screen against ground- and space-borne plasma weapons. Normally as clear as summer air, it now floated an opaque layer of ionized particles. That was the official warning to all air traffic that an alert was on and the Dome was up to its full, killing power. It also blocked all outside peeping, whether optical, electronic, or mimetic.

Unfortunately, when the particle layer was deployed, no natural light could enter the area covered by the Dome. A starless midnight fell, and the Palace's illuminations came on automatically.

As Follard's aircar approached, sending the correct recognition signals for the day, the black chord facing them began to swirl and a seam, a pair of vertically aligned lips, opened. The car passed between their roiled edges.

Bertingas turned his head and looked behind, where a flicker of blue daylight was dying in the night sky.

"What would happen," he asked, "if they didn't open that patch for us? I mean, it's just an e-mag field with some dust in it. It might damage our electrical systems. Might scratch the paintwork. But if we were moving fast enough, it wouldn't stop us. Could it?"

"I once examined a car that one of the Pang Fasters tried to crash a dome with. Not this dome, but one like it. The field is computer controlled. It stays passive when it has to handle a plasma burst—just absorbing and shedding it, absorbing and shedding. However, when anything metal gets past the missile defenses and pierces the shield, the control becomes overt. The electromagnets divide and reverse the field, which sets up a shearing counter-current and shreds anything caught in it."

"Anything ferrous, you mean. But who would build an aircar out of iron? Aluminum and resins"—Bertingas tapped the dashboard—"are not magnetic."

"Hemoglobin is."

Below them in the nighttime darkness, the street lamps and building floods lit the intersection of two major thoroughfares in a gauzy, jeweled cross. It was four kilometers long, end to end. Follard took the car down to the deeper shadows near the inside perimeter of the Dome. As he approached on instruments, a square of blue edge lights came up around his parking space.

"I never saw this before," Bertingas said. "Most of

the Government people drop off in Chancery Lane. I thought permanent parking wasn't allowed inside the Dome. Is this new?"

"No, just special." Follard switched off the engine and closed the fan vents, and the car settled on its extensible jacks. "We're on the roof of the Kona Tatsu Hall of Justice."

"Oh."

The dying whine of the turbine seemed to suck all other noise out of the cabin.

Follard led him at a brisk walk—because they were already latish—over to the roof's private elevator (concealed as an air-conditioning tower), past sentries whose somber uniforms blended with the darkness, down to a public loggia off the main entrance hallway, and out into the pseudo-night of the street. It was a fast two-kilometer trot to Nero's Golden House, where the current governor preferred to hold her meetings.

The House was much more impressive in the full light of noon, when its mirrored glass and fourteen-carat spider buttresses fairly glittered with reflections from the four petal pools surrounding it. However, a million watts of tuned halogen lamping could simulate the effect well enough, at least, that a fond memory could carry it off. In his thoughts, Follard called this building the Jewel Box. Open the lid, and a mechanical tone fork would begin to chime *Esmonee*.

It was far too civilized a setting for the squabble they were going to hear this morning.

Follard and Bertingas showed their credentials to the frocked herald at the West Door. He lowered his nose a fraction to peer at the holo likenesses, sniffed, and waved them through. In the outer circular hallway, they walked around to the Ten O'Clock entry door. Follard cracked it, looked through with one eye. They were not as late as he had thought.

Beyond the low curtain wall that backed the corridor, the Golden House was a single egg of space. A neo-Faberge egg. Tiny golden ribbon lights picked out the arches that soared upward among the glass panels, toward the crested finial. Tiny silver footlights picked out the ramps that descended past the gallery and mezzanine seating to the amphitheater stage. Well-diffused pinlights and backgrounders filled in the shadows. The overall effect was one of mellow brightness without direction and without glare.

On the stage was the council table with its parallel lines of high-backed, red-upholstered chairs. They looked like theater props for a banquet scene. Except there were too many people standing around it for the number of places. From a distance, the stage appeared to shimmer in a heat haze—sign of a portable dome on low power. When Sallee rapped the meeting to order, the aides and sideboys would retreat to the gallery and the dome would go opaque. More darkness. That's why the stage was also set with a ring of free-standing, self-powered floor lamps, refugees from some grand hostel. The long table had a central row of crook-necked reading lights, again self-powered.

The whole rig was probably as secure as Governor Sallee's staff thought they could make it, on short notice. To Follard, however, who knew about security, the effect was hurried and graceless. Opaque magnetic shielding was hardly the connoisseur's approach to privacy.

He and Bertingas hurried down the ramp and climbed the six steps to the stage level.

"Well, Follard! Going to join us at last?"

Halan turned to see Valence Elidor moving toward him majestically, like a land yacht under sail with outriders—his body guards, bestboys, and staff admirers. The Inspector General knew for a fact that Elidor carried fifty-eight years. Yet the appearance he gave was of a tanned and athletic forty-year-old. Biceps like a wrestler. No belly. Slim hips. His hearty grin and that hand-clap on the shoulder were meant to be manly, friendly, and at the same time dominating. Elidor had the firm jaw, flinty eyes, and trained expressions that executives pick up at conferences with each other and practice in front of the mirror.

"Had a bit of a detour. Business."

"More important than the you-know-what?" Elidor winked at him.

"What do I know?"

"Ahhh, Halan! Spoken like a real cop."

"Why not? That's what I am."

"And who's this up and coming young man?" Elidor turned a twenty-kilowatt smile on Follard's companion.

"Tad Bertingas, of Cluster Communications, currently the acting Director . . . Tad, this is Valence Elidor, Haiken Maru's Trader General for Aurora Cluster."

Bertingas made his manners with a gleam—of awe? of opportunity?—in his eyes.

Elidor shook hands with a vacant politeness, his attention already turning elsewhere.

Follard and Bertingas made their way toward the table. At either end government functionaries and various military brass were sorting themselves out. Near the head—which was reserved for Governor Sallee—the new and yet-to-be-announced Director of Communications, Selwin Praise, had claimed the first chair on the left.

With a nudge and a covert finger gesture, Follard pointed him out to Bertingas.

Praise was defending his seat against the Protocol Master's polite suggestions that he find a lower place: the Chief of Staff was due any minute. The ex-Playmate and Kona Tatsu operative was a small man, pale, with thin hair combed straight back from a too-high forehead. He had little eyes and a narrow mouth that, when opened in protest, showed pointed, mouselike teeth. The P.M. looked just about ready to push him sideways out of the chair when the Chief breezed in, nodded a greeting to Praise, and took the seat on the right. With a flap of his arms the P.M. walked off. Praise smiled to himself.

"There goes your chair, Tad," Follard observed.

"I'd better go find a place in the orchestra then." Bertingas touched his shoulder. "Thank you for the ride, Halan . . . and the advice."

"*Ni'evo,*" he smiled, and the other hurried off the stage.

Bread upon the waters, Follard thought. We'll see how fast Bertingas sinks.

The chair at the bottom of the table, opposite Sallee's—which made it the number two seat on the stage—had been taken by General Pollonius Dindyma, the Cluster Commander. He officially held a rank equal-to-but-slightly-below Deirdre Sallee's, his authority derived from military rather than political appointment. Another squabble broke out at this end of the table when Captain Malcolm Thwaite arrived feeling he was entitled to sit opposite the Governor.

As senior representative of the Pact's Central Fleet on Palaccio, Thwaite contended—and always had—that his minor rank was superior to any in the merely *local* administration. After all, as he liked to say, the Fleet's Base Gemini, in the otherwise uninhabited Kali system, was home to eight cruisers and more than twenty destroyers, while the Cluster Command could field no more than four overage destroyers and a planetary monitor whose hyperspace drive had been written off for years. All very well, Dindyma would be saying, but those four destroyers were just a whistle away, while who knew where Admiral Koskiusko was patrolling with his gunboats this week? Thwaite countered that those "gunboats" were the cluster's first line of defense in uncertain times, and furthermore . . .

Follard's attention drifted to the middle ranges of the council table. No little fights marred the order there. Valence Elidor claimed the central chair on the right side and flanked himself with two Haiken Maru staffers. The other leading conglomerates—Baranquilla, Daewoo, and Mitsui—took the remaining places at the table, and the lesser traders docilely drifted back off the stage to find seats beyond the ring.

On the left side, the latifundistas and small estate holders ranked themselves by precedence after Amelia Ceil, the matriarch of Greengallow Holding. Again, when the chairs ran out the little fish retreated to the auditorium seats.

Follard approached that side, coming up behind Rebus Jasper of Prentiss Fief, who was sitting on the edge of the military reservation. He tapped Jasper on the shoulder and, when the man turned, gave his humorless *gestapo* smile. The landholder popped out of the chair as if it had been wired. Follard sat down without a nod or thank-you.

Everyone at the council, he noted, was full Human. Not even the Gowta, the Deoorti, or the other "passers" with semi-illegal Pact citizenship had the coin to buy their way in here: the trust and tolerance that the red-blooded proto-primates from Planet Earth gave to their own, first and foremost.

The Two O'Clock door opened with a bustle of pages and heralds, and Deirdre Sallee breezed down the aisle with her entourage.

She was a tall woman with a straight, mannish figure. Iron-gray hair was pulled back from her face in a coif that, even here in Aurora Cluster, was several years out of date. Her face was weathered granite: hard lines across the brow; deep dents beside her mouth; nose prominent, like a ship's prow;

eyes dark and weary. She was seventy-two standard
years old. All of that.

The dossier said she had borne three daughters,
though not to her current husband, Regis Sallee,
who trailed her like a small white poodle. She had
six grandchildren—four boys, two girls—who remained
at Central Center "for schooling purposes." Hostages
against Sallee's good behavior in office, no doubt.

Who would hold the strings on those young lives
now, he wondered. Avalon Boobur? Someone closer
to the Heir? Someone secretly in the pay of Haiken
Maru? Follard made a mental note to find out.

She took her chair at the head of the council table,
helped not by Regis but by a liveried footman from the
Palace precincts who stood two and a half meters tall
and was muscled in proportion. He handled the high-
backed, dark oak chair like a cane-bottomed stool.

Sallee sat there for a moment in silence, like a
hooded hawk, appraising—with senses other than
sight—those around her. Her shoulders were squared
against the old brocade of the chair, her hands resting down in her lap.

"All right, let's have the dome," she said.

The stage went dead dark. The echoes of the Golden
House died away. Like smothering . . . Then, one
by one, hands found the switches on the table and
floor lamps. New, smaller noises—tap of finger, rustle of fabric, scrape of shoe—defined their space.

"Some of you will already know why I've called
this extraordinary meeting. Most of you will not. In
ten words, then: the High Secretary is assassinated;
the succession is in doubt.

"The remaining members of the Proto Council
have demanded that, as an electrix supremator, I
register my nomination in favor of Roderick. Immediately. Further, that all of you—as Pact military,
administrative, trading and holding members—second
that nomination. Also immediately.

"My staff has prepared coding for the appropriate signals. All that's required is your personal—"

"Aren't we being a bit hasty, Deirdre?"

The rich, reasonable voice of Valence Elidor cut across her gravelly monotone. Its echo left a deep silence.

"Wait until I call for discussion and recognize you, Haiken Maru," the Governor said formally.

"Discussion didn't seem to be on your agenda, my dear. However, I think this group has much to discuss. Our choices, for example, and how we can improve them . . ."

"We have *no* choice but to offer our—"

"Come, come, Your Excellency! If we voted according to the pro-formas of a mere caretaker council, who represent none but themselves and a group of decadent hereditaries and hangers-on—your pardon, Madam!—whose competence the entire handling of this assassination has called into question, and who happen to be a thousand light years and twenty-one jumpseconds away, why, then we would well deserve the political chaos that will follow throughout this interspatial agglomeration. We would be courting a—dare I say it?—a civil war that will make the Years of Ascension seem like peaceful negotiations."

As Elidor spoke this set piece, Follard watched not him but the others around the table. He saw agreement and doubt mixed in those faces.

"Are you quite through?" Sallee asked.

"I think others share my feelings."

A restless shuffling around the table bred first a word here and there, then a spoken aside to a neighbor, then a murmur of not-quite-dissent.

"What's this about a civil war?" Captain Thwaite asked, into the lapping tide of voices. "Not while the Fleet's on guard."

"Merikur," Amelia Ceil said aloud, to the table at

large. "He's all but taken control of Apex Cluster. He now holds fifteen others in fief if not in name. He makes open war upon Haiken Maru. Do you think *he* will sign these pro-formas?"

"Governor Merikur is no threat to Haiken Maru," Elidor replied.

"Haiken Maru is a threat to us all!" Abel Peller, a junior latifundist, shot back. "You promote this war, Elidor."

"If war comes here—however it comes—there will be no place for neutrals," the Trader General replied smugly. "Friends or foes. Take your pick. But choose the right friends quickly. Or earn yourselves a lot of trouble."

"Is that a threat?"

"If Aurora takes sides, she is lost," General Dindyma declared. "I haven't ships enough to defend Palaccio from a determined attack, much less this whole cluster."

"I have enough ships," Thwaite grinned.

"Don't think we'll forget the Ponsable Massacre, Captain," Ceil told him. "An entire planet fused—"

"They had aligned themselves with aliens. Wogs from beyond the Pact perimeter, another order of technology which—"

"So you say! None *here* ever saw them."

Tap, tap. Sallee's ring beat against the tabletop.

"We displayed the skeletons, the new metals, evidence of inhuman logics."

Tap, tap, RAP! The Governor brought her hand down flat.

"Forgeries!" Ceil said. "Inept ones at that."

"Order!" Sallee barked out.

"No one ever—?"

"I said *order!*" the Governor shouted.

The table fell silent.

"If this council cannot decide where its loyalty

lies," she said, "I shall be forced to reply for it. Our loyalty—"

"Not without our consent codes!" Elidor spoke through his teeth. His lips were twisted into the grim parody of a smile.

"This is bootless!" The Governor stood up and half the table rose with her.

"Take care how you decide and what sides you choose, Madam," the Trader General warned.

"And you take care with your treasons, Sirra!"

Deirdre Sallee gathered her skirts and swept off toward the edge of the stage. Two seconds ahead of her, the tall footman dropped the dome. The dark tensions around the table seemed to dissipate as mellow, gold-and-silver light flooded in to mark her exit.

Chapter 3

Taddeuz Bertingas: STRING PULLER

For half an hour they sat and watched the twenty-meter black egg on the stage as if it were an important but boring ritual. No one among the aides and assistants, the second secretaries and deputy directors who filled the audience seats felt so self-assured that he or she would stand up, move around, trade gossip, break out a deck of five spot, or otherwise pretend they were all cut off from the action by a wall of energy as thick as syncrete. But there was a lot of whispering, side to side.

Tad Bertingas had folded his hands between his knees and spent the time with his future. Having seen the new D.ofC. from a distance of forty meters, Tad loathed him on sight. Small, slick, furtive, prissy, mean—all those adjectives rushed forward to describe a man who would steal a chair and then argue about it. The man's low forehead, waxed hair, pale complexion, and rat teeth all supported those adjectives. The way his shoulders had hunched down when the Protocol Master tried to eject him implied a stubborn, ungracious soul. Tad could read signals, if not auras, and Selwin Praise was no leader. He would push from behind instead of striding out in front. Not a man to die for.

Oh, well. What else had he expected?

Bertingas had just reached this satori of acceptance when the dome dropped. Voices around him cut off in mid-whisper. No one expected Governor Sallee to emerge from the side of it like a great flapping bird. Her cloak fluttered around her shoulders as she charged off the edge of the stage. Her elbows jerked up as her foot came down unexpectedly on the air over that first step.

Her pace never faltered, her face never broke its mask of anger, as she almost broke her neck on the way down. There was a scramble in the orchestra seats as Regis Sallee and the rest of the Governor's entourage recovered from their surprise and rushed to follow her, already halfway up the aisle.

Amid the standing and the shuffling, the breaking and the running, Tad took a long look at the figures remaining on stage. Most still sat around the council table. A few had risen with the Governor's exit and now stood awkwardly, as if unsure whether the meeting was really over. Some faces were set in grim lines. Others looked woeful, like witnesses to a natural catastrophe. Halan Follard was staring into the middle distance, thinking, probably plotting, possibly amused. Only one face was actually smiling, and that was Valence Elidor's, the master trader.

How was Praise—? Oh, yes. He was sitting, head down, doing something with his hands, reaming under his fingernails, one by one, with a small knife. It winked and flashed in a subtle spotlight from an odd corner of the hall. Praise's mouth was set in a sneer of concentration.

Would this be a good time to approach and introduce himself? Well—when would *ever* be a good time? Like a man going into battle, Tad made his legs work to climb the steps onto the stage and approach the head of the table. The council members were leaving now. Some gave him a nod, others just pushed past him. Selwin Praise went on cleaning his fingers.

"Excuse me? Sir? Ah . . . Citizen Praise?"

The frosty eyes looked sideways up at him. The sneer changed to a half-smile. "Yes?"

"I am Bertingas. Your deputy. From the Ministry?"

"Oh?" The eyes clouded. "Yes. I remember reading about you. Born here in the Cluster, came up through the local admin, long time in the ranks. Yes. You're Bertingas."

"Yes, sir."

"I've read a lot about the organization you've been mismanaging in my absence, Bertingas. I have to tell you, quite frankly, that I am not pleased. Not pleased at all."

"In what way?" Tad felt a tremble—but whether of fear or anger he couldn't decide.

Praise pursed his lips. "What would you say the monetary value of the system in my charge is worth? In round numbers?"

"Well, that's hard to—"

"Just one, just start with one node in the Hyperwave Network, shall we? Would you say a million . . . ? A *billion* New Rands?"

"Closer to a billion."

"And we have thirty-two stations in the Cluster as of the last audit. Haven't misplaced any, have I?"

"No, sir—"

"And the Freevid? The Shadow Box? A lot of hardware there? A couple of billion in each system, maybe? All told?"

"Yes, sir, although General Accounting would know the exact— "

"I'm asking *you* to know, Bertingas. So, we have a communications system valued, by my quick estimate, at fifty-seven point three giga-Rands. Now, what's your expenditure on security, Bertingas? Don't waste my time with a guess because you don't know, do you? But I know—"

Fifteen point seven, Bertingas remembered. In millions.

"—that you don't spend more than twenty million New Rands a year. Mostly on guards who double as messengers and light clericals. It's there in your reports. A 'cost saving' measure. Which means that any terrorist or rogue trader or peeved alien can walk up to one of *my* nodes and *own* it. Now, how do you think that makes me feel? Do you think I sleep well at night?"

"I really couldn't guess about your sleeping habits, sir."

"You'd better start worrying about them, Bertingas. From now on there is one person in your life who can make you feel very fine or very not. That's me. . . . Now, after I finish some business here at the Palace, I am going to take my lunch, then I am going to inspect my nice new office in the Government Block. The one thing I hope to find there, on my nice big desk, is a report from you with a plan, fully costed, for a high-security force, paramilitary and quick-reacting, that can keep the creepers and the peepers out of my nice clean systems. Do you *ponimayesh*, Bertingas?"

"Yes, sir!"

A cold smile came to Praise's face. He looked at his fingernails again. "Very good. Good-bye, Taddeuz. It was nice meeting you."

Bertingas turned on his heel and walked off. His stomach was squirting hot acid. His teeth were grinding pale enamel—he could feel flakes of it on his tongue.

He forced himself to take a deep breath and calm down.

Now, where was his friend, Halan Follard? On the other side of the stage, talking to the old woman from Greengallow Holding. Tad approached them, hoping he could beg a ride back to the Block.

Follard broke the line of conversation and quickly introduced him to Amelia Ceil, then went back to what seemed like small patter about the Haiken Maru quote for metasheep at the Klondyke Lift Center. In the middle, Follard suddenly paused and wagged a finger at Bertingas.

"Reminds me," he said. "I've arranged a body-guard for you."

Bertingas felt he'd slipped hypersideways and dropped into a war zone. Everyone was talking security now. In sunny old Meyerbeer, City of Fountains. On white-cliffed Palaccio, where nothing ever happens.

"I don't need a bodyguard, Halan. Honestly."

"You don't *want* one, but that's not the same as you don't *need* one. She's waiting in your office right now. Treat her kindly."

"*Her?*"

"You'll see." Follard turned back to Amelia Ceil and stock prices.

Tad still needed to get back to Government Block or, considering the number of hours he'd already been awake—and ignoring Praise's promised report— to his apartment.

He walked up the aisle to the Four O'Clock door and out into the deep, false darkness of the Palace Dome. The space around the Golden House, however, was bright with the hidden lights that illuminated its arches and buttresses. Water played around him, cooling sprays from the petal pools. He could smell grass being cut by the green techs. Bertingas remembered that public aircars sometimes paused in Krasniye Square and, failing that, a well-camouflaged monorail stop was just beyond. He started in that direction when a fast set of footsteps came up behind him.

"Ah! Citizen Bertingas!" The voice was deep and strong and jovial. Tad turned to see Valence Elidor, minus his cluster of staffers.

"Yes?"

"An exciting morning, hey? Lots to think about. You look like a man afoot. For the pleasure of the walk? Or do you need a lift? After all, you came with—"

"I would very much appreciate riding with you. At least as far as Government Block."

"No farther?" Elidor winked as if that meant something. He made some hidden signal then, he must have, because with a soft *swoosh* a large, black car dropped out of the darkness and hovered, half over the plaza, half over one of the pools. Its airskirt flattened one of the fountains and kicked up its own curtain of water. None fell on the two men. The side doors pistoned open, and Elidor waved him aboard.

Haiken Maru did well for itself. The interior was faced with unblemished gray Dowda leather, soft as Human skin. Because the Dowda, of planet Kraal in Arachne Cluster, had an intelligence potential of point nine three, hunting or farming them as animals was a capital offense.

The side panels pulled down to make a communications console better than the one in Bertingas' office. His didn't have a wet bar with refrigerator. The tongs were silver, the glasses fused crystal.

The overhead was painted—by a living artist, not a reprobot—in a scene that, after some staring, Bertingas interpreted as *The Execution of the Traitor Rydin*. With a sense of shock, Tad realized that this wasn't even a copy but an offwork by Poreeter himself.

The rest of the car came into focus: patterned carpets, gold filigree, beveled quartz, matched mahogany from Earth. The appointments inside this vehicle were worth the lifetime salary of a government bureaucrat, even at Bertingas's level.

While he frankly gawked, the car rose silently and passed through the Dome into bright sunshine. Without being told, the chauffeur took it to 800 meters, outside the pattern, and made slow circles.

"Do you mind if we orbit the city for a bit?" Elidor asked. "I get so little chance to talk with someone in your fascinating profession."

"That's funny," Bertingas said. "For the second time in one morning my host would rather talk than fly. . . . Well now, I didn't know Communications was so interesting."

"I mean the technical end, the casting of illusions, the shaping of information, the creation of entertainment. . . ."

"Does a man in your position need much entertainment?"

"Well put." Elidor stroked the Dowda skin beside his thigh. "But I do need information. Often."

"I am fully conversant with the Baseform Scatter—"

Elidor barked out a laugh. "What I need isn't optically encoded. Oh no . . . Ah, hmmm . . . It's my impression that a man in your position juggles a lot of electrons, visual images, backgrounders, 'sound bytes' do you call them? You would also have access to files on just about everything that's gone out over the last, say—two weeks?"

"That's a fair assumption."

"Including the original, and possibly a dozen outtakes, of Governor Sallee's first Freevid address upon planetfall, the archival copies of her formal council sessions, and, presumably, some record of what we just witnessed this morning?"

"Most of that, yes."

"Your technical section, presumably, could blend some of these electrons so that, on the wire, in theory at least, Governor Sallee might appear to pledge her support for Chairman Borking's claim to the High Secretariat?"

Bertingas put his obvious answer aside and instead asked his own question, however audacious.

"What is the basis of Borking's claim? Why would he have a chance?"

"Cultural dynamics, Tad." Elidor didn't seem at all offended. He smiled with real pleasure. "The Pact is rotten at the core, from Central Center outward. We all know that. The authority of the High Secretary, the power to expand the Pact's spheres of domain, its markets, its knowledge, its technical capabilities—all of this is wasted in the palsied hands of congenital halfwits. Which is exactly what the Holcomb regency has become. To remain loyal to them is to remain loyal to chalk pudding. It costs you almost nothing and it nourishes you not at all.

"Villem Borking is a decisive man, Tad. He has a program to restructure the Pactwide economy along more vital lines. Put banking under the control of people who know how to use money, instead of just sit on it. Put the military on a paying basis. Put the unique capabilities of our alien populations to more creative use.

"With a strong economy and a unified political structure, we can begin again the outward expansion that is the heritage of every Human. The stars can be ours again!"

"I see." Bertingas nodded. "And Deirdre Sallee's support—or the appearance of it, at least—could really help?"

"One cluster governor backing our Chairman will be like dropping a seed crystal into a supersaturated solution. The other governors, who now lack direction, will unite behind her, behind Borking. The advance on Central Center will be quick and bloodless."

Bertingas shook his head. "An—impromptu—

broadcast could be denied later, by the Governor, in person."

"Not if the technical quality were—um—convincing. If you feel your people are unable to achieve that, be sure that Haiken Maru's facilities and staff are at your disposal. They are capable of quite a lot."

"I'm sure, but still—"

"The Governor's position is uncertain. She has not yet decided where her own advantage lies. That's what bred such confusion and disruption at this morning's special meeting. By helping her decide, you would be doing her a service. Anyway, even if she were to change her mind—again!—and repudiate the transmission, that would be politically . . . nonviable. No other force in contention for the secretariat would be able to trust her. Governor Sallee will be obliged to honor the commitments you will be . . . clarifying for her."

"I'm sure she would still find a way, in private, to reward me for forcing her hand. Administrative terminations on Palaccio begin with a hyperinjection of *nepenthe*, I believe? Beyond that, the details are usually clouded, but she might make an exception in my case."

"Not if a successful Haiken Maru promoted her to some capacity at Central Center—say, the Interspecies Commission on Commemorative Stamps?—and appointed a more sympathetic governor for Aurora. Not if that new governor made a startling discovery of who, in the Communications section, actually did all the work. There might then be a new director. Even a new planetary administrator."

"That's a prodigious collection of 'ifs,' sir. The future might not be that assured."

Elidor shrugged. "A bold man must take bold risks."

"You make it sound easy. And attractive. However—and please understand that I mean you no offense—

there is a certain sense of professional ethics and trust that one acquires after spending a decade in an organization. To turn all of that on its head, even in the name of fine-sounding things like 'cultural dynamics' and 'spheres of domain,' is just not in me. I'm sorry."

Valence Elidor pursed his lips and stared ahead for a long minute, then nodded. "I can understand that. Yes, I can appreciate your sentiments."

With the gentlest of bumps, the aircar grounded on the avenue outside Haiken Maru's offices in Meyerbeer. Bertingas could not recall any signal from Elidor to the chauffeur, nor even when they had stopped orbiting and started descending. The hatch popped up on Elidor's side. As he moved to step out, he paused, leaned forward and spoke into a metal grille. A silver one, Tad noted.

"Take the Deputy Director wherever he wants to go, Andre." With a faint smile and a wave that was almost a brushing gesture, Elidor completed his exit.

"Citizen?" the grille asked.

Bertingas asked to be taken back to the Government Block, and the aircar surged upward.

It climbed too fast, too long, too high.

"What's wrong?" Tad demanded of the grille.

The voice that came from the front was under strain: "I don't know—the controls—malfunction—"

Bertingas had no eye for heights, but the ground was a long way down. Maybe 3,000 meters? The Palace gardens looked like the pattern on a playing card, with a black stone in the center. All of Meyerbeer would soon disappear under his hand. So were they at 4,000 meters? Higher . . . ? And was the aircar's cabin pressurized?

When the chauffeur blew the bolts on the forward escape hatch, Tad thought the whole car was coming apart. The front end split in three sections like a melon, and the plush partition at the head of his compartment automatically folded back.

The chauffeur was a small man with wide shoulders, like an over-muscled monkey. He buckled on an escape harness, climbed out on the front skirt, closed his eyes, and threw himself off backwards, like a skin-diver tumbling into the water. Tad knew how the harness worked: as soon as the person was clear, it would unreel a hundred meters of braided metal pigtail; the battery pack would discharge itself, creating an electrostatic drag just like a personal drop tube. You fell from the sky with the crack of a thunderbolt. It was so exciting, some people did it for fun.

Not this time.

The harness trailed only three meters of its pigtail. Either it had jammed or someone had cut it. The pack gave one feeble blue spark then shorted out. Tad could hear the man's scream above the hum of the car's ducted fans. It went on a long time.

By the time the scream faded, the fans themselves had changed pitch. Above 5,000 meters, the air became too thin to support the car. In a second or two it would begin to sideslip. If it rolled beyond a certain degree . . .

Bertingas climbed into the open steering compartment and found the other escape harnesses. His eyes saw what the chauffeur's had missed: abrasions on the reel mechanism, cracked plastic, broken wires. Someone had worked them over with the blunt end of a hatchet.

The floor started to shift under his feet. The final sideslip was starting. He started to grapple with the control yoke. It *was* frozen; the driver hadn't been faking. So, either the personal aircar of the Haiken Maru Trader General was suffering an unbelievable set of malfunctions— throttle, steering yoke, guidance and escape systems— or someone had been willing to sacrifice a presumably trusted employee and a vehicle worth five times a deputy director's annual salary to do Taddeuz Bertingas in.

Damn it, these vehicles were made to be safe! Almost crash-proof! Just for instance, if the fans cut off or the rubber skirt collapsed, the car's underside was shaped like a lifting body. It was supposed to glide down to a low-speed, nose-up landing. So . . .

Bertingas found the turbine switches and banged them down. Whatever gremlin or Human agent had messed up the controls hadn't thought of a simple shutdown. The fans cut off, feathered, and braked abruptly; the skirt closed with a *whump*; and the air-car stabilized on its keel. He strapped himself tightly into the driver's position. The descent was at first invisible and silent—until the blown panels around the front cabin began to whistle, then moan, then shriek as the car picked up forward speed.

Did he have control now?

Some. The linkages between the yoke and a set of spoilers on the blunt end of the lifting body were entirely mechanical, and they were working. The best Bertingas could do, however, was pick his landing spot within about five degrees either side of straight ahead.

Straight ahead, however, and growing larger with every second, was the black bubble of the Palace Dome.

"Hello? Help?" He thumbed buttons across the traffic control comm set. He also flipped the switch labeled "Emerg Trans"—whatever good that did.

"Help? Anyone? This is—um—" He read the registration. "Haiken Maru 681 Staff. I've got a runaway aircar, here. Over the Palace. Can anyone hear me?"

Would the antimissile systems pop up and deal with him in their own blind way? He prayed the car's automatic transponders were saying the same things electronically that he was gabbling into the voice circuits. Only more coherently.

"Don't shoot! Please! I am *not* attacking anyone. I have a total systems failure. Please don't—!"

The Dome seemed to be rising to meet him, giving him the illusion that it was inflating, expanding, creeping outward to cover and darken the surrounding gardens. Just as he thought it was going to swallow him, the Dome began to color and swirl. Not just a single iris was opening in the blackness before him, the entire Dome was falling. The opaquing particles dropped like smoke being sucked underground. Below him were the embassy buildings, the Golden House, the three wings of the Residence, broad avenues, trees, and people looking up in wonder.

Try not to hit the people, Bertingas told himself as he twisted the control yoke. His line of descent now seemed to include a strand of ancient elms, a green knoll, and a lake. As good as he could do . . .

The underside of the car banged through the trees in a cloud of green leaves. One of the spoilers was unhinged and dug a furrow of turf across the top of the knoll. The body lurched forward into the lake, falling with a bellyflop that threw up a shower of water. The lake was deeper than it looked; the return wave sloshed into the open compartment around Tad's waist and kept coming. The car was going to sink right there.

There were three buckles on the straps holding him to the seat. His head was under water before he found and worked the last one. Then he swam to the surface.

Not two meters away from him was a flat-bottomed punt, carrying two guards in livery. One worked a sweep off the stern. The other held a military-issue repulsor rifle, aimed more or less at Tad's face.

Bertingas swam over and grasped the gunwale. The weapon did not move aside particularly fast.

"Who is it, Lieutenant?" A crowd had gathered on the lakeshore, and the voice that called out was familiar, almost known to Tad.

"He has a Communicator's uniform, ma'am. It looks like . . . it *is* Deputy Director Bertingas."

"Well, bring him in, you fool!"

It was the Governor's voice. The guard put aside the rifle and reached big hands down into the water. He lifted Tad, sloshing and dripping, straight into the boat. The other began working the sweep toward shore.

The flat bow grounded in the green reeds that lapped the water, and Bertingas stepped off. People pressed around him but, careful of their fine clothes and mindful of the duckweed and water still dripping off him, did not come too close.

"What a frightful experience, Deputy Director," the Governor said. "How did it happen?"

"Some kind of mechanical failure," Tad stammered. The morning breeze was cold. "It was the Haiken Maru Trader General's own car and, after he got out, somehow . . . Luckily only I was aboard . . ."

A murmur of gossip and speculation arose in the crowd. One voice cut through it.

"What about the driver?" asked Halan Follard. So he was still on the Palace grounds.

"The chauffeur, he—had an accident with the escape harness. Somewhere over there." Bertingas gestured vaguely off to the southwest, back along his line of descent.

More gossip. More questions were called out, but the Governor cut them off.

"That's quite enough, citizens! We'll know everything we need to, once the trader's car is raised and the Kona Tatsu technical people have a chance to examine it. In the meantime, the Deputy Director is cold and wet and probably suffering from shock. Halan, will you help him?"

With a grim nod, Follard took Bertingas's arm and led him across the grass, onto the ring avenue, and over to the Kona Tatsu building. There they went up to the second floor and the infirmary, where Follard got out a first-aid kit for his scratches and a fluffy white towel for his wet hair.

Follard called up for dry clothing, but when the duty officer brought it, he shook his head.

"Can't have you walk out of here in a prisoner's singlesuit. Wrong image. Can you stand that wet tunic and pants for another ten minutes, till we can get you home?"

"They're all right. Be dry by then and, really, I should get over to the office."

Follard shook his head again and took him up to the landing stage. When they stepped out on the roof, it was dark. The Dome had been raised once more.

"Don't you want to know what I think happened?" Tad asked as they settled into the little black car and Follard boosted the turbines.

"Not particularly. You told everyone enough coming in. I was even picking up your signals on my AID. As for the truth, we'll know that as soon as we pull that aircar apart."

"Oh."

"Funny," he went on. "I know how Elidor dotes on that luxy car of his. Shows it off. Even inflates the cost in his tax reporting. So, he must have been under a lot of pressure if he'd consent to using it for a murder."

"Then you *do* think it was planned."

"Of course. Didn't I say you needed a bodyguard?"

Bertingas was about to ask "Why me?" when the car grounded on the jutting airlip of Government Block. Follard popped just the one door on Tad's side.

"Aren't you coming?"

"You'll be in good hands in a minute." Halan smiled. "Try not to get killed on the way down to your office."

Tad climbed out, and before he was two steps away, the car had lifted, spun, and darted off.

The ED drop tube had the effect of beating some of the water out of his uniform. As he stepped out at the ninety-ninth floor, the faint globe of mist surrounding him continued its own descent. His boots still squeaked as he walked down the corridor.

When he entered the bullpen, the people of his section rose almost as one from their desks and gathered around him. After the early morning call, the senior staff meeting, rumors of an aircar out of control over the city, anxiety about a new director—and now their deputy arriving with weeds on his uniform and scratches on his face and hands—everyone looked nervous and unhappy.

"Is it true, sir? . . . About the High Secretary . . . Will there be a war, sir? . . . Were you hurt? . . . Is the new man any . . . Have the . . . ?"

Tad put up his hands.

"Please, people! It's been a long day—already—and most of us haven't had our coffee break yet." That brought a few smiles.

"Yes, the High Secretary has been assassinated. So we have our work cut out for us there. No, there isn't going to be any war. So those of you hoping to escape this place into a general conscription are out of luck." More smiles, some laughs. "I'm not hurt, but crash-landing an aircar from 5,000 meters does put me out of sorts. For those of you interested in details, I'm planning a series of lunchtime lectures on the subject—mandatory attendance"—groans, hisses—"over the next three weeks. With holovids." Outright booing, chorus.

"I've met the new man . . ." Tad turned his voice serious. "His name is Selwin Praise. He's from Central Center, of course. . . . He seems to be—um—a stickler for details. That's okay. That's *parfait*. We can all work with a director who wants everything done right, because that's the way we do things here."

Relaxed looks and a few knowing nods moved the faces around him. The tension had gone out of them—or gone underground.

"Now, if you'll excuse me . . ." He picked a strand of green weed off his sleeve, held it out for inspection. "I think I'll go plant these things."

The crowd broke before him, all but Gina Rinaldi. She matched pace with him on the way to the corner office.

"Tad!" she whispered, "what really happened?"

"Someone tried to kill me. Took a lot of trouble over it, too."

"Then don't go into your office."

That made him pause. "Why not?"

"Because there's a person in there who could complete the job. One-handed."

"Oh. Then let's meet her, shall we?"

Gina stared at him. "How do you know it's a 'she'?"

He had already gone in.

The person was standing at ease on the other side of the desk, by the window. The blunt body was either the most out-of-norm human he had ever seen, or some new order of humanoid alien. Almost a meter wide and half a meter thick, but scarcely 130 centimeters tall. A walking lump, with wrists like ankles and ankles like tree stumps. Flat slabs of heavy muscle concealed any trace of breasts, hips, or other secondary sex characteristics. The person wore no trace of make-up, and its—her—reddish blonde hair had been cut back to a thin bristle that showed golden against her scalp. She wore a singlesuit of monofiber. A hint of alien background there—possibly intentional? And a weapons belt.

"Good morning, sir," she said, stepping forward and putting out a hand that looked like a ship-side docking grapple. Her voice came from deep in that wide chest, a flat rumble, although the voicebox modulating it might, in another person, have produced a pleasant contralto. "My name is Patty Firkin. Halan Follard thought you would need my services."

He took the hand, felt it close gently.

"Thank you, Miss Firkin. I think we all do."

Chapter 4

Gina Rinaldi: *PAPER TIGRESS*

Not one day in Gina Rinaldi's life passed without pain.

The worst of it was the atmosphere on Palaccio. It had too little oxygen for her needs. So each breath, no matter how she filled her gillsacs, left her on the edge of a gasping convulsion. There were pills that helped slow her metabolism and reduce her need; and she kept a small injector nearby at all times to boost the oh-three content of her fluid stream. Neither remedy was as good as being really able to *breathe*.

The gee-pull here was another source of constant annoyance. Her musculature had evolved on a planet with a far deeper gravity well. Every move she made had to be choreographed in her head. Otherwise she would leap two meters through the air while the Humans around her shuffled along the ground. Without careful planning, the coffee cups she picked up would fly off their saucers toward the ceiling; the contents of file folders would sling themselves across the room. When she accidentally bumped a chair or a table, it skittered along like a fast beetle.

She thought of Palaccio as the *thin* world.

More serious, Gina found as she grew older that the planet's low gravity was changing her body. Her bones were becoming brittle here as they shed their alumina content. Her tendons were contracting, causing painful cramps. The specific gravity of her fluids was altering, precipitating the lighter metals, on which she depended. Gina began to understand why neither her poly-divergents, who had immigrated to Palaccio to work the fields of Pescador Holding, nor her diploids, who had moved into Meyerbeer as contract money traders, had lived much beyond fifty standard years. When the normal lifespan of a Deoorti individual was 250 years.

Worse than the physical problems was the casual contempt the Humans displayed. The "aliens" among them were valued only as convenience machines. Her gynamere had just been some kind of self-replicating agricultural tractor. Her mere had been a mechanical tallyboard. Gina herself was a walking AID, when she wasn't an automated sex toy. Tad might forget and talk to her like a real person, sometimes, but that *machine* mentality was always there, under the surface. What the Humans forgot was that, pound for pound in protoplasm, and outside the artificial boundaries of Pact politics, the "aliens" outnumbered them a billion to one.

For all that, the Humans fascinated her: they could doubt.

Deoorti Orthodoxy was almost a biological thing, based as much on commensalism as on Hive law. To *disbelieve* in a structured society, to *disobey* the common precepts, to *distinguish* oneself from the common good—these were unthinkable. A Deoorti might as well disbelieve in the stars, disobey the flow of time, or distinguish herself from sodium.

By contrast, the Humans were so diverse! They could disbelieve, disobey, and distinguish. Freely and at will. And from that raw material of discontent, they had created comedy, tragedy, music, war, commerce, and a thousand other interesting things the Deoorti had never dreamed of. Human life was a rich-smelling garbage heap of emotions and responses, some that didn't work at all, and some that worked better than expected. As much as Gina was repelled by the waste of it, she loved the variety.

Most confusing of all was the concept of politics. Two Human beings, both of good will, honest intent, and certifiable sanity, could disagree so violently on basic questions of public action and benefit. In her own department, the battles raged between privatism and macloohanism, between the Imageurs and the Veracitors, between the careerists like Tad and the appointees like this new man, Selwin Praise. *That* battle would be no different from the last, or the one before it.

After several years, she had learned that the words they used, the issues they fought over, the decisions that one would make and the other unmake, were not what they were fighting about at all. Behind the words was this mystical thing called a "position." Each of them, Tad and the currently appointed director, could have one. Neither could have the same one. In some way Gina could not understand, this "position" was linked to each man's view of himself in relation to the political structure of the Pact, to Human society as a whole, and to the universe of one hundred billion galaxies. Each Human had to invent this view for himself and defend it vigorously against all others.

Her Deoorti body may have been patterned on the Human, but some things the mind could *not* copy.

Of course, in all these battles, she sided with Tad.

Not for "politics," she reminded herself, but for "love."
That was another emotion the Hive had never produced. Love was something like Hive loyalty but
focused on a single individual. It was not, could not
be, the coupling of sex—although, for Tad, sex was
impossibly intertwined with love. Of course, sex with
a Human and sex among the Deoorti were two different functions: one social, the other biological.

It was all very hard to understand. At times, when
she was alone by herself, Gina thought it might be
easier to stop trying. To lapse into the *machine* role
the Humans seemed to want for her.

On another level, however, it was all very simple.
The movements of sex and the words of love had
brought her a permanent work permit and temporary authorization to live within the city limits of
Meyerbeer. In Human society, sex and politics were
survival. That she could understand.

"Gina!"

Tad's voice from the corner office, raised in a
shout when the intercom was six centimeters beyond
his fingertips. "Yes, Tad?" she called back.

"Come in here a minute!"

Inside, she found him sitting at his desk. He was
bent over his artificial intelligence device, fiddling
with the optical attachments.

"These lenses don't seem to work. I'm trying to
get a holo image, but they don't even show a blur."

Gina saw the problem in two seconds. He'd fitted
the microscanner instead of the macroprojector. Now,
how could she tell him this without making him feel
stupid? Well, let the machine do it.

"AID?" she queried.

"Ready!" it answered enthusiastically.

"Show pic."

"I can't. I'm blind. Has that idiot put on my mi-
cros again? If he has, then he'd better give me something to read inside a three mikey-mike focus, or I'm

going to sit here and recite the entire *Rig-Veda*. In Sanskrit. And leave out the dirty parts."

"Oh. Wrong lens," Tad said. "They ought to mark these things better." He switched them out and angled the unit across the corner of his desk blotter.

"Show pic," he commanded.

"Do you mean, 'Please let me see the image series we were discussing?' If so, that would be the polite way to say it."

"Just dump the data."

The center of his work area lit up with a blinking, strobing blur. It was over in six seconds. The images changed so fast, Gina could get only the most general idea that they were topo maps or structural plans of some kind.

"Slower, please," Tad said woodenly.

"Oh, you want *reading* speed," the AID cooed. "I thought you said 'dump.' My mistake. Sir."

Why didn't Tad just disconnect or reprogram the personality codes? Gina suspected that, in some way, he enjoyed being lipped off by impudent machinery. . . . Maybe that was why he kept *her* around.

The first holopic was a green valley, pierced by an ambling trout stream that flashed like metal in the sunlight. The image jumped back and forth between two frames, faking the ripple of water and the shiver of trees in a simulated breeze. At the center of focus was a white dome, made of prefab hexagon panels. It was a hyperwave relay station, somewhere on Palaccio, probably beyond the Palisades, far upcountry.

The next image closed in on the dome, showing a maintenance worker, for scale, and a truck sitting on its collapsed skirting to offload a rad-shielded probot. Moving into the image, a two-dimensional red arrowhead flickered across the station's vulnerable points: access hatches, the plasma tube and power buses, the Shadowbox wave dish for signal inputs.

A third image went inside, dissecting the station

like a tri-D grapefruit: containment shell, suspend-
ers, supporting framework, primary laser injectors,
cyber systems, and the probable locus of the singularity.

"What are we looking for?" she asked.

"Ways to get in."

"Door's on the left. There."

"No, I mean, if we weren't supposed to."

"Break down the door. On the left."

"That's what I was afraid of."

"Who would want to get inside a hyperwave station?" Gina asked. "Nothing in there to steal except
some industrial-class lasers and an old computer that's
so task-oriented you'd have to rebuild it to reprogram it. Unless you wanted the singularity itself, and
you'd need a portable mass synthesizer, a big one, to
grapple with it. And if you fumbled it—then you can
kiss off this entire planet as real estate. . . . No,
nobody would break into an HSN station."

"They might if they wanted to take control of the
Cluster's communications system."

"Well, yes, I suppose they could jack in at one of
the repeaters. That would put them in charge, technically, of just the one node and its two-way link.
Wouldn't it be simpler to infiltrate here, through this
office, and command the whole system? Our cyber's
a lot more versatile. More cooperative, too."

"I heard that!" the AID squawked. Gina rapped its
carbon fiber case with her knuckles. She couldn't
hurt it with anything less than a ten-kilo sledge, but
the machine shut up.

"Anyway," she said, "who's worried about break-
ins?"

"The new D.ofC. has a phobia about it. He braced
and grilled me after the meeting at the Palace. Says
he wants a proposal for some kind of military reaction force, complete with barracks sites, training program, costs and pay schedules—probably even a

retirement policy and a marching song—on his desk after lunch."

"So that's why you're sitting here in a soggy uniform, still hanging with pond weeds, and looking at twenty-year-old structurals. The Department decommissioned Delta Station nine years ago, you know."

"Um . . ."

"Look, don't try to do this thing reasonably, Tad. You're wasting your time figuring out how to get inside a hyperwave node and, from that, computing the military forces needed to defend it. You're neither a soldier nor a vandal. Instead, take a guess. Fifty men? A hundred? At each station? On each planet? Then multiply by the number of stations and other facilities."

His nose wrinkled. "That's a big force. There might not be that many trained soldiers available in the whole Cluster, outside of Dindyma's marines or the Central Fleet."

"So you recruit and train them. Takes six months."

"Train *whom*, exactly? We can't reclassify from our own staff; we're already short-handed. Other departments would feel the same. And the conglomerates and latifundias are all closed labor systems."

"Workers from the dole pool? They're certainly outside the system."

"Yeah, far out. Half of them thieves and the other half spies on retainer from who knows where. They're just the sort of ragtag army we'd be defending the stations against. Praise would like *that* a lot."

"What about—aliens?" It made Gina feel strange to use the word, especially when talking to a Human. . . .

"Aliens? Can they fight? Even if they could, why *would* they fight for us?"

Good question. Still, Gina pushed on. "I think they're capable of loyalty," she said slowly. "Great loyalty, sometimes."

"Well. Whatever. Put down an unspecified force, the make-up to be determined later. What else do we need?"

"Ummm—armored carriers to move them in. For weapons, you'd need repulsor rifles, HD coils, stun grenades, and portable plasma pots—"

"Where can we get them?"

"Beg them from the Cluster Command, buy them in the bazaar, import them from offplanet. At any rate, once you know the size of the force, just multiply everything else—transport, housing, training, salaries—out of that. The rest is economics. I can punch it up on a wristcalc in ten minutes."

"I don't know. This man Praise is pretty sharp."

"Sure. But he's not omniscient. If you come in with a snowstorm of numbers, it will take twice as long to break 'em as it took us to cook 'em. Gives us leadtime to do a solder and patch job on the project."

"You want to take a crack at it?"

"Sure. For what it's worth . . ."

"How do you mean?" he asked. "The new Director wants—"

"The new Director doesn't know blip about comm theory and practice. To do real damage to the system, you don't try to disrupt or censor just one node. You'd want to shape the information, skew it, rewrite the text and sculpt the electron flow with your own slant. That's the subtle, the cool way. A military attack is un-cool."

"Maybe." Bertingas stared thoughtfully at the holo projection of the station schematics. Then he shook his head. "It would be too easy to detect. The D.ofC. would clamp down before you got the project even—"

"Oh, really? Tad, the Director doesn't pre-sample a tenth of what goes out of here. He doesn't know or speak to any of the techies. When was the last time you saw one of the upper brass poking around in the equipment bays? We know who really runs the Department. You or I could fake a transmission, stash it in pieces in off-RAM, and spring it whenever we wanted."

"*You* probably could. . . . Hmmm. Do you think I'd find out about it?"

Gina felt a coldness in her lower bowel. She sometimes misread Human thoughts and emotions, having no emphatic waveform for them. However, the trend of Tad's thoughts was unmistakable.

"I—I don't know. Maybe not. Probably not."

"But that isn't what you told the Haiken Maru people, is it?" He swiveled his chair abruptly and lanced her with his eyes.

Some detached part of Gina's mind recalled that she could, with one stiff-armed blow, take the top of his head off—right across the weakened structure of a Human skull's eyesockets. She might even be able to get out of the building after she did it. Once on the streets . . . But Tad was more, to her, than some inconvenient blob of carbon-based jelly. Her shoulders sagged a millimeter or more.

"How did you know?"

"Twice in a single morning someone suggests to me, in a subtle way, that the images this department puts out might be doctored. The first person to suggest it goes to a lot of trouble to kill me when I refuse. And he, to be frank, knows less about comm tech than our new boss. I have to consider the possibility there's a link."

"What are you going to do?"

"Did you tell them to kill me?"

"No! I wouldn't—Tad!"

"Did they pay you?"

"No, it wasn't like that. A Deoorti Sister works in the Haiken Maru subculture. She was asking about my job, and my relationship, with you. We got to talking tech and she asked if I could scramble and fake the system anytime I wanted. I told her maybe, once, on something small. But anything too long, or a major message like a Palace transmission, and you'd be likely to find out."

"So they had to kill me."

"No—not—never . . ." Gina wailed. She dropped straight down to the floor, her legs folding into what the Humans called a half-lotus. For Deoorti, it was a surrender posture.

"We made *joke* about it. If I had to, I could tie you up and closet you for hour, for two. Or fuck you one-handed. To get job done. That kind of joke. Not kill, never kill Taddeuz."

There were tears, hot tears of lithium salts. Gina could feel them eating into the creme make-up she put on her face every morning to make her look more Human. She had to get control: her body, her language, her emotions were going back to the Deoorti pattern. That would alienate him. Still, she could help none of it.

"Why are you . . . ?"

"Oh, be hush you stupid man! I love, have loved you! Not Hive, not Sister, not Right Smells, but loved no less. And you think I would have you killed. Now that you love me no more. Not fair, Taddeuz, not fair to me."

He just sat there looking down at the top of her head, clearly wishing he were somewhere else.

"My—my people," she began again, "were patterned on you. To *kaqulendir*—to mesh—with you. How could I not love you? Not stop loving even when you do. Even though, to you, I am just a thing. A soft bitch. An *alien*."

"I don't—it's not like that," he said.

But she knew from his voice, it was.

Gina was about to explain how she, too, was loyal to the Pact, why she had to be, when a buzzer from Tad's desk cut her off. It was the special buzzer, from the 100th floor, which had not sounded in months.

"That's the Director. He probably wants to see me," Bertingas said. He sounded relieved.

She looked up at him. Her face was still wet with the Human emblem of tears, but her legs were loosening from their reflexive crouch, her shoulders lifting.

"Your uniform is mess."

"No time to change it, I guess."

"No . . ."

"Why don't you—ah—keep working on those figures? For some kind of military force."

"You trust me with that? After talking to Haiken Maru? After getting you killed?"

He made a small, tight smile. She suddenly understood how near to tears himself this Human had come.

"Not your fault," he said, "not intentionally. You're a good woman, Gina."

Good woman, almost Human.

She wiped the corroded make-up off her cheeks with the palms of her hands and returned his smile.

Then he was walking quickly out of the office. One dress boot squeaked with the damp still in it.

Chapter 5

Taddeuz Bertingas: *UNEXPECTED SUPPORT*

Tad's boots squeaked and his mind spun as he fast-stepped toward the lift tube. His right hand was clutching the startled AID, which he'd swept off the desk as he left . . . fled from . . . his own office. He squeezed the machine once, for reassurance. No good having to go back for it, not now, not there.

The bodyguard—what was her name? Firkin? —came out of the angle between two cubicularia and tried to fall into step with him.

"Just business with the bossman," he tried to smile. "Upstairs."

She didn't break stride. "I should check the—"

"Back off, muscle lady!" he snapped.

That froze her, her boot heels actually skidding on the tiles. Tad whirled on, his mind still spinning.

Gina had collapsed like a broken robot, or a puppet with the strings cut. Mumbling and raving by turns. All about a simple question of who knew what and how much about the Department, and who had tried to kill Tad over it.

Of course, he and Gina had shared a good relation-

63

ship. A kind of love. Once. He supposed it might have been as pleasurable for her as it was for him. Perhaps not. Aliens were wired differently, he knew. A phenotype so close to Human, as the Deoorti were, of necessity became successful mimics, able to simulate a whole range of Human emotions. Perhaps even feel them. Perhaps not.

After the scene in the office, Bertingas concluded Gina might be a very sick personality. Or a good actress.

Yet, who else was there for him to trust? Who else could think as clearly as she could? Who else could do the work? Who else owed him so much? Maybe, just maybe, by the time he returned from this meeting upstairs, she would be back in her sockets and ticking along like nothing had happened. He had to think that, just to get his brain straight for his next encounter with the new Director.

He stepped into the lift tube and felt its characteristic pull on the long muscles in his body. A leaden ache in the back of his thighs reminded him that he'd already taken a beating this morning.

The electrostatics pulled the last of the pond moisture out of his uniform, but that didn't make him look better. The black material was pleated and creased across his groin and armpits, and it chafed. He had a scurf of dried green weed, like tarnished braid, on his cuffs. He smelled like a bog.

In contrast to the hard surfaces and half-panels, clack and clatter of the ninety-ninth floor, the one above it was carpet and crystal, deep-grained wood and quiet. Sitting at a pulpit desk in the tube entry bay, a young woman wearing the uniform of Building Services checked his face unobtrusively against a holofile concealed in the counter before her. When she had a match, she pressed a button releasing the invisible repressor field that screened the head of the corridor into The Maze, on the far side of the bay.

She did all this as fast as Tad could walk the four meters from tube lip to corridor. If he chose to ignore her, he might never know he was being cleared.

That button cap under right thumb, Tad knew, contained a microcircuit set to interpret one set of finger whorls—hers—and one pH balance in the skin oils—also hers. If anyone else touched the button, not only did it lock but the field collapsed, sweeping everything not screwed down inside the bay into the lift shaft. And the shaft reversed to fast-drop. As a security system it was fairly crude, but no one had ever walked unannounced into the offices of the Combined Directors of Cluster Services.

The Maze was only confusing to first-timers, as it was meant to be. Actually it was just a double-ring of corridors, an inner and outer square, with the Directors' office suites aligned on the outer, window side; support staff and the building core were on the inner, non-window side. Selwin Praise's office would be three lefts and a right, unless he'd arranged to switch with one of the other directors. However, since that would involve a certain loss of face by the switchee, for agreeing to the whim of a new man, Tad could trust that the D.ofC. was in the same suite his sixteen predecessors had occupied.

He was right.

The secretary in the outer office was a man, possibly Human, possibly another Deoorti Sister. Tad's internal radar wasn't functioning too well right then. The man had the signs, wide-set eyes and coppery skin, but they could have resulted from Human genetics and a bad tan. The secretary barely looked up as he waved Bertingas through into the inner office. Behind him, as the door slid closed, Tad could hear a sniff and a chuckle.

Praise's head was bent over some work. He was actually writing, on paper, with an ink pen. He did it slowly and made it look hard. Praise didn't speak or lift his eyes for some minutes, leaving Tad to stand at rough attention in the center of the carpet.

"I thought I would have a report on my desk when I came in. At least the *outline* of a report." Still Praise didn't lift his head. "Something about security, I remember, which you were going to write for me . . . Or did you forget?"

"No, sir. But between then and now I've had a rather spectacular accident."

"Explain." Praise lifted his head and Tad got his second really good look at the man's eyes. They reminded him of a cold lizard—sleepy, slow, indifferent, deadly. Those eyes tried to show concern now, and failed.

"Leaving the Palace, I was the guest of Valence Elidor, the Haiken Maru Trader General." Tad saw the eyes flicker over the name—with envy? "He took me aside and wanted to chat with me . . ." Twist the knife. "About a communications problem they were having. Anyway, after we dropped him off at the H.M. city offices, the driver was heading back here when the car malfunctioned. Shot six or seven klicks straight up, began sliding around. Then came down inside the Palace Dome."

"Was that you?" Praise's eyebrows raised; the eyes themselves never warmed. "I saw the whole thing. Someone fell out of the car, didn't he?"

"The driver. Jumped with a bad ED dragline."

"Defective?"

"Sabotaged."

"Oh, dear. Then it was *you* who brought it down?"

"Yes—"

"You might have picked a less public landing spot," Praise sniffed. "No good having Cluster Communications attacking the Palace grounds. Even by inadvertence."

"I didn't exactly have a lot of choices."

Praise looked thoughtful. "No, perhaps you

didn't. . . . Sabotage, eh? Someone trying to assassinate the Trader General? That's bad news for us all."

"Or kill me? Elidor was already out of the car."

"Why would anyone want to dispose of you, Bertingas? To be sure, I couldn't do without you. Every minute I'm in this job, I see how much I'll be depending on my deputy. Still, being career service, you're hardly a *political* target, are you?"

"I suppose not."

"Still, that does raise a question of our vulnerability. To the accidents of time, at least. I'm just writing up a new standing order that will cover that. It calls for all Freevid transmissions originating with this department to be cleared by both you and me. Kind of a double check. How does that sound?"

Ghastly, Bertingas thought.

"More—secure, certainly . . . sir," he said.

"Ahh, and *that* reminds me."

About the security report, Bertingas prompted silently.

"About the report on security—you *are* working on it?"

"Of course."

"You've given thought to the composition of our fast-reaction force, haven't you? I thought we could make good use of some of the alien population. Here on Palaccio and elsewhere in the Cluster, perhaps."

"Why, that was our—my—thought exactly! The dole humans are too unreliable, unmotivated. However, the guest species—"

Praise was nodding, all but the eyes. "Some of them do look very efficient, with excellent reflexes and, um, physically powerful."

"Yes, and with the right approach—"

"How do you feel about aliens, by the way?" There was a hook in that question, somewhere. Bertingas could sense it.

"I suppose I like them. Well enough. I don't know that many of them. Or not all that well."

"You have no residual phobias, do you?"

"No, no. Quite the contrary . . . I think some of them get treated very badly, especially on the agricultural holdings. The *Zergliedern* system applied to labor gangs, for example, is—"

"Zerglee—?"

"Punitive dismemberment, sometimes disfigurement, for infractions of house rules. It started just with the species who had fast regenerative powers, but I've heard of cases where a symbiotic personality got severed. That's sadistic—and too brutal for any Human civilization."

"Ah, well, now. We can't change the world, can we? But I don't suppose you have many aliens in the Communications Department. Not above the solid-brain level, anyway . . ."

"One or two," Bertingas said. "There are limited opportunities in our field, what with this Cluster being so heavily demographed to the Human."

"Yes, exactly." That nod again. "It almost reminds me of Central Center. Not a lot, but in some ways . . ."

"About the plan, then, you would pre-approve using—and arming—aliens?"

"Of course. I suggested it, didn't I? And you should take your original estimates and quintuple them. We'll move right into training cadres with twenty percent of the first inductees. Get me estimates on your requirements for barracks space and materiel. We'll fund this out of your program planning budget, to start with." A grim smile. "That's usually over-allocated in an operation like this."

"If you say so, sir. Quintuple—that's a lot—"

"Don't worry about where the bodies will come from. We'll draw levies from the latifundists, if we have to." A dry chuckle. "You'll make the primary contacts and recruiting arrangements, yes?"

"I have an assistant who would be better—"

"I'm sure you have a whole platoon of mother's little helpers down there, but I want you to handle this yourself. *Ponimayesh?* If nothing else, it will get you familiar with the quality of troops you'll, um, command." Another chuckle, which Bertingas didn't like. "Now parallel your AID with the desk here. I have some contacts for you."

Bertingas set his unit on the contact studs and it handshook with Praise's artificial intelligence. The Director tapped in a dump code on his deskpad and the two AIDs duplicated certain memories. There wasn't much to file: their transfer was over in a fraction of a second.

"You have two names there." Praise must be reading minds this morning. "One is a gentleman of the warrens here in Meyerbeer. The other has a following, of sorts, in the rural precincts. From all reports, they should be able to help you."

"I may have to bargain for good-quality trooper stock. Even offer them individual inducements. What's our upper limit?"

"Oh . . . ." A shrug. "Tell them whatever you like. Whatever you think they'll accept. Of course, if the Governor decides she can't support it, she'll hang you out to dry like a hankie." More chuckles. "Fair enough?"

"Ahh . . . I guess."

"Good. Then you have your work cut out for yourself, don't you—Commander?"

"Yes, sir." Praise was, of course, being ironic. He had no more authority to hand out Central Fleet commissions than Bertingas did to make his recruits Pact citizens. Still, the implications—would it be fun to play at soldier? For a week or so? Somewhere, of course, where the glass beads weren't flying . . .

Bertingas gave a mock-sloppy salute and turned on his heel. As he heel-and-toed across the carpeting, Praise called out to him.

"By the way, Commander."

Tad turned. "Yes?"

"No Cernians."

"Cernians?"

"Yes . . . You know: little fellows, green skin, bad eyesight, worse breath. Don't take 'em."

Now *that* was strange. "Why not, sir?"

"Call it a whim. Say my sources indicate their loyalties are not above suspicion. Whatever. But . . ."

"No Cernians." Bertingas shrugged. "Whatever you want." He walked quietly from the office.

As he stepped into the drop tube's retarding field, he felt his thoughts rise in a jumble—along with his stomach.

They were thoughts of Selwin Praise, and when they settled again Bertingas had a pattern: the cold, grinning superiority; the cat-and-mouse conversations, with their hooks; the obscure whims and jealousies. The man reeked of secrets. Halan Follard was right. Praise was a Kona Tatsu agent, definitely, and this preoccupation with security forces was either a smokescreen or a deeply veiled plan.

Where did Taddeuz Bertingas's advantage lie? In playing along, just following orders? Or in dragging his feet, sabotaging the effort? Should he tell Follard about his guesses? And was the Department *really* in danger? How did the Haiken Maru assassination attempt—for that's how he thought of it—how did that fit in? Would the firepower of a regiment of alien fanatics have helped him any in that aircar crash?

Down in the ninety-ninth floor's tiled tube bay, Bertingas was brought up short. The bodyguard was waiting for him at exactly the spot he'd left her. He might have expected Firkin to be sitting on the bench there, working a puzzle, doing some knitting, reading a book, but no. She stood roughly at attention, or maybe just at ready. Waiting for—what? —half an hour while he was topside with Praise. Once again Bertingas asked himself if this wide person was exactly Human. If not, then a squad of her phenotype would be worth a legion of bubble-fingered agricultural workers.

She fell into waddling step beside him as he left the bay.

"Firkin, what do you know about the Cernians?"

"Trolls, sir?" In that flat rumble. "Or that's what some call them. They aren't exactly in the Pact. Well, there's a lot of bugs that aren't. But these Cernians have their own little cluster, about five worlds, outside the Pact. Who knows what they might have built it into, if they hadn't met the Pact coming the other way."

"Are they warlike?"

"Not particularly. Just hard to kill."

That appraisal, coming from a body as solid and tough as Firkin's, made the Cernians seem indestructible.

"Are they friendly, then? Say, with any political force inside the Pact?"

"Rumors, sir." Firkin shrugged.

"What do they say?"

"That the Cernians are mixed pretty deep in Harmony Cluster. General—now Governor—Merikur seems to have them under his spell. Or they him. Hard to tell, at this distance."

"Just rumors, eh?"

"That's all I hear, sir."

They walked side by side up to Tad's office, then Firkin pushed ahead. To check out this most familiar room.

Gina was nowhere in sight, neither in the office nor at her cubicularium. Any sign of their *encounter* this morning—scuff marks on the floor, the silvery tearstains—had been removed.

Bertingas found her AID, which she'd named Squeaker, sitting on her desk. It was talking to itself in alien whispers. He left a verbal message for her with it, giving Praise's approval of their plan to use aliens for the strike force. He also relayed the Director's order to quintuple their original estimates—whatever those might be. So Gina should think *big* in her planning. He then told her he was going back to his apartment, to change out of his ruined uniform and perhaps take the rest of the day off.

And that was about all there was to say. Except . . .

"Oh, and Squeaker—tell her I'm sorry. Really sorry."

Chapter 6

Patty Firkin:
ALARUMS AND DIVERSIONS

"All right, Firkin. Let's go."

Bertingas walked out of his assistant's cube and waved at Patty in his offhand way. He was like an overgrown boy: by turns helpless and tyrannical. It was becoming tiresome.

She went with him.

"Where are we going?"

"Back to my apartment."

Now *that* was a problem. If this young potato was still as hot as Patty figured, going to his published place of residence was not a bright idea. The people who had botched the out-of-control-aircar would probably have thought of something else by this time.

"May I suggest, sir, that . . ."

"Later. It's been a long day and I'm *still* wearing this stinking uniform. I want to change, get a hot bath, maybe a massage—you don't give massages, do you?"

"No, sir."

"Then a drink or three and dinner. Do you eat dinner, Firkin?"

"When it's offered, sir." She couldn't resist a small smile.

At the tube, he started to step into the levitator. Patty put a hand on his arm.

"Up, sir?"

"Of course. I've signaled for my car."

And given someone the notice and leadtime to set all sorts of surprises . . .

"Wouldn't it be safer to use the streets?"

"All the way out to the Satellite Villas?"

"Well, it's just, ah, not as far to fall."

"I see. Then you lead, Firkin."

She walked into the drop tube and pointed her toes: it made the trip marginally faster. She felt the pillow-plump sound of him entering the tube above her. They dropped amid the whisper-crackle of energy discharge.

At the ground floor, she had to show him where the street doors were. Was it possible he had never entered the building this way? No, his dossier said he'd started in the basement on the archival system. Perhaps this floor was recently remodeled. Were the tatsu-wardens still in place, then?

Out on the avenue, they bucked the flow of walkers, gawkers, and street hawkers that mingled and moved around the maglev stop. When a car came through going west, Bertingas looked both ways, shrugged, and waved her aboard. The car glided off on its suspensors along the ceramic beam twelve feet above the street's median strip.

Bertingas hooked his elbow into the strap like he was used to riding the 'rail. They were pressed by the crowd between two Humans in half-piped General Services uniforms and a Clotilden with a metal snake grafted to its cervical collar. The snake looked like business.

"Do you work for Halan?" Bertingas asked.

Now, how much did he know about Follard? The

Kona Tatsu Inspector General had suggested they were casual friends. Could she fool this petty bureaucrat? For how long?

"Not directly," she answered evasively.

"Are you a freelance, then?"

"Free—? You mean a mercenary? It's something like that."

"How good are you?"

"How do you mean?"

"Got any references?"

There was more than boyish challenge in his eyes. Patty remembered that this was the dude who had brought down a stalled aircar from seven klicks over the Palace and avoided killing anyone. Not even himself . . . Except for the driver. With her chin she worked back the jumper's wide sleeve on her strap arm. Far enough to show him the red line.

"So, you have a regraft," he said, after a hard look. "What's that supposed to mean? Other than you were clumsy—and lucky enough to lose it on the doorstep of a full med-ops. Where did it happen?"

"Battle of Carmel-Chi."

"Oh . . . You were—outside?"

"With First Drop, II Corps."

She could read the thoughts behind his depthless stare. II Corps Marines was the unit that had lasted through all ninety-six hours of the siege at Carmel Base. Toward the end, they were valving off their suits and vacuum-freezing pieces of themselves to ration the remaining pressure. Her squad had accepted the citadel's surrender on their knees and elbows. The only good thing you could say was, the defenders were in worse shape.

"I see, unh—Sergeant?"

"Colonel."

The monorail car floated out through the Embassy District to what, in Meyerbeer, on Palaccio, passed for suburbs. Each of the Satellite Villas was a discrete structure, although it was clearly meant to look more like the cluster-hutch of a Neapolitan hill neighborhood. Terraces, tiled roofs, airpads, window walls, and garden patches lay atop and beside one another like scales patterned on a snakeskin. The trick, architecturally, was that the building seemed to have more outsides than insides. Any student of solid geometry will tell you that, as an object grows in size, its volume expands faster than its surface area. The genius who designed the Villas found a way to reverse that.

The building, Patty knew, was hollow. Its interior grotto was faced with a reverse array of terraces and windows. Water was the theme: a fountain at the center fed a pumped stream, livening the space with dancing reflections and brook sounds. Sunlight came down from that mirror array near the ridgeline. Yes, the inside was nicer, in a controlled way, than the outside.

As the car neared S.V. IV, Bertingas started to tell her this was his stop, but Patty was already moving toward the door.

She led him in through the Villa's main lobby, beside the recovery pool for the inside stream. They took the lift tube up to Concenter Three, which was Bertingas's level. By that time, he was no longer trying to lead her, just following. As she had planned.

They were on the outside now, moving along a twisting garden path above one householder's windows and below another's terrace. Patty took out her AID and queried it subvocally.

"Trouble, Colonel," it told her through the bone implant.

"How big?"

"Fifty-point-nine kilos."

"Body temperature?"

"Thirty-seven-point-two Celsius."

"Is that estimated or actual reading?"

"Would I lie to you? She's been there an hour, so her temp's adjusted to the room. Tell your boyfriend he keeps his 'cycler too low. It's freezing in there. The lady's got her coat on, and he'll soon be wishing she'd taken it off."

"How do you know she's female?"

"Men don't walk on five-centimeter stilettos, do they? Makes a real clatter on the parquet."

"All right. Is she armed?"

"Yeah, two of them."

"Weapons, you wiseguy."

"Got a chunk of ferrous-something in her pocket that masses close to a kilo. Maybe she collects meteorites. But if it throws beads, look out for big ones."

"Thanks."

"You want her stunned or stone cold?"

"Neither, right away. Will she startle badly if we walk in?"

"Yeah. Pulse and respiration say she's on the edge of something pretty crude."

"Okay, we'll tippy-toe."

"Are you talking to Halan?" Bertingas asked over Patty's shoulder.

"No," she said. "Just doing some reconn."

"Of my apartment?"

"Sure. You've got a visitor."

"Unh—that's not possible. This is very expensive living quarters. The security system alone costs—"

"More than it's worth. Big puppydog. When I went through this morning, it rolled over on its back and begged to be scratched. With the right fingers, that is."

"*You* were in my apartment this morning?"

She watched him work the timing out in his head. "Since that crash at the Palace?" he asked.

"Yes," she lied.

"Oh, well then . . ." Lie accepted. Advantage Kona Tatsu.

"Do you have any girlfriends?"

"That's a little direct. Are you suggesting—?"

"The body in there displays female. Anybody you'd be expecting?"

"Human female?"

So that was his deep and dirty secret, hey? "Yes, Human or masked to pass for one."

"Then no."

"All right. We'll go in casual. Like we own the place."

"I do—remember?"

"Just let me lead. Unless you're wearing body armor."

He shook his head. "By all means, lead." She could feel his eyes reappraising her singlesuit and the shape of her flesh beneath it.

She might use the expensive sound system— twoofers, bleeters, floor amps, thousand-watt dazzlers, and a neural synthesizer—which she'd found in the apartment that morning and linked to her AID, for communicating with the woman inside. Patty decided against it. If the quarry was a friend of Bertingas's, then a sudden order issued by the walls for her to walk out with hands locked on top of her head would only confuse and frighten her. And if she was a professional, it would just tip her off. A dose of subsonics, however . . .

"Listen," she growled to the AID.

"Always, my sweet."

"Switch on the audio system in there—real quietly, and no twinkie-lights, if you can. Give me a sine wave at ninety Hertz on those big subwoofers. Start it below forty deeBee and raise it, gradually, over about thirty seconds to 110. Then pulse the loudness, real fast, over that range."

"May I point out that the Human ear does not hear clearly at that range."

"No, but sphincters and bowels do."

She caught a gleam in Bertingas's eyes.

"Beginning procedure," the AID said dutifully.

They crouched on the doorstep, huddled out of the greeter system's line of sight. Patty drew her repulsor, checked the charge and the load. After forty-five seconds, she told him: "Key the door."

He hit the latch.

She struck the heavy oak panel with her shoulder and ricocheted diagonally across the foyer, flying horizontally about a foot above the simulated flagstones. Landing on her hip, one knee, and an elbow, partly concealed by the foot of the archway into the lounge room, she swept a sixty-degree field of fire.

At the center of which was a blonde. She was trying to stand erect, but one hand was clawed into her flat belly. The other held a Schlicter rail gun, similar in design to Patty's repulsor—but a single-shot. It would accelerate a 100-gram pellet of uranium, jacketed in glass and suspended in teflon, at 3,500 meters per second. Tear a hole in a girl about two feet across. Through body armor.

Patty had a clear shot at the weapon. She could take it right out of the woman's hand, and the hand off right up to the neck. Not a neat solution.

"Friends-no-fire," Patty called. She clacked her own gun flat down on the flagstones—but kept a hand on it. That left her face, spine, and shooting hand exposed.

The woman spent ten seconds trying to raise the Schlicter above the level of her own hips, then gave up. The weapon thudded on the carpeting. She sagged onto the cue-form sofa and hugged her knees.

"Turn it off . . . off," she cried.

The subsonics were even beginning to get to Patty, and she wasn't at the sound system's focal point. She told her AID to shut it down. It was like a fog lifting in the room. The blonde intruder relaxed, stopped rocking and moaning, but didn't uncurl.

Patty walked over, toed the gun away, and waved Bertingas in from the front door.

"Know her?"

"Never had the pleasure," he said. "She does look familiar."

Patty studied the face: high and pointed cheekbones; straight nose with fully arched nostrils; a mouth more carefully painted than a Noh actor's; big gray eyes with the clearest whites she had ever seen—agate and alabaster; brows curved and shaped like the mud fenders on an antique Rolls; high forehead with not a line on it; hair layered and puffed and tinted in the fashionable semolina-and-sequoia shades.

It was a perfectly forgettable face. A thousand of them looked at Patty every day from the Freevid screens and holozines.

"That gun is Central Fleet issue," Patty observed. "The AID she's toting looks like it could open up and run Gemini Base. But she's not any kind of trained agent, not by my guess."

"Do you always talk about people in the third person while in their presence?" the woman asked. The voice was low, cultured, and had a slight hesitation, a catch, that Patty knew any man would find irresistible.

"Only when they've been shooting at me."

"I have never—"

"You were tryin'."

"Now, now, Firkin," Bertingas said, just about waving a finger in her face. "There may be extenuating circumstances. We can't know all the details."

"Exactly," the woman said. "Dire circumstances." She straightened herself on the sofa, but not enough to flatten the curves of her body, from Bertingas's perspective. The room curved around her, as that damned cue-sense furniture always seemed to do with the most beautiful woman in sight.

"I came to Counselor Bertingas," she said, "because I have reason to suspect the Haiken Maru are looking for him, too."

"You're a little late," Patty said dryly.

"Yes, the air crash, I heard about that. Terrible thing. The H.M. tried something a little less spectacular on me this morning. When I landed at the City Port, they rigged a bagbot to throw a restraining web and snatch me right off the exit ramp."

"Oh, my dear!" from Bertingas. "How ever did you manage to avoid that?"

The blonde's cool eyes tore themselves off the man and flicked over to her discarded Schlicter. "I had to damage the machine."

"Why, exactly, were they snatching you?" Patty asked. "Who the hell are you, anyway?"

"I'm Mora Koskiusko."

At last! Something *ugly* about the woman.

"I'm the daughter of Admiral Johan Koskiusko, of Gemini Base. The Haiken Maru were trying to kidnap me in order to have a hold on him."

"Now, why would they want—?" Bertingas started to ask.

"The H.M. corporate organization is moving for the Secretariat, of course," Koskiusko answered him. "Throughout the clusters they are aligning military support—by negotiation or force. And my father is loyal to the Pact."

"After the kidnapping, why didn't you go to the Central Fleet office in Meyerbeer?" Patty asked.

"I don't trust Malcolm Thwaite. Not completely."

"Huh! So you came here, right off?"

"Yes, I knew that at least one other person on this planet was on the same—"

"How did you manage to get in?" Bertingas asked.

"Well, your home system, it wasn't—"

"That AID of hers," Patty observed, "could convince your security system it was talking to the main net at Government Block, sell it twenty thousand shares of Pinkney Bendo, and *then* open it like—*Jesus!*"

The shock went up her right side like a bad muscle cramp.

"Sorry for the tase, Boss," her own AID said calmly, "but we have visitors in the garden, and you do tend to ramble on."

"How many?"

"Platoon strength from the tramp of little feet. Tell the homeowner he's not going to like what they're doing to his *Pachysandra nipponica*."

"All right. Everybody down on the floor."

Bertingas and Koskiusko slid down on the carpet. Patty saw the woman reach sideways and pick up her Schlicter. Patty let her. Bertingas had his hands over the back of his neck—not a very useful position—but his head was up and his eyes watchful.

"Open up the place," she told her AID.

The carpeting in front of the window wall flipped back along the lines Patty had cut that morning. The Manjack she'd concealed there erected itself and swiveled its 240mm repulsor coil toward the glass. From deep in the couch cushions, two HV directors popped up and pointed at the window. Two more of the little demons lifted from behind other furniture and aimed their discharge antennae at the other entrances to the room. At the AID's command, the window opaquing dilated.

"Just like Custer," Patty said under her breath, seeing the massed shapes in the garden. It was the splintering of wood, from behind her, that ignited the battle. She took aim with her own gun, told the AID to open fire, and shot at the window. Her service pistol accelerated a stream of aluminum-skirted glass beads in a repulsion coil. An energy pulse vaporized the metal into a slick of plasma, and the coil accelerated the beads to supersonic speeds. The window disappeared in a shower of sharp fragments.

Her shot was answered by a flurry of return fire, the *whip-whip-whap* of supersonic beads and the crackle of blue lightning from the creepers in the garden. She threw herself on the floor behind the couch and counted three.

Pfeet! Pfeet! Pfeet! The Manjack picked its targets and eliminated them. Its weapon was not particularly fast, but who needed to hosepipe a thousand projectiles a minute when one, cybernetically placed, would do the job? The Manjack could afford to ignore the incoming beads that caromed off or splintered upon its titanite tripod and spindle.

Mora Koskiusko, flat on her belly, was using the Schlicter two-handed, feet splayed behind her to take up the recoil. That was going to rip hell out of her nylons, especially at the knees. Still, she was doing a nice professional job on the intruders: single shots there, no blind firing.

The little HVs were laying down a high-voltage suppression field. Anything one-point-five meters above the floor got fried. It wasn't doing the apartment's plush decor any good, but the baddies were hanging back in the foyer and in the kitchen hallway. Bertingas finally had his head down.

Patty figured they could hold the room for, oh, another thirty seconds or so. Then what?

The *what* was a dragon. The heavily armored aircar came screaming down into the terrace garden. Titanium slats feathered its ducts. Quartz glass ten centimeters thick shielded the driver. Everywhere else it was angles and planes of cold-rolled steel, layered with ceramics and resins—except for its turret, where the business end of a plasma exciter poked through.

The weapon was a standard of space warfare. Deep in its reaction chamber, an enfilade of lasers would excite a deuterium pellet to fusion heat; electromagnets would channel the expanding ball of plasma out through the discharge port. It was, in effect, a unidirectional fusion bomb. Aimed into the room.

Patty didn't think, not on any conscious level. Pulling a sonic grenade from her sleeve sheath, and keeping her ass below the level of the HVs' continuing discharge, she crawled forward. Crossing the line of broken shards where the window used to be, she emerged from the dark cave of Bertingas's lounge into bright sunlight and straightened.

Step, step, *step*, and she had one foot on the forward lip of the aircar's metal-mesh skirting. Her knees slipped on the flat steel of the forward deflector. Her hand found a grip somewhere on the exposed ductwork. She climbed. The turret depressed, its horrible mouth trying to get an angle on her, but Patty was too close and too low. With her free hand she pushed the grenade into the locking ring around the ball joint. No time—nor clear space—to jump free. She flattened herself against the dragon's warm steel skin, almost tasting the metal through her cheek.

The turret made a violent jerk, as if trying to dislodge her packet. The car rose with a howling cry, as if trying to withdraw. Then her shaped charge went off, destroying the turret mechanism, fanning the air above her with pieces of metal. Patty knew the interior of the car would reflect and amplify the shock of the explosion and all its harmonics. It tended to shred Human tissues.

Set on some kind of delay, the ruptured plasma gun went off. Its plume of ionized gas lashed out above Patty's head, tearing out part of the apartment wall and an old apple tree planted in the garden.

The car was still rising—and moving backward under the combined force of her grenade and its own plasma discharge. It was falling away from the garden and sliding, sloppily airborne, faster and faster, down the terraced face of Satellite Villas IV.

Patty hung onto its steel flank and prayed.

Chapter 7

Taddeuz Bertingas: SOMETHING REALLY DIFFERENT

Bertingas watched white motes dance against a red sky and waited for his eyes to clear. The afterimage of the tank-thing's one shot was still doing a rolling boil against his retinas.

How much energy had there been in that white plasma burst? How much radiation? Maybe his vision wasn't ever going to come back. Did he even *have* retinas now—or were his optic nerves just telling him a story?

"Mora?"

"Yes, Counselor?"

"Can you see?"

"Of course I—oh! You were looking at that dragon when it fired. Here, let me help you."

A hand caught him under the elbow and raised him, turned him, pushed gently. He sat on what was left of the couch, put his head back and watched the motes reorient themselves against the motion. He spread his fingers on the cushion beside him and felt long rips in the material. The surface was seeded with grit and slivers of syncrete.

"How are your eyes?"

"Getting better." And they were. The brightness of the images was fading. Still, too much light was coming into the room, even with the window blown out, and the background was going from red to blue. Were his corneas playing some kind of refraction trick?

In a minute more, he saw an outline, a jagged curve at the edge of vision. He turned his head. The south wall of the apartment was missing, letting in the blue sky. It was very quiet, except for the scrape of Mora's shoes as she moved around what was left of the room. Somewhere, water trickled from broken pipes.

Bertingas looked down at his sleeve and saw more white motes. The dark material was flecked with pieces of the syncrete wall and fluffy spots of ash, some of them from burn holes in his tunic. He figured this uniform—which had been fresh and new that morning—was now a total write-off.

He lifted his newly functioning eyes and looked for Mora. She was poking one-handed—her other still holding the Schlicter—around the butt end of the Manjack while it auto-tracked a random pattern out over the garden. After a second she found its manual circuits and shut it down. The muzzle wobbled once and depressed itself.

Maybe four hours ago Ms. Mora Koskiusko had been dressed for a day of shopping in the arcades of Meyerbeer. Bertingas remembered her summer frock of staggered polysilks. Now she was barely covered in gaudy rags with large areas of burnthrough—although the colorful bodystocking she wore seemed to have kept most of it from reaching the skin. Bertingas didn't mind the *primitif* effect, but she was going to catch a lot of stares if they went out on the streets.

Was there something in his closets—perhaps something Gina had left? All women were about the same size, weren't they? But then, did he even *have* a closet anymore? No, the other side of that wall . . .

Bertingas shook his head and stood up.

"How soon do you think," Mora asked, "before they try again?"

"Who? The Haiken Maru? They probably think we're dead in all this. Emergency Services, however, has undoubtedly received calls about the blast and the crash of that—'dragon.' We should be seeing the first med crews in about three minutes."

"We don't want to be here then."

"Why not?"

"Well, for one thing, they're going to want you to fill out the *long form* on this mess. That's going to take time. For another, the H.M. almost surely have a tap into the Emergency Net, and as soon as they start sending in reports—"

"We're marked," he finished.

"So we disappear. Now."

"What about Firkin? Did you see—?"

"She went over the wall with the dragon. Very brave performance, but I doubt anyone could have survived that blast, plus whatever happens when a machine like that augers in sideways. No, really—we must leave this place, and quickly."

"You can't go out, not like that."

She looked down at herself, for the first time apparently, then at him.

"You haven't seen the back of your uniform, have you, Counselor?" A smile curled her lips. "Think hard. Don't your, um, nether regions feel a trifle breezy?"

"Well, ah, yes." That was why he'd kept turning to face her.

"We could borrow from our friends here." She pointed to the half-dozen bodies—all apparently Human—that were sprawled from the sill of his lounge window out onto the terrace. Those covered by an angle of wall had not been burned in the blast.

Between them, he and Mora found complete outfits. It was dole clothing: drab, monochrome fabrics with cheap plastic closers. Mora took a wrapshirt off a man who'd been headshot; it was a clean kill—one she may have made herself. Bertingas had to take a jacket-and-dickie combination that settled a thumb-sized hole over his sternum. They managed to find two corpses which hadn't voided themselves and so ruined their trousers.

Oddly, for all the cheapness of the clothing, every man had a good pair of black leather boots; Tad and Mora could take their pick. The garments themselves, while worn, were uniformly fresh-washed. The bodies beneath were in fit shape and fairly hygienic.

"What do you make of all this?" Bertingas said.

Mora toed one set of naked white buttocks, as if testing the now-flaccid muscles.

"I'd say they were soldiers, dressed to look poor."

"Mercenaries?"

"Of course. None of our Fleet Joeys would go into a battle like this—without armor, comm sets, and proper weapons."

"What happened here wasn't meant to be a battle," Bertingas pointed out. "It wouldn't have been, if Firkin hadn't rigged that Manjack. . . . This was just supposed to be a simple kidnapping."

"Anytime you take along a dragon," Mora observed, "you're expecting a battle."

"Oh."

"Now. Shall we *go?*"

As they walked out the front entrance onto the garden path, the first of the sirens was in the air.

They quickened their steps in time with the warbling beat.

Where to go? Tad's AID held the addresses and partial dossiers of the two recruiting contacts Selwin Praise had given him. That was the business of the moment. And, from the dedicated way the Haiken Maru had been trying to kill him, it looked like the sooner Tad had a medium-size army at his back, the longer he was going to live.

He did have doubts about taking Mora Koskiusko with him, though. She might indeed be the Admiral's daughter, although her equipment and weapons—a repulsor with which she seemed to be expert and an AID that had impressed even Firkin—hinted at a less delicate upbringing.

Which made her . . . What?

Either *another* Haiken Maru heavy—despite her story about surviving a snatch job on the landing ramp, which could simply be window dressing. Or another Kona Tatsu agent, possibly working covertly for Halan Follard, possibly not.

Maybe, just maybe, admirals' delicate daughters did go shopping with classified hardware and a 100-gram bead slinger under their arms.

"Look," he said, as they crossed at street level to the monorail stop. "I have some business to attend to. It could be roughhouse, but most likely it will merely be boring. You probably have something more interesting to do, some social engagements, or—"

She stopped walking, turned toward him. Her shoulders sagged. The cheap, mannish clothing made her seem younger, more waiflike, more helpless. Perhaps, too, it was the smudges of dust on her pretty face.

"It's not that I don't want you along," he said quickly, "but this is Department business, and—"

"I have no one else to go to."

"No friends in the city? Or—"

"I kept my address book on a sidefile of the Naval Net. Captain Thwaite has extraordinary access. Any of my friends will be known—and watched. Anyway, I don't want what happened at your apartment to be happening to them. They wouldn't be as—so well prepared to receive visitors."

Her mouth curled in a wry smile. Bertingas knew she was trying to be winning, and he was won over anyway.

"All right," he sighed. "We'll make the run together. For as long as the Haiken Maru will let us. Do you have any extra ammunition for that Schlicter?"

Mora popped the clasp on her bag, pulled out four flat-black cartridge drums and a power cell. She held them up to him with a grin. "Where are we going?"

"Chinatown."

"Oh." She slid the drums back into her purse slowly.

Whatever a "china" might once have been—and Bertingas knew the Baseform Scatter Platter held at least 15 references or variants—"Chinatown" was now the Pact-common term for any urban concentration of aliens, especially mixed types. Chinatown had the whiff of strange spices, sundown deals, hard coinage, corruption, and naivete. It was a fringe where even dole humans stepped carefully. The air was too thick there, and the law too thin.

They took a monorail car headed for the southwest side of the city, across the river, where the aerial line went underground and didn't come up again. The tube stop was called "Marlborough," from a time when the district had been something else.

They emerged into a swarm of bodies, humanoid and divergent, walking, running, and waddling on two or more legs, whips, or dervish pods. Everyone around them moved three beats faster than a purely Human crowd would, with synapses closing faster.

Tad and Mora walked in a cloud of impatient grunts, taps, and swerving bodies.

The smells changed with each step and with every storefront and shopstall they passed: oranges, raw liquor, abraded polymers, T4 cell fuel, blasting jelly, old fish, lithium salts, fresh rubber, lubricating oil, fresh earth, bokai mushrooms, burned steel.

Colors abused their senses: skins like chrome, or jungle leaves, or patterned carpet; clothing that fluoresced in the sunlight; in one shop, strands of meat hanging in a red lightbath and glowing with green flecks; a Messenger AID that navigated in black light and washed specks of fluorescence out of the street with its eyes; a four-armed holo-juggler whose lightshow pulsed with overtones of yellow and green.

Buildings in this quarter were old and close together, flatblocks of three and four stories. They were assembled from slabs of foamed gray concrete—not the whiter, stronger syncrete—which had been pumped in place and tipped upright. Cableways, conduits, windows, and doorways had been cut with shaped charges, later patched over, then cut again someplace else.

Marlborough held echoes of the original frontier city, poor and scrambling, practical and diverse, that Meyerbeer had been before it raised the monumental architecture of a cluster capital. No gardens were kept here.

Or maybe, in alien terms, the raw garbage that lapped the street *was* a garden. The purplish light strobing from a fixture in the wall above it might be a nutrient spectrum. Bertingas stopped in the crowd and stared for a minute at the dull wads of fiber and scraps of colored rind jelled in a waxy binder. He was trying to see a pattern, the order of a tending hand instead of the jumble of discard.

A foot, three toes in blue plastic sheathing, came down in the middle of it, withdrew, kicked once to shake off the debris, and hurried on. So it was just garbage after all.

"What are you looking at?" Mora asked.

"Nothing." He straightened. "Our first contact is a person named Glanville. Address is 22-24 Sextet. Should be down this way."

The address looked like a mistake: a commercial building in an empty alley. Its entrance and lower windows were covered with panels of opaque yellow plastic, fitted flush and bolted into the concrete. The feeder conduit had been dug out, capped, and tagged with shutoff notices from both the Water Supply and Energy Supply departments. If people were living in there, they were drinking from bottles and reading by squeezelight—if they drank and read at all.

"How do we get in?" Mora asked. "Are you sure this is the right address?"

"It's all the address we have. We get in when we find a way in."

Bertingas went to the entrance panel, spread his hands a meter apart, palms outward, and pushed. The panel flexed by about two centimeters and rebounded with a hollow drumming. It felt about half a centimeter thick. He'd need at least a drill and a saber saw, and about fifteen minutes, to cut a doorway.

From above them came a rasping noise. They stepped back into the alleyway, looked up.

"What do you want?" asked a voice.

Bertingas searched the blank windows until he found one on the third floor that was cracked outward. Behind the crack was a pale face—maybe Human, probably not.

"We are looking for a gentleman named 'Glanville,' " he called.

"No Glanville here."

"We have money for him," Tad lied smoothly.

Pause. Two. Three. "How much?"

"More than we want to discuss out here in the street."

"Wait one."

The shadow of a face disappeared. With another rasp, the window swung wide. A beam with a pulley bolted onto its end slid out through the opening. A fiber line was paid out, snaking down to the pavement.

"Make hitch," the voice called from inside. "We pull you up."

Bertingas picked up the end and put a quick bowline in it. He looked at Mora. "This is no time for ladies first."

"You're absolutely welcome to it."

"If you hear—"

"I'll run—"

"Right."

Tad put his foot in the loop and tugged once on the slack. "Haul away."

The line went up quickly, until his head was alongside the beam. Then the whole affair was pulled back into the building on a track arrangement. He swung his free foot up onto the windowsill and stepped through, kicking off the loop before he jumped down.

The room inside was shadowed. It echoed like empty space. The light, when it came, was from a kilowatt portable flood that blinded Bertingas. But before it had clicked on, he saw at least five biped bodies, in a semicircle, all ready for mayhem. In the glare, all he could see were scarred white walls, scraps of lumber in the near corner, and a camp chair by the window, probably for the watchman.

"Call your companion. Make happy voice so he come."

"No."

"Won't hurt you. We take money, for Glanville."

"No. You take me to Glanville."

"Glanville not here. Give money." The objective lens of a jeweler's laser settled next to Tad's left eye.

"What we have for him is not exactly cash. It's in the form of a business deal . . . which will lead to money."

"Wait one. Are you Bertingas? From Government Block?" The voice changed, dropping some of its sourness.

"Yes."

"Glanville told us about you. We will take you to him. Call your companion."

The floodlight clicked off, leaving Bertingas blind in the dark of the room. He turned to the window, where the early evening sky was fading.

"Mora! It's all right—I think. Come on up."

Still blinking, he felt hands on his upper arms, moving him aside so they could work the pulley. The first thing he could really be sure of seeing was the outline of Mora Koskiusko, the curves of hip and arm and shoulder, with the evening light behind her cloud of blonde hair, as she stepped through the window. She let go of the rope and dusted her hands.

"Trouble?" Mora asked him.

"Mistaken identity. All fixed." He turned to the others. "Well, shall we go to Glanville now?"

The apparent leader, a pale-skinned Human male with a broken nose and a knife scar distorting his upper lip, hesitated.

"He sleeps now. We wait six hours, then take you."

"That's a long time to wait. We'll go about our errands, and then come back." Bertingas made for the window and the rope end, but a hand caught him.

"You must stay. See too much already."

"What have we seen but an empty room?"

"Faces. Our faces."

"I have a bad memory for faces."

"Pocket brains take holos." He gestured at the

AIDs both Mora and Tad carried. "Run their own games. We keep you till business over."

"Well, what are your accommodations like?"

Another empty room. With a table, a cold water basin, and an airbed that wheezed mightily when Bertingas tried an experimental bounce. The room also had a thick door with a lock. It was nothing an alert AID couldn't con, but enough to discourage casual visits around the building—or ungracious exits.

"Well, it's been a long day," he said, sitting on the edge of the bed and bouncing gently. "If you count receiving the news of one assassinated High Secretary, attending an executive council session to settle issues concerning same, meeting a new Director who's also a slimy turd, landing one busted aircar from seven klicks up, and—for recreation—enjoying a spell of target practice in my own living room. And it's not even vespers yet; I'd call that one of my busier days. How about you?"

Mora perched on the edge of the table, lightly.

"Let's see. Fighting off kidnappers at the port this morning. Running and hiding the length of Meyerbeer. Helping you and your friend with target practice. Making an unexpected visit to Chinatown. And getting hauled through the third-floor window of an abandoned building. Yeah, busy . . . I'm hungry!"

"We can't eat here. Chinatown."

"Our hosts look Human enough."

"I thought I saw a pair of hooves among them. Anyway, no telling what their metabolic balance is, nor their tolerances. We'll eat elsewhere, after we see this Glanville. Meanwhile, I suggest we get some rest."

"Are you offering me the floor?"

"Wouldn't you rather use the bed? It's big enough for two."

Those perfect eyebrows raised slowly, and her eyes widened, but her mouth was smiling.

"We'll both be fully clothed," Tad said, "and I'll leave a foot of space between us."

"Very well." Did her smile fade by a fraction? "I *am* tired."

Bertingas dutifully rolled to the far side of the airbed. She came over and lay down, primly, on her side, facing away from him. He watched the curve of her hip and upper arm rise gently and fall with her breathing until his eyes closed.

"Get up!" The voice entered his consciousness as part of the dream he was having. He had fallen asleep at a staff conference and his mother, with three day's growth of beard and a knife scar across her mouth, was shaking him awake and shouting in his ear.

"What time is it?" Mora asked, through a yawn that she barely hid with one slender hand. Her hair looked loose and breezy and still beautiful.

"Three hours after midnight," the watchman said. "Glanville wakes."

"All right then." Bertingas sat up, and felt a muscle pull in his back like a kinked slipknot. "Let's—agh—go."

Mora went over to the table and dipped into the basin of water. She touched the corners of her eyes experimentally.

"Don't bother," the houseman said. "We wash you."

She gave him a startled look and left the table.

He led them to a room that was fitted out like a primitive medlab—cold white porcelain and chrome-faced equipment. "Take off clothes."

"Oh, come now," Mora temporized. "We're not going to—"

Now she was looking into that jeweler's laser. "Glanville is allergic to Humans. You do it our way."

Her fingers found the clasps on the borrowed

wrapshirt. It fell open on wider vistas than Tad could remember seeing in a long time.

"What are *you* looking at?" she demanded.

"Everything," he said with a shrug and got busy with his own trouser tabs.

Soon they stood naked and shivering on the concrete floor. Tad tried to do strategic things with his hands and forearms, but Mora just stood there proudly, wrapped in glory. The guard, who treated them like sides of cold meat, pushed Bertingas toward a man-sized cabinet. It was an ultraviolet bath, without goggles. Tad stepped in, covered his eyes with the heels of his hands, and took a hard, microbe-killing dose. Then it was a diffuse laser-flash that burned the top layer of dead cells and body hair off his skin, followed by a disinfectant shower. When he stepped out, the escort gave him a loose-fitting gown of stiff white cloth, tied at the neck but open at the back, and a pair of rope-fiber sandals.

He felt like a mendicant on pilgrimage to the Fountains of Outre. Bertingas reached for his clothes and got his hand slapped.

"We give later. After Glanville."

"At least let me take the AID."

"You trust own voice. Glanville speaks Lingua."

"It has important data that—"

"Later." He bundled the AIDs into their clothes and boots and stuffed them all into a sack. Mora's Schlicter, its spare powerpack and drums of beads went in on top. The guard didn't seem either impressed or bothered by her weapon.

"Now what?" Tad asked.

"Now Glanville." The man took them back into the corridor, down to another door, opened it on a perfectly darkened room and stood back for Tad to enter. He hesitated for one second, then swallowed his misgivings and stepped through.

Into a drop shaft with its mass cap set far too low.

He dropped at about fifteen meters a second. Starting from the third floor of the building, he expected to reach the basement within about a second and a half. In a bone-breaking hurry.

Two seconds into his own drop, he heard Mora call: "Tad? Ta-aa-aiiyee!" Then she was following, somewhere above him in the darkness.

He tried to remember the drill for drop tube failure. Something about keeping your head up, flexing your elbows and knees, and trying to reach a superhuman state of relaxation while expecting a hard impact at any second.

Four seconds into the fall, and he had stabilized at what felt like a constant twenty meters per second. At the fifth second, and counting, a repulsion field grabbed him and shoved sideways. He did a sloppy forward judo roll, flopped over on his face, and came up standing in another corridor. This one was dimly lit with blue safety lights. It was cold down here.

Mora came shooting out of the access behind him, feet first, the white gown flaring, and struck him at the knees. They both went down in a tangle.

"All right. All right." She pulled herself up without his help. "Where are we?"

"About ten stories underground, near as I can figure."

"Which way to this Glanville character?"

"Forward, I guess."

"Then lead on."

He walked forward, one hand near but not touching the wall on his left. It wasn't a made wall, he decided, but the banded sedimentary rock that underlay Meyerbeer's valley. The stone had been bored out and fused with a plasma cutter. It sweated with the cold. The lights overhead were connected with ribbon conduit. Energy Supply was hooked up down here, if not in the shell of a building above.

After a hundred meters they passed: a cabinet,

which was locked; a dark side tunnel drawing negative air pressure down it; a desk with a guard. He either wore a grotesquely ridged helmet and breastplate, or grew his own grotesque beak and carapace. He either grew lenses instead of eyes, or wore some kind of light-amplifying goggles. He looked them over silently and waved them on.

The corridor bent and widened, the ceiling rising until they were in a blue-lit cavern perhaps thirty meters across. It was large enough to have its own chill breezes. People stood about in small groups, all more or less facing a shelf of the native rock on the far side of the cave. As his eyes adjusted, Tad saw that the bodies were mostly alien.

A number were hoof-footed Satyrs. Here, however, they were careless of their usual disguises. No shoes with plastic prostheses to fill in their missing arches and toes. No loose pants to hide the backward bends of hocks and pasterns. No artfully combed curls to conceal the points of ears. No make-up pencil to draw away the slant of eyes. Nothing to hide the permanent smiles that creased their lips.

Several in the crowd were the beak-and-carapace creatures, like the desk guard. It was a type Bertingas had never seen classified. They reminded him, however, of upright-walking lobsters. Their shells were mottled yellow, some shading to blue, some to green. They had subtle, articulated hands, like a multiform robot's. They had six jointed knees for each leg. Their faces were unreadable.

One or two in the room were green-skinned Cernians. Small, short-headed, clannish. Otherwise, they conformed to the Five-Point Process: bipedal, bilaterally symmetrical, clustered sensorium, articulated limbs, tool using. It was the usual "humanoid" form—which had so surprised the Humans when they first encountered aliens in venturing beyond their Home Cluster.

At the end of the room, however, was something really different.

On the rock shelf was a shallow bowl about a meter across, covered with a glass dome. Inside, as Tad and Mora approached and bent to look in, was a sluggish liquid that bubbled slowly. A Satyr stood by with a rag to wipe off the frost that kept forming on the dome. Whiffs of vapor puffed out of the holes where the wires went in.

Half submerged in the bath, with steel probes poking into its rind, was a cactus. Or it looked like a cactus: fluted, barrel-shaped body; stubby arms at right angles; white spines along the ridges. The disconcerting thing was its color, a more Human fleshtone than even Gina Rinaldi could manage. At the top of the body was a single fragile flower, maroon and white, reminding Tad of an origami paper lantern.

"I am Glanville." The voice came, not from the air, but from inside his mind.

Tad looked quickly and saw that, behind the bowl, the leads from the steel probes were connected to an AID, which in turn was hooked into a standard telecoder. Somebody had wired up a vegetable for a joke!

"Of course you are," he articulated in his head, adding the muscle pulls for a mammoth sneer.

"It would be easier for you to speak normally. And leave out the histrionic gestures."

So it was a smart AID. Sensitive, too. Tad still wasn't going to believe in a talking vegetable.

"Why not?" the voice in his head asked. "At cryogenic temperatures, many substances become superconducting and 'sensitive.' Why do you believe this is impossible in that order of life you Humans choose to call the 'Plant Kingdom'?"

Riffles of laughter went around the cavern. Apparently the 'coder was broadcasting one or both sides of this conversation.

Tad found his voice. "You can speak for these—?"

"For these members of the 'Animal Kingdom'? Yes, I think they will accept my advice. Now, you have a proposal for me, don't you, Counselor?"

"I have most of the details in my AID . . ."

"I know. We're questioning your little mechanical friend right now. However, you can give me the general outline—yes?"

"We are . . . that is, the Department of Communications is . . . recruiting a ready defense force. Its objective will be to protect the Hyperwave Satellite Network and other communications assets of this Cluster in the event of civil or military crisis. We need three thousand capables, all trained or trainable in weapons technology, amenable to military discipline, and able to take direction in Lingua and respond in same."

The seconds ticked by and Glanville was silent, not even carrier noise from the 'coder.

"When you reach my age," it said slowly, "you learn that life, even the short lives of animals, is precious. Some of these 'capables' will have the opportunity to die—yes?"

"They may."

"You are trying to project onto my mind the images of an easy life, Bertingas. Barracks living, idle hours, paperwork, games, routine, plentiful food. A few alarms, for drill perhaps, but no real fighting. Yet those are dishonest images, aren't they?"

Tad closed his eyes and blanked his mind.

"Essentially," he replied.

"Your department would not budget to pay for such a force if you did not expect to need it. You yourself would not come here, through the barriers of distaste and personal inconvenience we have set for you, if you did not see bloody conflict in the near future. You are more disturbed by the death of the High Secretary than you thought—yes?"

Tad could feel Mora watching him. He shifted his eyes and caught her look of concern.

"He was your High Secretary, too," Tad said, "if your species is a Pact signatory. If there is a war for the succession, it won't be Humans only."

"But it will be Humans mostly—yes? So, what will you offer these recruits that would compensate them for casting their lives into probability?"

"Human pay scales, for starters. The right to choose their own company-level officers. However, all will be ultimately responsible to the Director of Communications, with me as his second in command."

"Full Pact citizenship," Glanville countered. "Extended to families in the event of personal death. The right to live as Human equals at discharge, with no restrictions in space or time. The Bans will be broken for those who volunteer. Veterans will have first call on all new permanent positions in the Communications Department for which they may be qualified."

"I can't promise all that."

"You will do your best—yes?"

"Well, yes. I suppose I can try."

A glassine chuckle echoed in his mind.

"That may be good enough, Counselor. You will have my best, too. The troops you seek, half of them, are even now being mustered and moved to the barracks sites selected by your capable Rinaldi—"

"It's too soon—we're still in the planning—"

"Our true master," Glanville's mental carrier rode over him, "has sent the order down. It will be carried out. . . . The other half of your contingent you will obtain from my brother, Choora Maas. Go to him."

With a silvery *ping*, the carrier shut down and the room seemed to lose an extra dimension beyond shape. Bertingas stood there, looking at just a rind of cactus plant frozen in a bath of liquid gas.

He turned toward Mora, saw the rest of the room, all those aliens with hidden smiles.

"I guess that's it," he said to her.

"Did you get what you wanted?"

"Most of it."

"Then let's *go*, shall we?"

He took her hand and led her back across the cavern. The knots of onlookers melted away before them, the crowd meeting his eyes with amused stares. As Tad and Mora were about to step into the tunnel arch, the telecoder switched back on.

"One more thing, Counselor." From a distance of thirty meters, and with the bowl hidden by the intervening bodies, Glanville's mental voice seemed depthless and blind. "And 'No Cernians'—yes?"

The aliens in the room shared the laughter in his voice, especially the Cernians themselves.

Before Tad could reply, the carrier clicked off again.

Once in the corridor, the lobsterman who had been at the desk—or another of the same color—took them to a lighted side tunnel. Cut into its far wall was the opening of a drop tube. The bony ridges of the guard's hand settled on their shoulders . . . and shoved.

Tad, Mora, and a kick of dust from the corridor floor spun into a lift field set far higher than any building was allowed by license. The loose white gown rose up around Tad's hips; he sacrificed his equilibrium to use his hands for modesty. Mora just let her gown float and met his eyes with her woman's secret smile.

In ten seconds the field slowed and balanced them opposite an entranceway. Tad swam out and put a foot down onto the loading dock and cold storage area of a large restaurant. He reached back in and pulled Mora onto the solid flooring.

Still hand-in-hand, they walked out into the steamy

kitchen area. It was bustling with Satyrs. Amid steam and the clatter of pans and pots, they chopped, mixed, kneaded, baked, and boiled. What they were cooking, Bertingas couldn't figure out. It looked like green bamboo, or maybe papyrus reeds. It smelled like a glue factory, with overtones of honeybucket.

Satyrs had a Pactwide reputation as gourmands. Perhaps that was more concealment. Perhaps, too, they were cooking here for a herd of Gitchoos.

One of the Satyrs spotted them, paused with his cleaver high, tucked it—still dripping green sap—into his hairy armpit, and dug a bundle from under his chopping block. He brought it over and put it in Tad's hands.

They pulled on their clothes. Tad's AID, when he set it on a counter, squawked about rough treatment and "the bulls" giving him "the third degree." Whatever that meant. He supposed it had been dropped and damaged somehow. Mora's military service model AID was discreetly quiet.

"Now what?" she asked, bent over and tying her bootlaces.

"Now we go find Choora Maas. And get away from this *smell!*"

Chapter 8

Hildred Samwels: XENOPHOBES

Castor and Pollux were the strangest configuration that Captain Hildred Samwels had seen in fifteen years of service with Central Fleet. They still drew his eye every time he looked up through the wall of ten-gauge pressure glass behind the Admiral's head.

It was clearly an ephemera, a condition of instability that could not last. . . . How long *would* it last? As a programming exercise Samwels had once fed what was known about the pair into his AID and asked for a prediction. Fifteen hundred years, plus or minus two hundred, was the answer. Barely a strobe flash in the history of this system orbiting around the star named, ominously enough, Kali. Yet the Pact had happened to put a base here at the precise moment of grandeur.

Castor was a massive gas giant, the primary about which Gemini Base orbited at a distance, far outside the chaff of rocks and moonlets that circled the giant. Castor's small, dense companion was Pollux, which orbited fast and close to the larger planet's limb. Little Pollux was more than moon and less than twin—and Samwels knew enough preclassical mythology to make the connection.

Between the binary planets flowed a bell-shaped tube of gas, the atmosphere of Castor bleeding off to Pollux, lagging under the speed of the latter's orbit. Under most conditions, a laminar flow of nearly pure hydrogen would be invisible against the black of space. However, the tube was more than a gas stream, and the gas was more than pure hydrogen. Fierce energies flowed between the two bodies. The atmosphere of Castor contained a high percentage of the noble gases: neon, argon, krypton, xenon. They absorbed those energies and discharged photons at random and gorgeous frequencies within the visible spectrum.

Worms of red and orange wrestled with cloudbursts of green and blue. For Samwels, it was better than closing his eyes and watching the phosphenes dance. More color.

What would happen when, 700-odd years from now, Pollux tipped the gravity balance with its weight of stolen atmosphere? Would the flow reverse? Would the revolution of master and moon reverse—and Pollux become the primary? That would create instabilities which Gemini Base, even at this distance, would be better off not experiencing.

What was Pollux, anyway? A cindered-out dwarf star? A lump of pure uranium? A fist-sized fragment of neutronium? Gemini Base's electromagnetic scanners were vague on the matter, but the probes that Samwels had sent down to the surface of Pollux disappeared without a squeak. A pauper for data, his AID was rich with speculations. It was almost a hobby with the machine, one that Samwels encouraged.

The bridge between Castor and Pollux was a reminder to him. This system, with no inhabitable planets—no planets at all except for this antic pair—in an empty corner of the hyperbubble called Aurora

Cluster, could harbor such a sight, a waterfall of light to please the Human eye. It told him that the universe was a huge place with its own designs and purposes. The universe was self-minded, ever changing, sometimes cold and indifferent, sometimes generous with surprise. . . .

"Do you follow me, Captain?" the Admiral demanded.

"Of course, sir. The—ah—the succession, and its effects on Central Fleet policy. Yes, sir."

"Hmph! 'Effects.' The High Secretary *is* our policy. Of course, you're probably feeling a bit out of your depth here, in a staff job. Not as simple as your usual post in Engineering. There you take direct action: assess, make plans, do. Got a burned out condenser under the pinch bottle? Then you figure the man-hours in watches, line up dockage space, and fix it. Well, that's my preference, too, Captain."

"That's—"

"But here we have to be pol-i-tick. Can't specify and predict these civilians' actions the way you can order a Tech Spec-2 around. Politicians are going to do what they want and figure it's our duty to run after them with a magnetic wipe. Damn them."

"What will the envoy from Arachne Cluster want, sir?"

"His head patted every fifteen seconds, I'll wager. Governor Spile is a man of limited capabilities, from what I've seen. The sort who'll keep toadies and send them all over his neighbors on social calls. I'll take care of him in half an hour. Then, Samwels, we must talk more about the situation out of Central Center. Decide what we're going to do if that blind puppy Roderick is allowed to sit on his uncle's chair."

"Yes, sir . . . Uhhh, is there any word about Mora—Ms. Koskiusko—sir?"

"Damn girl! Goes shopping in the cluster capital and disappears. I've asked Thwaite to look for her, quietly. Not a man I'd trust alone with her, you understand. Not a man I trust entirely on anything— too involved with the landsiders, the traders, the political people." The Admiral paused. "You keep *that* kind of knowledge in this office, Captain. Still, Thwaite is on the spot, and he does have a company of Marines on Palaccio. He'll find her. Unless she's disappeared herself and is shacking up with some bar stud. Kill that girl. Daughters are a heartbreak. When you marry, Samwels, have only sons—and that's an order." The Admiral smiled at his own joke.

"Yes, sir."

"All right, go and get Spile's errand boy. See what kind of fish oil he's selling."

The envoy from Arachne Cluster was a war hero— from a war Samwels had never heard of. The man walked and gestured with multiple prosthetics, his spine encased in glass and tapped with electrodes. A small compressor strapped to his lower back drove the hydraulic pistons on his skeletal limbs. Above this walking machine was a face as pale and thin as winter.

Samwels invited the envoy into the Admiral's inner office, and the man strode past, sparing him not even a glance. A whiff of machine oil and the purr of pumps went with him. The captain withdrew and shut the hatch.

In the outer office sat the envoy's retinue: a woman in civilian dress and two men in the uniform of Cluster Command. They were older, with a gray hair here, a wrinkle there, and had the aura of a team of strangers thrown together, from different special interests, to make this official visit. Samwels read anxiety in their eyes. Their focus shifted nervously around the reception area and yet, when these people occasionally traded a word with each other, their eyes did not meet.

Samwels was crossing to his own adjutant's office,

across from the admiral's, when one of the men spoke to him.

"Captain, what kind of armed strength would you be having here at Gemini?"

"Enough. This is a Class 2 Cruiser Dock and Cluster Resupply. We have the cyber capacity, energy equivalents, and manpower here to patrol and protect a fifty-planet unit. Or administer a ten-planet cluster directly, in a crisis."

"You must have the power to win those planets, too, by conquest, I'll bet. Very useful."

"Ahhh. The question isn't likely to come up, is it, sir?"

"Sooner than you think, boy."

"Surely, we're past those days—sir. That's the whole point of the Pact."

"The Pact is just a bookmark in the pages of history. Just a breathing space for those who have the will to believe in—argh! Get off! Bugeyes!"

While the man had been talking, Pasqual had come up and touched him. The Dorpin was a heavy-gravity creature, built low to the ground like an earthly turtle but without the hard shell. He was nominally in the ranks as a swabbie assigned from Maintenance and Repair; his pushbroom was parked out in the corridor. Samwels knew Pasqual as a gentle soul and an innate Human psychologist to whom the noncoms and deckies took their personal problems. The touch, with one forefoot, was an aid to his hearing. (Samwels had personally seen that same foot, armed with four-inch stiletto claws under those moistly wrinkled pads, score metal in an airlock emergency.) Pasqual must have sensed a troubled spirit in the Arachnean's face or gestures and wanted to help.

"He only means to be kind, sir," Samwels said.

"Well, he's disgusting. I won't be pawed by an animal." Almost as an afterthought, the man pulled back his fist and punched the Dorpin in the snout. "Teach you, Bugeyes."

"Stop that!" Samwels ordered. "He is *not* an animal."

Without hearing a word of this but sensing the emotional flow, Pasqual looked up at Samwels. The captain waved him off. Using the two-finger language that Gemini Base had learned for Dorpins, he made the sign for a pile of waste. Pasqual replied with a push of his nose, sweeping up said pile, and made a smile.

"They're all animals," the Arachnean concluded grandly. "Those under alien influence—even such as Merikur, who's become a little too big for his reputation—will get what they deserve from the rest of Humanity."

"Really?" Samwels said coolly and began to turn away.

"But tell me, Captain," said the other man. "What kind of support for the Pact do you have among your other ranks? Everyone as uniformly loyal as you?"

"You may assume the answer to that, sir."

"Come now! Central Fleet's position is not so strong that you can turn your back on all of us. There will be places in the new order for all men with latitude of vision. Even outside the confines of Arachne Cluster. Even for former captains. We will need young men who can see their rightful loyalties."

"I doubt you'll find many here."

"Don't hesitate too—"

"Be still, you fools," the woman hissed at them. "This young fanatic will be putting us all in irons, before Quintain has a chance to convince the old fanatic inside."

The three cackled among themselves, although their eyes never met.

Samwels went into his office and had almost closed the hatch on them. Suddenly the facing hatch into the Admiral's office popped open. The envoy, Quintain, emerged in a series of fast jerks, his evident anger overriding the governors on his steel limbs. The three aides gathered themselves quickly and followed him out into the corridor.

"We'll be back, Captain." The man who had punched Pasqual stuck his head back into the room and leered. "Don't you—"

"Come!" Quintain barked at him. They all bustled up the passageway in the wake of the pistoning machine-man.

Samwels waited a moment, then drifted back toward the open hatchway of Admiral Koskiusko's office. It was shameless to invite himself that way, but . . .

"Captain Samwels!" the Admiral called.

"Yes, sir?"

The older man was sitting behind his desk, smoking a *Nicotiana hydroponica* cigar so hard and fast that the coal on the tip fairly crawled toward his mouth. And the Admiral had been trying to give them up.

"Do you know what that slimy piece of—of machinery tried to do to me? Suborn me, that's what!"

"How did he—?"

"Told me I could 'reaffirm my loyalty to the Pact' by immediately putting Gemini under the command of Governor Spile. Those people must have worms in their heads if they can confuse a minor proconsulship with the High Secretary."

"Of course, sir. I found his retinue to be—"

"I told *him* that neither my loyalty nor the chain of command was in question, and that neither one would permit me to even consider such an act."

"Good for you, sir."

"So he says that Arachne Cluster *is* the Pact in this quadrant, and Aaron Spile is running it. Or words to that effect. Gemini will be 'reduced' if it doesn't submit. . . . Now what kind of Cluster Command forces are going to take—and beat, mind you—eight heavy cruisers and twenty destroyers?"

"Well, sir, we do have a problem with some of those old Mark I batteries, basically a lack of parts. The drive of the *Sochi Gorod* is out. But—"

"Then get it fixed. Anything on this base that isn't taut and ready for battle, fix that too."

"Yes, sir . . . But, this envoy, Quintain, it wasn't just his bluster, was it, that—?"

"At the end of our interview, when he was oiled up and really making threats, I got a little hot under the collar. Offered to see him in Hell before I broke my oath to defend the Pact. Then he suddenly went all smooth, and smiled at me like some kind of stalking cat. Said when he got there, he'd greet my daughter for me."

"Mora? What could he know about—?"

"Exactly. Unless he and his thugs have taken her."

"Perhaps we should bring her disappearance to the attention of Auroran civil authorities, or to the Kona Tatsu."

"I don't know, Captain. After this Spile thing, I don't incline to trust any of the locals. I think they're all a little zoomy. Now that the succession may be in doubt, they've all got visions of empire. Even Deirdre Sallee will go unstable, you'll see. And the Kona Tatsu—no, not them. Not yet."

"Then we must call on Thwaite, sir. Have him muster his Marines and take Palaccio apart to find her. If you can't trust him completely, sir, then send me. I can rescue your daughter for you. With or without the Marines."

"No, Captain . . . Hildred. I appreciate your enthusiasm, but your place is here. My best engineering officer. I need you to get my squadron up to battle readiness. I believe we have hard times ahead of us."

Pushing back his disappointment, Samwels let his

eyes flick past the Admiral's head, to the glowing bridge of noble gases that bound Castor to Pollux. Ephemera. Seven hundred years. Such a fleeting time to enjoy this grandeur.

"What do you keep looking at, Captain?" The Admiral turned and stared out the window. "Those planets aren't *going* anywhere, are they?"

Samwels smiled briefly. "No, sir."

Chapter 9

Taddeuz Bertingas: FIELDS OF ALIEN CORN

Tad and Mora left the Satyrs' restaurant by the back way, past bins of green marrow and barrels that leaked brown sauce with a piquant smell. The clientele was definitely Gitchoo.

Outside, they turned from a short alleyway into a main street, still somewhere in Chinatown. Tad immediately sensed a change in the atmosphere. Where before there had been roar and bustle, now there was a tense hush. It reminded him of the high country, or a forest, moments before a rainstorm swept through—or the front edge of a terrible fire.

A Satyr, one of the cooks, stepped into the alley behind them. He leaned against one wall, pulled a roll of tabac out of his apron, and took a bite with his flat grinding teeth. The slow smile of addiction spread across his big-nosed face—then faded. The Satyr sensed it, too. Tad saw him spit the wad, still fresh, behind a barrel and hurry back into his kitchen.

Tad looked left and right, up and down the street: shopkeepers quietly shutting their fronts, steel mesh coming down, vendors' carts wheeling around corners, *jongleurs* stuffing balls into their pockets and hurrying along. This part of the city was closing up, and it was just midmorning. Only scattered knots of people, Human and alien, the *innocenti*, still walked normally or stood looking into the display windows of the big stores.

"Well, which way do we go?" Mora asked. She hadn't felt it yet.

He strained his ears, trying to sense. . . . From the right, from a side street half a block down, came a sudden blast of noise, shouting, a clatter, the high jangle of breaking glass. Two men walked out into view, moving backwards, using the measured steps of crawler handlers guiding a big rig. Perhaps they were more like parade marshals. When they were well into the center of the pavement, a hundred feet down from Tad and Mora, the first of the others, the mob, broke from the side street in a tangle of heads and arms, waving sticks, and hoarse voices.

"What is *that?*" Mora asked.

Tad shook himself, took her arm, and tried to fade back into the alleyway. But it was a dead end; the Satyrs had shut and locked their kitchen door. The mob had already spotted Tad and Mora.

The handlers seemed to be directing it. The two men pointed and stepped back, and a pocket of the riot moved in their direction. Tad noticed, however, as he turned away, that when others picked up an abandoned pushcart and made to heave it through the front window of a Quality Mart store, the marshals blew whistles and tased them. The errant rioters dropped in a twitch.

Tad and Mora fled down into the alley, as far as it would take them. He was trying to make the space behind a steel drum big enough to hide both of them when the first of the rioters dashed in. Rough hands pulled the two out into the street again, pushed them up against the spalled concrete of a wall. A ring of angry faces surrounded them, all Human. Most had the scuffed look of dole receivers, and a high percentage were bleary with alcohol or gleaming with stimulants. Except for the men who moved like handlers: they wore fresh clothing, of padded shockcloth, and had brassards that were engraved with the serpentine insignia of Haiken Maru.

And Haiken Maru, Tad thought distractedly, was sole owner of the Quality Mart chain and a dozen other local distributors. Ah-ha!

The first blow came from the rioter opposite Tad, a tall, red-haired, thick-muscled man with a wobbling gut and a hanging, unhinged jaw. He slurred a threat as he swung a piece of heavy wooden batten at Bertingas's head. Tad pushed Mora down and ducked his head. The club rang like iron as it struck the concrete and rebounded.

The second blow was already launched from somewhere else when Tad reached up, grabbed the belt of the nearest marshal wearing a Haiken Maru badge, and pulled his head into the flight path. The blow stopped in mid-stroke.

"Hey, watch the hands, Alien Lover!" the marshal protested.

"Do you recognize this face?" Bertingas said slowly and distinctly. His fingers keyed the AID, which still had its holofocus attached. The head of Valence Elidor materialized in the air before them. Lips pursed, looking judicious, he was saying, "—Governor made a startling discovery of who, in the Communications section, actually did all the work. . . ."

Although the edges were blurred, the background dark, the image was a startling likeness. And those defects were to be expected when recording from a non-holo camera: the scrap of video had been taken from Tad's left retinal implant, the sound from a tap off his auditory nerves. Once installed, his Auto Track had saved Bertingas hundreds of hours of taking notes at important meetings, but he'd never expected it to save his life.

The marshal gaped at the head. Tad let the implications settle in. When they did, the man turned to the ring of rioting Humans and shouted them back, making strategic use of his taser. They turned and scattered, with the Haiken Maru hireling trailing the pack. Tad and Mora were suddenly alone in the alley.

Bertingas sank against the wall, making an effort to touch all points of his back—lumbar vertebrae, short ribs, shoulderblades, nape of neck—to the cool concrete. He'd heard it was good therapy for tension. It seemed to work.

Mora talked.

"I *knew* the H.M. were stirring up trouble. The last time Father and I were planetside—it was in Thwaite's outer office, now that I think of it—they actually tried to petition him—bribe is more like it—something about using Gemini as an auxiliary dock for their transports. But that must have just been a cover. Then, when I went out that day, some men seemed to be following me. One of them had a notch in his ear, where the graft was peeling away. I noticed that very particularly. And now, today, it's the same man. . . . Well, wasn't it?"

"Who?"

"The one you laid hands on. You were wonderful, Tad. Do you mind me calling you that? Tad . . . Anyway, the same rough man. And he works for Haiken Maru. And they are trashing the alien quarter. Now what do you make of that? I wonder if they're the same ones who tried to kidnap me yesterday. And Thwaite's in on it, I'll bet. This riot—which didn't do all that much damage, did it?—is probably just a put-on. And the real purpose was to snatch me again. Kill you and snatch me. And then—"

"Mora?"

"Yes, Tad?"

"Would you hold that thought? Please? Just for two minutes? I need some time to think myself."

"Oh. Yes. Of course." She closed her mouth with a snap and stood there in a sulk.

Was the Haiken Maru out to kill him again? No. If the marshals of that riot had been given specific instructions about Taddeuz Bertingas, then no implied relationship with Elidor would have scared them off. The whole affair had to be random violence. A crisis builder. Chipping away at the social stability on Palaccio—and at the political position Governor Sallee held. If the H.M. were going to wield mob rule like a club, it became more important than ever for Communications to get some kind of defense for its installations. Tad might have to hold open their last links with the rest of the cluster, and to Central Center.

"We still have to find this Choora Maas," he said finally. "Somewhere out in the plantations."

"May I speak now?"

"By all means."

"If you're going to travel with me, Counselor, then you will have to take me seriously."

"Eh?"

"You dismiss my observations, opinions, and theories. You discount my ability"—she raised her military-issue repulsor—"to defend us, especially in that last little tussle. Yet you're pretty generous with your eyes, when the occasion arises. You treat me, in general, like baggage. That is going to stop. Now."

"Well, all right. Sorry . . ."

"Sorry isn't good enough, Counselor. I am kin to—and a confidante of—the admiral commanding your local arm of the Central Fleet. Either that's good enough to be partners with a Level 9 Cluster Bureaucrat, or I walk my own way and you can find your precious Tyoura Moss with a compass and a dowsing rod. *Comprends-tu?*"

"Right! Yes! Okay! I understand!" Bertingas made an effort to modulate his voice, getting control. "So—how do we get out to the Plantations? Where, may I point out, it is in your interest to go. Because staying within the precincts of Meyerbeer has so far proven hazardous to your continued health—and mine. Notch Ear or not."

"You have a car at Government Block, don't you? That goes with the deputy director's job, I know."

"I can hardly show up there in these clothes. Borrowed and, ah"—he fingered the hole in his front—"strategically damaged."

"We could use public transit."

"The levitrail doesn't extend as far out as we're going."

"Then rent an aircar."

"The rentals all have transponders. Two minutes' thinking and a little tapwork will put us right into the hands of your friends and mine."

"Then *buy* a car."

"Using what for money? I've got about four Rands in my pockets, the price of a stale meatroll and cold tea."

"Betty has some secret funds." Mora tapped the AID hanging at her belt.

"Then let's find an agency."

They walked, surface level, on cobbled and tiled streets that were still partly deserted, toward the outer edges of Chinatown. There open space allowed the dealers in various forms of transportation to display their wares under the hot sun.

Tad stared out over acres of dusty, dented metal, glazed airskirting, and flaking paint. He saw fan ducts with blue scorches that suggested burned bearings and bad fires. He saw patched plastic and mismatched paint around junctures that suggested ejection maneuvers and salvaged bodywork. He saw leaking fuel pods and dribbling oil.

"Do any of them fly?" he asked the nimble-footed Cowra, the lot's owner and chief sales negotiator. The furry alien was doing its autonomic two-step in the aisle between these marred and sagging hulks.

"Oh yess, Effendi. All caars fly. Fly very weel."

Bertingas hunkered down to look underneath an old red Forza. It had been a two-person sports model—before someone tried to take the turbine out of it sideways. Maybe someone had put it back. Maybe not. The car's long body had a sloped nose and curving airfoils. There were hints that it had been race-prepared.

"Take a look at this bus!" Mora crowed, pointing to a green Bundel. Tad lifted his head long enough to see that its fans were missing half a dozen blades, like broken teeth. The unbalanced forces would make it shed a dozen more the first time the Bundel was fired up. Tad bent back to the Forza.

"Say, that's a *cute* little car!" she said, after a minute. She was winking at him and hiking her head back toward the Bundel.

Bertingas suspected Mora was just trying to dupe the Cowra with phony enthusiasm. Give it a sense of overconfidence—as if anyone could stuff a backbone into their moist little personalities.

"I don't know . . ."

"Most exceelent choice, Memsa'b. Lots of liift. Very faast. Take you kliick-klick."

"But there's not as much *leg room* as in the Bundel, Tad." She rolled her eyeballs at him, trying to signal something—what, he didn't know.

"Blades are shot," Bertingas said absently. He ran a hand along the Forza's red plastic bodywork. "Can we try this one out?"

"Aaahh. That is very haard, Effendi. Flight test requires a bond, registration forms, indemnities, traf-

fic control codes, airworthiness checks and stickers.
Much paaperwoork. You understand? Once you own,
we can comply with all formalities very quickly. But
not, unfortunately, on an unregistered vehicle. You
understand?"

"Perfectly. Well, Mora, I think this is the car we
want."

"Let's see what the price is, shall we—dear?" Again
the winking and blinking. He tried to signal back,
but didn't know what she wanted.

In the prefab booth that the Cowra called his
"orfice," Mora put her AID on the table and coupled
its beam with the lot's inventory and sales computer.
While the three of them looked on, the two machines dickered in pancode. At the end, the lot's
computer gave a long whistle and spoke a figure for
the Humans and the Cowra.

The latter's bushy eyebrows came down. "Your
maashine is very smaart, Memsa'b. Too smaart. Take
me for loong ride." He tapped its case with one long,
abraded claw. He seemed to be memorizing the
Naval serial codes molded into its top surface. "Too
smaart."

He went about setting up the change of ownership
through his computer, fingering the keyboard with
the pads under his eight claws. The lot's automated
guidance system put the red aircar into a smoky
hover and brought it around to the front. The Forza
settled down with a slight list to port.

Mora and Tad climbed in over the airskirting and
pulled down the hatches. The interior smelled of
cracked leather, resins baked in the sun, and ancient
oil. Tad thumbed the controls and the little car shot
vertically into the outer circles of the Meyerbeer
pattern. The onboard computer seemed to have a
good relationship with Air Control, so Tad let his
AID punch in their destination, out in the country.

The car lifted its nose like a horse and spun off to the south.

"I'm still wondering how you're going to do it," Mora said, after a few minutes of silent flying.

"Do what?"

"Seduce me in such a small car. The Bundel would have been much more practical for that."

Ah-haaa! "Seduce you? Is that what I'm trying to do?" he asked innocently.

"Well, aren't you? You've been leering at me and acting like it ever since we left your apartment."

So, now what? If he denied the intention, this spoiled girl would take it as a personal affront. The results of that were unpredictable. She might lapse into a stinging silence—which was not the worst of all possible outcomes. She might decide to leave suddenly, via the ejection seat and ED harness. Or she might shoot him. And if he got too chummy and played up to her obvious advances . . . Well, their forced partnership would get sticky. And there was a Central Fleet admiral somewhere in the background of *that*. Relations with a Human girl were a lot more complicated than they had been with his Deoorti pretender.

He wished he could drive the car manually for a while. Something to do with his hands.

While Bertingas considered his reply, Mora changed the subject. As if nothing had been said.

"I do hope Daddy isn't having more problems with Governor Spider."

"Who?"

"Spile, of Arachne Cluster. That's what I call him. It fits. He sits there, at the center of his plots and plans, sending out agents, threatening everybody. He's quite mad, you know."

"Why do you say that?"

"He wants to dominate the entire Pact. Says it outright in his speeches. It's only the problems he has in his own cluster, two or three rebellions a year, that have kept Central Fleet from taking direct action."

"So, why is he a danger to your father?"

"Because Spile has backers. The Haiken Maru for one. I have the proof here in Betty's hindbrain. They're providing him with ships and men."

"Warships? But the H.M. are commercial. How would they get hold of warships?"

"I don't know, but they must have ways. I'll wager that's why they wanted to snatch me."

"Because they're selling munitions now?" Tad was getting lost.

"No, dummy. Because Betty and I penetrated their scatterbase and know how the scam works."

"You've told your father about this, of course?"

"Wasn't time. Betty only mentioned her findings on the flight here."

"Maybe, for your own safety, you'd better tell your AID to wipe it."

"Oh no! I'm going to present this before the High Secretary, when one is finally elected, and expose the Haiken Maru's treachery once and for all."

"And if the Secretary happens to be a Haiken Maru candidate—what then?"

Mora looked at him sideways, then down at her lap. "Then, I suppose, I'd better wipe Betty."

"Good thought."

The car was descending, according to the coordinates in Tad's AID, toward a grove of mutated *Sequoiadendron compacta*. They were on the highland border between two latifundia. Bertingas maneuvered to avoid the largest trees and set down in what he thought was a clear spot. Mora sprang her hatch and swung a leg over the airskirting.

"Oops! Trees on my side."

"Well, don't step on them, unless you want a hole in your foot. Walk between the shoots."

The tiny trees were genetically altered from stock

that, elsewhere on Palaccio and on other Human-dominated planets, grew to be mighty pylons. Here, with a twist of guanine and an extra adenine, that bulk had been turned inward and compressed without diminishing the cell structure. The resulting boles, in lengths of fifty to seventy millimeters, were stronger than any plastic or ceramic, stronger than many metals, but they had no magnetic field and were virtually non-conducting. They were used for everything from non-sparking dynamic bearings to high-tensile logic probes.

They left the car and walked downhill toward a bogland clogged with fruit mallows. These grew in such profusion that only the grid of electric heating wires showed this was a working farm. Thirty meters away, a head popped up and stared at them. The dark goggles masked all trace of expression—wonder, warning, happiness, or hostility. From the short stature and greenish skin, Bertingas knew that their observer was a Cernian.

"Excuse me!" Tad called.

The head sank slowly, as if into a crouch.

"I say!" Tad went on. "We're looking for someone. Maybe a friend of yours. Name of Choora Maas. Can you tell us where to find him?"

"What do you want with Ser Maas?" The voice was high pitched and anxious. It took Bertingas a minute to figure out that the alien was a youngster.

"We have money for him." It had worked before. . . .

"You are a liar! Nobody from the city brings money here. Not to Ser Maas. Now you go away."

"It's not money, exactly, but a proposition that could lead to money. If we can strike a deal."

"Go away."

"We don't mean to hurt—"

"You will, though. Go away."

"Really, this is—"

"Hoori? Hoori!" It was another voice, lower and

more mature, from somewhere deeper in the mallows. "Whom do you have there?"

"Strangers, Father."

"What kind of strangers?"

"Man and woman. Human. One brown head. One yellow head. Rough clothes. Smooth voices."

"What do they want?"

"You, Father."

The kid made a terrible guard, Tad decided. Exposes his position, tells all he knows, gives away his commanding officer and daddy in one breath. At least he wasn't trigger happy—if he was even armed.

"Well, ask their names," the older voice said reasonably.

"We are Taddeuz Bertingas, Deputy Director of Communications for this cluster, and Mora Koskiusko, daughter of the admiral commanding Central Fleet in this cluster. We have business with Choora Maas."

"Distinguished visitors," the voice said. "And not unexpected."

The youngster stood quietly among the mallows, looking at them through those dark goggles.

"You may walk forward," the voice said. "A hundred paces south along the line you've been following. Then two hundred east. You'll know when to stop."

As he spoke, the youngster's head sank among the plants. Within a second or two, Tad could no longer say exactly where he had been.

They walked, keeping as straight a line as they could, pushing aside thick leaves and walking around bunched stalks. As they brushed past, the plants exuded a heavy, sweet perfume, like hot cider. Tad tasted a smear of sticky purple sap on his sleeve. Strawberry jam.

He offered Mora a lick, off the end of his finger. She sampled it with a delicate lap of her tongue, smacked her lips and smiled at him.

On or about the two-hundredth pace of their eastward leg, they came to a thicker growth of the mallows, concealing what looked, at first, like a low hill in the wetlands. Up close, Tad could see it was a collection of shacks connected with makeshift passageways. The walls were pieces of rough wood, bats of insulation, uneven pieces of sheetmetal, loose bricks, and tiles. Whoever had built the huts seemed to have knitted these materials together, like a bird's nest. The only incongruity were the baffles—newly made, square, cut from some light, white metal—that covered the glazed windows. The insides of that hut would be dark as a cave.

A nailed-together oblong of boards swung upward on pneumatic struts, and a Cernian stood in the doorway. He, too, wore the dark goggles. The Cernians' delicate eyes could not tolerate direct sunlight, Tad knew.

"I am Choora Maas, whom you seek."

Somehow Bertingas had expected Maas to be another wired-up Ice Plant. After all, Glanville had called him "my brother." Now what was Tad to make of this business? Selwin Praise's orders had explicitly excluded Cernians, and here one of his contacts *was* a Cernian. What was going on?

"Won't you come in?" Maas stepped back and ushered Tad and Mora into the house with a clasped-hands salute.

They passed through a black curtain that baffled the door. Inside, it was warm and dark, musty with the odors of alien cooking and alien hygiene. The light, what little there was, came from patches of green luminescence around the top of the walls. It might have been an electrical effect, or a biochemical reaction, like the light of fireflies and deepwater fishes.

It took Tad a minute to discover that the main room was packed with still and silent people. Some

were Cernians, but many other kinds were repre-
sented, too. As his eyes adjusted to the gloom, Tad
could make out a clutch of Satyrs; two Cowras in one
corner, holding paws; an elegant Deoorti, looking
almost Human and proud of it; a scaly Bidoo; three
Wright's Jugglers, whose hands were in constant motion; and a Dervish, who sat completely unmoving
for minutes at a time, then leapt up, twirled its body
around three times, and sat down.

"Now, why have we been honored with this visit?"
Maas had come up behind them, and Tad turned.
The other had taken off his goggles, revealing his
eyes. The pupils were at least three centimeters across
and glowed faintly. Or perhaps it was a reflection
from the bioluminescence. It was like looking into a
cat's eyes at night. Disturbing.

"We, uhhh, that is, I have come with a proposition
for you to consider. From the Department of Communications."

"You are looking for a guard force. You have come
here to recruit."

"Why yes! Ahh, how did you know?"

"Surely you know, Counselor, that electromagnetic signals travel faster than aircars. My friends
hear. My friends talk. To me."

"We are prepared to offer Human pay scales and
choice of officers. And—as we negotiated with
Glanville—for veterans or survivors there will be full
Pact citizenship, complete with unrestricted move-
ment, no place, no time. If that can be arranged . . .
I'll certainly try."

Those great eyes considered him. The Cernian's
mouth barely smiled. Tad could feel Mora draw back,
behind his arm.

"That won't mean much to us, will it?"

It took Bertingas a moment to absorb what Maas
had said. "But . . . I thought . . . citizenship, Hu-

man rights, lifting the Bans, aren't they what every alien dreams of?"

"Dreams are not always practical, Ser Bertingas." Maas's eyes blinked slowly—a shrug.

"Well, sometimes. In this case, however—"

"Let me show you an example of *this case*." Maas led them over to a low settee, where an old woman, a Cernian with deep wrinkles in her face, sat upright with her hands folded on her lap. Where Maas's eyes glowed with depth, like wine in a glass, hers were dull, clouded. A milky fluid behind the lens made them seem like blank stones.

"This is Saara. A woman of my race. In her youth and beauty, she once failed to please the overseer of this plantation. As punishment, he applied a lesser form of the *Zergliedern*. He withdrew for three days the *privilege* of her smokes."

"Smokes?"

"The eye protection we Cernians all must wear on Palaccio, or on any other planet with a Human-normal incidence of ultraviolet radiation. Within two days, she was blinded for life."

"That's terrible. But she could have—"

"What? Left the land to which the Bans had bound her? Worn her smokes in secret—*at night* perhaps? Killed the overseer? Killed herself? The range of her options was limited."

"I don't deny there have been abuses. As full citizens, however—"

"That was not my point, Counselor. This latifundia is owned, indirectly, by the Haiken Maru. Many on Palaccio are. And throughout this cluster. You may promise opportunities to work in your department. Go ahead. We are pleased to accept. But it won't help more than a fraction of a percent of those who, citizens or not, un-Banned or not, will still serve on the land. Haiken Maru land. Operated by Haiken

Maru overseers. Who are pleased to do *this*." Maas
pointed at the blind woman.

"There are systems of justice. There could have
been a claim and a prosecution."

"City justice. Far away. Very costly. With Haiken
Maru's picked legal staff to defend the overseer.
And, if he had lost in open court, Haiken Maru thugs
to come in the night . . . Not much justice."

"What do you want of me?" Tad asked.

Maas turned away from the woman and faced
Bertingas.

"We are ready to believe. Always too ready. A
young man, full of ideals, like yourself, comes among
us and speaks of freedom and justice, and we do
believe. The hatred has not settled in our hearts. We
are not hardened, so we believe. But not this time,
Counselor."

"Well, I could—"

"You can do nothing. It is your government, your
society, your race that condones the Haiken Maru.
You condone them, because you do not fight them."

"It's not as easy as you make it sound."

"No, it never is."

"I am just one person. Twice the Haiken Maru
have tried to kill me, because I would not take part
in their plotting. Perhaps that makes us, you and
I—ahh—brothers."

"Fellow travelers, perhaps."

"Yes, well. So I understand about the Haiken Maru.
I also know how strong they are. One person, two, a
conspiracy, could never—"

"Your new governor, Deirdre Sallee"—Tad noticed that the Cernian did not say *our* governor—"is
reputed to be descended from the old Pact, when
'equality' among the starborn was more than a word.
She is also rumored to be a person of some honor. . . ."

"I believe she is."

"Then the Haiken Maru will not let her live for very long, will they?"

"That's to be—"

"Her position is in grave doubt, Counselor. . . . I ask you, how should we be persuaded to join your cause? When you yourself are already fleeing for your life. And when, in a matter of weeks or months, the government of the Cluster will be in the hands of this trading cartel. Which already has the power of life and death over us. We would be fools to contend with such strength, wouldn't we?"

Tad was suddenly tired. The fatigue poisons and old adrenalin from the past thirty-six hours dragged at his limbs. The stuffy air inside this cave soured in his lungs. The confusion and disappointments clouded in his mind.

"So, my mission has failed. Shall I go now?"

"I didn't say that," Maas said. "We look for a sign from you. Something more than bright words about justice and equality."

"What sign?"

Maas smiled, the corners of his mouth turning *down*. His eyes widened and actually gleamed.

"The Haiken Maru work busily at their island fortress, Batavia, on the other side of this planet. Have you ever visited there, Counselor?"

"Once, eight or nine years ago, when I helped them diagnose a sick data base . . ."

Bertingas had a flashing memory of shallow seas green as an apple, of low islands, and the sucking mud of marshlands.

Rising from the deepest water was a single construction of syncrete and steel, square miles of smooth white walls and white-tiled courtyards. Batavia. Rising above the walls were domes and towers, evaporators and landing cranes, antennae and null-field generators. Wharves and docking bays ringed the walls at the waterline. All had been shuttered with steel doors that closed on hinges as big as a man's body. The salt air worked endlessly to etch the syncrete and rust the steel, and the Haiken Maru bond servants—Cernians among them, treated no better than slaves—worked constantly to patch and scale and paint. As a paid consultant, Tad had been treated well enough in the week he spent there: bright accommodations, good food, entertaining companions. Overall, however, he had found the place depressing.

"The Haiken Maru have converted Batavia, reputed to be the single most hardened military facility in Aurora Cluster, into a munitions factory," Maas said. Others around the room nodded, and Bertingas remembered the fragment of information Mora's AID had uncovered. "They are calling in freighters, scouts, and miners from all over and refitting them with missiles, defensive shields, and plasma weapons. They will have a fleet to rival any in the cluster and many outside it."

"That is valuable information," Tad said. "I must get word of this back to my government."

"How will your government react? What will your Deirdre Sallee do with this information?"

"I don't know. Confront the Haiken Maru in Council, I suppose, ask them to—"

Maas shook his head. "One reaches an age, a state of understanding, when councils and the forms of law seem like a reasonable alternative. I have reached this age, after having seen much blood shed in very stupid ways. Yet I can tell you, the law will not be enough. If you and your government are to survive, you must attack Batavia, destroy this new force."

"I don't know if I can get the Governor to see it that way. Even if the attack could be successful, the Haiken Maru have grown so powerful, they practically run the economy of Aurora Cluster. There would be chaos."

"And you bureaucrats are allergic to chaos, aren't you? Who knows what might arise? Many comfortable niches might be disturbed." Maas smiled, downward.

At the word *niches*, Bertingas had another flash: a tunnel wall, perhaps a stone wall, interrupted with the arches of upright tombs. The entrances were bricked over. Torches flickered on brass plaques that looked like a government roster. The niche Bertingas had carved for himself in Communications over the years—a tomb?

Was Choora Maas using a telecoder to put these images into Tad's mind? He couldn't see any wires, like those on Glanville. And yet—

"I said we look for a sign, Counselor," Maas was saying. "A sign of strength from those of you who claim to govern Aurora Cluster. When your law breaks down, what strength do you have?"

"I'll do what I can," Tad said slowly.

"That is all any sentient being can do. If you are successful, then we can talk about recruits for your defensive force."

Chapter 10

Regis Sallee: AT THE NURSERY DOOR

The ringing of shrill, happy voices was still in Regis Sallee's ears, the touch of lithe, knowing hands still upon his flesh as he walked away from the establishment. Large and patient eyes, small and supple mouths played in his memory as he started to walk up the darkened side street toward Martingale Avenue.

"May I stroll with you a way, Citizen?"

Regis stiffened, then recognized the voice of his control. He began to turn, to greet the man.

"It would be best if you just kept moving ahead. That's it. Now, what news do you bring me from the Palace?"

"Deirdre is playing a very subtle game."

"I'm sure. With whom?"

"Against the Haiken Maru. She is planning to name Amelia Ceil, of Greengallow Hold—"

"I know what Amelia owns!"

"To the Water Board. You know how Ceil hates the H.M. So she should neutralize their maneuverings."

"Is that what Deirdre thinks? Or what you think?"

"Deirdre says it."

"But does she *believe* it?"

"I don't see why not!"

"Hmmm. Block the Haiken Maru—in a small way—without an open breach. For Deirdre, that *is* subtle. Now, what about my plan for a reconciliation?"

"She's not buying it, I'm afraid."

"Not buying—? You've explained to her, I take it, the advantages to Aurora Cluster of being on the right side of Governor Spile when he moves?"

"As far as I can, without arousing her suspicions."

"That must not be very far."

"Look, I told you. I can hint. I can suggest. I can't advocate, not with my own wife."

"Apparently, that's not the only thing you can't do with your wife."

"Now, see here!"

"Keep your voice down, Citizen. . . . What do the little charmers cost you, I wonder, for their tiny favors?"

"That's none of your concern. Besides, having—encounters—with alien species has been ruled to be neither immoral nor illegal."

"Yet the Venturans are so delicate, so trusting. So like children. . . . Have you ever touched a Human child, Regis?"

"No. Of course not!"

"Would anyone who knew you had a taste for Venturans believe that? Would Deirdre believe that?"

"You mustn't—must not—"

"I won't. Trust me, Regis, I won't. But I do want you to put forward, in the best light possible, a reconciliation with Arachne Cluster. Perhaps a state visit?"

"The only way, really the only alternative"—Sallee licked his lips in the cool evening air—"would be to create for them a dual allegiance. Say, to a third party. As allies. Still on opposite sides, but part of a

greater union. Say, one controlled by the H.M. Then
Deirdre's personal feelings about Aaron Spile might
be—"

"Ally herself under the Haiken Maru? Dream on,
Regis. It becomes apparent that I must speak to her
on the matter myself."

"With all respect, I doubt she'd listen."

"Oh? And why? She gave me the appointment we
both wanted me to have, didn't she?"

"That was not as easy as you may think. It took a
lot of persuading. A lot of advocacy. Deirdre doesn't
like you."

"I don't know of many people she *does* like."

"I could only convince her because your deputy—"

"That puppy!"

"—is knowledgeable about the functioning of your
department. He's also loyal—as far as anyone can be,
these days. 'If it weren't for Bertingas'—those were
her exact words at the time. So I wouldn't push her
too hard, if I were you. She only trusts you because
you haven't raised your head enough to draw her
suspicions. Yet."

"Then, since I am so ineffectual, I suggest you do
your job and get her on the right side of Spile. Or it
will be worse for all of us, one day."

Regis Sallee had reached the corner onto Martingale Avenue and turned right. Behind him, without
a word, his control must have turned left. The man's
steps faded into the night.

Chapter 11

Taddeuz Bertingas: TRACERS

"I *have* to get this information back to Gemini Base," Mora said, the minute her backside was plunked down in the little red aircar. She had been holding her peace, with some difficulty, on their walk up the hill from Choora Maas's cavelike collection of huts.

"When Daddy learns the H.M. not only tried to kidnap me but have also been building up their own private navy, he'll call down a first strike from high orbit. Pow! Push that island—what's it called? Batavia? —right under the water. Let them even *think* about arming a bunch of merchant hulls against Central Fleet. It's certainly a breach of the Pact. And if it's not, there must be something in Fleet regs, probably under 'civilian uprisings.' One way or another, Daddy will *nail* them."

"Do you want to slow that down a bit?" Tad asked. Her talk, her attitude, was making him uncomfortable— and a little angry.

He punched the starter sequence and brought the car's fans up to speed. When they had settled and synched, he gave his AID codes for the shortest route to Meyerbeer and sat back. The car rose with a surge and nosed around to the west.

"What do you mean? This is an emergency!"

"No, it isn't—it's a rumor. A story told to us by an alien—one whose species does not have the best political odor right now, either. I'll admit that Maas seems to be a sincere and even—ah—saintly character. However, his motives for making mischief with the Haiken Maru are pretty obvious. Do you think we want to go and incinerate a private trading installation on *his* say-so?"

"He corroborates the data Betty uncovered."

"If you choose to see it that way."

"I tell you they're selling warships to Governor Spider. You ask where a commercial trader would be getting warships to sell. Maas says they're building—or at least retrofitting—them on the premises. . . . *Now* you're saying it only adds up if you've got an active imagination? How much of a map do you *need*, fella?"

"Simply . . ." Bertingas began. "Fairly—*legally*, we must give the Pact some kind of proof before taking direct military action. Has anyone seen these warships? Does anyone have an accounting of missing commercial hulls? Has there been an attack anywhere?"

"You'd wait until they *use* the ships?"

"I'd wait until there was an investigation, a verified finding of criminal action, and a specification of charges before dropping on them 'from high orbit.' You people in the Fleet have the Central Center viewpoint: that everything happening out here in the clusters is a sort of barbarian uprising. Cauterize first and ask questions later. Well, the Haiken Maru, for all their faults, are the underpinning of the economy in this cluster. You chop them off *here*, and something will fall over *there*."

"Sounds like you're defending them—after two assassination attempts. Or three, counting the riot in Chinatown."

"No, not defending. It's just that—who's involved? Who's working as H.M.'s agent? Who's neutral? Who's an innocent bystander? Deirdre Sallee is *supposed* to be uninvolved, and above local connections, but can we be sure? She could have been turned five minutes after landing on Palaccio—or five years before. So, in this atmosphere, getting an investigation started against the biggest conglomerate in four clusters, is going to be a delicate matter. We want to be sure of the political winds."

"Oh brother! At that rate, the H.M.'ll be picking their teeth with you before you lift a finger."

"That's as may be. The alternatives could be worse. Especially if we show up in Meyerbeer with a lot of incriminating stories and tell them to the wrong people. For instance, would you trust taking this to Captain Thwaite?"

"Ouch!" Mora said. "I'd forgotten about him. I'd have to get back to Gemini without going through him, wouldn't I?"

"Can you do that?"

"With a private yacht . . . maybe. Betty has the base approach codes. Does your department have courier ships, service vehicles, mail capsules, anything like that?"

"Sorry, it's all done with light beams and hyperwaves. Anything above the atmosphere, we go to the Cluster Command for help with transit and hardware."

"Well, do you know anyone with a yacht?"

"Sure—Valence Elidor owns one. The Governor has the *Aurora*. I don't think either one would lend it to me for a weekend jaunt and no questions asked."

"I'll think of something."

"Well, just don't go making open charges. Follow my lead on this—okay?"

"Okay . . . I'll give you five minutes' warning, when I plan to break it. All right?"

"Ten minutes? At least."

"Make it seven."

"Uh—deal."

They crossed the city's perimeter. Air Control electronically tagged them and put them in the appropriate traffic slots.

"What are we going to do in Meyerbeer?" she asked. "Still running and dodging?"

"No, that's got no future. Instead, I'm taking us to the one place Haiken Maru can't touch us. Should have gone there first."

"Where's that?"

For answer, Bertingas put the aircar's nose over and dove toward the pyramid of Government Block. He pulled up a thousand feet out and on a level with the 123rd floor landing stage.

"So—'smile and salute,' " he told his AID.

"Right, boss!" The machine made electronic arrangements with the stage's valet system.

"We're going in there? Dressed like this?" Mora protested, plucking at the pants leg of her dusty, stained, worn, borrowed clothing. She pushed at her hair, which hadn't seen a brush or a comb in twenty-four hours. She dabbed at her face, peering into a bright piece of chrome for a mirror.

"You look fine," Tad said, with too much of a smile.

She gave him a look full of death daggers but stopped fussing.

They set down on the narrow ledge and climbed out. Mora gasped at the height and grabbed for his arm. Bertingas led her to the drop tube.

At the ninety-ninth floor, they were met by Gina Rinaldi and Patty Firkin. Gina looked as cool and graceful, elegant and poised as always. "Metal doesn't get messy" flashed through Bertingas' mind. Beside her, Firkin was showing signs of wear: a white bandage across her forehead and her left arm in a sling. Not bad, considering her wild ride on the front of a dying dragon. Which she had killed with her own hands.

"Mora, this is Gina Rinaldi, my secretary. Firkin you've met—and had a shot at. Gina, this is Mora Koskiusko, daughter to our admiral. She needs a place to clean up and some fresh clothing. You look about the same size . . . You have a dress and things here you could loan her, don't you?"

"Ahh—" Gina blushed slightly, as much as Deoorti skin can color. "I'll think of something, Tad." She took Mora's arm and turned away, then turned back.

"By the way, we're starting to get a stream of recruits at two of the bases you asked me to set up. Someone has to go out, inspect, and settle them. Since it's your project, I volunteered you. And the Director said he wanted to see you the minute you surfaced. He knows you're here, too. You are to go right up. His orders."

"Oh my! Then, I'll need a fresh uniform, a shave, and a five-minute update. Can you—?"

"Ladies first, sir." Gina smiled sweetly and took Mora off down the hallway.

"Can't you dress yourself?" Firkin rumbled at him.

"Used to be more fun the other way," he grumbled and headed for his office. Patty trailed him, and he noted she limped as well.

Inside of six minutes, he was ready to face Selwin Praise. He rode the drop tube up alone, walked across the security bay with its young Building Services cerberus, and threaded the Maze to the Director's office. Praise's secretary, still the doubtful man, announced Bertingas and ushered him into the presence.

The D.ofC. was studying a holoprojection on his desk. The diffuser axis was aligned with Tad, so he saw only a blur of colors which could be anything from architect's plans to naked ladies. Praise tore his attention away as if it were the latter. His eyes, like small agates, focused across the desk on Bertingas.

"I *still* do not have. On my desk. A report on security conditions. Signed by one Taddeuz Bertingas. Who seems to be among the missing. Around here. More than among the active-duty employees. I ask myself: what has he been doing with his time? Screwing the hired help? Do you know, Bertingas?"

"In the field, sir. I've been making those contacts you gave me—for the recruits."

"You were gone two days? Without leaving word? On that assignment?" Praise harrumphed. "Should have taken you two hours. Or twenty minutes on a lightbeam."

"I went in person."

"Your physical self? How charming. I'm sure your alien friends appreciated the—um—politeness of that."

"They didn't seem to be the sort to own Shadow Boxes."

"This *is* a backwater cluster. . . . Well, how successful were you in your negotiations?"

"I've got fifteen hundred mixed aliens coming in. Down payment, as it were, on a promise of three thousand. Those are from your contact 'Glanville,' who is really strange—"

"Fifteen hun—! That's *all?* What about Maas?"

"He had some reservations. He seemed unsure about our good faith toward alien species. He asked for 'a sign.' "

"What kind of sign?"

"He . . . ah . . . didn't say. Not in so many words."

Now why, Bertingas asked himself, did he resist telling Selwin Praise about the Haiken Maru war fleet, Batavia, and Choora Maas's demand for an attack on the installation? For that matter, why did Tad keep silent about the fact that Maas, to whom

Praise had personally directed him, was a Cernian—a species which Praise had personally proscribed on this project?

The answer to both questions was that, of all the people in Meyerbeer, Tad distrusted the new D.ofC. most. His internal radar could not penetrate the man. And Selwin Praise reeked of secret alliances and midnight promises.

". . . well, you'll think of something," Praise was saying. "Although I must say I'm disappointed. I send you to recruit thousands, and you come back with mere hundreds."

"Yes, sir, but those hundreds are coming into the training bases even as we speak. The numbers will grow. We couldn't handle thousands of recruits right now, anyway. No capacity at the bases."

"Hmmm. So you say." Praise was studying his desktop. "Well. I've revised my estimate of our need. We'll want 30,000 troops under arms inside of two weeks." He raised his eyes to Bertingas, in challenge, and they fairly gleamed.

"Thirty thou—! That's almost impossible." And it's almost, Tad's internal censor whispered, twice the manpower of the Cluster Command. A virtual private army.

"You're making the right promises?" Praise asked.

"More than enough. Some I don't think I can keep."

"Don't let that stop you. Get the bodies. Get them trained."

"May one inquire why the sudden need?"

"One may not. However, under a confidence, I would say we are on the verge of a crisis situation. The death of His Excellency the High Secretary has thrown into motion forces that may not be stopped, short of direct military action. . . . If one were to ask."

"I see."

"You do *not* see. I did *not* say. However, you *will* leave this office, Bertingas, with the imperative need of this Department for skilled troops *burning* in your mind. Won't you?"

"Yes, sir."

"And you will go at once to inspect this base of yours, at . . ." Praise paused to study something in the holoprojection. "At Cairn Hollow, in the Uplands. You'll begin training your recruits. Won't you?"

"Of course, sir."

Praise waited a three beat, his eyes still down, then looked up.

"Then what are you still doing here? Get a move on!"

"Right away, sir." Tad nodded once, vigorously, turned on his heel, and double-timed across the carpet for the door.

It wasn't until he was fieldfalling in the drop tube that Bertingas started to question Praise's whole performance: the D.ofC. had at first doubted the number and kind of Tad's recruits, yet he had the name of their first base, Cairn Hollow, literally at his fingertips. What was going on?

Mora was waiting in the foyer of his floor, dressed in an ankle-length sheath of tiny silver scales backed by russet satin. She made a small pirouette.

"What do you think?"

It was hardly becoming to her blonde hair, her pale skin, or the time of day. Tad recognized the dress and knew whose coloring and accents it *did* become. Was that truly the only clothing his secretary could find for their guest? Or was Gina sending a subtle message?

"It looks wonderful. But where we're going . . ."

"Where's that?"

"Above the Uplands. To meet the first of Glanville's troops."

"Then this is perfect! Gina is so thoughtful."

"Eh? That's a ball gown. Perhaps for an evening at Chez Dorsey, but—"

"It's also overlapping plate armor with a Rockwell C rating of 58, a superconducting coating, and a compressible underlayer. You could shoot me point blank with the Schlicter and just raise a bruise. And the coating drains off the charge from a high-voltage field. It will take anything but a direct plasma burst."

"Too bad it doesn't have a hood."

"Rolled into the neckline," she said, demonstrating. "Patty wishes we had one in your size."

"Not my color. Anyway, where is Patty?"

"Checking in with somebody, she said. Ah, here she comes." Mora raised her voice to the approaching Firkin. "Tad says we're going above the Uplands."

"To the training base, right?" the colonel growled.

"Yes," Tad nodded. "How did you know?"

"It's all over this floor. 'War footing,' someone remarked to me. A stranger, yet. In the latrines, for Kali's sweet sake. If this army of yours is supposed to be a secret, your security stinks."

"A secret? Well, I suppose so . . ."

"You don't know?"

"The Director didn't mention it."

"Trimurti!" the woman sighed.

"When do we leave?" Mora asked.

"Right away," he said. "I'd better tell Gina."

"Gone," Firkin said.

"Where?"

"Just gone. Didn't say. Didn't look happy, though."

"Why are you in such a rush?" Mora asked him. "We just got here, and you—we, both of us—have business to discuss, if you remember." She winked at him. "Perhaps with your Director, if now's the time—"

"No!" Tad barked. "Now is *not* a good time to bother Selwin Praise."

"Did Praise order this inspection?" Firkin asked quickly.

"Yes."

"He's really keeping you busy. Out of the office for—what? Two days now?—on one pretext or another. I wonder what he's trying to hide?"

Bertingas looked at her, shook his head slightly, but didn't say anything. To make his meaning clear, he moved his eyes around the four walls, pantomimed looking up and down the drop shaft.

Firkin closed her eyes. "Right. Security. Well, how do we get to the Uplands?"

"Car's waiting." He tapped the AID at his belt.

"Not that little red job we bought?" Mora asked. She unconsciously smoothed the dress over her thighs, clearly remembering the high lip on its door. Or perhaps she was thinking of color clashes with her new gown.

"No, I have a staff car. Big enough for all of us. Shall we go?" He made way for them to step into the tube.

Mora Koskiusko pointed her toes and rose like a silver arrow. Firkin followed, her toes dangling. Tad brought up the rear.

In the bulky, black Department car, hovering just beyond the landing stage's apron of approach, Bertingas linked up his AID and gave directions for Cairn Hollow. The car wheeled and started north immediately.

"You know how far that is, Boss?" the machine asked.

"Over the Palisades, in the—"

"I *know* that. It's 2,298 klicks."

"Good! Take about nine hours, time for dinner and a catnap. I'm overdue on my sleep cycle. That should get us to the base about two hours after midnight, and—"

"Two hours after never," it said. "The range of this

car is about 1,500 klicks, on full cells with spares in the outboard cradles. Which you don't have. We're gonna spend a long night in the woods."

Firkin put her chin forward. "Rinaldi ordered a waystation to be installed."

"Give the damn thing its coordinates," Tad said wearily, "and let's hustle butt. Okay?"

The drone of the fans put him under long before the car could serve up its prepared meal. He slept through the refueling and didn't open his eyes until, in utter darkness with only the stars above them, the car descended on the base perimeter at Cairn Hollow.

By its lights and beacons, the training base was laid out in a pentagram: five wedges in a compact figure, separated by broad avenues lit with the green glare of sodium brights. The landing strip was at the center, with the entire land width of the base to shield vulnerable landings and takeoffs from snipers and rocket attacks. It was a good configuration for wartime security, except this wasn't a war and it only meant heavy troop buses passing over everyone's head at all hours.

On the ground, Bertingas and the women were met by a tall Satyr with mellow eyes and grizzled chin whiskers. He had sergeant's chevrons pinned to his utility vest. The sergeant assigned them to temporary quarters in the officers' quad and took them down a road labeled simply "A2." Even in the sickly artificial light, Tad could see the surface wasn't tar and gravel, or any composition he recognized. It looked like fused cinders. Maybe the engineers used some plastic as a binder in the pour.

He asked the sergeant about it.

"No, sir. No time to go *pouring* surfaces here. Miz Rinaldi wangled use of a destroyer from the Cluster Command. They just brought it down to high hover at ground level, lined up its main batteries, and burned in the landing strip with six shots of plasma.

They cut these radial roads with about three shots each, out at right angles. Surface is a little uneven at the joins. We'll have trouble with weed control in the spring—if we're still here—but they work."

Beyond the lights, Bertingas discovered that all the buildings were not only temporary, they were inflatable. Tubes and ribbing under continuous positive pressure supported panels of some kind of frothed ceramic. Even the floors were raised on air pressure, which made them springy.

Between the grumble of aircraft coming into the strip and the whine of the building blowers, he got no sleep at all. Reveille was a bleak three hours after their arrival.

The same Satyr sergeant met them as they stumbled out the door of their quad. Mora had found some military-looking coveralls and had stowed the gaudy dress. Only Firkin looked unruffled and at ease.

"Miz Rinaldi signaled," the Satyr told him. "She said you'd want to inspect the corps early, sir."

"What about breakfast?"

"The recruits're all lined up, sir."

"Well, coffee? At least?"

"Afterward, sir. We'll get you fed." The sharp-faced alien smiled.

The landing strip did double duty as parade ground. Almost 2,000 bodies were standing there in not-quite-parallel lines. Tad had thought they would be grouped by species, but some old military mind had put them in order by height.

Filling out the end that Bertingas and his party approached were mostly Ghiblis and Cowras. The former squatted solidly on their three-toed pads, a sheen of spittle glistening and dripping on their constantly exposed, half-meter fangs. Beside them the timid Cowras performed their nervous little dances—

even when ordered to attention. Their tiny eyes never strayed far from those Ghiblis' teeth.

At the other end of the lines, toward the back, a group of long-necked Foolongs kept bunching up, trying to herd. Their species functioned best in a group dynamic with a telepathic element. In a cadre, they could be stronger than any Human or other alien unit, but as individual soldiers, perhaps cut off from their fellows, they would wilt into a near vegetative state. A recruiter took what he could get.

"What am I supposed to be looking at?" Bertingas whispered to Patty Firkin.

"Check their weapons," she suggested. "Any sign of neglect, like dirt, oil, low charge, or packing grease, and you flick the back of your hand against the trooper's shoulder. If he's got one. Near the neck, at least. And—ah—*gently* with the Ghiblis. They've got some hard-wired reflexes. The sergeant will handle discipline later. Anyway, it shouldn't be a problem. These weapons were just issued, too new to have seen much abuse."

Tad went down the lines. He peered into coil tubes and thumbed the action on reloaders. He examined new collar tabs and freshly burned tattoo brands. He peered into the polish on boot toes and hoofs and hindclaws. Occasionally, mostly for show, he flicked his hand for real or imagined infractions. Just to keep his new troopers on alert. No one protested the demerit, however; no one questioned his judgment.

By the end of the inspection, he was enjoying himself.

"What's next?" he asked the sergeant.

"Buildings and stores, sir?"

"Very well. Lead on."

So they inspected buildings and stores. Tad keyed through on the comm gear, let his AID query the cybers, ran his fingers along cooking surfaces, stared at sealed machinery, poked into bins and bags, initialed manifests, signed chits. At one point, he even got his cup of coffee, while sampling the chow in the mess hall.

They went to the improvised target range and watched their recruits put glass beads, steel bolts, and static discharges through hologram targets. For all their visible ferocity, the Ghiblis were lousy shots—compounded by bad eyesight and a short attention span. And the Cowras fidgeted too much to hold their weapons steady. But the Foolongs, provided you gave them two minutes to consult and pat each other beforehand, were devastating. They would aim and shoot as one being. Tad was reminded of soldiers from his reading of history: British redcoats in long lines—one kneeling to fire, one standing to fire, two crouching to reload—who advanced in a clockwork human wave punctuated by volleys of lead balls and blue smoke.

He began to feel some enthusiasm for this experiment. Perhaps a picked body of aliens, given the right weapons and instruction, could support them in the coming crisis.

By ten o'clock they had exhausted the camp's possibilities. Mora, who had probably accompanied her father on hundreds of inspections, was shifting foot-to-foot. The sergeant was looking haggard, and even Firkin seemed bored.

"Is that everything?"

"Oh, yes, sir," the Satyr affirmed.

"Then why don't you call our car and we'll be getting back to Meyerbeer?"

Once they were in the air, he plugged the AID into the controls and collapsed into the seat with a sigh.

"This soldiering is hard work," he said to Patty.

"Right."

By daylight, Bertingas could see the kind of country they were crossing. A thousand meters higher than he normally hiked through, but still familiar. Granite ridges with stands of what looked like fir trees between them. The soil would be black loam, he knew, and thick with needles. Occasionally, in the higher meadows, he could see shoals of orange flowers, trembling in the late morning breeze. In the lower valleys he could see stands of white-skinned trees, like birches. It was good country. Clean air. Sweet water. Cold nights.

"We got company, Boss," the AID said suddenly. "Three vehicles, big ones, on a closing vector behind us."

"Something you arranged?" Bertingas turned to Firkin.

"Nobody I know."

"What about Halan?"

"He said I was working solo this assignment."

"You want to assume they're hostile?"

"Seems like a safe bet," Mora said, "considering recent history."

"What weapons do you have?" he asked the AID.

"Are you kidding? This is a staff car, outfitted for embassy calls. I've got champagne and *foie gras* in the ice chest and a box of deckle-edged notecards, suitable for all occasions, under your seat. Perhaps you want to write somebody an invitation?"

"Okay, cut the sarcasm. What are our options?"

"Immediate surrender," the machine replied.

"You say those are heavy vehicles." Firkin leaned forward. "Troop carriers?"

"Mass is about right," the AID said.

"All things considered, we may be faster. Can we outmaneuver them?"

"Worth a try," Mora put in.

"Maybe if you jettisoned the party tent and picnic equipment," the machine responded.

An idea was forming in the back of Tad's brain.

"What's their range?" he asked.

"Hundred and ten kilometers."

"That's outside the horizon of your traffic radar."

"I got the word from a friendly intelligence in Hemisphere Satellite Survey. 'Someone to watch over me.' Need it in this business, Boss."

"Are those troop ships working us from the same source?"

"Uhhhnnhh—" Where did his AID learn *that* verbal tic? "Could be, Boss."

"So we could assume they can't scan us with a lot of sophisticated equipment—yet."

"I don't feel any probes," the machine agreed.

"All right. Mora, Patty, there are drag harnesses under your seats. I'm going to do a slow roll and let you two out. You fall for two hundred meters and *then* pop your pigtails, on full discharge. Our friends back there can't trace your plume, yet. Get down in the trees. Wait one hour until this circus is well past. Then turn on your beacons. A party from Cairn Hollow should come get you inside of two hours."

"You want us to *jump?*" from Mora. "Into the woods?"

"What about you?" from Firkin.

"I've got a few tricks left."

"But Follard made it clear that—"

"Halan isn't here now. You must go with Mora. She has important information pertaining to the survival of the Pact. I want you to help her, protect her, and see that she gets that data into the right hands. Clear?"

"Well . . ."

"Do it, Colonel."

Tad overrode the AID's control and put the car into a long roll that wouldn't show up on their trackers' instruments, if any. The two women strapped into their electrostatic discharge harnesses. Mora patted her Naval AID, Betty, to make sure it was secure. Tad blew the roof. They dropped into the screaming airstream.

As the car came around upright, he brought the rear cameras into focus and watched until they showed the telltale blue lightning of a high-voltage ED unit. One crackle, then another, at the right time, right altitude. It was a clean drop.

Now what? Continue at the same speed and heading, as if he suspected nothing at all. Let the followers come into his computed radar horizon. At that point, pour on the speed, as if he were startled, panicking.

Then what?

Then improvise.

Tad kept the controls, for something to do, and let it happen as he had planned. When the three troop carriers first pinged on his screen, he waited three or four seconds, as if he were just figuring out the situation. Then he opened the throttles wide and shed his altitude, as if diving for cover among the granite ridges. The airspeed indicator rose to 350 klips. The rush of wind screaming across the open canopy rose to a higher, frantic note.

The troopships moved that much faster. Suddenly they were closing on the screen at a visible rate. Tad's staff car could never outrun them.

On his right quarter he got his first visual. The black speck loomed up and paralleled his course. As it edged closer, it grew from speck, to fly, to beetle outline. It was a big vehicle, fifty meters long and broad in proportion. Its shape was boxy, hinting at a large interior space, with a high center of gravity. Its tough, rindlike surface was armored with ablative ceramics. Mounted on the nose, well forward of the first fan scoop, was a nine-centimeter swivel gun. It was trained left, tracking on Tad.

He kept an active scan on the radio, but no one had hailed him yet.

The other two cars seemed to be hanging back, out of range. But out of range of what? Tad had no weapons.

Well, one.

From initial distances in kilometers, that first car was now within a hundred meters and closing slowly.

Let them come.

What were they making of his broken roofline? Might they suspect that someone had already bailed out? Let them. In a few seconds, it would not matter what they knew.

Fifty meters. Tad took a new grip on the control yoke with sweating hands.

"You're planning something," the AID said accusingly.

"You bet."

Twenty meters. Were they going to try *boarding* him? Did they actually think he would hold a steady course while two or three armed villains leapt across into his cockpit? And did that mean they hoped to take him alive?

Ten meters. Time to move.

Tad's hands wove a complex pattern on the yoke. His car bobbled in its high-speed airstream, like a stone skipping across water: left side high, right side low, passing to right side high, left side low. The maneuver brought his right fender up, hard, under the troopship's airskirting.

At the sped they both were traveling, the time needed for recovery was just too short. The other vehicle flipped over on its back, like a box turtle in the sun. Its fans were suddenly working against the mechanics of flight. The pilot was still trying to recover when he spread himself across a cliff face. There was surprisingly little fire, just one orange flash and then broken pieces tumbling down.

Tad contoured the land, looking over his shoulder to see where the other two troopships were. That was his only trick, and it would work just once. When the others caught up with him, they would probably shoot him down.

"Well, old friend . . ."

Bertingas mentally reviewed the memory content of his AID: people's addresses and Shadow Box codes, mostly for business; two month's worth of meeting notes, all boring; some new building plans and specs; the early work on their security force, although Gina's AID had the bigger picture now; all the details on next year's budget. He decided that, altogether, there was nothing he either hadn't backed up or couldn't afford to lose.

"Yes, Boss?"

Bertingas started pulling on the ED harness, one-handed. "I want you to take back control now."

The machine did. Without being told, it duplicated the aircar's hill-hopping, zigzag flight. Smart machine.

Bertingas quickly closed the last clips and checked the dragline power settings. He armed the front part of the canopy and rested his hand on the eject lever.

"Just keep flying like that. Low across the hills. When we get a minute of visual cover, I'll jump."

"Who is going to drive the car? When you disconnect me, that is, and take me with you."

"I am not going to disconnect you. You must continue flying this same pattern, so our friends back there will think I'm still on board."

"Oh." The AID paused for several million nanoseconds. Call it five years of subjective time for a Human. "What will they do, when they catch up with this aircar?"

"To you? Nothing. They probably won't even notice you. And when they return the car to Government Block, I'll fetch you."

"Oh good. For a minute there, I thought you were abandoning me."

"I wouldn't do that." What does it cost to lie to a machine? "Now, that half-sized mountain up ahead. You curve low around the west slope and I'll go."

"Right, Boss."

At the last minute, he decided not to blow the rest of the roof. Instead, he climbed around to the rear and stood in the hole Mora and Patty had gone by. With the car still flying upright, he had to push himself up into the airstream. It shoved him diagonally as he took three steps across the skirting and threw himself face forward. Even before he was off the side, he broke the dragline's restraint tabs and yanked. The pigtail pulled hard and crackled with its miniature thunder.

It was a hundred meters down to a steep gravel slope. Tad made his body a loose ball, hit on his shoulder, and rolled bonelessly. The pigtail was still flaring blue and pulling against his fall as he rolled in among the fir trees.

What would those who followed see? From half a kilometer back?

They would catch a trailing flash of the ED discharge. They would notice—but possibly miss—a speck on the slopes, which might be a man, or a deer, or a falling rock. The aircar would still be ahead of them, caroming through the mountains. Those pilots and observers would need superhuman intelligence and reflexes to interpret what they saw, figure out what he had done, break off their chase, and circle back to lay down a barrage across his position in the trees.

No, the psychology of pursuit was on Tad's side. Probability said they would follow their main objective, the aircar, and not break off for him.

And after they had destroyed the car? Would they fly home and report their mission accomplished? Or would they remember the flash, the speck, their suspicions?

Of course they would come back. Probably in five minutes. Maybe in ten. The troopships could hover above that gravel slope and offload a squad of searchers. The ships couldn't settle on the slope, for fear of a slide, so they wouldn't be able to bring in heavy equipment, a command center, a full-scale manhunt. Unless they went down the valley and found a clearing. That, however, would take time.

While he worked it out, Tad slipped out of the ED harness and threw it as hard as he could downslope, into the branches. He took the metal out of his pockets—small coins, stylus, chrono repeater, nail knife—and scattered these things left and right. The searchers would have ferrous spotters and resonance detectors.

But wait. His clothing was loaded with metal—snaptabs and closers, silver foil in his uniform braid, heel plates in his boots. He stripped and scattered everything he was wearing, down to his underwear. That was a single skintight weave of thermal monofilaments, guaranteed to be without metal and having a resonance that was reasonably close to his own body's.

Only trouble was, without an outer layer of clothing, his skinnies wouldn't hold much body heat. The nights got down to zero Celsius in this latitude, at this altitude, at this time of year.

The searchers would also have infrared detectors, probably, to trace his body heat. Tad knew from past experience, however, that these hills had a lot of large fauna, all warm blooded and radiating hotter than the rocks. Such instruments would give more false readings than true. Let half of his trackers go chasing a hungry Wampit on the prowl. He hoped they'd find it, too.

Tad quickly moved off the slope, going diagonally, deeper into the forest. His body picked up the jog-trot-walk routine that would, he knew, take him

farthest, fastest. As he moved out, Tad pondered his
situation.

He was six or seven hundred kilometers from anywhere in particular. He was unarmed and nearly
naked. And within the time of a hundred heartbeats,
a dozen or more angry men would be swarming over
this area, trying to kill him.

On the plus side, he was back in the hills he
loved. He *had* been planning a vacation ramble up
here for the last three months, hadn't he? Time away
from the grinding details of the office. Time to breathe
fresh mountain air. The vacation had just come a
little sooner this year.

As his pace cycled into a walk, Bertingas began
whistling. Quietly.

Chapter 12

Hildred Samwels: UNDER ATTACK

Samwels always expected to hear echoes. The enclosed space where Gemini Base docked and repaired its squadrons was big enough—3,000 meters in diameter—but it had no atmosphere. Of course, pressurizing this huge volume would make it easier to work on the ships. Anything small enough to fit in the docking bay was transatmospheric, designed and built for direct touchdown on a planet's surface. Having some air pressure in here would simplify the procedures for opening access hatches, testing fluid lines, applying paints, and doing delicate work without the clumsy suit gloves.

But, of course, not even the Pact's Central Fleet could afford to put 14 billion cubic meters under pressure.

It would be better—not optimum, but second best—if they could get a real, hard vacuum in the bay. Clean nothing, the very opposite of pressure. But even that would cost too much.

So sparks and smokes from the electrostatic welders, leaks from the air curtains and pressure locks, fumes from adhesives and cleaners, spills from the ships' environmental and sanitary systems—it all floated through this space in a light fog. Every hour or two he had to wipe his faceplate, creating a smear and bringing his glove away damp and slippery. It was like working in a toilet.

Of course, a captain and an admiral's aide didn't normally pull duty on the docks. But Samwels wanted a private word with Captain Bennington, of the freighter on the third resupply cycle. Bennington's next stop would be Palaccio, and Samwels wanted to commission him, privately, unofficially, in the search for Mora Koskiusko. It had been five days since she had disappeared there.

Samwels especially wanted Bennington to probe the connection between the Arachnids and Mora's disappearance, at which Spile's envoy had hinted. Hildred Samwels was beginning to suspect that something was really rotten on Palaccio.

"Hand me that skip gauge, would you, Captain?"

A gloved paw with six fingers and two thumbs stuck out of the guts of the mass inverter. When Samwels was two seconds slow in finding and passing the right tool, all eight digits wiggled impatiently.

"Thank *you*, sir," the mechanic said when Samwels found and passed the gauge. Just on the edge of insubordination.

The little Capuchins in his work crew didn't seem to mind, particularly, the slimy fog in the docking bay. They were permanently mad at everything.

Capuchins were a continual wonder to him. Aside from the even-fingered hand, they were dead ringers for the Earthly species *Cebus capucinus*. They had the small, lithe bodies covered with long, reddish hair. They had the prehensile tails and flat faces, with beards and cowls of black or gray tufts. They had the quick hands and treetop agility, making them perfect for mechanical work in tight quarters and varying gravity conditions.

They might have come straight from the long-vanished Amazon forests, except they had evolved on a planet more than 4,000 lightyears distant in realspace. Their similarity to Earth monkeys had caused Human scholars to run in circles, inventing new theories of evolutionary convergence and space-borne proteins as the cradle of all life.

Differences showed up, however—mostly in the psychological dimension. The Capuchins were not social. They had not a hint of the monkey troupe in their background. Each was a stalwart individual: suspicious, thorny, superior.

And the Capuchins were smarter than Humans—in some ways. What tests could be devised showed that even the slowest among those who would work in the Pact scored over 200 points on the Human IQ scale, certified geniuses. The bright ones were off the scale, untestable by any instrument. But all that capability was intellectual: memory retention, comprehension, computation, and organization. They were morons along the dimensions of creativity, social skills and interaction, or empirical application. Capuchins made fine mathematicians, clerks, and mechanics—and that was about it.

If their social life and creative impulses had developed in concert with their raw intelligence, the Capuchins might have conquered hyperspace, opened up the star clusters, fought their wars, and eventually formed the Pact. Instead of the Humans.

Or, given the demands of a social order and its necessary curbs on the unpredictable genius, the Capuchins' great intellects might have been leavened. They would probably have ended up no brighter, along any psychological dimension, than Humans.

Still, for all the unveiled contempt they showed

him, Samwels was glad to have a Capuchin working in the bowels of this cruiser, PPS *Dawnlight*. A sick mass inverter called for a specialist, one who could juggle transcendental equations in his head and oppose six fingers and two thumbs on one hand.

The mass inverter's theory of operation was simple. It canceled the volumes of empty space inside and among atoms. Whatever lay within the inverter's sphere of influence shrank, instantly and in perfect proportion, inside its own Schwartschild radius. This artificial concentration of mass popped through the thin fabric of spacetime into another part of the hyperspace probability that constituted a cluster. The stars and planets that constituted a Pact cluster were not adjacent in realspace but in the folds of hyperspace.

That was the easy part. The trick came in distorting the collapse field so that the pilot could predict just where, in hyperspace, the ship was going. When its distorters started to drift off synch, the inverter became unpredictable and couldn't jump. The *Dawnlight*, disabled this way, could move out of the docking bay on her inertial thrusters and even push around the Kali system—both planets. But she wasn't going anywhere useful.

The Capuchin poked his head, absurdly small by Human standards, out of the inverter's main space. His helmet, like those worn by all his kind, was transparent so that he could display the gray-and-black status banding on his cowl.

"I can't fix this thing." The Capuchin scowled.

"What's wrong?"

"You wouldn't understand, Captain."

"Try me."

"Well, the Theta function overlap should be in three-phase at sixty degrees, except the Lambda is holding irregular on two channels. You with me so far?"

"Sure."

"Irregular bandwidth, irregular phasing, so we can't hold in the sixties as we should."

"You know what's foxing the Lambda?"

"Of course I do."

"What then?"

"Time."

"Oh."

The Capuchin was going to be inscrutable. Which probably meant it didn't really know. Samwels had enough experience with Capuchin vanity not to push it too far into admitting ignorance or a mistake. They were ornery enough to bite when piqued. And they held a grudge long enough for this one to get to atmosphere so it could shed the helmet and *then* bite.

"There's your supply freighter, Captain." It waved a gloved paw at the dark shape of the *Salmo Iridium* cutting through the bay's access field. "Why don't you go pester Bennington and quit hanging over *my* shoulder?"

"All right," Samwels smiled, making sure that he showed his teeth. "And why don't you just knuckle down and fix this thing. 'Time!' When did anything quantifiable ever stump a Capuchin?"

The scowl deepened, and also showed teeth. "Don't play psychological games on me, Captain."

"I wouldn't think of it."

Samwels backed out of the access hatch, sighted on the docking grapples toward which the freighter was heading, and kicked off with his packjet. Twenty meters out, he remembered to light up his radar beacon so the scooter and tow traffic wouldn't run him down. Any ships moving under thrusters and magnetics, however, were his problem to avoid. They couldn't spin that much mass just to keep from impacting a Human-sized object, even if he did have an inherent right-of-way within enclosed space.

This was a busy morning inside the docking bay.

Gemini had put out six destroyers, in three sections of two, and two cruisers on routine patrols in the cluster. The remaining fourteen destroyers and six cruisers in Koskiusko's squadron were inside, either for crew standdown or repairs. It was practically a full house.

The Admiral chewed about the repair cycle, which got deeper and deeper every quarter. What he chewed on was Samwels' butt. The way appropriations from Central Center were trending—and likely to falter even more, what with confusion over the succession— the repair situation was only going to get worse.

The markings on the freighter, now that she was under the bay's klieg lights, were not exactly what Samwels had expected. Bennington's ship had a lateral line in dusky red, with the dorsal surfaces speckled in gold on powder blue. They were the transit line's colors. Samwels would never have noticed, except for the comment Paol Bennington once made, about them miming the rainbow trout of Placer Colorado, which were the his favorite fish to catch and eat.

Except the lateral line on this freighter was not red but a dull brown. The speckles were more yellow than gold, too.

Now, what kind of stellar radiation, or atmospheric abrasion, or nebular gas titration would be likely to so affect the ceramic dyes which saturated the ship's hullmetal? Samwels was still trying to figure it out as he braked for rendezvous with the forward manway lock.

He considered for two seconds the possibility that the freighter was not the *Salmo.* Her access transponder must be giving the right codes, however, or she would have closed down the entire base. Perhaps it was a different ship from the same line, an older ship perhaps, that Captain Thwaite on Palaccio had hired at the last minute. That might make Samwels's call a bit embarrassing—and his morning in the docking bay a waste of time.

As he spun on a timed jet burst, the ship slid into its grapples and the aft cargo hatch began to open. That was faster than usual for radio checks. Someone up in the Comm Shack must have been on her toes and cleared the ship before it had penetrated the access fields.

Samwels reached the lock handholds, tugged away the last bit of his forward momentum, and started to dial for pressure. The telltales stayed dark. The lock was shut down.

The first of the ten-meter cargo pods was coming out of the open hatch aft. With a curse under his breath, Samwels pushed off toward it, not bothering with the packjet. He was rehearsing the bawling out he meant to give the shiphandlers for lousy portside procedures.

As he glided aft, the pod drifted sideways toward the base's cargo crews, who scattered before the plowing mass. No tether lines, no bounce pads, not a finger to keep it from ricocheting out into the busy docking bay. Hildred Samwels cursed aloud inside his helmet and decided he was going to lift somebody's license.

The plastic pod split open *before* it hit the base's inner wall. Instead of puffing out atmosphere and packaged goods, it spilled men in vacuum suits. Men armed with repulsor rifles.

The intruders spread out quickly. They shot at the retreating freight handlers. One of the riflemen faced an oncoming scooter and picked off the ensign riding it with a single plasma-banded bead. Another saw Samwels drifting down on them and shouldered his weapon.

Samwels did an impossible pirouette in mid-trajectory and hurled himself against the hatch coaming. The shooter was a second behind him. The string of glass beads the rifleman fired clanged off the hull a foot from Samwels's helmet and exploded in crystals at a flat angle away from him.

"Security. Security." Samwels thumb-clicked the master override on his helmet radio. "All sections. Intruders at Port 14. Firefight in progress."

Within three seconds, radio chatter picked up about two hundred percent, backed by the internal alarm siren.

Rather than give the man with the rifle another shot at himself, Samwels shoved off from the hull for the ensign's scooter, drifting twenty meters away. He wasn't thinking of escape; he wanted a ramming weapon.

Four bead streams bracketed him on the long fall for it. Three missed and the last one cut his suit across the calf. He felt a sudden coldness there—vacuum, shock, and evaporating blood. He didn't pause but snagged the scooter and keyed it over. A mist of red and sticky filaments drifted up around his knee.

A fifth line of glass beads clanged on the machine's thrust canister and exploded it, putting the vehicle solidly out of commission. Samwels was an upright target in a shooting gallery. He braced for the next shot, which would surely take him in the chest.

"*Damn you!*" shrieked a high, thin voice on the proximity channel. A small, silvery ball of suit cloth flashed by him going the other way, toward the knot of intruders. The distinguishing feature was the clear acrylic helmet over a cowl of gray and black hair. One arm, bent behind the Capuchin's back, worked frantically at something. Before the captain could figure out what it was doing, intruders, Capuchin, and pod halves evaporated in a yellow flare.

Later, at his leisure, Samwels decided the mechanic had used an electrostatic welder to burn through, alternately, the small green bottle of emergency oxygen tucked into his suit's environment unit and the fuel tank of his packjet. Only a Capuchin could have performed the mental calculations to know, without looking, how many searing touches were needed to breach the two tanks at the precise moment ending that long jump. And only a Capuchin would know why an antisocial genius would sacrifice himself to save the life of a Human officer he didn't even much like.

But those thoughts came later. Before the expanding ball of flame and gases dissipated, Samwels had snagged a loose repulsor rifle from one of the dead intruders and kicked off the scooter toward the open cargo hatch.

Inside, other pods had split apart, and more suited men were setting up a portable plasma gun. It was a twenty-megawatt model, with a serious enough heat plume to do real damage to the unprotected hulls arrayed around the docking bay. Samwels picked his shots, taking two of the gunners in the helmets and then, as his approach vector shortened, making the rest keep their heads down.

When he had the chance, he put random pellets into the still-sealed pods at the back of the freighter's hold. Sometimes he was rewarded with puffs of air and cereal grains, sometimes with fresh blood crystals.

Just as he drifted into the hatchway on the last of his momentum, and fired off the last of his rifle's ammunition drum, the first of the Fleet's Marines charged out of Port 14.

The destroyer in the dock across the way unlimbered its uncollimated plasma battery and put a single shot into the freighter's drive unit. The recoil from that shook the hatchway around Samwels and his Marines as they descended in a swirl on the remaining fighters. He prayed aloud that the gunnery officer on that destroyer wouldn't try a second shot for a clean kill on the bandit ship. And that the flight crew aboard the freighter wouldn't try to get away by a single hyperspace jump. Either one, from inside the docking bay, would blow the air-curtained manways leading into the base and gut Gemini's relatively fragile interior.

The vibrations from that single plasma discharge were damped out by a deeper, more ominous tone, a deep buzzing from inside Samwels's left mastoid. He had only heard it twice before, as a test. Gemini Base was about to crash-launch its full complement of destroyers and cruisers.

In his peripheral vision, Samwels could see the translucent flex tubes, fore and aft on the ships in cradles, tremble with the impact of hundreds of feet and hands. Sailors, gunners, engineers, trackers, officers, programmers, magnetic handlers, navigators, talkers, captains, and cooks were climbing cheek-to-butt up to their ship stations.

Was Admiral Koskiusko overreacting to the threat of an intruder fire team loose in the docking bay?

Possibly.

But why now? Samwels had the situation almost under control aboard the false freighter.

Or was worse damage being done somewhere else in the base? Holy Trimurti—! Was Gemini being evacuated!

"We're holding this deck, Captain." A Marine sergeant saluted at his elbow.

"Well, get your men under cover. The base is about to dump the squadrons."

"Yes, sir!"

"Samwels to the Plot," said the bug behind his ear. "On the double—sir."

"On my way," he replied on the command circuit. "What's the situation?"

Samwels spun on his heel and slapped the packjet. The blast doors had automatically come down on all the air-curtained cargo ports, so he was going to make a 200-meter jump to the nearest security lock. It would take him thirty-two seconds. Still, it was the fastest way—unless the launch went off before then and filled the bay with a maelstrom of reaction mass at near plasma temperatures.

"Globular attack," was all the talker had time to tell him.

It was enough. The War College taught that the globular attack—a large force of ships dropping simultaneously out of hyperspace around a tactical objective—was almost unbeatable. The only defense was a crash-launch, meeting inward force with outward. The trouble was, any competent attacker could calculate the maximum at-rest number of ships, n, which the objective could dock. Then pour $n+1$ ships into the globule.

Twenty-five seconds into his jump, the security lock started to close. The hullmetal door slid left to right. In the last meters of his trajectory, Samwels skewed his shoulders right to left and ignored the proper braking bursts. He scraped through the gap at 9.75 meters per second and still accelerating. The impact against the far wall of the lock gouged him in the ribs, smashed his radio and the suit's environmental controls, and put a star crack in his helmet shell. The slow, whistling leak was a mosquito-whine in his ears.

The crack would be serious, even deadly, in any other circumstances. In these, however, he planned to be out of the suit and on the run two seconds after the lock finished cycling. The gobby red mass along the back of his right leg was more of a worry. When the suit sealers pulled free, that was going to bleed like a butchered pig. Hurt, too.

In the partial pressure of the airlock, Samwels

heard a muffled thump. He felt it through his bootsoles. The crash-launch. Fourteen destroyers, five cruisers, and the *Dawnlight* with her disabled mass inverter were now thrusting outward from Gemini's lower bay. The whistling from his helmet shell seemed louder.

Once out of the lock, Samwels took an extra half second to slap a medipad on his calf and jumped into the nearest drop tube, headed for the base's combined command center and situation room, called simply "the Plot."

Admiral Koskiusko was bent over the TAC—the Tactical Analysis Computer—display, which was subordinate to the real-time, holographic images of the Central Zone Repeater. The Admiral's brow was furrowed. He straightened when he caught sight of Samwels entering the compartment.

"There you are, Captain. We've got something strange here. Damned strange."

Samwels hurried over, doing his best not to show a limp.

"The CZR shows an attack by upwards of one hundred large ships," the Admiral rumbled. "They dropped out of hyperspace in the classic globing formation. Damned tight, too. They were on us in a span of twenty-three seconds." He turned to a nearby watchstander. "Twenty-three sound right, Lieutenant?"

"Yes, sir. One-oh-four ships in two-two-point-eight-niner, to be exact."

"All right, so we're dead. Total wipeout. No defense for *that* kind of engagement. Even a crash-launch, at an attack:defend ratio of five-to-one, is a hopeless gesture. And after they deal with our fleet, their combined firepower can overload our own deflecter system. Then the base vaporizes. Dead . . .

"So, Captain. Why aren't we dead?"

"They aren't attacking?"

"Sure they're attacking. Giving our destroyers and cruisers hell. But not enough hell. In the time you took to get up here, we've already licked our own weight in bogies. We shouldn't, but we have."

"How many have we lost, sir?"

"*Fortinbras* is half-blind, and the old *Dawnlight*'s taken a major pressure loss. Everyone else is still flying and fighting."

Samwels bent to peer into the TAC. He toggled two keys to switch it from radar image to universal transponder. The analysis held: their attackers coded out as large, both heavily armed and heavily shielded, destroyers, cruisers, and even three planetary monitors. The Admiral was right. Gemini should be dead.

"Perhaps their intention is not total victory. Could they be trying to scare us?"

"Hrrumphh," the Admiral said. "Central Fleet will not be cowed."

"Yes, sir. Do they know that?"

"They ought to—unless they're bandits from far outside the Pact Perimeter."

"What do they call themselves?"

"They've made no formal challenge."

"And their transponders don't identify. Whom do we suspect? What does the Intelligence say?"

"It's read my logs. It says we're being attacked by Arachnid Cluster Command. Ninety-percent probability on intention. But—"

"But Spile doesn't have any hundred heavy fighters, even if he's managed to co-opt Scorpio Base."

"Never. Admiral Pozzolan is as loyal as I am."

"Of course, sir. I only raise the point to dismiss it."

"Look!" Koskiusko pointed into the holographic repeater. "Double burst. Two more gone . . . A third!"

"They don't seem to fight very well," Samwels observed. "Their maneuvers seem—well—sluggish."

"Hit on the *Gloriosus*, sir," a talker reported. "Starboard polar deflectors are—secondary concussion! Guns down. Nav down. Drive down. Pressure failing . . . Sir, the *Gloriosus* has ceased transmitting."

Almost as an afterthought, the zone repeater showed a small winking star. Gemini had lost the first of her children to war.

"Damn!" from the Admiral.

As if encouraged by this initial kill, the attackers suddenly rallied. For the first time in the battle, four and five ships were engaging each of the base's defenders. The Arachnids—if that was what they were— seemed to be teaching themselves coordinated tactics as they fought. Talker chatter from the panels behind Samwels and the Admiral suddenly doubled and tripled. In the span of five minutes, they lost three more ships.

"Sir?" Samwels ventured. "Perhaps we should summarize this development and send a hyperwave signal to CORECINC."

"Are you throwing in the towel, Captain?"

"Not at all, sir. We must, however, allow for all eventualities. Even for—demoralizing—possibilities."

The Admiral's face hardened. "Send the signal."

Samwels snagged a talker out of the line and dictated his orders. The sailor nodded once and left the Plot for the Comm Shack.

When Samwels turned back to the CZR, it flickered and went black.

"Damn!"

"Interfrequency flutter, sir!" one of the techies called. "They're jamming us."

That meant the base battle computers were blind. The captains out in the thick of the fight were getting no tactical projections. Or worse, they were getting invalid projections.

"Clear it!" the Admiral barked.

"Can't—sir."

"Use the chaff overrides," Samwels called.

"Ineffective."

"Hand the token over to *Roselight*," the Admiral ordered. "We'll piggyback from her bridge consoles. At least we'll get to watch."

"If the cruiser is destroyed—sir?" Samwels prompted.

"Then we pass down to the next ranking cruiser captain, then to destroyers—if their equipment can handle the load. By then, there might not be much of a fight left to track, anyway." It was the first defeatist thought Koskiusko had voiced.

Seven more ships went out, harried by their attackers through the damage stages, from failed magnetic shielding, to failed gunnery coordination, to failed maneuvering, to failing pressure, and finally to death.

As he watched this ballet of the dying, Samwels began to see a pattern.

"Look, sir! One of the attackers always holds back. Just behind the others. Still it consistently scores more hits on our ships. The others in the fight are just harriers, window dressing, essentially amateurs. But, in each case, that ship which is keeping its distance—that's the professional."

"Relay that to *Roselight*. Add coordinates where known."

"Yes, sir."

"And see if the base batteries can train in from the bounced perspective of the cruiser."

"I'll tell Lieutenant Carnot it's never been done before. Then he'll find a way to do it."

The Admiral grinned.

Within ten minutes, under battle control from the *Roselight* and aided by Samwels' deductions, the base defenders were taking a heavier toll among the "professionals." In fact, they had cut the enemy almost in half. The less skilled of the attackers were still taking an occasional destroyer, but more by luck than tactics. The Gemini captains were getting tired, and the battle computers on the cruiser were fearfully overloaded.

At the end of twenty minutes the first of the patrols, including the cruiser *Aurora*, had popped back on emergency recall and tipped the balance.

"We're down to three cruisers, five destroyers, Admiral," one of the talkers reported. "You wanted to—"

"Yes, yes. Tell them to begin a staged withdrawal to the base inner circle. Pull the enemy behind them, north and south, into range of our polar batteries. Signal Carnot to prepare for full autofire in—"

"Forty seconds, sir?" prompted Samwels.

"Forty seconds it is."

"Aye-aye, sir."

The feint began, played to look as if the wounded defenders were making a gallant retreat. Thirty seconds into the maneuver three more destroyers popped out of hyperspace, behind the closing enemy, joining with the *Aurora* and her squadrons in a classic pincers.

"Now!" Koskiusko husked in a dry throat.

Inner ring of defenders and outer, supported by the base's own guns, they all switched to a coordinated autofire under cyber control. The holofocus lit with a white glare. Samwels and the Admiral had to shield their eyes. Talkers on the other side of the Plot turned away.

When the glare died down, the holographic repeater was clear. Only the Gemini ships were indicated on either side of a dead zone. The zone itself was empty.

The image was a computer's lie, of course. In the eye of his mind, Samwels could see cubic kilometers of hanging, eddying debris. Ceramics, plastics, metal, and meat floated, charred, and broken, in the dissipating wisps of cooled plasma.

"Dispatch *Aurora* to rescue duty," the Admiral

ordered. "Tell Captain Worley to give it two hours. If he isn't finding survivors in that time, there are none to find. Rest of the ships and base crews to stand down . . . And tell the men, well done."

Samwels nodded and started off.

"Oh, and Hildred—thank you."

"My duty, sir."

"Nonsense, Captain. Do you think we don't monitor emergencies from up here? I saw what you did in the docking bay. I figure you headed off a Trojan horse maneuver that might have tipped the balance when we had to launch."

"It was the Capuchin, sir."

The Admiral shook his head. "Stupid sacrifice. Alien psychotics. He wasted himself for at most four men. You alerted us to the situation, called for reinforcements, then charged right in and cleared that freighter's entire hold, including an operational plasma gun. Clear thinking, teamwork, and courage in the face of the enemy. That's what saved us, and my report on this action will make certain recommendations to CORECINC. Good work, Captain."

"Thank you, sir."

As a coda to the fight, Samwels sat in on the Admiral's board debriefing the Gemini ship captains. The report from Captain Worley of Cruiser *Aurora* made interesting reading. Although he had recovered no survivors, Worley had picked up enough residue from the final seconds of the engagement to do a computer scan and make a statistical analysis.

"Merchant ships. I'll stake my commission on it."

"But their transponders—" Samwels protested.

"I don't care what their radio codes were rigged to show. I've got a couple of tons of hullmetal, most in pieces about a meter square. It's not as thick as a warship's. Plus I've got four or five hundred cubic meters of fittings and equipment fragments. Some of it's military, sure, but on a ratio of ten-to-one, it's civilian stuff—cybers, cabling, thrusters, servos, hydraulics, suit packs . . . We even got *serial* numbers, for God's sake."

"You've traced those, have you?" the Admiral drawled.

"Of course, sir. Some of it's Arachnid Cluster Command. Some from the Bovari Trading Group. Most, however—sixty-nine-point-eight percent—is Haiken Maru. I'd bet platinum Rands on them being the owner of registry."

"But those ships were *fighting* us!" Carnot cried, from down the table.

"Sure, quick retrofits with plasma shooters and a magnetic field source," from Worley. "Scrape your crews up from the beach. Get enough of them in the sky, and you can even take on squadrons from the Central Fleet."

"Or try," Carnot countered, with some pride in his voice. "We mopped them up, in the end."

"I don't think they expected as much fight as they got," Samwels said.

"Oh, yes," from Worley. "We've all heard about your exploit in the bay, Hils."

"What did it prove?" Carnot insisted.

Samwels raised his eyebrows at the lieutenant.

"As of 0600 today, we have four ships of the line that can jump space. The rest are all leaking atmosphere or down for repairs. Whoever is converting those freighters—"

"Haiken Maru!" someone said aloud.

"Bovari!"

"Governor Spile!"

Samwels put up a restraining hand. "Whoever it is, they've tapped into a cheap source of naval power."

"Not worth much!" from Carnot.

"No, not much," Samwels agreed. "Yet with every engagement, the value of our own ships rises. Five or six hundred percent in the last twenty-four hours, by my estimate."

"Say a thousand percent," the Admiral grunted.

"Yes, sir. At some point," Samwels went on, "our ships become too valuable to put in the field. We'll withdraw before a shot is fired. We'll hoard them. They'll become hangar queens, every one of them."

"Whoever is supplying those armed freighters," the Admiral said, "has rewritten the rules of engagement in this sector as of today."

"We're neutralized, sir," Samwels agreed.

Chapter 13

Taddeuz Bertingas: WALK IN THE PARK

It hurt his feet to scrabble against the bark of the tree. His hands were still strong, the skin lean. But after running for nine hours, barefoot, his feet were swollen and cut.

Bertingas's progress had been swift, once he got going and had spent less time hiding. In the early hours, his travel had been interrupted by the need to fade into small copses or thick stands of rhododendron or other undergrowth, holding his thudding breath and waiting for a patrol to walk past. And they always would—whacking the bushes with the butt ends of their repulsor rifles and making noise enough to drive the forest before them. (For two days afterward, Bertingas saw no animal large enough for him to eat.)

Once he got elbow room and a nose for his general direction of travel, however, Bertingas moved swiftly down the game trails. He would still cut at odd moments—or when his instincts told him—cross-country through the brush. The instinct to part with the trails was damped by his situation: trails were easy underfoot, packed dirt and young grasses; the brush was thorny with stems and sticks and sharp rocks.

His feet were strong, as he was accustomed to hiking, but they were soft, being more used to the insides of boots or shoes. The white flesh of his soles was scored pretty badly by that first night, so that he was leaving blood marks on the grass and working dust deep into the open cuts, where it would tattoo the skin in time.

The scramble to climb a tree, where he could wedge himself into a forking limb and doze the night in relative safety, added crumbles of black bark and a smear of pitch to his feet's dirt coating.

Wedged there finally, without dinner and with no water except what he had scooped from a stream or standing pool while on the run, Bertingas took stock.

Hungry and cold and still thirsty, yes. His feet would either get better and toughen up, so that he could begin again in the morning; or they would stiffen so that he could barely hobble. Then his pursuers would surely find him.

Now, was that such a terrible prospect?

Yes. The people who were looking for him played rough. The attack on his apartment—what? Only two days ago? Three? That attack had been no attempted detention or kidnapping. They meant to kill him, rub him out, bury the pieces.

Perhaps by tomorrow or the day after, some of the trackers afoot in these woods might also be friends. Searchers from the base, out looking for him along the line of flight that Patty Firkin would certainly be able to describe. If Patty and Mora had escaped unobserved and unharmed.

Without his AID to analyze and link signals with them, however, Bertingas would have to trust his instincts and fade back into the undergrowth. Glide silently away at right angles. Not show the pale skin of his face toward them.

If his feet did cripple up, so that he could not go on for another day or two, would he be able to stay in this tree?

No. The soldiers or bully boys or whatever they were who chased him would sooner or later notice that they were driving the large animals out of this area. Then they would bring in their infrared equipment again—and begin to believe it. Then they would find him up a tree where no Wampit could climb.

So, the first order of business was his feet, care and feeding of same.

Bracing with his right heel against the bole, he crooked his left knee—it grated like a rusty hinge— and brought his foot up into his lap. The fingers went to work, flexing, massaging, rubbing around the cuts. He had no water to clean them, but he could drip spittle upon his fingers and rub that into the gashes. It stung a little, and the moisture cooled the heat in his flesh.

Pain, of one kind or another, was going to be his companion for a long time.

The garment he wore—aside from the slippers Bertingas had fashioned out of stiff bark that first morning he had climbed down out of a tree—was a single weave of monofilament. It could not be cut with any tool he could make of stone or wood, but it could be unraveled.

In the fading light, with a cold wind rising from the northeast, off the mountains, he swore to make a fire. It would be small and smokeless, no more than a glow of embers from dried twigs, he promised himself. Still, it would give some heat to bear him through the night.

To make his fire, Bertingas needed a notched block, a bearing pad for his palm, a drill, and a bow to drive

it. He had the various pieces of wood at hand, cut
and shaped with a sharp sliver of flint he had picked
up for a knife. He also had a pile of dried leaves and
shavings for tinder, a supply of sticks for burning.
Everything was ready except a string for the bow.

A twist of green grasses had no strength to it—
he'd tried that.

If he had killed an animal, even a small one, then
it would yield skin and sinews for a string. So far,
having just his hands to hunt with, he had taken only
grubs.

They were soft and dry, and squirmed in his mouth
until his teeth had come down a dozen times. The
taste wasn't bad, like sweet resin and powder, but
they gave him nothing to make a bow drill with.

So he attacked the edge of his underwear just
above the ankle. The rough edge of the flint abraded
the material enough to get a ravel going. In a few
minutes, as the dark closed down, he had pulled a
thread around and around his leg, taking the hem up
his calf. Then he snapped it with his teeth.

Bertingas doubled the thread over three times and
tied it to a notch in the bow. He bent the stick
across his knee and tied the other end. Without
pausing to admire his workmanship, he crouched
over the notched block, holding it with his bare toes.
The drill stick fitted into the notch, and the pad
fitted over the top of the drill. A loop in the doubled
thread gripped the stem and whirled it around as he
sawed back and forth with the bow.

The block wobbled, and he pushed harder with his
toes to steady it. The top pad wiggled on the drill
until his hand found exactly the right angle and the
right pressure for holding it. His stroke with the bow
smoothed and found its rhythm: not so fast that the
point of the drill rode up out of the notch; not so
slowly that it dug into the wood and stuck.

Back and forth, back and forth. The sweat rolled

down from his armpit and soaked the cloth along his side. Then the wind came and made that place cold.

Back and forth. He was about to give up. The old books were wrong. No Human had ever made wood smoke and burn this way. It was the wrong wood. Too much sap. Or not enough.

A spark suddenly tumbled out of the notch, fell on the rock. Bertingas dropped his tools and covered it with a promising leaf. The spark went out.

He quickly picked up drill, pad, and bow; found his angle; began sawing again.

In another minute or two, the blackened pit of the notch smoked and gave forth another spark. Bertingas ignored it. Then two or three sparks. He sawed faster. The tip of his drill flared into flame.

He dropped everything again and bent down. He blew on it, and the flame rose up the width of his little finger. Without looking, he reached for a piece of leaf and pushed it into the notch. It burned quickly. Another, and another. He piled on his tinder, then his small sticks.

It made a light by which he could see the backs of his hands, sense the reflection off his gaunt cheekbones. He could just feel a beginning of warmth against his face when a sound caught his attention. A crackle of brush, a tramp of feet. Far off now, but growing.

With a hiss that was almost a curse, Bertingas spread the fire and batted the flames out with his hands. He kicked shavings and tinder to the four corners of the wide spot where he had crouched, and a growling noise came involuntarily from his throat. There were tears in his eyes, and not from the smoke.

Taddeuz Bertingas was ready to sit down right there, slump cold and exhausted, and wait for his pursuers—the first patrol he had heard in two days—to find him.

Let them take him to some place with light and

warmth, even if they had a lock on the door and chains on his legs. Let them take him to real food, even if it was a crust of dry bread, and his last meal. Let them kill him. At least he would be warm for a moment.

But these thoughts passed in an instant. He gathered himself to himself. He slipped on his bark shoes. He picked up his drill, his bow, notched block, and flint blade. And he faded into the trees.

Chapter 14

Regis Sallee: TICKLER

Regis Sallee chose his moment exactly: two minutes into the melon course of a state breakfast. The honorees this morning were the Latifundist Association. Salt of the earth, the landholders, but boring people. More interested in labor fees, title law, export prices, and weather control than in real politics.

What must it be like, to live and strive for half a corona more on the price of *beet juice,* and care not a fig for *dominance?*

This was the perfect audience before which to drop his grenade.

"I say, m'dear . . . ?" The vocipulators picked up his voice and carried it, as they were intended, through the bubbles of conversation around the table.

Deirdre turned, a wedge of yellow pulp on a spoon halfway to her mouth. The look she gave him was not that of a loving bride.

"Have you reached a decision about the nomination?"

"There never was a doubt of it, Regis." Her voice

183

came back through the same system, and everyone in the room could hear. "We are pledged to Roderick."

"Pledged, but not bonded."

The cattleman sitting at Regis's left put down his spoon, wiped his mouth, and turned to look at the Governor.

"A mere technicality. I will have the consent codes, I am sure, from all *loyal* Pact subjects. I am glad to report that the—um—majority of our friends here have graciously provided me with their codes."

Around the table, spoons tinkled onto plates and a smatter of applause echoed. Some of it was muffled by napkins clutched in one hand or the other.

"Majority, m'dear? Some but not all? Of our loyal friends?" That was according to script.

"Indeed."

"Do they have doubts, do you think?"

"Certainly not! They know where their loyalties lie—and to whom. I am sure they have merely been too preoccupied with matters of business, the harvest, taking care of their bondworkers, to provide the codes in a timely manner. An oversight, I assure you."

"Yet some have doubts." Regis looked right and left with his eyes. This was *not* according to the script. He noted subtle hesitations among both the guests at their food and the servants moving plates.

So there were spies in the Palace staff. Well, he knew that already, just not who all of them were. He made a rapid catalog of faces and badges—the names would come later.

Amelia Ceil threw down her napkin.

"We support you, Deirdre. You can trust that. We support order, peace, law, and a settled market. But Roderick . . ."

"He's a puppet," someone on the far side of the table said sharply.

"Better than a combination of the traders," someone else whispered.

"I know My Lord Roderick ten Holcomb . . ." Governor Sallee began.

"Rather too well," Regis supplied in a grunt, deep in his throat, unheard by the vocipulators.

"He has his father's values. He appreciates the work that all of his subjects, but especially you stewards on the land, have done to promote and defend the Principles of Pact. Once elected, he will continue the program of expansion and development that his father—"

"Grandfather," from down the table.

"*Great*-grandfather," from the other side.

"—supported with his every waking thought."

"When he was sober," in a whisper.

"Which wasn't often," in rejoinder.

"We will not have a war, Deirdre!" Amelia Ceil barked.

"Of course not!" the Governor replied.

"But others will. Spile makes open war for the Chair. He has support from many sources."

"Mad dogs and traitors," from Deirdre.

"Of course. The man is mad himself," Amelia Ceil conceded. "No one denies that. Still, he leads by example. There are others, no less ambitious and not at all mad, who would push him along his course, as far as he can go, watch him burn down to a greasy spot both himself and everything in his path. . . . Then they would slide in behind him with real strength."

"If you have evidence of such plotting against the Pact," the Governor said, "it is a crime to withhold it, Amelia."

"Of course I don't have evidence! But I know what everyone knows, if they have eyes to see and a brain to think."

Regis noted a white-coated waiter drifting close to

the Mistress of Greengallow's shoulder. The man—
for he was a Human—had big, loose hands and held
them about at the level of Ceil's neck.

"Roderick and the Central Fleet will stand against
all such mischief-makers," Deirdre Sallee affirmed.

"If he gets our consent," from Ceil.

"You have given yours."

"An indication of willingness only, Deirdre. Not
my promise. And not my code."

Others around the table were nodding and mur-
muring agreement.

The waiter with the big hands turned away sharply
and made himself busy at the sideboard, preparing
the protein course. It was steak and eggs with a
salmon sauce. Regis wondered how many here could
eat it, or keep it, after this interchange.

His mission was well accomplished.

Chapter 15

Taddeuz Bertingas: TAKE-OUT

Thick and hot, the blood ran over Bertingas's lower lip and trickled through the beard stubble on his chin. He stopped only long enough to wipe it back with the heel of his hand, then licked his palm. Immediately he set again to ripping chunks out of the animal's liver with his teeth.

When about half a kilogram was choked down, and the gorging frenzy was off him, Bertingas paused to consider.

Was it an animal?

It had moved on four legs, each tipped with a single callused pad that might have been a hoof in the early evolutionary stages. It had grazed along the forest floor and the lower tree limbs, nibbling anything green and flickering its short, black-striped tail. Its eyes were on the sides of its head, like a herd animal, a sky watcher, a prey. Not toward the front, like a predator. It might have been a sort of proto-deer, except its high, domed skull was innocent of any horns. Its white hide was covered with short, stiff bristles, like a hog's.

When he had met it on the trail, the animal—call it a Bristle Deer—had stared at him stupidly. Someone not so hungry might have said its stare was more . . . thoughtful. The creature had hardly flinched when Bertingas put his flint-tipped spear against the yoke of his throat and pushed once, hard.

As far he was concerned, the Bristle Deer was a dumb animal. He saw no possibility of it being an undiscovered intelligence. It was just an unclassified fauna of the Palaccio Uplands, possibly very rare, but also very tasty.

He could feel the nourishment pour through him from the broad, glistening organ he thought of as the liver. At least it had been in the right place for a terrestrial mammal's liver—once he had hacked through the skin of the belly with his spear blade and pulled the carcass open with the help of a short stick.

The Bristle Deer—call it *Odocoileus bertingasi*—was wealth, health, perhaps life itself to Bertingas. He would mine the flanks for steaks, to supplement the berries and grubs that had been his diet for the last week. He would strip and scrape the hide for a sturdy outer garment and moccasins, to make up for the cloak of dried grasses he was wearing next to his ragged underwear and his bark slippers, which were thin and falling apart. He would peel the tendons for a bowstring, slice the intestines for food pouches, chip the top off the skull for a water cup, crack the long bones for arrowheads and fish hooks. He would boil the small bones for glue and shave the bristles to fletch his arrows.

With this deer, he could continue the long trek indefinitely. He felt like thanking it for the gift of his life.

What a difference a week in the wild country had made in him. Would any of his friends recognize this savage who had killed an animal with a sharp stone and ripped its meat with his teeth? Would they believe it was the same Deputy Director of Communications for Aurora Cluster? Formerly the archivist of the Baseform Platter and adherent of Veracitor principles? A svelte urbanite of Meyerbeer and resident of the plush Satellite Villas. Rubber of elbows, almost, with Central Centrists such as Deirdre Sallee and Selwin Praise. Would anyone believe it?

Yes, Halan Follard would. He knew all about Tad's penchant for escaping to the high country, to the winds and the deep woods. Still, Follard knew Bertingas went on his treks with the latest in gear: a tent of thermal silk, a ground roll of spring fibers and memory-malleable airbeads, boots of moleskin with steel shanks, nutrient syrups with the savor of a banquet if not the substance, a convection heater with leaves of light metal that folded down to the size of a candle in his pocket.

What Follard didn't know was that Tad had also studied the old ways—of the Sioux, the Yakut, the Inuit, the Polynesian, and the Wahabi—for surviving on the land. It was from them he had learned to chip flint, strip a sapling, and wait along a game trail for the first unwary mammal.

It had taken a week to bring down his first deer. To be honest, he'd had more than mere survival on his mind. A dozen times in the waiting and walking Bertingas had been interrupted. Where he expected the delicate footfalls of an animal large enough to kill, he heard on the trail the crashing, crackling, limb-snapping progress of a Human patrol. One not trained to the woods and to silent stalking. Therefore, soldiers.

As his hands worked on the deer, picking the parts he wanted, his eyes and ears scanned the perimeter of this place among the trees. If anyone came upon him before he had time to prepare a cache pit and hide the remains—even the blood-soaked soil from beneath the carcass—he would have to run very fast.

It would help to have advance warning, just a whisper on the wind or flash of movement along the hillside. And . . .

What was this?

Right at hand, not five meters from his dinner table, a Leila tree grew. Bertingas had been looking for one since he had tumbled out of the aircar. Of the thousands of known and classified flora on Palaccio, this was one of two that were known to be poisonous. The other, *Nerium khan*, was pure death to touch in any form—root, bark, leaf, seed, sap. A drop of rainwater falling from the smallest leaf of *Nerium* was a Borgia's cup.

The Leila was more friendly. Its sap, on entering the bloodstream, caused drowsiness, disorientation, and a stupor lasting some hours. That interaction, however, neutralized the sap; so flesh from an animal or bird taken with a Leila dart was still wholesome and untainted. Game killed with a smear of *Nerium* was inedible.

Bertingas had planned to make some birding arrows, once he found something to fletch them with. A blunt stone weighting the tip would stun birds and small animals among the treetops without rending the small bodies or pinning them among the boughs. Leila was better. A thorn or bone sliver, tipped with the sap, could be blown from a short pipe. If he had a short pipe . . . perhaps carved from a shinbone of the deer, or cut from a stout reed.

As he policed the area of his kill, making the ground smooth and clean, he took a cutting from the Leila. While he continued down along the path, he used a piece of sharp flint, left over from his spear making, to cut and smooth and hollow out his selected shinbone. He could make a flute, if he knew how to play one—or a deadlier instrument.

When the bone was to his liking, Bertingas stuck it in the back of his grass belt to dry and grow hard.

His hands, always moving, went to work on the Leila cutting. He peeled away bark and cambium, and split away strips of the inner wood. Each fresh surface he rubbed with the side of his thumb to coax the sap out, making first a gummy curl, then a tight brown ball of sticky narcotic. He dropped these into a sack of deer's intestine.

Toward evening, when his legs were about walked out, Bertingas arrived at his destination. During the last three hours he had been climbing. For anyone lost in the woods, he knew, this was generally a bad policy. Downhill, following the natural course of water, takes the weary traveler to the lowlands; to the place of social, intelligent beings; to the sea, if there is one on the planet. Uphill takes you to the peaks, the dry rocklands, the interior wastes. Yet Bertingas was following no haphazard trail.

He knew, without his AID to tell him, that he'd abandoned the aircar within 200 kilometers of the Uplands Hyperwave Station. It was one of the few in the system that were planet bound, instead of being lodged on a moon or free-floating asteroid. Since capturing, suspending, feeding, turning, and shooting laser messages through a massive singularity was potentially dangerous work, the stations were placed beyond the pale of civilization. On a new planet like Palaccio, that was about 500 klicks out of town.

Bertingas had been moving toward it, more or less, for the past week. He had been interrupted only by the need to avoid hostile searchers and find water sources along the way.

On a scarp about thirty meters above him, the station grew like some giant puffball feeding on the rocks. The round containment for the singularity gave the building its shape. From the cover of the trees, Bertingas studied it. He noted the waveguides that traded microwave signals, through repeater stations, with Meyerbeer. He listened for the background rumble—barely audible above the light wind—of the fusion generator. The power system was under autonomous control, with backups. And, if the worst of bad days happened and the backups went down, the system would automatically switch over and draw 500 megawatts of power through the microwave signal system. Uplands Station had every priority it needed to maintain its power stream.

If it ever failed, and the field that suspended the singularity dropped, Palaccio would die.

No one had ever seen a planet collapse from the black cancer of a gravity singularity eating out its core. Aurora Cluster's permit for Uplands Station still called for a systemwide evacuation in the event of a fifty-percent power fluctuation.

There, in the fabric of the cliffs, he could feel it: the rumble-tumble-grumble of the generator. All was well.

Oh no it wasn't!

As Bertingas watched, the groundlevel hatch undogged and swung wide. A Human in some kind of uniform, dark green coveralls with heavy boots, stepped out and looked around. He walked over to a flat rock about stool high and sat down in the evening sun. He propped a repulsor rifle against the rock and loosened his bootlaces.

Slowly, careful not to make a sound on the loose pebbles underfoot, Bertingas faded back in among the trees. Just as slowly, he sank down into a crouch, then put his stiffening legs out, and rested his back against one of the trunks. Through the intervening branches, he could still see the station and the soldier.

Only one, but Bertingas was fast gaining an appreciation for the military mind. There would be more inside the station. How many? At least two. Maybe five. Unlikely to be more than that, or he would see another outside.

Group dynamics predicated that when more than

four or five Humans gathered in any setting, social or otherwise, and the location provided for more than a single space, say an inside and an outside, as here, then the group tended to clump. In any body of ten people, one person would not casually break off like this—unless he was in a sulk or on guard duty. This one's body language showed neither solitary anger nor special alertness. So, if a large number of people were inside, two or three would more likely be out here. Or that was the theory Tad had absorbed in his reading.

The man's green uniform was nothing he recognized. Nothing from any of the Auroran services, and not Central Fleet. It could be the military command from one of the other administrative clusters, of which Bertingas's knowledge was imperfect. Or it could be the chosen uniform of his new security brigade, which Patty had neglected to show him on their inspection.

In that case, he could just walk up, identify himself, and ask permission to tap his access code into the microwave channels. There was—what?—a one-in-ten chance they would let him. And that, piled on the one-in-ten chance they weren't part of the search teams he had been dodging for a week, made the odds about one in one hundred that he would be able to walk away from the encounter. Unless he acted aggressively.

But not *too* aggressively, in case they turned out to be his own people, waiting for him after all.

Bertingas massaged his legs and worked out a plan of action. No sense in moving now, when he was tired and the soldier was alert. He would wait until full dark, past dark, almost dawn.

As he prepared to enter a light doze, Bertingas's restless fingers found the haunch of his deer, still hanging from his belt. Already in the heat its flesh was softening and becoming—unh—flavorful. He plucked bits of it and chewed them raw. As he chewed, his fingers worked out the tendons, peeled them to long, tough strings, and began braiding them. Within an hour he had a meter or more of knotted sinew. It would make a workable bowstring, when he found time to cut and shape a bow. Or sewing thread for his deerskin garment, if it ever got made. Or something more aggressive. In another hour, with his head tipped against the tree, Bertingas slept.

His biological clock woke him automatically at the darkest part of the night. His joints creaked and grated as he moved, again in a crouch, toward the edge of the trees. He paused to stretch the tiredness out.

In the starlight, the white dome of the station glowed. In its side he could see the still-open hatch. On the foreground, darker than the native rock, was the solitary soldier—perhaps a guard, after all. His head was down, sleeping.

This was going to be easier than Bertingas had thought.

Shedding his impediments—the haunch of deer, the grass cloak, the bark slippers—he crept forward and climbed toward that guard. Like a shadow among the stones, Bertingas moved around the man, whose head rose and fell slowly with each breath.

Behind him, across the hatchway, Bertingas tied the sinew string to the bottom hinge on one side and to the dog clip on the other. The string cut an invisible line, almost level, about fifteen centimeters above the lower lip of the hatch.

Bertingas plucked it once, to test the tension.

Thwunk! the string said softly, one low note in the night.

The guard stirred but didn't rise or look around.

Bertingas's smile showed teeth.

From the pouch at his belt, he fished out a ball of Leila sap, now slimy from resting inside the deer guts. He reversed his spear and, with his thumb, worked the sap well into the nibbled edge of its flint head. Then he crept forward, toward the guard.

The man stirred again, not really awake. He seemed to sense the presence of another Human.

Bertingas extended the spear, reaching for the neck. Just as the man started to rouse, he jabbed obliquely, right below the ear. A line of blood, black in the starlight, showed before the hand came up to cover it. The man cursed aloud and surged up, swinging the rifle around. Bertingas flattened himself on the ground.

The guard swung the muzzle past Tad's head and continued in a circle, a loose pirouette, until his left knee buckled and he fell with a clatter.

"Corl?"

One word, called hesitantly, sleepily, from inside the station.

The last thing Bertingas wanted was for them to hole up inside the building, prepared to hold him off. He seized the rifle by its stock and coil, pried it loose from the guard's twitching hands.

"Out here! Help me!" Bertingas called hoarsely, then dashed over to stand beside the hatch. No light came on inside, as he'd expected it would. That gave those others the same night-sighted advantage Bertingas hoped to enjoy. Not a good sign. It meant they were professionals.

The first of the other Humans came through the hatchway on the run. By chance his stride took him over and clear of the string. That fouled Bertingas's timing.

He had expected to bring the rifle stock up in a short arc to the man's stomach as he pitched forward. Now Tad had to change grip and bring it down on the base of the neck as the man moved out into the darkness. The blow fanned air behind the man's head. The soldier skidded to a stop, turned, and caught a hard, level jab with the butt full in the face. He flopped on his back.

The second man through the door found the stretched sinew with his leading ankle and did a cartwheel out into the night. He plowed solidly into Bertingas's back and tried to hold on, but Tad twisted around, bringing the rifle stock up into his short ribs. Once. Twice. And the man fell away to the left.

A third man hung back in the shadowed hatchway. In the starlight, Bertingas could see a rifle muzzle poking out, hunting around for a target. Slowly, silently, by centimeters, he glided out of the line of fire and over to the side of the doorway. Then with the speed of a striking snake, he grabbed the coilguide and pulled it through.

Whap! The rifle discharged into the stony ground.

As the man behind it stumbled forward into the string, Bertingas brought up his bare foot, toes curled down for an instep kick, into the man's groin. The other gasped once and rolled on himself. Tad sealed the deal with a downward chop of his hand against the exposed neck.

Then he froze, listening.

No sound came from within the station. That meant the fourth man inside was either very cautious or nonexistent.

Bertingas had only one way to test it. Holding his newly captured weapon at the ready, but loosely, he stepped through the hatch.

No movement, no attack.

He walked once around the service foyer.

No challenge, no scuttling steps.

He turned on the lights, exposing the opened door to the emergency relay office. Through it, he could see the ends of a couple of sleeping rolls and a litter of cooking equipment. A scorched mark on the tile floor showed where someone had made a fire.

"Put down your weapon," came a call from inside the office, "or I'll trip the field!"

Bertingas edged closer to the door. A shadow, moving on the floor, hinted at someone just out of sight, beside the station's master console.

"You know what that means!" the voice warned.

Bertingas held his silence, moved closer.

"The black hole will fall straight through to the core!"

Step by step Tad moved, creeping up, silently.

"I'll destroy this whole planet!"

He was half a meter from the doorjamb, now, but still off the line of sight of whoever was inside.

"I can do it!"

Tad popped through the doorway, rifle leveled, with a good pound of pull on the trigger. "No you can't!"

The man inside, some kind of officer by the braid on his collar, raised a pistol at Bertingas's face.

Bertingas shot his arm off, at the shoulder, with an explosive rip of glass beads.

The officer pinwheeled back against the console in a spray of blood, then slumped to the floor.

Bertingas put down his rifle, grabbed up some of the bedding, and tried to compress the flow from the open side of the man's chest. In a few seconds, the material was soaked through, and still the blood and other fluids poured out.

"How—did you—?" The dying man's eyes found Tad's.

"There is no switch for the gravity field," he explained. "No reason ever to drop it . . . I'm sorry."

"Ohh." The body struggled once, and then released. A stench from the relaxing sphincters reached Bertingas's nostrils.

He left the dead man to tend the live ones. A tap on the back of the head put down those who were gaining their unsteady feet. Then he cut strips from their own bedrolls to bind them. Within ten minutes he was in total possession of the station.

"Priority Interrupt Q-2," he tapped into the keyboard, cutting across the flow of microwave traffic from other dimensions down to the memory banks in Meyerbeer. "Execute lock-on search, Comm Dept staff, Rinaldi, Gina."

Within thirty seconds he had a voice-only link.

"Tad? Tad! Where are you?"

"Uplands Station."

"That Firkin woman said you were dead. An attack on your—"

"Not so. I bailed out."

"What have you been doing for a week? We've had so much—"

"Hiking in the woods. Look, Gina, whom do you trust right now?"

"Nobody. After—ah—"

"Wrong, my dear. You trust—I trust—Halan Follard. Get a secure line to him or, better yet, try to meet him in the flesh. Explain where I am, and say I need his help. Plus reinforcements."

"What about the Director?"

"No! Do not tell Selwin Praise. Let him still think I'm dead. In fact, after I close here, you are to wipe the last half hour's feed from this station."

"Tad!"

"Do it, Gina. Purge the banks. Everything."

"All right. Are you well?"

"Never better."

He closed the link and purged it from his end, putting the whole station off-line until further notice. Then he sorted through the soldiers' gear, looking for any kind of civilized food. He came up with three energy bars and a packet of cocoa powder. Within five minutes he had a small fire going in the burn mark on the floor and a cup of water bubbling away, ready for the powder. Breakfast.

Within two hours, as the first light of dawn was coming across the mountains behind him, the aircars started to land. In the lead was a dull-gray bus with the gold flashes of the Kona Tatsu. Halan Follard stepped out, flanked by two heavyset men in anonymous coveralls.

From upcountry a second vehicle circled around and landed. Patty leaped clear before it had fully touched down. Behind her came a trio of fierce-looking Ghiblis, the poisoned spittle dripping unconsciously off their fangs. The driver of her car was a Cowra that seemed to have calmed down: its hands were competently steady on the controls.

Behind Follard's bus came a transatmospheric boat of the Central Fleet. It landed upright on the flat space behind the station dome and discharged a squad of Marines. Leading them, a bright spot of color against their field gray uniforms, was the admiral's daughter, Mora Koskiusko. Either she had patched up her suspicions about Captain Thwaite, or she'd stolen the boat from under his nose.

The three sets of rescuers converged on Taddeuz Bertingas and his bound hostages.

"Tad!" Follard shouted and rushed toward him, arms outstretched. The Kona Tatsu chief stopped three paces away, breathing shallowly. His arms came down slowly. "It's—so—good to *see* you."

Mora came up to him, paused, wrinkled her nose, and backed off two paces.

Firkin beamed at him. "Grub any good in these woods?" she asked.

"Fair, when you can find it," he answered.

"Put up much of a fight?"

"Not if you surprise it."

"Who are these guys?" She bumped one of his hostages with her booted toe. "Dinner?"

"You tell me. Halan, have you ever seen a uniform like that?"

"Not local, is it?" Follard shook his head. "Maybe something private?"

"Could be."

"Do they talk?"

"Haven't tried them yet," Bertingas shrugged.

"We've got things in the bus that'll take care of them . . . Ah, Tad?" He coughed. "Aren't you *cold*?"

Bertingas looked down at himself. Bare feet. Tattered underwear. A belt of woven grasses. Dirt. He stroked his jaw and felt the dried blood and grime crackle in his beard.

"Do you want a blanket?" Firkin asked.

"How about a hot shower?"

"We've got that in the bus, too," Follard said. "Come on."

Chapter 16

Halan Follard: ROUNDUP

As he led the flight of airbuses and the ship's boat down toward the landing pad at Kona Tatsu headquarters in Meyerbeer, Halan Follard ordered the building sealed.

"Say again, Chief?" the duty man at the comm console, one Special Agent Cobb, asked.

"Close the visa office, clear out the waiting rooms, lock the front door, put out the un-Welcome mat, and cancel your afternoon tea. Go to full security. With sidearms. Chop-chop."

"Unh . . . Yes, sir! May one ask why? Sir?"

"One may not. I am bringing in a little lost sheep who's survived half a dozen recent attempts on his life. Also in my custody are three soldiers, fully armed and combat trained, whom he brought down with a piece of string and a stone spear. The fourth one died trying to take out this lamb."

"And you want us mobilized to hold onto this guy, right?" Cobb asked.

"Wrong. I want you mobilized in case the people who are trying to kill him try again. I would find it intensely embarrassing if this Service were to lose possession of a protected person inside its own Cluster HQ."

"Yes, sir!"

"Short of atomic attack . . ." Follard mused over the open circuit. "In which case, you'd better rig the Elsewhere button. Put a remote in my office." He knew it was a purely theoretical precaution, because no one had ever tried, or seriously tested, the Elsewhere system.

During the building's construction, Kona Tatsu architects had buried—between the second and third subbasements—a mass inverter. It was a Fleet-rated device, big enough to jump a naval cruiser through four phases of hyperdimensional space. Of course, no one had ever jumped, intentionally, from the surface of a planet. No one had ever jumped a structure as fragile as a planet-bound building, a gravity-supported framework of stone and steel, woodwork and plastic panels, cableways, piping and waveguides, cornices and carpeting. Neither had anyone ever landed from such a jump, at ground level—not two meters above—in otherwise unoccupied territory, under an atmosphere.

Follard suspected that the *pop* on arrival would be just as loud as the *bang* going away.

On the one hand, Elsewhere was some paranoid planner's brainstorm of the ultimate defense maneuver. On the other, no one had ever thought of a better way to defend a Human-made structure against atomic assault.

"Yes, sir. Activate Elsewhere," the console jockey repeated.

"*Wait* for my order, if and when, to activate. For now, just rig the button. Understood?"

"Yes, sir."

"Follard out."

He put the two buses on the roof and directed

Mora Koskiusko's pilot to land the ship's boat in the square that fronted the building. It wasn't exactly a warship, but the twenty-millimeter plasma pump in its nose would hold off ground forces. Its re-entry shielding of ablative ceramics would take a certain amount of pounding.

A squad of K.T. Storm Troopers met them at the tube shaft. Follard pointed to the three unidentified soldiers being carried out, now thoroughly webbed and drugged.

"Take them to the receiving chambers. Wake them up, gently, and find out who they are. Full details. Down to their mothers' maiden names."

The troopers laid hands on Bertingas, who had dressed in the dark green uniform of the dead officer. It was almost whole, except for a ragged seam on one shoulder, and had been hurriedly washed of its stains, blood and otherwise. It was a bad fit, but better than the ragged thermal bodystocking and stinking animal skin they had found Tad wearing.

"Not him. Counselor Bertingas goes to the infirmary for a complete physical. Pump him full of vitamins, check his head for lice, and put him under the narcolights for an hour of total rest. Then bring him to my office."

The lieutenant leading the troopers nodded, saluted, and whisked their charges away.

"Shall we go down to my office and await developments?" he asked Patty. He also signaled an aide to bring Koskiusko up, once she had her admiral's barge jacked upright and depressurized.

Firkin hesitated, looked back at the collection of beings who attended her.

"Bring your lieutenants, of course," he urged.

She tapped off two Satyrs and a Ghibli, all armed. The latter carried what looked like a portable plasma gun across its back. The rest she instructed to wait with the bus.

Follard took them to a room on the third floor that embarrassed even him. It was twenty by forty meters, with ceilings fifteen meters high, hung with white-frosted plaster drapes and cupids. Two chandeliers, in brass and purple-tinted crystal, took the shape of bunches of Earth grapes. This space had originally been the ballroom, for formal receptions with the Governor and other Central Center dignitaries.

The last Inspector General had cleverly rescheduled those celebrations into nearby public halls, finally abandoning them as formal K.T. functions. Then he had appropriated this room for his office.

During Follard's administration, as the rest of the building filled with secondary staff, sub-directorates, third and fourth bureaux, new data analysis techniques and equipment, a records retention section, and a complete library, it had become impossible for him to move out of this space without setting off a chain reaction of office bumping that might not settle down for two years. So Follard ran the local K.T. station from a lone desk, a worktable, and half a dozen visitors' chairs that huddled in one end of a space that could string three foozleball nets and hold the Cluster Semifinals, complete with Freevid coverage.

Mora Koskiusko entered with two Marines who wore sergeants' chevrons and carried repulsor rifles at port arms. She walked over and took one of the circle of guest chairs, at the center, without being asked. Patty hung back, near the door, uncertain. Follard could guess she was feeling less than social with him.

"Please, sit. All of you."

They filled the circle. The Satyrs' short shins and long metacarpals, like a horse's or a goat's, made their legs work the wrong way for a Human chair. They weren't, however, about to pass up the honor of being treated like real people. They sat precariously on their narrow shanks and tapped the floor lightly with their splayed hooves for balance. Koskiusko's Marines laid their rifles quietly on the parquet floor. The Ghibli just squatted on the left side of the desk and drooled.

On Follard's blotter, carefully placed in the center, was a cordless black box with one red button, covered by a locking bar, the Elsewhere switch. The bar could be unlocked with a seven-notch security key, the only copy of which was in Follard's pocket.

He moved the black box to one side without comment.

"Now, Mistress Koskiusko, tell me . . ."

"Yes, Inspector?"

"How did you manage to convert a platoon of Central Fleet Marines to your cause? Under Captain Thwaite's nose, as it were."

The two sergeants exchanged uneasy glances but held their peace.

"They are not Captain Thwaite's men to command," she replied primly. "They were fresh landed at the port from the destroyer *Thermopylae*. They know me from duty on Gemini and agreed to help."

Follard looked at the men. "This is true? You had business on Palaccio, but not with your liaison office?"

"We were on—ah—shore leave, sir."

"Do you doubt me, Inspector?" Koskiusko demanded icily.

"It's my business to doubt everyone, my dear. I'd prefer my Service were not charged with complicity in the theft of Central Fleet property and kidnapping of Central Fleet personnel. You've met Captain Thwaite, no doubt?"

"I have."

"Then you understand my concern." Follard made his most charming smile.

Mora Koskiusko smiled in return, and the temperature in the room lifted.

"What about those three captured soldiers?" Firkin asked.

"The mindscan should take about an hour. They have no choice but to let us know all they know."

The intercom on his desk buzzed.

"Yes?"

"A Captain Thwaite to see you, sir. He says it's official and urgent."

Follard shot a glance at Koskiusko and her Marines. She glanced back demurely.

"Send him up."

The captain came through the door at double time with his head down, as if walking into a stiff breeze. He rounded on Follard's desk then stopped, surprised at seeing a full house, complete with Ghiblis. He looked from one to another, then his eyes focused on the Marines and Mora Koskiusko.

"So *there* you are! Young lady, I ought to have you spanked. The Admiral has been burning my butt for the last *week* over your disappearance. You sneak down planetside, commandeer the gig from an active-duty vessel, *plus* a squad of assault troops, fly all over hell's half-acre, and then you leave them in a public square. To come hobnob with police agents and aliens. When your father—"

"Captain?" Follard interposed. "You didn't come here just to report a missing ship's boat, did you?"

"Eh? No, not at all. Or not till I came over and saw where she'd parked it. I had an—ah—a report that you've taken prisoner someone I want to see."

Follard took out a pen and fiddled with some notepaper. "Name of prisoner?"

"Bertingas, Taddeuz. Formerly of the Cluster Communications Department. He was the deputy director, I believe."

Halan put down the pen. "No such prisoner here."

"Oh, then, perhaps I'm—"

"Misinformed? That's a possibility. Where did you hear this incredible story? And why do you say 'formerly'?"

"Well, I thought certainly if he had been charged with some crime . . ."

"No charges have been preferred against the counselor."

"Then do you know where he is?"

"Why, he's here, resting. This morning he was rescued after an ordeal on the Uplands, attendant upon an aircar crash. My Service was of some help in the rescue, as were your Marines—operating under the directions of Mistress Koskiusko."

He nodded at Mora.

She nodded back.

Thwaite eyed them both.

"May I ask why you are so eager," Follard continued, "to see the counselor?"

"We have had an interruption in our normal interforce channels. Possibly natural causes. More likely sabotage. Whatever. I wanted to access the Cluster's communications facilities."

"So you came to interview a supposed prisoner about this? Why not deal with the director, Selwin Praise, himself?"

"That's a matter of—um—security."

"You don't trust Praise?"

Thwaite eyed them all: Firkin, the Ghiblis, the Satyrs, his own Marines, Mora.

"Speak freely," Halan urged. "Here if anywhere."

"I don't know whom to trust anymore. The traders, the holders, the puppets from Central Center. At least Bertingas is—well—"

"Too naive to be anything but loyal?" Follard offered.

"You put it nicely."

"Why else do you think we worked so hard to get

him out of the woods? Now, you suggest your own comm channels are down by sabotage. What reason do you have to suspect it?"

"The last message we received—fragmentary—from Base Gemini implied they were going under attack by an unknown force. We've heard nothing for thirty-six hours and, until *Thermopylae* rounded this planet, had no patrol vessel to send on recon. Then somebody made off with the captain's gig." Here he glared again at Mora.

She had gone white from shock.

"And Daddy?" she said. "Don't you have any—?"

"The piece of coded report we picked up indicated an englobement by more warships than, frankly, I thought were spaceborne within three cluster diameters. If that's true, there may no longer be a Base Gemini to reconnoiter."

Halan Follard watched the captain more than the girl's reaction. Thwaite was taking pleasure in scaring her.

"But I have to—" Mora started to say, then faltered.

Into this lapse, Follard's lab attendant knocked twice on the door and admitted herself.

"Inspector? We have results from the prisoners. If you'd care to take them."

"Display them here," he said, gesturing to the large screen hung against the back wall, between two preoccupied cupids. "The condensed form, please. Just the results."

The technician nodded and turned to leave, bumping into Tad Bertingas, who was coming through the door.

Aside from a few scratches and broken fingernails, the counselor was looking as sunny and urbane as always. Instead of his usually immaculate clothing he wore a field uniform, sans rank or insignia, borrowed from Follard. It fit well enough, except for three tuck-rolls at each cuff.

"H'lo everybody." He smiled and waved to them all.

"Tad!" Mora had found her voice. She jumped up, ran over, and put her arms about his neck. It took Follard a second to decide that this wasn't an over-enthusiastic greeting, but a huddling for protection.

"I'm glad to see you, too," Bertingas said.

"It's not that, Tad. Gemini's been attacked. Maybe wiped out."

"My goodness!"

"By many ships. A *lot* of ships. A whole fleet of them. A fleet such as we—"

"Oh, no!" Bertingas said. "Omigod. Are you thinking it's . . . What Choora Maas told us . . . about . . ."

"Hai-ken-maru." The voice was mammoth, slow, slurred, frozen. The screen lit up with a face, one of the captured soldiers. He had slack, liver-colored lips and vacant blue eyes, swimming with tears. As they all watched, a hand come into focus with a gauze pad and blotted the eyes.

"What was your assign-ment?" asked a muffled voice, offscreen. It spoke with a singsong, metro-nome beat designed to insinuate itself into the mindscan pulses.

"S'cur-i-ty."

"Where was your assign-ment?"

"Aitch. Cue."

"Aitch-cue? Where is H-Q?"

"Hai-ken Maru's is-land."

"Why were you up-country?"

"To dis-rupt their comm lines."

"Yet you failed to do that."

"We went to find the trai-tor."

"Went to *kill* the trai-tor?"

"Find him, too val-val-u—"

"Who then is this trai-tor?"

"Braid-cuff cub."

"Why is he a trai-tor?"

"He knows the se-cret."

"What is the se-cret?"

"No one tells the se-cret."

"What is the se-cret?"

The lab tech broke in. "There's more of this, Inspector, but it goes in circles. You've heard the best of the most lively one. These boys are, on the whole, unaware. About twenty percent, I'd say."

"Thank you," Follard said. "Close them down."

He turned to Bertingas, who stood with Mora, staring at the screen.

"You might have tried harder to save that officer," Follard told him. "We would have had the best chance of getting something useful from him."

"Sorry. He also had the best chance of taking me out."

"So what's the secret, Tad?"

"That the Haiken Maru are using their island fortress, Batavia, to arm merchant vessels. Getting themselves a big fleet, fast, for a good price. Makes them a military power, equal in size, if not in skills or battleworthiness, to anything the Central Fleet or Cluster Commands can float. Choora Maas told us all of this, about ten days ago, but I didn't know exactly who to warn. It looks like I waited too long . . . I'm sorry, Mora."

"Who is Choora Maas?" Follard asked.

"One of my alien contacts, a Cernian, recommended as a source of recruits for this security force we're building to protect the Cluster's communications system."

"Recommended by whom?"

"Selwin Praise."

"Then perhaps you had reason to hesitate?"

"Perhaps. Still, if I'd told you, or Thwaite here—"

"How do you know *he's* loyal?" Mora interrupted, and Follard let her.

"Well, I don't. But . . ."

Koskiusko turned to Thwaite and bored in on him.

"What have you done, Captain, in particular, just lately, to keep Aurora Cluster loyal to the Pact? And what are you prepared to do?"

"Why, with what forces I have," he stammered, "which are one medium-size destroyer of uncertain battle readiness, back from extended patrol, two more that are currently out of contact, a ship's gig, and a brace of Marines who are given to deserting their duty roster—why, I'm not sure just *what* I can do."

Bertingas was watching the captain closely. "Of course you know, Terrel. There's something we *all* can do—"

"Inspector!" the comm box on Follard's desk interrupted. "One of the prisoners just expired. The other two are dying fast, and—"

"Not now with that!"

"Yes now! The dead one is transmitting, somehow, on about four frequencies we can read and maybe a lot more we . . . Perimeter watch informs me they're tracking a low-flying aircar, without transponder, that will not answer our challenge. What shall I—?"

Before she could finish, Follard had made a swooping dive for the surface of his desk. One hand retrieved the anonymous black box, the other fished in his trousers pocket for the key to the locking bar. As he came up with it, they all could hear, through the room's tall windows, the falling whine of a pair of ducted airfans. Halan Follard flipped back the bar and jabbed down on the red button.

A hollow *whump* filled his ears—louder than he'd supposed it would be, heard from inside a collapse field.

Chapter 17

Taddeuz Bertingas: DESPERATE PLOY

Anyone who had ever traveled off planet knew the feeling immediately: the null moment. When a body's physical dimensions passed a certain lower limit during an inversion collapse, electrochemical responses in the central nervous system ceased. For the duration of an interstellar jump—which *had* been measured, once, but the findings were contested—the body was clinically dead, as it was at the instant of a sneeze.

Bertingas knew the feeling, although only in the context of a web couch on shipboard. He had never jumped standing up, and never inside a building. The result was he fell on his ass. And got the breath knocked out of him when Mora Koskiusko landed on his stomach.

Kona Tatsu headquarters shook and swayed around them as the floor and walls found new equilibrium. A sifting of plaster dust from the ceiling drifted into Bertingas's face. In one corner of Halan Follard's office, a chiseled garland and the angel that held it crashed to the floor. The wallscreen, where the Haiken

Maru soldier had appeared during mindscan, split and released a crackle of pent-up energy.

The Ghibli, clearly distressed, roared and snapped over its shoulder at the sound.

"What was *that*?" Bertingas asked. "An earthquake?"

Patty Firkin sat up on the floor where she, too, had fallen. "We jumped, by God, we *jumped!*" she said.

"Where to?"

"Not far," Follard replied, from behind the desk. "About fifteen kilometers up the valley. That's all."

"And why?" Bertingas said.

He rolled Mora off him but kept an arm around her, for support and protection.

"I'm afraid that's a classified—" Follard began.

"Crippled Kali!" Bertingas shouted at his friend. "We've left a hole about ninety meters wide in the middle of downtown Meyerbeer. Even Regis Sallee could figure out *how* it was done. So spare me the long form and explain the *why*, okay?"

"That last report, from our perimeter watch, indicated an unidentified aircar closing on the building. Our threat analysts predict that's the most likely way to insert an atomic device through this building's defenses."

"Did it go off?"

"No, I got to the switch that activates a mass inverter inside—"

The double doors to the room slammed open and three aides, armed with repulsors, crowded the opening.

"Is everyone all right in here, sir?" the lead one asked Follard.

"No injuries, small damage. Deal with it later."

"Very good, sir."

"Did it go off?" Bertingas repeated, this time to the Kona Tatsu attendants.

They just stared at him.

"The bomb in Meyerbeer. The one aimed at us. Let's find out if there's still a city back there—and a Cluster Government."

The three heads swung toward Follard.

"Do it—discreetly. Launch our prepared cover story for the disappearance of this building."

The trio nodded and withdrew.

"You have a *cover* story?" Bertingas asked, skeptical. "I wonder if I'd believe it. Something about a rogue space warp, no doubt. By the way, *were* you expecting company?"

"On your behalf," Follard said. "It's the pattern. Wherever you go, Tad, assassins seem to follow."

"I know—'the traitor.' But traitor to what? I have—Mora and I had—the secret of Haiken Maru's bogus battle fleet. That doesn't make me a traitor—not to the Haiken Maru. And not to the Pact, either." He shot a look at Terrel Thwaite.

"Just before we jumped," Follard said, "you were making a point about taking action. 'Something we all can do.' What is that?"

"Well . . ." Tad searched his memory. "If there's one common thread in this whole affair, it's the Haiken Maru. Elidor, their Trader General, tried to suborn me. Remember that day I crashed in the lake at the Palace? He was trying to kill me when I refused to cooperate—I'm sure of that. Then, too, the Haiken Maru have a heavy investment in Arachne Cluster. Their presence is as deeply rooted there as it is here in Aurora."

"So, you're saying they're in league with Spile?" Mora asked eagerly.

Tad paused, then shook his head. "Not unless it's a diversion. Spile has ambitions, certainly, but he's too unstable to take—and hold—the High Seat. Elidor is pushing for his own Chairman, Villem Borking, to be voted the Secretariat."

"Or given it in default after Spile starts a civil war," Follard said.

"And ends it how?" Bertingas asked.

"He's started well enough," Thwaite observed, "with a classic surprise tactic and support from a fleet of tricked-out merchant vessels. In the long run, however, Spile can't win an open battle against the combined forces of the Cluster Commands and Central Fleet. Eventually, he'll lose."

"After getting how far?" Bertingas asked. "Look at how much damage he's done in the englobement on Gemini. He'll go as far as the Haiken Maru want him to."

"Unless?" Follard prompted.

"Unless we intervene. Now. Choke off this third military force at its source."

"I can't go on the offensive against Arachne!" Thwaite cried. "That would start the civil war Elidor wants."

"Not against Arachne. The real traitors here are Elidor and the Haiken Maru. I say bring the hammer down on Batavia. Stop their yards from converting any more ships."

Thwaite squinted at him.

"That's a bit ambitious, isn't it? We'd need more firepower than I can command at this moment."

"We can call on Dindyma and his forces in Cluster Command," Bertingas pointed out. "They have ships."

"Some. Not very good . . ."

Firkin was nodding thoughtfully.

"We need a coordinated plan of attack," she said, "details on the island's defenses, and a better feeling for the logistics. Haiken Maru have done well to place their headquarters half a world away, with the only close dropfields under their complete control."

"So take them out from orbit!"

"Same problem, then—no ships."

Follard pursed his lips.

"Your plan, Tad, is technically an offense against private property. The Pact has very strict regulations about freedom of individuals and corporations to conduct their business. We'd need airtight proof against them of treason. Governor Sallee won't approve any move by Cluster Command otherwise."

"How about supplying arms without an export license?"

"I'm sure the H.M.'s licenses have been carefully worded to cover every conceivable charge we might lodge."

"What *I'm* hearing," Mora said haughtily, "is a distinct lack of backbone. If you want to stop these creeps, then do it. If you win, the Governor can put whatever face on it she wants. If you lose, then Borking's in the High Seat and we're all traitors anyway."

Thwaite looked at his shoes. "She has a point."

"Halan?" Bertingas turned to his friend. "The Kona Tatsu maintains a separate judiciary. You're technically both a judge and grand jury, if I remember one of our drunken conversations correctly."

"Technically . . ."

"Could you prepare some warrants, restraining orders, sigils of arrest, or whatever the proper documentation is? Something for the 'proprietors of the privately held property known as Batavia' to 'show cause why they should not cease and desist the manufacture and sale of armed vessels,' etc., etc."

"I could, I suppose. But how would you serve them?"

"With an army," Tad smiled.

"Which one?"

Bertingas pointed at the aliens who had accompanied Firkin.

"Nay, sir," shied one of the Satyrs.

"Not us, sir," said the other shaggy-legged recruit.

The Ghibli just growled and leered at him.

"You're signed for a proper hitch," he told them. "To follow orders and see action at the discretion of your commanding officer . . . Me."

"We're really not very good, sir."

"You seem to be learning surprisingly fast. At least to my eye."

"Appearances are deceiving."

"Patty? Can they move in battle formation? Will they stand in a pitched conflict? Can they *fight?*"

The heavyset woman looked at the three aliens with narrowed eyes. For a moment, as she weighed details in her mind, the colonel that she had been in another life shone through.

"Some will. Most will."

"Then, Halan, we'll serve your warrants—or knock out that island trying."

"And Deirdre Sallee will see right through this sham. She'll roll me, you, the Kona Tatsu, and your whole department up in a tight little ball and hand us all over to an outraged Valence Elidor. To dispose of as he chooses."

"No, she won't," Tad said with a grim smile. "She won't have the option."

"How do you know?"

"Leave that to me."

The gray service truck, salvaged from the garage of the displaced Kona Tatsu building, touched down on the lip of the airpad on Floor 123. Normally, the valets who ran the pad would wave a vehicle like that on. This truck, however, with its simple double flashes on the lower skirting, was the sort that most people believed ferried prisoners to and from the Down Camps. The valets tried to ignore it.

Passing over the city center, Tad had briefly inspected the hole where the Follard's headquarters had been. It was a neat hemisphere cut into the rich, dark earth. The sun was still baking out the mois-

ture, turning the soil into crumbly brown clods—
except where a broken pipe was pumping in water.
The hole's bottom showed a crosshatch, the sheered
ends of support pilings that, in this river valley, had
to be driven to bedrock—such as it was on a light-
matter planet like Palaccio. Tad had caught a glimpse
of other fractured connections: sewer, power, and
communications lightguides.

They wouldn't be able to jump the building back
to its original site. Not at all. Probably have to aban-
don that pile of stonework and plaster that lay up the
valley and rebuild it down here.

What a lot of trouble Follard had gone through to
protect him! Bertingas was starting to feel grateful—
which was a bad feeling for a conspirator to have.

From the air, Tad had used the truck's anonymous
AID to signal Gina. Now she came out to the pad,
stood and looked at the truck uncertainly, then got
in.

He lifted off and went into a parking orbit south of
the Palace. She would not turn toward him for a long
time.

"We all thought you were dead. Or a prisoner."

"I know. It seemed safest. How is Director Praise
taking my disappearance?"

"He smiles a lot. Of course, he always smiles a lot.
He says you were a good man, but that you can be
replaced."

"*Has* he replaced me yet?"

"There's talk . . ."

"Who?"

"Me—but it's just talk. Coffeebreak badinage. You
know."

"Sure." Tad let it hang there, then went on. "Should
I come back?"

"You mean just—? Well, I wouldn't fight you. I'd
work with you. I'm not sure I'm ready for rank."

"I appreciate that, Gina. Really . . . How would Praise react if I came back?"

"Disappointed, I think."

"Still, I'm his only link to those recruits he wanted so badly, am I not?"

"He seems to have lost interest in all that."

"Ahh. Busywork for the bad boy in the department. A classic political gambit."

Gina nodded, then looked at him.

"You seem leaner. More alive. More sure of yourself."

"It's getting shot at—without result. As Sir Winston Churchill once said . . . We're still getting funding for those training bases, aren't we?"

"Yes, the Director seems to have overlooked discontinuing that."

"Careless with Department money. That's not like him. Can you guard my rear and keep those budgets open? No matter what he does?"

"I guess I can. Unless Praise gives me a specific order to close them. Or until he finds out and challenges me on them. Why? Do you need the money?"

"No, I need the bases, the troops, and their equipment kept intact for a while. No matter what Praise wants."

"Are you in some kind of trouble?"

"Since the very beginning, Gina. We all are. If I'm reading our hints and guesses right, those alien—excuse me, non-Human—troops could be all that stands between the Pact and all-out civil war."

"I'll do whatever I can."

"Good, there's something more I need." He reached inside the tunic of the borrowed uniform and pulled out a sheaf of handwritten notes. "You remember the discussion we had—it seems so long ago—about the Haiken Maru?"

"Do you think I would ever forget?"

"No, of course not. I need it done, now, what we talked about then. These notes explain the subtext;

follow and fill in as you have to. You'll know how to handle it. The names are in a kind of substitution code, in case anyone takes these papers off you. Hint to get you started: read this as if it came from the Palace. Then all should come clear."

"From the Palace. That's dangerous, Tad."

"Of course it is. I told you, we're all that stands between the Pact and chaos. Be careful."

"You must trust me very much. After everything."

"Of course I trust you," he said.

I have no other choice, he thought.

Bertingas brought the truck around and down in the street near a rail line that would take her back to Government Block.

"Be careful," he told her, "but don't be too nervous. We always agreed that you could get away with this where I, being more visible—and now a hunted man—never could. Right?"

She nodded, all serious.

"If anyone asks," he went on, "you haven't seen me, don't know about me, wish I was truly dead, and want my job. Right?"

Gina tried to smile and couldn't. One last time she put an arm around his neck, drew him close, and kissed him. Tad could taste the strange sweetness of her lips, like brass and silver mixed in a crucible and cooled. He kissed her back.

She finally let him go.

"Be careful yourself," she said and slid out the door.

Tad fed power to the fans, leaving her in a downdraft that swirled her skirt and streaked her hair. Gina waved once, then turned and walked off.

Patty Firkin poked twice at the tarpaulin covering herself and rolled out from under the side bench in the back of the truck.

"You are *smooth*, Bertingas," she said, sliding into the seat Gina had just left.

"Yeah, too smooth."

"Do you think she'll do it for us?"

"Sure. For me. She'll get caught in the shakeup after she does it. She'll be pulled apart by people not quite as gentle as Follard's. And she knows all that. But, yes, she'll do it."

"That's all we want, Tad."

"For the God-damned Pact."

"Right, for the God-damned Pact," Firkin replied. She was rubbing her upper arm, where Bertingas had once seen a thin red scarline.

Chapter 18

Pairs in Private: CONFUSION

The offices of Cluster Command were impressive.

As Terrel Thwaite was locked through the main public entrance, led down corridors of chrome and granite, voice-IDed, retina-IDed, thumb-printed, pinky-printed, blood-sampled, and body-scanned, he let his cool mind count the ways by which Dindyma's people were trying to impress him.

First there was the physical separation. No suite or set of floors in the bland monolith of Government Block was distinctive enough for them. No adjunct to the Palace, itself an architectural confection in glass and steel, was private enough for them. No ornate private building like the Kona Tatsu's, with its stone and rococo plasterwork—now happily removed from the city—was elegant enough for Cluster Command.

No, they had to stake out a hundred hectares of rolling hills north of the city, fence it with wire and scan-guides, and begin building their own collection of structures.

Second, the buildings themselves. The pattern, Thwaite had once been told, was a Cistercian abbey of the early second millennium, B.P., from somewhere in the Earthly nation-state called France. Every dimension from the original plan had been multiplied by a factor of 2.471—but why that particular number, no one seemed to know. In the original model, the dark stone had been cut into blocks and stacked. At these new, larger dimensions, the architects had to create an underframe in steel and concrete, then face it with polished granite, outside and in. Where the supply of stone, or the mason's art, had given out, the carvings, cornices, gargoyles, and finals were reproduced in chrome. The effect was austere, brutal, callous, dark—everything a collection of play-acting soldiers would want others to think of them.

Third was the rigmarole. Thwaite had presented his electronic credentials at the door. Taking samples of his bone marrow—painful as the procedure might be—could prove nothing more about him.

After walking half a mile, under heavy escort, mostly under cover from the sun and air, Thwaite was led into the presence of General Dindyma. And wasn't *his* office grand? Grander than the converted ballroom where Halan Follard held court. Almost as grand as the pavilions from which Deirdre Sallee directed the Cluster's political affairs.

The commander's office was the main chapel—or maybe the term was *cathedral?*—of the old abbey. Columns of banded stone and metalwork soared above the inlaid floor and met overhead in a branching parody of low-gravity trees. The screenwork at the far end, however, was original. Carved, blond wood depicted some kind of ritual torture of a nearly naked prisoner. It was impressive—and dusty.

Before the screen lay a block of chiseled black stone, whose upper surface was supported by the figures of thirteen robed and bearded old men. Pollonius Dindyma used it for a desk. The insides of the block, Thwaite knew, had been hollowed out and held sophisticated equipment: a Battle Tech AID, star recorders, tactical holograms, a strategy tank— all to keep track of four destroyers and a monitor that would never leave this system except under tow.

Now, now, Thwaite chided himself. Make nice with the old man. Best behavior.

"Ah, Terrel!" Dindyma half-rose from his chair to meet his guest.

"General! So good of you to see me on such regrettably short notice."

"My pleasure." The older man tipped his head politely. "Always ready to do a courtesy to our brothers in arms."

"Yes. Well. More than a courtesy, this time."

"Eh? You have a request of some sort to make?"

"Oh, no. I've come to thank you for your swift responses."

"In the matter of . . . ?"

"Ah! This room is secure, is it not? Even one's closest aides and attendants must represent some risk of espionage, at times. All these columns and dead spaces—" Thwaite waved a hand around the great room "—must make a sweep . . ."

"We sweep daily, sir." The General puffed up his chest and sniffed broadly. "Have no fear of your confidences. Out with them, man!"

"Certainly. I'm referring to your preparations for aiding Central Fleet in its defensive actions against our mutual objective."

"Of course, no trouble at—'mutual objective,' you say? What might that be?"

Thwaite dropped his head and looked at the General from under his own quite impressive eyebrows. "You did receive the secret orders from Her Excellency did you not?"

"Hah-hmmm—er—of course. I can assure you we

have the most cordial—*secret* orders? Yes, but—humm—no. No secret orders."

"Ah!" Thwaite contrived to appear embarrassed. He covered his eyes with a hand. Revealed them to smile again. "I must commend you on your discretion, General, your dedication to the canons of secrecy. You shame me with your sense of propriety."

"You're too kind, Terrel. I'm sure it's all a dreadful mix-up. Something to do with that new chief of staff at the Palace. Tell me, if I *were* to have received such orders, would I then be in a position to know 'our mutual objective'?"

"Of course, sir. You would be positively brimming with enthusiasm for it."

"Would I? I would!" The General all but clapped his hands in excitement. "Now, supposing that we have suffered a mere clerical disqualification . . . could you divulge to me the nature of that objective?"

"Certainly. It's military."

"Ah! Military. Right in our line. Hardened?"

"Some would say."

"Susceptible to reduction by tactical forces?"

"Eminently."

"Does the objective have a name?"

"It does."

"Might one hear it?"

"Haiken Maru."

"Haiken—! Surely not! Their financial and mercantile transactions are the strength of the Cluster."

"As their base perfidies will be the undoing of this cluster," Thwaite rejoined.

"I'm sure the Governor would have indicated . . ."

"The Governor is, in these delicate times, under a certain amount of restraint."

"Of course, of course. Haiken Maru, you say? Well, I never would have suspected. You have proofs, certainly?"

"Ten ships destroyed or damaged in a mass attack.

All signs point to the H.M. as responsible. We have even taken prisoners."

"Incontrovertible."

"No—talkative as well."

"Ah-hmmm. Yes . . . Our preparations, Captain, such as they are, must of necessity be meager. We have four superannuated destroyers, and one planetary monitor whose capabilities are less than ideal—"

"Each branch of the military serves as best it can in this crisis, General. Even if that service is limited to an honorable surrender in the face of overwhelming force."

"Hmm? Ah—well put, Captain. Without hyperdrive, however, our *Charlotten Broch* would be a sitting target in any orbit. Less effective even than your Gemini Base—with the usual apologies, of course."

Thwaite nodded his head grimly at the old jibe.

"So you can see . . ." The General flapped his hands.

"The objective, this time, is no more mobile than your *Broch*, sir."

"Ah? A sort of counterpart Maginot, your hardened objective?"

"As it were."

"Under control of the Haiken Maru?"

"Exactly."

"There is only one facility in the Cluster which meets that description. Certainly the Governor is not suggesting . . ."

"Not openly. Not yet."

"Will she give her authority, at the appropriate time?" The General chewed at his mustache with his lower teeth.

"I am assured of it."

"Then I will look into the preparation of a suitable plan. For our mutual defense."

"Excellent, General."

Thwaite knew enough not to press the advantage. He stood quickly and bowed himself down the length of the chapel's nave, toward the narthrex.

"One second, Captain!" Dindyma called. "What if we *should* be met with overwhelming force? Surrender, even on honorable terms, is not an option defined in the regulations of Cluster Command!"

"Why then, General," Thwaite replied, with his butt not three meters from the door and safety, "we shall all have the privilege of paying for our commissions a second time! Good day to you, sir!"

"Try it again."

Patty Firkin slipped her hands into the player's gloves attached to the Battle Tech and began rallying her ground forces. In the deep holo focus, under control of a competitive AID, were the shadowy walls and turrets of the fortress. It may once have had a natural shape, the shoreline of the island—revealed as Palaccio's inland sea receded into mud and marsh—but now it was all hard lines and defensive angles. Star-shaped bastions and tall bartizans, scarps and counterscarps, machicolations and merlons toothed the water's edge. Batavia was all towers of iron and ramparts of reinforced concrete.

Or, that was the Batavia which their Battle Tech knew, and it was drawing on century-old plans retrieved from the Kona Tatsu archives.

Patty went for a pincers approach, splitting her brigades to bring one over the land bridge—which would surely be mined—the other on a low air attack. Feint, foil, and fight.

The plasma projectors on the two flanks of the bridge cross-fired and wiped out a third of her attackers. The loss was just yellow and blue markers in the machine. But it would be flesh and blood—or whatever ichor the Cernians, Satyrs, and Ghiblis of her new army used for blood—when the real action came.

"I didn't know you could do that!" she protested, pointing at the crossed lines of fused nuclei in the tank. "The magnetic charges ought to cancel each other."

Halan Follard shrugged. "The Battle Tech should know. Control of the plasma stream within the projector is magnetic, certainly. Once it's past the orifice, however, the stream is inertial. It'll go where you point it."

"This is a waste of time," Sax observed. The Surian shifted her coils.

"How so?" Follard asked.

"It's almost certain they have a black-layer refraction screen over that installation by now. Even if your archives don't note it."

"Cost a lot of money to raise one of those on a whole island," Patty said. "Look at the screaming that went on when they did the Palace."

"What is the Haiken Maru except money?"

"There's an energy penalty, too," Firkin said. "A lot of their power reserves would go into maintaining the field, and they have no nearby grid to tap."

"Money is energy in other form," the Surian whispered. "Their published accounts over the past ten years show unexplained gaps. That money went somewhere. Perhaps into building and powering a dome."

Patty had no natural fear of snakes. At least she didn't *think* she had. Yet even the most . . . animal . . . of the many aliens who associated themselves with the Pact worlds usually had some endearingly . . . Human . . . quality. It helped to focus on that quality, and remind yourself that sentience relates to mind, not to form. The Surians seemed to have no such qualities.

Sax was, in form and manner, presence and mind,

a cold-blooded reptile. She was a twelve-meter-long anaconda whose scales scraped and rattled on the floor tiles as she shifted her coils. Patty could not believe that flat, narrow head—which was mostly gaping mouth, jaw hinges, and eyepits—harbored a brainpan large enough for intelligence. Yet the wisdom and memory of the Surians was legendary. The characteristic that griped Firkin most was the "autonomic weave"—that hypnotic, side-to-side waddle the Surians did with their heads as they focused first one eye, then the other, on any object of interest.

It made Patty seasick.

"We can add a dome to the simulation," Follard agreed. "But how big do we make it? And where do we put it? Outside the old mechanical defenses? Inside, covering the core administration areas and the landing fields? Somewhere in between?"

Sax seemed to consult her gods. The nictitating membrane closed slowly over the near eye, then flicked back.

"Then place it beyond the outer walls," she said.

"Gee, thanks," Firkin murmured under her breath.

"Don't mention it," the snake replied coldly.

Adding an energy dome to the simulation made any attack with the ground forces Patty had almost impossible. Recruits toting repulsors and portable plasmics over unfamiliar ground, backed by limited air support, were barely competent against fixed emplacements in the hands of a 110-point Binet-rated AID. Giving that AID control of a blackout screen that could also block any metallic intrusion fixed the odds against her.

"Increase the spectrum response," Sax told the AID. "Take it up into the ultraviolet and down into the infrared. There is no point in limiting ourselves to mere Human senses."

"No, none at all," Patty said sarcastically. There went her IR snoops and her field data wipers.

As she began again with the gloves, Halan asked the Surian: "Have you collated the reports on the Haiken Maru's weapons production at the island?"

"We have rumors only," Sax corrected him.

"Well, then, the rumors?"

"They have made up their losses since the Battle of Gemini."

"That's bad."

"Yes, it is."

Firkin's puppet brigades fell left and right to a sonic resonator. She removed her hands from the controls.

Before she could speak, two Cernians came into the room unannounced.

"We have it, the purloined intelligence."

"From the dis-indentured recruits?" Sax asked.

"Yes, one of the automechs brought her right hand over with her." The Cernian waved an articulated glove, like those that controlled the battle simulation.

"Plug it into the AID."

The alien did so, and the holo image deep in the tank reformulated. As it rebuilt, Firkin noted subtle differences: new angles to some of the battlements, realignment of pieces in the weapon systems, and a new perimeter to the refraction screen. It cut across some of the outflung redoubts in the wall but kept most of the island within its circumference. So the dome was a real part of the defenses, not just hypothetical.

Firkin sighed.

"What are the specs on that dome?" Sax asked.

The Cernian consulted with the AID. "It extends farther down into the infrared and up into the ultraviolet than this system has ever encountered."

"Can we hit them with microwaves?" Follard asked.

After a pause: "No. There's a patch across the likely wavelengths."

"I don't suppose we could hit them with short-wave radio?" Patty suggested. "Send in six or seven hours of old speeches from the Secretariat? Bore them to death?"

"Very funny," Follard said. "All right, let's try it again."

Regis Sallee shifted uncomfortably from one foot to the other. Deirdre rarely invited him to pass time with her anymore, not in any setting, and never in her boudoir. The evening boded ill.

"It's the most amazing communication I've received since we arrived," she was saying. "From that pompous old fraud—doubly so."

"What fraud is that, m'dear?"

"Pollonius Dindyma."

"Dindy—?"

"You remember. He runs the local military establishment. Cluster, not Central. Technically, I suppose, he's *our* general, while the others are merely their own."

"I see," Regis nodded vaguely—to conceal that he already knew the contents of the General's letter. Damn him! Dindyma would sink them all with his foolish garbles and speculations. "What did he have to say, m'dear?"

"That 'per your instruction'—which is *mine,* presumably—he's preparing for defense against a threatened uprising. He makes reference to the late attack upon the Central Fleet's base. That attack seems to have rattled the old fellow pretty badly, although I take it that in normal circumstances there's no love lost between the two branches of the service."

"I should say not."

"The curious thing is his choice of words—an 'uprising.'" She picked up a brush and began working through her hair. "I thought we had definitely established that the Gemini affair was a clash with that madman Spile. Strictly between him and Central Center. Not our affair at all."

"Dindyma may be feeling useless. An old war-horse, you know. Has to stamp and gnash the bit when he hears trumpets far afield."

"Hmmm. Do you think so?"

"I stake my life on it. He's become senile. Perhaps you should consider replacing him."

"That's odd, Regis, because he certainly was not merely 'gnashing the bit.' He's got a particular enemy in mind. Not Spile, and not some generalized saboteurs nor rebel forces nor terrorist malcontents. He believes our enemy is the Haiken Maru! And here is where the syntax becomes strange, because he does not merely insist they *are* our enemies, but that *I* believe them to be our enemies and want him to prepare defenses against them."

"What did I tell you, m'dear? Senile. Wires all crossed up."

"Perhaps. That thought did occur to me, at first. On reflection, I believe Dindyma may have pinpointed just that facet in the local political medley that will focus disloyalty to the Pact. Underneath their placid, apolitical, trade-and-trinkets exterior, the H.M. are ambitious and aggressive. Elidor is not an Aurora man, and clearly not Center. He's loyal in ways and to causes I can't fathom. If Dindyma has seen through him, that's brilliant deduction, especially for the military mind."

Damn, damn, damn the man!

"Do you think so, Deirdre? Seems muddled to me. I know you argue with Elidor in council . . ."

"I never argue." The hairbrush stopped in midstroke.

"Well then, fail to reach agreement."

"Always." She started brushing again.

"That doesn't mean he harbors treachery."

"Valence Elidor *breathes* treason."

"Well, perhaps. Certainly that doesn't mean he would engage in military adventures. Bad for trade. Bad for trinkets."

"Unless he can win."

"Win *what*, my dear? And how? He could buy guns, arm the peasants, and even lead them in stumbling circles for a month or two, I suppose. Yet, when it was all over, even if he had bloodied us badly, he would still be just a merchant. The Cluster Governor would still be appointed by Central Center. And the Fleet would crush him to powder. End of story."

"Is it so simple, Regis?"

"Of course, m'dear. He knows enough to leave politics to the people who understand them. We can leave trade to the people who don't know anything better."

Deirdre gave him an uneasy look in the mirror, then turned her attention to her hair again.

"I'll try to keep that in mind."

"Al-*loy* . . . al . . . loy . . . Loy-al . . ."

Click-click.

"Reality . . .uh-*ty* . . . Loyal-ty . . ."

Click-click.

"Impact . . .uh-*pact* . . .thuh Pact."

Gina Rinaldi stared into the two-to-one editing tank with absolute attention. She was watching Deirdre Sallee's face and lips—or a holographic image of them—as the Governor spoke these word fragments.

"Haiken Maru . . . Mar*u* . . ."

With one hand on a trackball and the other on a pitch bender, she darkened the pixels across Sallee's eyes and simultaneously raised the frequency on that final syllable by a half-tone. The AID controlling the editing suite's functions absorbed these commands and redubbed them into the master imaging file. The result was an apparent squint and a note of stress, passing for distress, as the Governor said the name of the trading combine.

Experts would be able to detect Gina's fakery—if they were ever called upon to testify. By which time it would be too late, probably. The mass audience would see and would believe.

She lifted a hand from the ball and rubbed between her eyes. Working clandestinely, in the dead of night like this, was straining her. She could feel the cells of her body burning at an advanced rate. Part of it was concentrating on the tank and the words, and at the same time trying to listen outside— for the Block's janitors, for any late-staying Department staff, for the new Director's spies. If she were discovered, and her work correctly interpreted, it would mean more than the failure of this project.

They would probably make her disappear.

She shrugged the tension out of her shoulders, bent her head over Tad's handwritten notes to work out the next phrases in the speech.

"Vile treason beyond any . . ."

Now, "vile" she could reshape from "while." Although the lip movements would take some digital surgery, the sounds were easy. But where, in the combined catalog, could she find "treason"? Start with "reason" and add a dental to it? That would work.

Gina set the AID to hunting up her candidate phonemes while she went to work on the Governor's lower lips. This was going to take a *long* time.

"I don't *want* to go."

"I know, I know."

Tad held her close, wrapping her in the darkness.

"But I can *help* you," she said.

"You can get killed—"

"Alongside you!"

"Hush now. Yes, alongside me. Always."

"You'll be in the same danger."

"That's different somehow. It's a danger I've created."

"I helped. It's my war, too. Right from the start. And you've got no way of knowing, Counselor, whether those first shots—back in your apartment—were fired at you or me."

"Your father wants you back in Gemini. He needs you."

"He needs to know his little girl is safe. I'm not his 'little girl' anymore—"

"I know *that*." Soft laughter in the darkness.

"—and nowhere is safe."

"All right. You tell him what you want."

"I know how to handle admirals."

"And bureaucrats."

His arms went tight again.

The aircar lifted into the night from one of Meyerbeer's smaller parks. For so big a machine, its ducted fans were almost silent, coming and going. Selwin Praise settled into the plush leather, smoothing it idly with his hand. No sign of water damage. It must have been replaced, like most of the coachwork, after Bertingas had smashed this car through the trees and into the lake at the Palace.

"Aren't you going to offer me a drink?" He gestured at the open bar, the half-empty glass near Elidor's hand.

"Take what you want."

"And be damned to me?"

"I might be tempted to put something in your glass besides alcohol. Rid us all—"

"Oh, really? You wanted a meeting to poison me? I should have guessed when you suggested an evening ride. This vehicle has seen a lot of service recently."

"Don't be smart-mouth with me."

"Don't you be threatening with *me*, Elidor."

"What possessed you to put Bertingas up to recruiting an *alien* army?"

"You know about that, do you?"

"We've had him followed, of course."

"He's a puppy," Praise said. "Totally naive."

"He's a *dangerous* man. Resourceful. Intelligent. Physically brave. And now suspicious of us."

"If he's suspicious, you have to take some credit for making him so. Your people haven't just been following him; they've been trying to take him out. Clumsily. Several times. Not that I would disapprove of your success along those lines—if you had any. However, I deplore the pattern you've been spinning for him. Now, you can save us all a lot of time and trouble if you'd tell me where he is."

"You don't know?"

Praise closed his eyes and counted ten. He only got to three. "No, Valence, you've finally run him to earth."

"We've lost him."

"Worse and worse."

"Not necessarily. You are in control of this army he's created, aren't you? Disband it. Cut off its funding. Close the bases."

"That will take time. My control is at the level of the paperwork, the authorizations—not at the day-to-day, operating level."

"Damn!"

"I still don't see why you think this is such a problem," Praise said. "We're talking about a bunch of scaly wigglers and green-skinned morons. They're not even citizens. And they're led by a bureaucratic pencil pusher whose only tactical training is what he may have read in a book. They'll shoot at each other and sow confusion among the Cluster's forces."

Elidor just looked at him from under heavy brows.

"Well, I think it's a stroke of genius," Praise went on, "to create a diversionary force within the framework of government and to finance it with cash that costs us nothing . . . Because that government will soon be in a position to honor nothing, including its own checks."

The Trader General's stare never broke.

"They're barely mechanized," Praise insisted. "They will never stand up against experienced Human troops."

More stony silence.

"They're a *police* force, for Cybele's sake!"

"That 'bureaucratic pencil pusher,' " Valence began slowly, "overcame a squad of armed men using nothing more than a stick and a string. He's got help from a renegade Marine officer. And we have reason to believe he has the backing of the Kona Tatsu . . . Now, tell me, Citizen—how well do you know this Taddeuz Bertingas? Well enough to entrust him with a few thousand 'scaly wigglers' under arms? I think not."

"I still say he's—ah—politically naive. He doesn't know where to lead those troops."

"If he has the sense to lead them against us, we will be in a very deep hole."

"He could hardly justify, or persuade, an attack against his own department head."

"I do not include you among 'us.' "

"Now, be subtle, Val. If Bertingas and his army of renegades were to attack the Haiken Maru, on any pretext, it would give you a grievance you could ride all the way to Central Center. You would have justification for any action you wanted to take in—and against—Aurora Cluster."

Elidor grunted.

"Do I interpret that as a murmur of gratitude?"

"Interpret it how you like. But let me assure you: if this blows up in my face, I'll have you peeled back, layer at a time, until we come to a bloody pip. Then I'll squeeze that pip between my fingers 'till you *pop!*"

The hush of the fans wound down, and Praise could feel the aircar slide in for a landing, somewhere. He tossed off his drink before leaving. Mentally, he was scrambling for a last word, to take the sting out of the Trader General's threat.

"Oh, be *subtle*, Elidor!"

Chapter 19

Taddeuz Bertingas: STRIKE FORCE

The inside of a dragon was more crowded than Bertingas had imagined. Armored ductwork for the fans squeezed the control space fore and aft.

"Why do they put such heavy plating around the *inside* rim of the fans?" he had asked the Capuchin who was ground chief for the vehicle and flew as gunner and number-one fixit. "I wouldn't think you'd take many hits from that shallow an angle."

The Capuchin raised its eyebrows—a Human gesture which distorted its facial markings into the parody of a sad clown. Tad had quickly learned this expression was one of disdain.

"None at all. But you take *one* heavy bead, at any angle, through the fan and it will shed some blades. At 35,000 revs they will travel the length of the ship without slowing down. *You* need the armor, unless you want to wear holes."

The sides and overheads of the space were squeezed with equipment, control panels, gauges, lights, and screens—for navigation, defensive ranging and detection, offensive ranging and targeting, turbine read-outs, generator read-outs, control surface indicators, plasma-beam focusing and firing, and communications.

As soon as they climbed aboard, Mora had found a flip-down seat and settled into it. She pulled her knees up and hugged them, making herself small. Aside from Tad and the ground chief, the crew consisted of two other Capuchins and a goggled Cernian pilot. For any one of them to move, two others had to slide out of the way.

The only clear headroom was the throat of the turret. It was choked with the target chamber of the plasma gun, which was the size of a prize-winning pumpkin.

"I've never seen one of those up close before," Tad said. They had a long ride before them, nothing to listen to—yet—but the drone of the fans, and too much to think about—if he let himself. So he intended to ask questions.

"Not much to see, Counselor."

"Can you tell me how it works?"

Again that sad-clown stare.

"Crude device, really. Pre-Pact technology by a thousand years or more . . . Back here is the laser ignition system." One small paw, with a wrinkled, black-skinned finger that looked almost Human, pointed to a cylinder that stuck out of the rear of the spherical target chamber.

"It's a carbon-dioxide pulse laser. Puts out about 200 watts in the infrared. Very tight beam. Very hot. These here"—the Capuchin pointed to a series of six graduated pipes that angled off from the working end of the laser, came forward, and angled into the chamber—"are the mirror splitters and the beamguides. And these jackets here, here, and here are photoflash amplifiers. They pump the beam up to about four megawatts on its way to the target."

"What's the target made of?" Tad asked.

Crouched on her seat, Mora smiled and rolled her eyes at him.

The Capuchin reached up, flipped open the lid on an injector that looked like a toothpick dispenser. Out came a steel whisker.

"The chamber is hollow." The alien tapped it. It rang. "The exact center is where those six beams all come to focus. Now, this whisker has a glass bead at one end. Can you see it?"

Bertingas stared. He saw something that might have been a bubble of spit. Maybe it was just a reflection off the steel. He nodded.

"The bead is filled with a mixture of deuterium and tritium. Both isotopes of hydrogen. Get the right mix and it'll fire every time. That bead isn't glued on too tight. This mechanism"—the Capuchin tapped the injector—"flexes the steel and snaps it in synch with the laser pulse. That shoots the bead—actually a whole string of beads—into the chamber, right into the focus as the pulsed beams arrive there. . . . Then what happens, Counselor?"

"With four megawatts coming down on it, the bead goes *poof!*"

"Right, but it's more complicated than that. The glass shell has two sides: an outside and an inside. As the bead vaporizes, the outside goes flying away to anywhere—but we don't care about that. It's the inside surface we need. That side has nowhere to fly to except more inner, you see?"

"Sure."

"That creates pressure. Now, we already have heat from the laser beam. Together, heat and pressure set up a perfect reason for those hydrogen isotopes to fuse into helium."

"There can't be much hydrogen in that tiny pellet."

"Don't need much to get the fusion bang we need. Okay. What's a hydrogen bomb? Just an expanding wave front of plasma, moving fast—"

"And the pressure," Tad picked up, "pushes it out the firing tube at the front end, right?"

"Wrong, Counselor. Not unless you want to burn hell out of the inside surfaces of the chamber—and get just a drip of cold plasma out of the firing tube for your trouble. You have to control the wave front from the start. That's what these bulges are for."

The Capuchin ran a hand down the polar ridges that gave the target chamber its pumpkin shape.

"What are they?" Bertingas asked.

"Electromagnets. They create a magnetic bottle inside the chamber. Its envelope both contains the plasma and pressurizes it. An opening in the field conducts the superheated fluid out the tube and toward the objective."

"What about radiant heat—the infrared? That chamber must be pretty heavily insulated and cooled, eh?"

"It still gets pretty hot in here." The Capuchin shrugged. "Hot enough to crinkle fur."

"I see. Uh—thank you for the explanation."

"Oh, that's not all. I've added an improvement or two of my own to this gun."

"Such as?"

"See these rings on the firing tube?"

"More magnets?"

"In a way. Those are the stators of a magnetohydrodynamic generator. They pick up a charge as the plasma leaves the gun. I've fed the current back into the power supplies for the laser ignition, the bead injector, and the magnetic bottle. At peak firing rates, this gun is almost self-powered."

"A perpetual motion machine?"

The Capuchin grimaced. "Until you run out of deuterium beads."

"Of course."

Bertingas clapped a hand on the alien's shoulder—a

gesture from which the little Capuchin shrank. Then Tad turned to the Cernian pilot.

"You don't have to draw me out with your questions, Counselor," the pilot said. He sounded cold, but beneath the dark goggles of his race, he was smiling. "We're on course for Batavia. Over the inland sea now. The deepest part. Which isn't too deep for any deep-water sailor."

"Where are the boats?"

"They're already on station. Playing at their cover. They even have nets out."

"They still have their guns under wraps, I hope."

"They'd better. At four klicks, they're inside electronic surveillance range by the island."

"With surprise, maybe they can knock out the dome generator . . . ?"

"Not unless they level the island. Those spinners are buried deep."

"I guess so."

"But you're right, sir. . . . Once the refractor dome goes up, then we're outside, they're inside, and the war's over. So, what's our plan for dealing with the dome?"

"Maybe we can get them to drop it."

"How—by asking nicely?"

Bertingas smiled and changed the subject. "How's our wing holding up?"

The Cernian—whose name was Turkhana Maas, but no relation to Choora—tuned his ranging screens and studied the pattern of transducer blips. Tad watched over his shoulder.

Two hundred air vehicles, some paid for but most stolen, spread out in a shallow vee behind them. The brightest blips were the hardened fliers in the line: armed dragons like their command car, armored personnel carriers, a few ship's boats with ablative shielding. Weaker images showed where the lines were reinforced with transports, cargo trucks, commercial carriers. All were loaded to the slats, Bertingas knew, with the Department's security troops. Each body sagged under the weight of assault gear—repulsors, bolt guns, static chargers, concussion and fragging grenades, comm sets, flares, ropes, pitons, picks, and hammers. Seventy-eight hundred fighting personnel, freshly trained and eager. Soon the sergeants and psychers would pass among them, recalling signal examples of offense and insult, chanting the names of those who were dead and maimed under the *Zergliedern* system, whipping up the troops' enthusiasm for the coming attack on the Haiken Maru.

"Those old buses you dealt for are barely holding formation," Maas said. "And in another ten minutes they'll be switching to reserve tanks. If they're going to land ground troops, we'd better get them over something you can walk on. Soon. Our wing isn't going to be attacking the causeway, is it?"

"No, that's Follard's objective."

"Thought not. Then I'd say we're going to have a couple of loads of our effectives *swimming* for Batavia."

"Can we do midair refueling?"

"On a modified city bus? You're kidding, Counselor. Somebody should have worked all this out before we lifted off."

"There wasn't time to think of everything," Bertingas said smoothly.

"There never is, especially when its *our* lives at stake."

Tad held his silence at this jibe. He exchanged a look with Mora. She shook her head.

After a pause, Tad said, "Could we have some Freevid?"

The pilot jerked in surprise. "Unh—which channel?"

"Any one will do."

The timing was impeccable. As the holoscreen

settled its long-distance static, they could make out the ornate, four-color seal of the Governor of Aurora Cluster. A deep male voice was saying, ". . . for an important message from Her Excellency Deirdre Sallee."

Very formal. Subdued crisis atmosphere. A nice touch.

The screen dissolved into the face of Her Excellency, lined with cares and wrinkled with concern. It was a face that Bertingas was sure Madame Sallee had never—either intentionally or by mischance— shown to a pickup lens. He mentally gave Gina a gold star in electronic make-up.

"My fellow citizens and subjects of the Pact," the image began, with just the right note of sadness.

"It is my solemn duty, and one I fulfill with deepest regret, to report to you an instance of intolerable transgression among one whom we all had believed to show loyalty to the Pact. Evidence has been placed before me that one of our—formerly—most respected trading organizations, the Haiken Maru, has aided, armed, and supported elements currently in rebellion against Pact authority. The receiver of this support, the officially deposed Governor of Arachne, Aaron Spile, has used it in a vicious and unprovoked attack, with heavy casualties, on a loyal Central Fleet base in our Cluster."

Bertingas glanced around the dragon's control space. Mora was staring with open-mouthed wonder.

"The Governor would *never* acknowledge—!" she began.

Tad smiled and shushed her.

"This was, for the Haiken Maru," the screen went on, "no simple mistake of trade policy. *Caveat emptor* does not apply. This was a calculated act of vile treason beyond any explanation or justification. Valence Elidor and his fellow traders have made a cunning choice, to support a rebel and a renegade, in defiance of established order."

The image of Deirdre Sallee took a breath. A long pause.

"As your Governor, I must make *my* choices. As of this date, this hour, the Haiken Maru are disbanded. Their offices and emporia are closed; their inventories, assets, and records confiscated; their contracts with any and all parties abrogated. I take this action under the authority invested in me by the High Secretary, both the late Stephen VI and his futurely elected successor.

"At this moment, loyal units of the Kona Tatsu and our own Cluster Command, as well as remnants of Central Fleet—"

"Remnants!" Mora hooted.

"—are effecting this order. If you, as citizen or subject, have honest dealings with the Haiken Maru and experience an inconvenience under this civil action, I urge you not to attempt interference. Opportunities will be made available at a later date to obtain redress."

"Whatever that means," the Cernian pilot muttered.

"As of this date, this hour," the screen said, "I am electronically publishing a warrant for the arrest and detention of Valence Elidor, Wynan Corfu, Abraham Wile, Pers Glomig, and John Does 1 through 250 who may be proven to be Haiken Maru agents and administrators."

"Thank you, Gina," Bertingas said aloud. "Now my ass is officially in a felony."

Mora giggled.

"The miscreant Aaron Spile will be dealt with under military action at the appropriate time and place. . . . It is my wish, as your Governor, that the current civil actions may be completed in a timely fashion and without undue disruption of honest Pact business."

"Whatever that means!" Mora, the pilot, and Tad all chorused.

"I thank you for your continued support," the Governor's image finished and faded.

Bertingas reached over to the communications panel and turned off the receiver.

"That's our go signal," he said to the pilot. "Proceed to full speed." He keyed to the operations frequency for his own wing of the expedition: "Blue corps, pick it up, follow on me." Then to the command network: "Red Leader, Green Leader, go and go."

"Roger that, Blue," Halan Follard replied. "Tell Gina that was a beautiful piece of work. The Governor won't be able to withdraw or deny her position now."

"We hope . . ."

"Four minutes to the boats," Patty Firkin cut through.

"Do we have a dome yet?" Follard.

"Not this side—whoops! Just went up. Tuned to full black."

Bertingas glanced into the miniature strat tank that was tucked in between the pilot's station and the comm panel. It was tuned to accept coded and scrambled sitreps from the sensor equipment on Follard's and Firkin's lead ships and collate them with data from Bertingas's position in the attack. The tank, which a moment earlier had shown a tiny holo image of the sawtoothed island, now held only a mute, black hemisphere. It was fringed with Batavia's outlying defenses and the shallow green sea beyond her docks. It looked like a huge tumor exposed on a surgical field of green cloth.

"I see it," Tad said.

Mora craned over from her sideline seat.

The first wave of their assault—troop carriers, old

trucks, and city buses—slid onto the fringes of the island. Armed and eager aliens from Bertingas's scratch security force poured out and infested the quays, docks, and empty warehouses outside the dome.

The plasma batteries of Batavia's external defenses tried to depress far enough to take out these insignificant attackers. Yet the guns had been sized and aligned to ward off approaches from the sky by cruisers and destroyers, at least. Low-flying aircars and ground troops moved beneath their swivels with impunity. The one or two gun captains who tried to fire on the attackers only vaporized seawater a hundred meters beyond the docks.

Within ten minutes, the officers leading the assault reported the enemy's outlying guns captured. Beyond that, however, they faced the deep black curtain of the dome.

The "fishing boats" opened up with their plasma beams. One, two, three lines of sputtering white fire arced up to touch the dome. Without effect. After a minute or so, the rocking, pitching vessels were able to bring their beams together into a single spot. That spot began to turn gray, then milky, then almost transparent. Then the ships' fire drifted slightly. The spot dissolved. The dome's face turned black again. One by one, the attackers' impromptu navy ceased fire.

"End of game," Mora said quietly.

"Not quite," Bertingas replied easily.

"What do you mean? Those things are impassable. Missiles, ballistics, and ships moving at any speed just get deflected. You can pump plasma into one all day, and it only feeds the generators, makes the shield stronger."

Bertingas smiled at her. To the network, he said, "Did you two crack the formula for that virus?"

"Virus?" Firkin's deep voice rumbled, surprised.

"Never thought of it that way. More like a dose of poison—"

"Whatever," Follard responded. "To answer your question, Tad, yes. Once we got hard data on the field strength. My forward tactical eldef is releasing the drone now."

"Can they see it?"

"They literally won't know what hit them."

"Roger that. We will observe from this side."

"What—?" Mora began, but Tad just smiled and pointed into the tank.

One the far side of the dome, a small missile darted forward from a lumbering aircar in Follard's van. Kona Tatsu technicians had loaded the ship down with electronic defense gear and this one strange weapon. The tiny missile approached the blank, depthless curve of the shield and exploded about 300 scale meters short.

Mora groaned, but Tad just smiled harder.

As interpreted by the strat tank, the detritus of the missile showed up as a thousand tiny stars, bright points of light drifting forward against the dome. Tad knew, from the theory explained by Follard and Firkin in one of their late-night sessions, that the reality was much less impressive: the stars were microscopic metal filings, shreds of a ruthenium-nickel-ferrous compound that had no place in nature.

Each scrap of metal was a cultured magnetic monopole.

When the sprinklings entered the outer layers of the dome, its computer controls began their mindless routine. The resident AID divided and reversed the electromagnetic field to rend any body within it. As the field reversed itself, each monopole reversed it again, locally. The computer re-reversed the field. The monopole reversed it. And reversed it. And reversed it.

While Tad and Mora watched, the smooth black curve mottled with a thousand tiny dimples and bumps, like abrasions on a black curve of glass. Each dimple snapped out into a bump, each bump sucked in to become a dimple, back and forth, in and out, until a quadrant of the dome began to glow with yellow incandescence. The local interference spots began to grow larger and merge together into one uncontrollable spot that flexed in and out. When the surface of the dome finally tore, it was like a weather balloon coming apart. The rent split the dome halfway to its zenith and spread like a white grin over a blackened face.

"Overload!" Firkin crowed.

"Well done!" from Follard.

"How soon until they can reconstitute the dome?" Mora asked Tad, shaking her head.

"Not until they go in and pull our rogue filings off the propagating antennae," Bertingas told her. "One by one. With tweezers." Over the net, he said: "Suggest we begin making evasive. They've still got firepower."

"Roger, Blue Leader."

"Tell the boats to open up again."

"Relayed."

In the strat tank, the exposed surface of Batavia was notched and ridged with more gun turrets, landing pads, and ship cradles. As his dragon jinked side to side along a descending curve, Bertingas swept the island's image with one eye and counted at least forty war vessels in various stages of construction. From what he could see, about half looked able to move, at least suborbitally. He compared the strategic holo with the screens reporting from his own ship's slit cameras. The latter added details of real life: non-military vehicles moving on the causeway, inert cargo hulls lying in the water alongside the island's quays, swarms of Human technicians and their alien servitors working on the warships in cradle.

A lancing flash of ionized gas from one of the fishing boats cut across this scene. One of the towers in the center of the strat tank sagged and fell.

Two more lines of plasma came from the attackers' boats, doing more damage to Batavia's superstructure.

Then a dozen surgical beams cut out from high points on the island, criss-crossing the patch of water where the boats rode.

A cough from inside the control space caught Bertingas's attention. The Capuchin was seated at the control horns of their dragon's own plasma gun, eyes screwed into the targeting cups. The alien coughed again, loudly.

"Fire at will," Bertingas ordered.

The pumpkin sphere made a muffled *whump, Whump! WHUMP!!*

The forward cameras of the dragon went white with light overload, and the vehicle's forward motion slowed with the reaction from the blasts.

"Gold and Silver Teams move forward," Tad ordered on the command net. The ground assault would begin, building by building and cradle by cradle, until either his attackers or the Haiken Maru's defenders ran out of troops and firepower.

From the center of the island, two warships rose slowly. They began firing streams of plasma in among the warehouses where Bertingas's attackers were concentrated. When one of the fishing boats tried to return a ship-killing plasma stream, the warships' own e-mag screens dropped around them like black eggshells. Then they pulsed open again to shoot down among the island's outer structures.

The Capuchin swiveled and fired on the nearer of the low-flying ships. That seemed to arouse it. Its return fire lanced straight at them. The Cernian pilot put the dragon into a barely controlled tumble around the stream of liquid star matter. Bertingas heard a grainy, fizzy crackling from the port side of the ship.

"Ablative shielding," the Cernian said. "From where the stream brushed us."

"Don't do that again," Tad said, to no one in particular.

"I won't!" both gunner and pilot answered at once.

"Gotcha!" Mora crowed.

Tad turned toward the strat tank in time to see one of the warships, its shield coming down a fraction of a second too late after a salvo, take a square hit amidships from one of their boats. White fire splashed on its hull; the metal flashed from red to white to blue incandescence, but it held its shape. After the plasma stream had dissipated, they could see the glow on the ship's side fade.

"Damn! Nothing," Tad cursed.

"Watch," the Capuchin told him.

Stressed by the uneven heating and cooling, the bruised hullmetal crystallized. In a few seconds, it blew out like a weakened embolism on an artery wall. Ship's partitions, fuel, and a spew of jetsam came with it. The warship sank back on the island's crown and exploded in a greasy ball of flame.

Everyone aboard the dragon cheered.

One ship down, but three more had risen into the airspace above Batavia. Their plasma batteries were more than holding their own against the second, third, and fourth waves of attack.

For the next ten minutes, the tank was a random pattern of gas streams, pantomimed troop movements, and colored markers dilating and contracting around the island's perimeter.

"Can you break this stalemate?" Mora asked.

Tad checked the chrono on the bulkhead. "Not for another three minutes."

"What happens then?"

The command network answered for him, with Halan Follard's voice. "Skyfall's come early!"

Within the tank, the random pattern of plasma shots stabilized in an unusual pattern: *down* from above, out of the upper range of the tank's reports. A *lot* of beams were coming down. The armed merchant ships drifting over the island were starting to direct their beams upward, firing longer, exposing their delicate skins more to the stabbing beams.

"What is *that*?" Mora asked.

"Friend of yours," Tad replied. "Code name Skyfall."

Chapter 20

Terrel Thwaite: SUMO MOVES

Thwaite was in real trouble.

The Planetary Monitor *Charlotten Broch* was falling through the thin upper atmosphere of Palaccio much too fast. Something had gone wrong in the computer systems as they had retro'ed to put her in a lower orbit. Instead of a ten-point-two-second burst on the secondary thrusters, meant to nudge the huge ship into a deep suborbital skim over Batavia, the circuitry had gone haywire. The main reaction drives had burned for a perilous thirty-one-and-a-somethingth seconds. Full braking.

He was re-entering a ship that had never been meant to touch down on a planet's surface. One whose internal bracing was designed to withstand the stresses of reaction and battle maneuvering—but never to support their own weight against the pull of gravity. They had two minutes and forty seconds to impact.

The plan had been so simple.

Terrel Thwaite had gone aboard as part of the joint "defensive preparations" with Cluster Command. His personal gig was still attached to the 270-Degree docking port—and would probably shear off its moorings when this wild ride was over. Thwaite had been on the bridge when a message had come over the command circuits for the monitor's own commissioned captain, Colonel Bernoit. It was an operations message directly from "the Governor."

"Colonel, we have an emergency situation here." Pause.

"Yes, ma'am?"

"A commando team under my orders is at this time invading the Haiken Maru stronghold at Batavia. They should be coming up on your horizon in 140 minutes." Pause.

"Indeed so, Your Excel—?"

"Good. I want you to turn over tactical command of your ship to Captain Thwaite, whom I understand is aboard. He has personal experience with the maneuver I have in mind. Captain . . .?" Pause.

"Yes, Madam Governor?" Thwaite responded.

"At the Battle of Niosh, you commanded a monitor similar to this, did you not?"

"I—"

"Over a light-metal world such as Palaccio? And you brought your vessel into a technical re-entry without actually landing?" Pause.

"Yes."

A further pause. The Governor looked just past Thwaite. "I want you to effect the same maneuver, starting immediately, to bring the ship at perigee over Batavia. Your orders are to eliminate any large, spaceworthy vessels that may be defending the island while you avoid damaging any atmospheric craft—no matter what their posture and distribution. Can you do that?" Pause.

"Yes, I believe we can."

"Very good. I am granting you acting command of the—um—*Broch* for the duration of the maneuver.

Good shooting, Captain." The Governor had given a regal nod of the head, almost a salute, and the transmission had ended.

If it was a forgery, as Bertingas had claimed he could arrange, then it was a damn good one. Peremptory tone. Air of contained excitement in crisis. Short pauses for inconsequential answers. Masterful. If it was, indeed, a forgery . . .

Then Thwaite's career was at an end. Now he wasn't merely trading word puzzles with old Dindyma. Thwaite had, as an officer of Center Fleet, taken command of a Sister Service vessel under fraudulent conditions. Of course he could claim, with Colonel Bernoit, that he had believed the Governor's transmission, but too many witnesses were still alive— Bertingas himself, Mora Koskiusko, Halan Follard, Colonel Firkin, surely others, too—who would know that he knew the transmission was a fiction.

Even if they all held steady beside him and told the same story, this gaffe with the main thrusters would end his career for him—if not his life.

"Put the e-mag screens up to full power," he ordered the Defense Section.

"Going a little deep, aren't we?" Bernoit drawled.

"We are."

"You might want to consider—just as a thought—" the Colonel said sarcastically, "swinging the ship, putting the main thrusters back on, and getting us *back up to orbit!*"

"I would, Colonel, except that precious pile of sticks and sliding beads you call a computer system can't seem to get the ignition circuits reset." He pointed to the condition read-outs, which were red, bright red, and had stayed red ever since that thirty-one-second burn had chopped off so raggedly.

"Well, you can't re-enter a Diplomat-class monitor."

"I know that! If you had a workable inverter in this bucket, we could punch out of this problem sideways, but you don't. So we're going down. At least, our defensive screens will absorb the worst of the heat and neutralize most of the atmospheric buffeting."

"It's neither the heat nor the buffeting I worry about, but the hole we're going to make when you finish this wild ride. A ship this size doesn't even have landing jacks."

"Right. You're going to lose a couple of lower decks, aren't you." Thwaite snarled. "I suggest you go and start placing your non-GQ personnel topside, get them under restraint and shock mounted. They'll live longer that way." He turned his attention to the rest of the bridge crew. "Plot! Give me an angle on that island."

"Eighty-eight degrees, Captain. We're right over them."

"Screens, release gun portals along the forward limb."

"Hull heating, sir!" the lieutenant at that station reminded him.

"So, *let* the hull heat up a bit. We still have a mission to perform.

"Guns. Select your targets on declination minus ninety. Nothing smaller than a G-class freighter, per the Governor's orders."

"Aye, sir. Three targets in range and closing rapidly."

"Fire at will."

The monitor's quad batteries opened up. Thwaite could feel a slight trembling beneath his boots, but whether it was the guns or the hull's first contact with the denser lower atmosphere, he could not tell.

"Targets returning fire, sir."

"Noted. Keep them busy. Plot. What's our, um, elevation?"

"Above the planet, sir?"

"Yes."

"Instruments show—twenty-eight kilometers, sir."

"Rate of descent?"

"Now at 548 meters per second, sir. Fifty-one seconds to planetfall."

"Fire secondary thrusters, if you can."

"Secondaries now firing."

Thwaite breathed out a quiet sigh. "Thank you, Kali," he muttered.

"Rate of descent slowing to—231 meters per second. Planetfall in 113 seconds now."

"Maintain thrusters. Guns. Widen your attack. Pick off hardened targets on the island itself: gun batteries, shield termini, communications. However, avoid the graving docks and power centers. Coordinate your targets with the computer's navigational profiles for that installation."

"Aye, sir."

"Sir!" from Guns. "One ship down."

"Excellent. Continue firing."

The *Broch* bored in, with no further change in her rate of descent, firing almost steadily on the island and its puny, inadequately shielded defenders. She destroyed two more warships in the air and an unconfirmed three on the ground. After a minute more, Colonel Bernoit reappeared on the bridge.

"Captain, may I suggest . . .?"

"Yes?"

"That we retire to the emergency control center and let the bridge personnel strap in?"

"Good idea. Which way?"

"Through here, into the core stack."

"Guns. Cease fire. Defense. Close the shield. Tune to maximum gauss and radius. Then evacuate this compartment. Well done, everyone."

"Come on!" Bernoit pulled at him.

The collision harnesses in the emergency center were old-style primitive: a steel cocoon lined with a body-shaped membrane to be pumped full of high-viscosity jelly at three atmospheres. A glazed rubber mask covered the face and provided a breathable mix, under pressure. Once the occupant was in place and squeezed, the cocoon rotated to put the body's longest axis at right angles to the impact. That spread the shock over the widest possible area, like a *judoka* flattening out in a fall.

"Will these things stand up to an impact at 800 kilometers per hour?" Thwaite asked, halfway into the can. He was holding the mask in one hand and probing the lower reaches of the interior membrane with his bootsoles.

"Better than my hull!" Bernoit snapped.

The hood slammed down on hydraulics. A great, gooey hand gripped him around the feet and fingers, wrists and ankles, thighs, groin, chest, neck, and shoulders. The hard edges of the mask pushed against his chin and forehead. It pumped cold air against his face.

Nothing . . .

Relax, he told himself.

Nothing . . .

Limp, like a rag doll, he made himself.

Nothing . . .

Thwaite's stomach suddenly fell against his backbone. His spine bent like a sapling in a high wind. His lungs collapsed under a surge of pressure. The face mask pressed against his eyeballs, igniting a dance of white fire.

Like pulling a boot out of deep, sticky mud, his body rebounded from the shock. Then a secondary pressure wave caught him and pushed him back. Once more he unbent. And that was it. The cool jelly was sucked away from the membrane about his body, and the hood slammed open on the pod.

They were in a noisy red darkness filled with drifting, acrid smoke. The loudest sound was the shriek of twisting metal, overlain with the screaming of sirens.

"Damage report!" That was Bernoit.

"Sir! Yes, sir!" A jumble of voices answered him, separated into individual reports by the communications computer. "Circuit paths below Deck 33 are nonfunctional. Southern hemispheric defense screens are down. All thruster engines report dynamic interruptions. Quad batteries from infra starboard to infra port are not responding. Medical reports fourteen deaths, thirty-six injuries—mostly from improperly activated harnesses. Hull breached in twenty-two separate places. Deck 31 reports . . . flooding . . . with water, sir. The *Charlotten Broch* is . . . sinking!"

Bernoit and Thwaite made their way out of the core against an unusual force—planetary gravity. They actually had to walk on the deck surfaces, and the ship wasn't even under spin. Those surfaces slanted at what, to Thwaite's newly adjusted inner ear, was about a thirty-degree angle. He could feel that angle steepen as the ship settled lower in the . . . water.

The bridge looked unchanged. Only the drifting smoke and a pattern of darkened control panels— where certain offensive and defensive systems, and the entire bank of reaction engines, had been damaged beyond response—showed that the ship was not in normal space. Crew members were filing in, staggering against the unaccustomed gravity, and finding their stations.

"What's the status on our—um—buoyancy?" Bernoit called.

"Where's the island?" Thwaite asked simultaneously.

"What difference does *that* make?" the Colonel demanded. "If this ship fills with water and sinks, we all drown."

"Where's the damned island?" Thwaite repeated.

"Bearing 160 degrees, sir," the Defense talker called. "Range 5,600 meters."

"If I correctly recall our charts of the objective," Captain Thwaite said, "the waters surrounding Batavia are relatively shallow. At this range, they are no more than thirty or forty meters deep. The *Broch* is 525 meters in diameter, is it not, Colonel? So your ship should—"

A mild shock came up to them through the deck plates.

"—be settling on the bottom about now." Thwaite turned to Guns. "Do we have any functional units on the northern hemisphere?"

"Ten batteries, sir. Six quads, four singles."

"Power for them?"

"All the power you need, sir."

"Then lock on the island. Same targets as before. Fire at will." He turned to Bernoit, who was slumped against the navigational station. "We still have our mission, Colonel."

Chapter 21

Taddeuz Bertingas: MOP-UP

Without thinking, Bertingas scrambled over to the dragon's top hatch and undogged it. Enough with the strat tank—he wanted to *see* what was happening. With the hatch open and a gale pouring over the forward coaming, Tad put his head out and craned his neck, searching the hard, blue sky overhead.

Directly above, he saw a glittery point of green-white light. It was sputtering like the fuse on a Birthday sparkler and slowly widening, or getting longer. He had a hard time telling the difference from his angle of view—right below it.

So far, there was no sound at all.

Something tapped his chest and he pushed back against the hatch coaming. Mora brought her head up alongside his face.

"What is that?" she asked, raising her voice above the wind and the noise of the dragon's fans.

"I think it's the Cluster Command's planetary monitor, *Charlotten Broch*," Bertingas shouted back.

"They're re-entering."

"Looks like it."

"They shouldn't do that."

"No, they're evidently in trouble."

"Are they going to hit us?"

The offside hatch slammed back, and the Capuchin gunner stuck its furry face through. Clearly, it had heard her question.

"Bah!" the gunner snorted. "If the trail of ionized gases is not completely foreshortened from your point of view, then you're several thousand meters from the impact point."

"Will it hit the island?" Bertingas asked.

The Capuchin squinted a gunner's eye at the falling warship. "No, southwest of us."

"Then the operation is safe."

"Everyone except our troops on Batavia."

"What? How so?"

"If that thing hits at sea—and it will—it's going to push a lot of water. A tidal wave. Right over the top of the island."

"Quick!" Bertingas started to duck back inside, became wedged in the hatch opening against Mora's chest. He got an arm out, placed his palm on the top of her head, and pushed her, gently but firmly, down into the ship. Then he ducked in and called to the pilot.

"Relay to the command network. 'All personnel on Batavia to seek shelter in—' " He returned to the Capuchin. "How long?"

It shrugged. "Three minutes? Make it two."

Back down to the pilot: " '—in ninety seconds. Expect tidal wave.' "

The Cernian nodded and repeated the order.

Tad looked back up at the glittering light. It had grown brighter and wider. He could begin to see a dark, curving limb inside the flare of incandescent gases.

"Will that thing damage us? Shock wave? Radiation?" he shouted to the Capuchin.

"No data." It shrugged.

Bertingas dropped inside the hull and pulled the hatch shut after him. A secondary *clang* told him the gunner had the same thought.

Tad and Mora braced against the comm panel.

A deep sound like ripped canvas—the frayed mainsail of an ancient clipper coming apart under a bellying wind—jarred their airship. The fans raced as air was sucked sideways across their ducts. The dragon lurched.

In all the turbulence off the *Broch*'s flightpath, they never heard the splash.

The gunner went over to the keyboard shelved beside the strat tank and began pecking in numbers.

"What are you doing?"

"Getting an estimate of wave damage."

"Good thinking."

Distance, water depth, the *Charlotten Broch*'s tonnage (guessed from her navigational offset masses), and her impact velocity (guessed from a reasonable estimate of her orbital speed and braking capability). The tank's AID came up with a wave twelve meters tall. It would damage the wharf area and drown out Batavia's peripheral batteries. If the assault teams had all gotten the message and found shelter, then the drenching would do more to disorient and dislodge the defenders than any trick Bertingas and company had tried so far.

He studied the effects in the tank. "As soon as the wave passes," he said to the pilot, "put us down on the spine of the island. Bring in the rest of the airbornes then, too. We go hand to hand."

Two minutes later, Bertingas's command dragon was grounded near the refit cradle bays. He took a repulsor rifle from the rack by the topside hatch and climbed out to join the operation's fire teams. Mora Koskiusko was somewhere behind him, also with a weapon.

By this time, any aliens who worked on Batavia had surrendered to the advancing army of their compeers. Left to fight were the Human executives of the Haiken Maru, fanatics without hope.

Tad and Mora slid off the dragon's forward airfoil and had just found their feet when the first shots bracketed them. One heavily weighted pellet blew a shallow crater in the syncrete beside Tad's heel, the other punched a ragged hole in the dragon's fiberglass outer skin four centimeters from Mora's left hip.

He pulled her down and under cover—at least visual cover—of the airfoil.

"How long can we stay here?" Mora asked.

"Well, until—"

"From the angles, those shots had to come from the cab of that crane at two o'clock," she said. "Give me a second ammo drum."

"I don't have a second—"

"Then give me the magazine from your weapon."

Tad popped the drum out of his rifle's breech.

"Now, when I step out," she said, "you climb back inside and get *four* cassettes of ammunition and *two* chargepacks. And another weapon. And a handful of those grenades I saw."

"What are you going to do?"

"Don't look. Just go."

With that, the woman he loved, or was starting to love, walked out into the line of fire, planted her feet wide, raised the rifle to her hip, and shot the entire drum into the crane cab. Tad could hear the *whap-whap-whap* of 15.5mm glass beads going supersonic. Followed by the *thud-thud-thud* as they punched holes in the rolled steel and plex of the cab.

"Get your ass in gear!" she snarled at him. Then she ejected the original drum and shoved in his.

More *whaps* as Tad climbed back over the airfoil and into the dragon. There was no return fire from the crane. He scooped up the armaments she'd ordered, told the Capuchin gunner—too late—to cover them, and ordered the Cernian to get back in the air twenty seconds after he left.

"Relay this order to all units," Tad said. " 'Preserve as many of the ships in cradle as possible.' We may need them."

The Cernian nodded and Tad climbed out through the hatch again.

Outside, Mora was standing in cleared space, turning slowly on one heel, her repulsor still riding high on one hip, its muzzle seeking new targets. She was magnificent.

Bertingas landed beside her, slung a belt of drum ammunition and a chargepack around her waist, stuffed grenades in her pockets, and went back to back with her, to cover half of their exposed area.

"Now what?" she asked.

"They're going to take the airship out of range, and we're going to find the—"

Tad's voice was drowned out by a hollow, splintering, crackling sound, like sheets of fiberglass and steel being crumpled and crushed at the bottom of a deep well. He instinctively turned his head toward the dragon, but it was unmoved and untouched. He looked up.

A lancet of purple-white light hung low in the sky.

Bertingas closed his eyes immediately. "Don't look!" he shouted to Mora.

The colors were so intense, he was sure his retinas were damaged. Maybe permanently. Maybe only temporarily. If he sensed any fading of the image in—say, fifteen seconds or so—then he would feel better.

As he waited for his eyes to clear, Bertingas studied the afterimage. The colors had overridden all other visual impressions. How wide the plasma stream had been, how far away, he had no way of knowing. Unprotected as he and Mora were below it, their lives might depend on being outside the critical five-meter diameter of the plasma's path through medium atmosphere.

"Are we dead?" Mora asked in a whisper.

The image across Tad's eyes was beginning to fade. He looked up and around.

"That stream must have come from the *Broch*," he said slowly. "Top batteries. Fairly elevated on the curve of her hull . . ."

"We're pretty high on the island," Mora observed.

"Right, but if we can find the target . . ."

"If it hit anything."

"So, what's changed on the skyline around us?"

"That tower over there." She pointed to the north, the right direction for anything that was on the receiving end of the plasma stream Tad had seen. "Wasn't it . . . taller? With some kind of antenna thing on top?"

Tad studied the tower. He vaguely remembered a horned antenna, a section of parabolic seen edge-on, atop it. The horns were still there to be seen, but lower, across a thicker part of the tower. Then what he was seeing came into focus. A perfectly circular bite had been taken out of the middle of the tower. Syncrete and structural steel had vaporized under the wavefront of plasma. Tad could detect no fallen wreckage, no hanging pieces. Clearly, as the top of the tower collapsed, it had sagged into the still-pumping plasma and had also been vaporized.

A sheathed stream of ionized helium, heated to one million degrees Celsius, would do that.

Yes, the cut in the tower looked to be at least ten meters up the side. Bertingas pointed this out to Mora.

"So we're safe, as long as the *Broch* keeps picking her targets carefully," she said. "You were saying something about where we were going . . .?"

"The docking control center."

"Why there?"

"I want to shut this whole area down."

"Oh."

"This way."

Tad led her across the hardpan and under the bows of a stubby merchant vessel—or perhaps it was some kind of reaction tug—that was missing half of its hull plates. The loss was the work of welding arcs and wrenches, not military action. As Tad and Mora went, no one shot at them, no one ran from them. For the middle of a pitched battle, it was strangely quiet.

They moved quickly along a high wall, part of the revetment separating the docking bay they were in from the next one over. As they neared the end of it, Tad heard footsteps—at first thinking they were an echo of his and Mora's—before anything else.

From the other side of the wall: running feet, the clatter of bootsoles on syncrete; then voices, high and whooping; then the click, snap, and ping of weapons brought to the ready.

Bertingas took out a sonic grenade, tore off the restraint tab, flicked the spoon, and hiked the pear-shaped canister high over the wall.

Two seconds later, even Tad and Mora were slightly stunned. The sound came in four parts: a bass element, like the kettledrums in a marching band; a treble, like crunching metal and breaking crystal; a sibilance, like steel cables sliding across each other; and a ringing like all the bells of creation. It came in four parts all jammed together into a single *blat* of noise that their bruised ears would take a minute or more to sort out.

Tad didn't wait for his head to clear but ran around the end of the wall and began firing, low at first and then raising his aim.

Four men, already reeling and holding their heads, danced with his beads until they flopped down. They wore the same green uniforms as the soldiers Bertingas had overcome at the hyperwave station after his long walk in the woods. He checked to make sure all were dead, and put a single mercy shot through the head of a man whose legs were gone into twitching tassels of blood, bone, and tendons.

Mora came up behind him.

"How did you know," she asked, "from the other side of the wall, that these weren't our own soldiers?"

"I—uh—didn't. Actually." Tad was embarrassed. "That's why I threw a sonic stunner, instead of a concussion or fragging grenade. But I guessed right."

"You're *dangerous!* Even in a war." Her voice showed exasperation and pride, mixed. "Now what?"

"Up that ladder over there."

"I'll go first—"

"What? Why?"

"You get off to the side and cover me. If we both go up at once, we're both helpless."

Bertingas nodded. He put himself in firing position against the smooth syncrete wall. Mora slung her weapon and began to climb. When she reached the top, a pair of hands came down and lifted her bodily, legs kicking, off the ladder.

Tad ran out and took aim, but Mora was gone.

He had no alternative but to climb up himself.

Bertingas went up cautiously, hand over hand, listening and peering upward. The hands came over the top at him. He shifted his rifle and took clumsy aim against his left forearm. Then a face followed the hands—the square face of Patty Firkin. Tad let his rifle slide loose on its strap.

"What are you doing up there?"

"What are you doing down there?" she answered. "All the action was topside."

"Not *all* of it."

"Yeah. Halan and I got to watch you at work. You're dangerous."

"That's what everyone says. . . . What's left to do?"

"We've pulled the plug on this area. That shut down all the doors and drop tubes. Now we have teams going from level to level taking surrenders—or making more permanent arrangements."

"So we've won."

"Looks like it."

"Where's Halan? For that matter, where's Mora?"

"I sent her up to the control center. Where he is."

"Which way?"

"Over here." Firkin started off, her boots ringing on the dense syncrete.

"What's the damages?"

"On which side?"

"Ours first."

"Of 15,000 troops landed," she said, "we have 7,000 responding to the roll and another 3,000 under medical care. On a closed field like this, an island, with its defense force fragmented and gone to the cellars, we have to presume the remainder of our effectives to be dead rather than deserted or captured."

"I see. That's bad."

The Colonel shrugged. "They won. First-time troops. Against a hardened objective. *How* they won is, ah, secondary."

"Go on. What's the condition of facilities here? Specifically, those merchant ships in cradle."

"Still evaluating. I sent a team of Capuchins in to scope out the equipment the H.M. were putting aboard. They're jerry-built, for sure, but they still did some damage in that battle at Gemini. Are you thinking what I'm thinking?"

"Find out how many of those ships are operable," Bertingas said. "And have the Capuchins work over these cradles. We'll see if Gemini's damaged destroyers—maybe their cruisers, too—can retrofit here."

"They can't."

"Why not?"

"Because Gemini Base is under blockade. Nothing moves. We got word of that ten minutes ago."

"Ouch!"

They had arrived at the glassed-in control center—now missing a lot of its windows. The equipment looked mostly undamaged, except for crystals of tempered glass scattered over everything like big diamonds.

Mora was there, with Follard. They both looked grim.

"Who is it that has Gemini?" Bertingas asked. "Spile?"

"Has to be," Mora answered.

"Then this was just a diversion. . . ."

"No, we've choked off one source of easy weapons," Follard said. "We've also broken the powers of his best ally, at least here in Aurora Cluster."

"Not to mention," Firkin began, "making a political breach that will—" She stopped when the traffic board lit up.

The young Capuchin that had taken it over and dusted off the glass fragments called out: "Incoming party of five airships. Transponder on one says it's the Governor. Others make noises like the Cluster Command. Do you want to believe them?"

Follard looked suddenly tired.

"Yeah. We'd better," he replied. Then, to Bertingas: "Now's the time to explain your little trick with the Freevid."

"If I can . . . It would help if we had someone important here, like Valence Elidor, this station's manager, or even the head of ship repairs—whoever's surrendered to us—to formally turn Batavia over to Governor Sallee."

Follard looked at Firkin. "See if you can find someone with gold braid and a contrite look. Meet us on the field. And—um—explain to this person, carefully, that if he—or she—begins to lodge a protest with the Governor, he won't outlive the interview. Make it convincing."

"Sure, Boss." The square-set woman went off.

"Still going to be your party, Tad," Halan said.

Bertingas nodded.

"Then let's go down."

The traffic board brought the Governor's line of aircraft down on the open blastway to the north of the docking center. Upon debarkation, Deirdre Sallee was surrounded—and a military eye would have said shielded, too—by ranking uniforms of the Cluster Command and the heads of department from throughout her government. The brains of Aurora Cluster, or at least the figureheads, were gathered in this one spot, vulnerable to a single concussion grenade. Bertingas looked quickly up and down the strip, at the blown-out windows and open doorways of hangars and outbuildings. One surviving Haiken Maru office boy with a repulsor could change history here.

As Halan, Tad, and their subordinates approached, one of the shielding group broke away and came toward them. Bertingas recognized the sleek head of Selwin Praise.

"You are under arrest!" Praise shouted. He turned to one of the Cluster Command brass. "Colonel, take that man prisoner!"

The officer, whose attention had been on the Governor and what she was saying, looked over in surprise.

Praise advanced on the assault team.

"You've precipitated an unprecedented attack on a sovereign conglomerate, Bertingas. And why? Why? If any of the Haiken Maru's ships *had* been used in the raid on Gemini, it was under a lawful sale of merchandise to the Arachnids. Not a military act, certainly. But you've given them cause now. When they are through dealing with the Central Fleet base, those ships will come here, to Palaccio and reduce it to slag. There's not a hope in Hell that Governor

Spile will ignore this cluster now. He'll wipe us up with the bloody rags of Gemini Base. Unless we throw ourselves immediately on his mercy. You've reduced our options to that and that only. You've given us noth—are you listening to me, sirra?"

Bertingas shook his head.

"Isn't that for the Governor to decide?" he asked quietly. "We've given her back the Cluster, or at least the military advantage in this part of it. If she wants to hang me for that, then she will. If she wants to turn me over to Aaron Spile and his Haiken Maru henchmen as a peace offering, then that's her prerogative, too."

Bertingas tried to walk around the man.

"You can't evade your responsibility for this," Praise shouted. Tad suddenly understood that he was speaking a set piece, for other ears.

"Oh, yes!" the D. of C. declaimed. "We know it was you. We took your accomplice, the alien Rinaldi. She admitted to creating that utterly false and treasonable transmission at your direction. It put Her Excellency the Governor in a terrible position. We have Rinaldi's working notes, also in your handwriting. There's proof that—"

"You must not blame Gina," Bertingas said wearily. "She was working totally under my orders. Simply a technician. You cannot prove she even knew what she was preparing, or why."

"Very brave of you," Praise sneered. "Very gallant. And very much after the fact."

"What—?"

"The creature barricaded herself against our lawful arrest procedures and then, in captivity, resisted our questions. I'm pleased to say she did not survive her injuries."

"You killed her."

"She did it to herself." Smugly.

Under other circumstances, in his earlier life, Tad

would have collapsed under this onslaught. A tongue-lashing from his direct superior would have brought tears to his eyes. The news of a colleague—a friend—done to death in a cell, beaten, drugged, dying to protect Bertingas himself, once would have driven him nearly insane with remorse. Now he was a different person. He had been abandoned naked in the woods, been hunted and shot at, and had killed men of his own volition, with his own hands. Now he just looked at the grinning face of Selwin Praise.

He could push it in.

The butt of his rifle would move so fast—up from the hip, across his body, into bone and cartilage, and then back again to parade rest. One flicking motion that even Halan Follard, who was standing right next to Bertingas, couldn't be sure he'd seen. Tad would then call for corpsmen, the roving Satyrs with white circles and red crosses on their jackets who had come in with the fire teams. He would tell them the D.ofC. had suffered "a stroke"—which was the perfect truth. They would link Praise's hands across his stomach and lug his body, perhaps still twitching, perhaps limp, away by the shoulders and heels.

But wouldn't there be repercussions? Praise might not die from the blow. He would certainly use it to expand his complaints against Bertingas. The blow itself might be construed as proof of Tad's guilt in the conspiracy with Gina. (What the hell! He *was* guilty.) The blow might be used as a pretext for holding him in irons, in a cell, under torture—at a time when the Governor, Halan, Patty, all of them, needed him. Hovering in the back of Bertingas's mind were the breathless words "You're dangerous!"

So his rifle remained at his side.

Selwin Praise kept looking at him with that triumphant grin. Tad shook his head and walked around the man at last. At that moment, the group of men and women around the Governor broke and came toward the party from the docking center.

"My dear Follard!" Deirdre Sallee said, taking the lead and extending her hand to the Inspector General. Halan took the hand and kissed it. "And Counselor Bertingas! Still alive!"

"Yes, ma'am." He took her hand and copied Follard's courtesy.

"Despite the worst they can throw at you," the Governor said, "you seem to float over it all."

"Yes, ma'am."

Bertingas could feel Praise gathering himself, rounding on this knot of dignitaries, ready to renew his charges and call loudly for Tad's arrest.

"This latest misunderstanding is a perfect case in point," Sallee went on. "Why, I was actually furious with you. Furious I say! To think that you had contrived to falsify the formal address which precipitated this action on Batavia. I was on the point of ordering your arrest and immediate execution—would you believe? But then I called in my science advisor, Doctor Craxi, to see if there might be some other explanation, other than treasonously criminal actions by one of our most loyal counselors. That is when he explained to me the temporal nature of the Hyperwave Network. I'm sure I don't have to explain it to a technical expert like you—I'm not sure I fully understand it myself, even now—how a message in the network can sometimes travel through time as well as through space. . . ."

Bertingas was on the point of demurring, of explaining that, while everything she said was true, the falsified address had been broadcast on Freevid, not Hyperwave. He kept his mouth shut a moment too long.

"Dr. Craxi explained to me that, because the attack here took place in conformance with the message, it was proof that message came from a—a 'rogue temporal wave' was how he put it. Sometime in the future, or in an alternate now, I *did* make that address to the people of Aurora Cluster. And you, Halan Follard, and your brave crew, acting independently—if a trifle prematurely—fulfilled the commission I had set—or will have set. So the circle is not broken. Time, as the doctor says, has healed itself."

Two or three of her courtiers, standing on the edge of the crowd, raised a small applause. The Governor beamed and nodded in their direction.

It was all nonsense, of course. "Rogue temporal waves" and "alternate nows" did not work that way. They could not precipitate actions in some offstream past that blended with the present. Bertingas knew this. He suspected that Deirdre Sallee and Dr. Craxi knew it, too. However, the Governor's nonsensical story would become the official version. It would also save Bertingas's skin.

Even if it was too late to save Gina's.

"Some people," and here the Governor glanced significantly at Selwin Praise, who fumed on the other edge of the group, "have said that this action 'limits our options.' That now we will come under the Arachnid hammer and must beg for mercy. Ladies and gentlemen"—her voice rose dramatically— "Aurora shall not submit. We shall stand loyal to the Pact, as we always have. Our best course of action, now, is to make sure there are no 'bloody rags' at Gemini with which to begin an invasion here."

Deirdre Sallee turned to Mora and laid a consoling hand on her forearm.

"My dear, we shall turn this base to our own uses. We shall launch these ships"—the hand went up to sweep across the rows of converted merchantmen in cradle—"captured here in brave battle, to assist your father."

"I'll find the crews for them, Deirdre," snapped

Amelia Ceil, the matriarch of Greengallow Holding, "if I have to strip the land to do it."

"Very well said. I thank you. General Dindyma?" The Governor's eye sought out her Cluster Commander, another of the dignitaries in her party.

"Yes, ma'am?"

"Will you contact your planetary monitor, *Charlotten Broch*, and determine her status?"

"Ma'am, I already have," said Patty Firkin, who had come to them from across the landing strip. "Captain Thwaite and Colonel Bernoit report her grounded in shoal waters little more than five klicks from here. The hull is breached, but reparable. Most of her gun batteries and missiles are operable. Her reaction drives are largely undamaged . . . but of course they will never lift her to space. Not from a planetary surface."

"She could lift," Follard put in, "if her defective mass inverter were made operable. Just punch her into deep space and then use the drives to accelerate into whatever orbit you need."

"Do you suppose," Dindyma asked, "that this facility has the resources . . .?"

"I begin to suspect," Firkin said, "what the Haiken Maru have created here is a complete forward base for Governor Spile. Inverter technology would be a standard—"

"Gentlemen," the Governor interrupted. "And Colonel," with a nod to Patty Firkin. "The *Broch* will be my flagship in this venture. I will leave you to work out the details—after you give me a tour of inspection of this facility."

"Of course, ma'am," they chorused.

"And then we shall take a council of war."

Chapter 22

Hildred Samwels: GADFLY PATROL

The grid of diamond pinpricks around Gemini Base had become as familiar to Hilred Samwels as the pattern of constellations that shaped the night sky around Kali system. The pinpricks, sunlight reflecting off the hulls of blockading ships, seemed to regulate and tame those unnamed star clusters. They threw a measuring square across the glowing gas tube that spanned Castor and Pollux. Gemini Base had acquired, by an act of war, its own celestial sphere, with latitude and longitude, azimuth and declination to any point in the sky.

Samwels let his attention wander from the Captains' Council long enough to glance out the room's undamped port and make this comparison.

Where the base had been able, once, to fight off an englobement by an Arachnid advance force backed with Haiken Maru and Bovari auxiliaries, it was now stalemated in blockade. And these blockading ships were no cut-and-fit merchant hulls made over into sometime warriors. This was the full battle fleet of the Arachnid Cluster Command, supported by units captured from at least four other clusters. More than three hundred ships patrolled in delicately intersecting orbits around the focus of Gemini Base.

"They won't be drawn, Admiral," said Niorn, one of the destroyer captains. He and Captain Sudelich had taken their ships out on gadfly patrol, testing the defenses and willingness of the Arachnid fleet.

It had been a dangerous maneuver, when the entire base complement included only six destroyers and three cruisers capable of navigating hyperspace and eight more destroyers that could only move and fight in realspace.

"We engaged at two adjacent points, a coordinated attack," Sudelich elaborated, "but it never rose above ship-to-ship dueling. The others wouldn't break their formation to fight us. When those we had attacked began to drift off station, they withdrew and moved to fill the grid. I'd say they were extremely disciplined."

"Is that all it is?" Koskiusko asked.

"All, sir?"

"Could they be conserving missiles? Or fuel?" the Admiral demanded.

"They might, sir." Sudelich frowned. "However, with five clusters to resupply ship's stores, and all of Kali system open to bring them in, I'd say conservation was their last priority."

"What do they want?" Koskiusko asked, more to himself than to his assembled captains. "They could have mobbed us five days ago. One rush and the base would have been open to them, or destroyed. But no. . . . They form their corps de ballet and keep station. What are they waiting for?"

"Perhaps they are afraid of our guns, sir?" That from Carnot.

"Go on," the Admiral growled.

"I've run an analysis on that fleet. Ninety percent destroyers, a couple of cruisers, one fighter mothership that may be their flag carrier. No planetary monitors, nothing big."

"Monitors," someone down the table interrupted, "haven't been a factor in free-fight tactics for thirty years. Too slow. They're defense only."

"Exactly!" Carnot exclaimed. "What is a blockade like this, except defense? A monitor is the only single vessel that shoots with batteries big enough—and enough of them—to do us serious structural damage. Those ships out there are keeping out of the range of our plasma streams. That also gives them maneuvering room to dodge or destroy our missiles."

"Which *we* are conserving," the Admiral said.

"Of course, sir."

"That many ships, though," Koskiusko observed. "They could still englobe us, combine their firepower, and fight our batteries to a standstill. Why don't they do it? They would only lose. . . . How many, Captain Carnot?"

"Minimax—forty-two percent of engaged. Say 144 ships."

"Not a bad price for an Alpha Class free-orbiting base, is it?"

"Maybe, sir, it's a higher price than Spile is willing to pay," Samwels put in. "We have to be looking at most of his effectives right now. That's the fleet he has to take all the way to Central Center, plus what he can capture and convert on the march. He would be shy of losing almost half of it to subdue one base in one fairly out of the way cluster. Even an Alpha base, sir."

"Then, if we're as unimportant as you seem to think," the Admiral growled, "Spile could go around us."

"And leave the Central Fleet—at least as much of it as will remain loyal—a rallying point in his rear? You might take the risk, sir. I or any other military man in this room might. But Spile is a civilian in braid, sir. He's cautious. It has taken him a long time to plan this revolt. The death of the High Secretary was merely the trigger, and even that caught Spile by surprise, I'll wager. Spile is conservative. Doesn't know when to gamble on a decisive move, backed with confidence in his tactical skills."

"He's done pretty well, so far. Brought us to our knees."

"That was with overwhelming force in a surprise attack. One he must have mapped out and gamed a dozen times. Perhaps over years. See how, when it failed of complete success, he grew suddenly cautious. His whole advance has slowed down to this—containing Gemini Base. We have the man, immobilized, sir."

"Much good may it do us," one of the captains muttered.

"We can leave, but we can't take resupply or accept reinforcements," Koskiusko said aloud.

He was stating the obvious. The radius of the blockading sphere, which averaged 500 kilometers, was too narrow for any ship to jump into. The standard of navigational accuracy in any hyperdimensional maneuver was to achieve the arrival point within five G-solar diameters. Anything closer than that was pure luck.

Halan Follard's little jump with his headquarters building—whose fame had already reached Gemini—sent cold shivers down the spine of any experienced shiphandler. The Inspector General had been as likely to orbit his pile of bricks anywhere on the near side of Palaccio's primary as he was to drop it elsewhere on the planet. The luck of fools had held for him.

Any of the Gemini ships could jump *out* of the Arachnid's web of ships, of course. Anytime. To return to the base, however, or to bring in reinforcements, they would have to fight their way back through the blockade.

Central Fleet HQ had been informed of their predicament and had promised a relief action—soon. As soon as the Fleet's "other engagements and commissions" were fulfilled. An open-ended commitment the brass might feel free to extend into the next century.

"Captain Worley," the Admiral began, "what's our sustain time?"

The new provost captain cleared his throat.

"With our missile fabrication shops working three shifts, we will have exhausted our parts stores within the next ninety-six hours. That will leave our batteries—uhh—" He called up some calculations subvocally from his AID. "Just under 2,100 units to fire. Our stores of deut-trit pellets for the plasma batteries are adequate for—3,600 combined salvos. Or something over 15,500 independently targeted shots. We can stretch that almost indefinitely if we divert deuterium and tritium from the base fusion generators and attempt to fabricate our own pellets. But we'd be using nonstandard techniques, and I can't vouch that the product will implode accurately enough to fuse."

"Humph!" from the Admiral. "What about the fusion plants themselves?"

"Forty days, sir, at nominal load. Less if we continue to maintain general quarters around the clock, with all systems at peak."

"How much less?"

"Eight days, sir."

"Eight days less or eight days total?"

"Total, sir . . . As to food, water, and breathable," Worley went on, "we have exceeded our 120 days' supply. Still, that's no problem. Early on, we brought the waste recyclers up to full production. We're living almost exclusively off our own, er, byproducts."

"There goes my lunch!" one of the captains whispered.

"Going? Or coming?" someone else sniggered.

"We can survive this way indefinitely, of course," Worley plowed on against the hecklers.

"No, we can't," from down the table.

Admiral Koskiusko rapped for order and glared around at his captains. "Gentlemen, this is serious business."

"Breathables *are* a concern, Admiral," Worley said "because of the hits we've been taking from those sapper raids. Every meter-plus-wide breach in the outer skin—allowing for the harassment and lost time the repair crews experience—evacuates, on average, 200 cubic meters of gas at one atmosphere's pressure. Negligible in itself, against the enclosed volume of this base. If the raids continue at their current frequency, however, we'll have to either lower the system pressure or begin closing off decks."

"You're maintaining your postings?"

"A full squad of Marines, suited sans helmets, at every second lock. The minute we sight a skimmer, they seal up and lock through. But too many of the raids are blindsiding us."

"How is that possible, in an englobement?" Koskiusko turned to Samwels.

"The skimmers are invisible to our radar, Admiral," he said. "Plastic frames and one-shot reaction tanks. These are suicide squads, sir. Armed only with satchel charges and repulsors. Once they land on the hull, all they can do is fight—or valve to vacuum."

"They might try surrendering."

"Not if they think we're too stripped to accept prisoners, sir."

"Spile must be able to command their absolute loyalty," Koskiusko mused.

"Or threaten something they fear worse than death," Samwels replied.

"Hmmm." The Admiral paused in thought. "So,

Provost Captain, what's the summation? The maximum on your minimum profile, please."

"Six days, sir. Based on current weapons usage."

"Captain Carnot?"

"Sir?"

"If we took three days' worth of fuel to the base generators and fused it all at once, what would the blast radius be?"

"I presume you mean with effects that might disable a medium-sized warship? Say, a destroyer or a cruiser?"

"Yes."

"Calculating . . . Six hundred klicks. With a shockwave overpressure of seven standard atmospheres at a mean temperature of 5,000 Celsius. Not counting fragmentation effects from this structure. Is that acceptable, sir?"

"Captain Samwels, you will rig detonator charges around Numbers 2 and 3 reserve tanks. Set to trigger on my command."

"Yes, sir." Samwels nodded grimly.

A rustle of shifting bodies and suppressed comment moved around the table.

"Ahh, sir?" Hildred ventured. "What about the base complement? You don't intend a suicide—?"

"Of course not, Captain!" the Admiral snapped. "We'll load all personnel aboard the remaining hypercapable destroyers and cruisers. They'll have strapdown space, won't they?"

The assembled captains did some quick mental calculations and agreed.

"Right. Then, thirty seconds before detonation, we jump straight from the docking bay to the far side of Castor and Pollux. Don't tip our hand to anybody. And after the base is—gone—we come back and pick off as many of the survivors as we can. Acceptable, gentlemen?"

Most of the group nodded or murmured assent. Not Samwels.

"Is that the best we can do, sir? Blow the base and hope to rupture—how many, Carnot? A dozen? Twenty of Spile's ships?"

"More than that, certainly," the captain said.

"All right, but not all of them. Not even most of them. We'll fight the remainder until we begin losing badly. Then we'll withdraw, for the sake of the civilians aboard our own crowded ships. You know we will."

"Come now, Hildred," the Admiral said softly. "It's an honorable—a barely honorable—defense."

"But it leaves nothing—nothing!—behind Spile. No Pact-loyal forces that he need fear. Governor Spider'll be free to drive straight on to Central Center and the High Secretariat."

"Given the circumstances," Koskiusko said. "It's all we have left to us."

Chapter 23

Taddeuz Bertingas: DROP KICK

His null moment passed, like the blankness after a sneeze. Bertingas rose into consciousness with a violent sideways twist. The light webbing of the jump couch tightened along his right side, then slapped his left hip and elbow into the steel subframe. His head snapped over and cracked against his own shoulder. Tingles of pain ran down his arm. His neck muscles screamed. He thought he could feel blood run out of his ear.

The air on the *Charlotten Broch*'s operations deck pulsed red. It hooted and warbled with three different kinds of alarms.

"What happened?" he asked aloud. Was it Follard to his left, or Thwaite? Was Mora all right?

"Collision! Several of them." Thwaite answered him, speaking low. He clearly was able to read the ship's warning and alert systems.

"How could that happen? We're in free space, aren't we? We didn't—*did we clear Gemini?*"

"Pipe down, Tad," the Captain growled. "Neither

one of us can do anything from here. Let the bridge crew handle it."

Bertingas freed his right arm and felt his ear. It was hot but dry—and would probably swell up like a blooming rose. Sensation was coming back along his left side.

"Well, *that* was exciting." The voice was Deirdre Sallee's, cutting across the questions, calls, alarms, and groans in the red darkness. "Would someone turn off those braying sirens, please? And start giving me some reports."

The compartment went silent.

"Ah—bridge here, Your Excellency," General Pollonius Dindyma answered over the intercom. He clearly was unused to deferring, from his own bridge, to a higher authority aboard. "We seem to have jumped to a point that was, um, previously occupied by two, possibly three, inert bodies."

"You mean asteroids, General? Or gas clouds?"

"No, ma'am. Ships."

"Not our own!"

"No, of course not. They apparently were holding in some kind of orbital pattern, Your Excellency. We deduce they were part of the force blockading Gemini Base."

"What is their current disposition?"

"Beg pardon?"

"What happened to them? What happened to us?"

"We seem to have sustained no structural damage at all. The enemy ships have . . . Well, with the difference in our masses being so great, the *Broch*'s sudden displacement seems to have rolled them into their own Schwartschild traps."

"In plain language?"

"We've sent them through hyperspace. An unprepared and unlogged jump. They may not return."

"Thank you, General. Where are we in relation to the base?"

"Coming up in your navigational tanks now, Your Excellency."

By this time, everyone on the ops deck had unstrapped and was standing. They were covertly exploring pulled muscles and bruises.

Half the government of Aurora Cluster seemed to have shipped aboard the flagship. Regis Sallee, the Governor's consort, was there—taking up space for no reason Bertingas could perceive. Selwin Praise was there—officially keeping watch on his hot-headed deputy. And Bertingas himself was there at Halan Follard's polite suggestion to the Governor.

Mora came to stand beside him. Her hand quietly found his. They joined the general drift of the crowd forward to the ten-meter holocube that showed the *Broch* and her surrounding space for a distance of a thousand kilometers.

Hanging at half that distance, scaled like a melon to the planetary monitor's grape, was the Central Fleet base. Around it, and intersecting the *Broch*'s current position, was the Arachnid's globular formation of ships. Sketched into the distant perspective, below everything, were the bulk of Castor and Pollux.

"How extraordinary," Bertingas said to Mora. "We broke the blockade in a single move. On the first jump."

The plan, as Dindyma and Thwaite had outlined it at the Governor's council of war, had been to use the planetary monitor as a psychological battering ram. (To use it as a *physical* ram they had thought would be beyond the realm of statistical probability—or good fortune.)

Their plan had called for the huge ship to pop into the space near Gemini, creating confusion in the Arachnid formation with their sudden bulk and firepower. Under cover of that confusion, they would cut close to the base and, in the monitor's field shadow, resupply whatever Gemini needed from the *Broch*'s huge stores and take off the civilians and wounded. Then they would get distance and pop out.

They could repeat this maneuver any number of times, until the siege broke. Meanwhile, the remainder of the Cluster Command's squadron, supported by the hulls captured at Batavia, would harass the Arachnids from behind the lines.

Unfortunately, the unexpected collisions had thrown off the timing of this first run by several minutes.

"Move!" Thwaite called out. "Start the run on Gemini!"

"Captain!" the Governor exclaimed, shocked. Then, to the bridge: "General, ignore that order. We must assess—"

"Too late," from Thwaite. "Here comes their countering stroke."

As everyone on the ops deck watched, a spherical wedge of the besieging formation dimpled and collapsed about the planetary monitor. It shaped a smaller englobement, identical to the one about Gemini. Except this one was closing, tightening, concentrating to increase the strike's firing density.

"General?" Sallee spoke to the air above her head. "Please send my greetings to Admiral Koskiusko, at twenty to one speed, and then raise the ship's screens to full intensity."

"Done, ma'am."

"Thank you. As we've already managed to eliminate three of Governor Spile's war fleet, I think we can forgo the formalities of a formal challenge and open fire at your convenience."

"Yes, Your Excellency."

Within the tank, the round body of the *Broch* sprouted lines of violet fire, plasma streams lashing out in thirty different directions to splash against the shields of their attackers. The blips of fifty missile launches arced outward. Some wound back and forth like snakes to evade physical and electronic counter measures. Some spiraled around and through the plasma lines. All sank home in a series of shattering fusion explosions.

At such close range, less than twenty kilometers, the separate blasts merged into a white glare. The *Broch* disappeared beneath it.

When the radiation effects faded, the local englobement was shown to be breached in three places. Still, missiles and gouts of plasma were already streaking in from the Arachnid survivors.

"Jump!" Deirdre Sallee commanded.

Dindyma must have prepared for just that order. He jumped without the usual ten-minute warning horns, and without the delay of bagging equipment and strapping down personnel. He jumped standing up.

Bertingas could actually see the image of the *Broch*, deep within the tank, begin to shrink. Before the simulation could collapse entirely, reality caught up with the AID controlling the tank—and with Tad's brain function.

Reality sneezed.

As he came out of the null, Tad found himself still standing, but his balance was off, one knee slipping sideways. Instinctively he clutched the railing around the navigational cube and hung on. As did everyone else.

In front of their eyes, the tank was filled again. Not with stars or ships, but with a random pattern of colored light, like candy sprinkles on a field of white ice cream.

As the AID struggled to regain its mechanical senses, the first image to appear was the most massive—the bulk of Gemini Base. Except now it was on the far left side of the tank, instead of the right. Dindyma had jumped clear across the formation. As the rest of the field came in, they could see that the *Broch* was inside the blockading globe of ships.

"Raise shields and—urk!" Governor Sallee's order was cut short.

Bertingas looked up, looked across the navigational tank to where Deirdre Sallee was standing.

It was comical. Selwin Praise was standing behind her in a clumsy embrace. His left arm was thrown around her gaunt midsection, just below the Governor's bony ribcage and superannuated breasts. The right hand was raised along the side of her face, in a stiff caress. What made it so funny was that Deirdre was a head taller than the D.ofC., so his arms were at strange angles.

The Governor was not struggling, not even protesting. Her eyes were wide with shock and fear.

Then Tad saw the glint of metal next to her left eye and understood why. Praise held a fingerknife pressed to her temple.

"All right!" Praise shouted, looking out around her shoulder. "I'm in charge now and . . ."

The side of his head went soft. It dimpled in, partly collapsed, and blossomed in blood. Praise's right hand twitched, leaving the barest scratch by the Governor's eye. His arms slipped, and he slumped to the deck.

An instant of awful silence passed into a welter of voices.

"Open fire! Fire at will!" from Thwaite, to the bridge crew.

"Get that blade! Analyze for poisons!" from Follard, to one of his aides.

"Teach him to touch my wife . . . in public," from Regis Sallee, to anyone at all, as he put a tiny coil gun back in his pocket. Bertingas recognized it as the kind of short-range self-defense weapon that fired exploding pellets.

"Close screens and jump!" again from Thwaite,

whose eyes had never left the strategic picture un-
folding in the tank.

The null moment caught them all in motion.

When the instant of disorientation passed, half the
personnel in the ops chamber were sitting, lying, or
sprawling on the deck. That mental sneeze had thrown
them all off balance.

All except the Governor, who was still standing—
tall and imperious—against the railing around the
tank. She touched the line of blood along her temple
and glanced at her fingertips. The she looked around
for Regis Sallee, who was also on his feet. When the
ship jumped, he'd had nowhere to go.

"Thank you, my dear," she said clearly, smiling.
"You always have my interests at heart, don't you?"

"You mean more to me than anyone will know,"
he replied, and returned the smile.

Deirdre Sallee's face turned serious and she stared
into the tank.

Up on the bridge, General Dindyma was clearly
following a pattern with his jumps. Against all the
vagaries of hyperspace navigation, he was trying to
quarter the blockade: first from east side to west,
now to the north pole of the englobement. Once
again, the Arachnid ships of the local quadrant were
collapsing around them.

"Screens up!" the Governor ordered. "Full power.
Rotate 120 degrees and fire main engines. Drive
through them to the base. Batteries, pick targets and
shoot at will."

Within the tank, the miniature, stylized *Broch*
spun on its own center of gravity and dove down
toward Gemini. The monitor blazed with missile
launches and plasma streams. Their course inter-
sected head-on with one of the blockaders, a small
frigate.

At the moment of simulated impact, Bertingas felt
a shudder go through the fabric of the ship. The

huge *Broch* was barely affected by the collision. The frigate, even with her e-mag screens at peak power, could not survive. Fractured keelsons and beams, ruptured hull plates, bashed equipment, and broken bones would take their toll. The tank showed a drifting oblong whose screens, coded green in the strat key, quickly faded to black.

As the *Broch* bulled her way through the blockade, Gemini opened up with its own defenses: long-range nuclear missiles, flare jammers, sun dogs, and the most powerful plasma weapons in the Pact arsenal. The surge of the *Broch* and response from the base pulled in the Arachnids. Their orderly englobement fell apart in a swirling, dodging fight as they tried to intercept the planetary monitor. Confusion deepened as the rest of the Auroran fleet—the fully capable warships of Aurora's Cluster Command and the converted hulls from Batavia—dropped into realspace outside the globe and attacked the Arachnids' rear.

As Tad and the rest of the Governor's party watched in the tank, the fight rippled back and forth. Knots of color—the green of e-mag screens, the purple of spouting plasma, the red and gold of missiles, the white of overload when a ship occasionally flared into vapor—blazed against the black of intrasystem space.

Two, three and four warships came together in duels and dogfights. Up on the bridge, Dindyma's nav and tac teams flew and fought the *Broch*. Sallee and Thwaite told him where and when. But as the pace of battle intensified, and the lights of clashing duels spread like a stain across the failed englobement, the strategists on the ops deck had less and less to say.

It was every ship for itself in the melee.

"Move in on the base," Deirdre Sallee called. "Get the lower docks ready to pass them some containers. See what they need."

"Aye, ma'am."

Like a fat lady at the ballet, the *Broch* slipped and dodged through fight and dropped into the shadow of Gemini. When she was within one ship's diameter of the huge base—a distance that was geometrically shielded from attack—Dindyma dilated the screens on her lower quadrant. The Gemini defense techs opened a matching space. Handlers down at the ship's receiving tubes strapped brainless thrusters onto prepared cargo containers and kicked them toward the Gemini's wide-open docking bay.

What was in the containers?

Bertingas could guess: ordnance, flasks of deuterium and tritium, highly compressed breathable gases, packets of protein and fiber that only a sailor would eat, blocks of silicon and the tailored bacteria to work it into cybers, prefab missile components. The most difficult substance to send them—and the one they would probably need most—was water. It was virtually incompressible at the temperatures and pressures any available container materials could withstand. And it was heavy. The handlers had orders to kick over two or three megaliter bladders of water, but that was barely a drop for a full Central Fleet installation.

In return, Gemini offloaded her civilian personnel. They came drifting over, in issue suits, moving heel to helmet along spider lines rigged by the handlers. Forty-seven people came aboard on that first pass.

When the exchange was completed, the *Broch* raised her screens and spun away.

Immediately she was in two short-range duels, one spawned on either side of her bulk. Like a master swordsman, Dindyma fought off both attackers at once and still kept moving along the line he wanted to follow. His ship edged out, to the extremities of the battlespace, ready to jump for a neutral star system.

Tad watched the parallel fights unfold: cut and thrust with streams of fire, double and treble the screen layers to repel counter blows, sneak in a fast missile when the battle AIDs thought they detected a soft spot in one of the opponents' defenses.

The portside duel suddenly flared up, and it seemed the Arachnid frigate there was expending everything: hose-piping her plasma and spewing missiles in a single reckless display. The *Broch* had to redouble her screens, which almost closed off her own offensive fire. That side of the hull warmed slightly under the glare of splashed fire and thermonuclear detonations held harmlessly at bay by the fields of the e-mag screen. Of course, no mere frigate could do much to damage a planetary monitor—even if she hurled herself bodily into the *Broch*'s electromagnetic barrier and then fused her engines.

In the tank, the monitor looked like a fuddled badger beset by a maddened rat. Not retreating, but hunkered down and waiting for the fury of tiny teeth and claws to end.

It did. As if cut with a knife, the barrage ended. The last missile, fired at perilously close range, wobbled off course and exploded a hundred kilometers to galactic north.

Then the frigate dropped her screens.

With a swiftness beyond human calculation, *Broch*'s battle AIDs conferred and fired. One fusion flare and the frigate's hullmetal vaporized. Armored plating, titanium substructure, bulkheads, and engine hulks, all went to gas in a nanosecond.

"Relay that!" Thwaite shouted.

Somewhere on the bridge a hand closed over a relay and dropped the AIDs into an electronic catatonia.

What Thwaite had seen, what Bertingas in his concentration had missed, was the strange stillness all across the battlespace. Half the ships had gone dead, hung nose down, unscreened, unpowered. The destroyer on the *Broch*'s starboard side floated at the same odd angle.

The navigational tank showed only a flare here and there as the Auroran forces, or the batteries of Gemini, picked off a belated target. Most of their captains had paused, undecided. Their own screens were still bright, of course, and their AIDs cried out to take on the helpless targets. Yet still the Aurorans, outnumbered as they were in this fight, withheld their fire.

"What has happened?" the Governor demanded.

"They've stopped fighting," Thwaite replied.

"I can see that. Why?"

No one had an answer. The crowd around the tank murmured, but no one spoke up—until Halan Follard did.

"It was just a rumor . . ." he began, almost to himself.

"What is that?" from Deirdre Sallee.

"Something from the training camps . . . Colonel Firkin?" Follard called to the bridge. Patty had taken her place there, with the other Cluster Command officers. Even if she was not of their corps, it was her station.

"Yes, Halan?"

"Do you remember the messages you brought me? From the Upland's training base? About—"

"About an alien alliance? Yes, of course, but you dismissed it. You said no 'brotherhood' could arise among—what did you call it?—'siloxane and hemoglobin, stewed in misery.' You waxed very poetic about it, Halan."

"So I did. But look out there."

"I'm looking. I was right, wasn't I?"

"You were, Lass," he agreed.

"Would somebody, please," Governor Sallee interrupted, "tell me what you two are reminiscing about?"

"When we were training the alien troops who fought at Batavia," Follard said, "Colonel Firkin discovered evidence of an alien organization, encompassing many species. It was underground, of course, but did not seem to be structured toward the usual fitfully hopeless rebellion."

"I should hope not!" the Governor exclaimed.

"They *were* rebels," he went on. "Out there, aboard the ships from Arachne—as aboard our own—are aliens of every sort. Despite their intense xenophobia, the Arachnids and their Haiken Maru colleagues know they need the aliens as wipers, sparehands, flashmaskers, fetchits, and playmates. The Humans who pilot and command the ships dismiss these aliens as menials. So they are: the aliens do every sort of low and dirty task. They also go everywhere, see everything, touch everything, know how everything—"

"Works. Yes, Kona Tatsu. And we have made our decision."

The voice came from against the back wall of the operations compartment. It was a low voice, wheezy, but with carrying power. The screen of Human bodies on that side of the room parted and the owner of the voice came toward the tank.

It was a Dorpin, turtle creature from a high-gee world. Bits of human waste—a scrap of paper and a twig butt—clung to the side of its beaky nose. They had obviously stuck there as the Dorpin went about its assigned task, which would be cleaner and maintenance tech. As if removing a disguise, one heavily clawed and padded paw reached up and brushed off the scraps.

"You are—?" Governor Sallee asked, with some embarrassment.

"My shipboard name is Squeezebox, Your Excellency. For obvious reasons. My proper name is Rashid

. . . Eighth Elder Rathid, of the Star Shorn Clan. Before I came into Pact space, I was planetary regent for nineteen systems. That was over four hundred of your years ago, of course, but I believe we can still deal as equals—my dear."

"How do I address you?"

"In your own language? 'Lord Rathid' will be sufficient."

"What Follard says about an alliance—it's true?"

"Most certainly. In fact, I had wondered how anything so big, and known to so many, could fail to become general knowledge. Then I came here and understood. Humans have a reflexive view of the universe. They are dream tellers. They see—their minds make them see—only what they want to. Or what they need to. Mostly what they see is themselves. You have a fraction of your population which exercises this talent so strongly that even you are made aware of it. You call them schizophrenics, and say they have a disease. I think, personally, they are merely your most developed specimens. . . .

"But I ramble. The answer to your question is 'yes.' "

"What does this alliance intend?" Here the Governor waved a hand at the navigational tank, where the battle still hung suspended.

The Dorpin waddled forward and lifted briefly on its hind legs to look down into the tank. To Tad, the movement looked painful.

Lord Rathid dropped down and seemed to consider.

"To cure you?" the alien asked tentatively. "That's a long-range goal. It will require millennia, I think. In the meantime, we have many opportunities. Too many."

"But what about that fleet?" Sallee asked, an edge of hysteria creeping into her normally cool tones.

"Oh, that. Blink of an eyelid. We couldn't very well let the schizophrenic among you, that man Aaron

Spile, come close to his private dreams of power. That would set the patient back . . . centuries."

"So you are supporting Aurora?"

"No."

"Then you are, after all, loyal to the Pact?"

"Not especially."

"Then what . . . ?"

"My dear, we—those among us entrusted with making decisions—are loyal to a conviction. That you Humans, with your nascent creative talents, can be brought to a larger, well, what some of you used to call 'world view.' Think of it as 'galactic view' now, because worlds are so insular.

"Not all of us share this conviction to an equal degree. Some of our members are innately hostile to you. The Deoorti, who might almost be your brothers, must overcome incredible inhibitions even to associate with you. The Ghibli, on the other hand, whom you despise and fear for their appearance, are very hopeful for you."

"And the Dorpins?" Follard asked, softly.

"Dorpins don't project. Or not more than once in a long lifetime. We observe, but don't judge . . . Now you should pay attention to that wonderful gizmo there." Lord Rathid poked his beak at the navigational tank. "Because we are at the end of even the most optimistic estimates."

"Estimates of what?" the Governor asked.

"Of the time our brigade could hold out on Spile's flagship. He has surrounded himself with some very dedicated men. Men who don't mind burning through doors and flesh of *any* composition to get what they want."

"Right now his intentions would be—?" from Follard.

"To leave this place," the Dorpin replied.

Bertingas looked into the tank quickly. One of the blips, bigger than any of the others, was supposedly the Arachnid flagship. It would be cruiser-size, the largest they had brought against Gemini. And where in the space of the tank was it? Tad searched the field rapidly; his eyes compared sizes, weighed anomalous movements. One blip, quite a large one, was swinging slowly around its own center of gravity. Its screens were still down—which meant, by the twisted physics of hyperspace navigation, that it could jump freely.

"There!" He pointed. "Quadrant—"

"Twenty-two, thirty-nine," Captain Thwaite sang out. "All ships, open fire. Salvo. Salvo!"

From two, three, four points adjacent to the cruiser the plasma streams sprang forth. Without a second's delay, the flagship's screens snapped up, giving the lie to her dead play. They smoothly doubled to absorb the incoming attacks, going deeper into the green.

"Keep them hot," Thwaite ordered. "Overload them if you can."

By chance, the point of battle was not beyond the reach of Gemini's batteries. The Central Fleet base added the power of its weaponry along one hemisphere. The flagship was wrapped in the white fire of continuous detonations.

"Even if the screens admit only radiation in the visible spectrum," Follard observed, "it must be getting pretty hot in there."

Thwaite grunted.

"You can fry them that way."

"I intend to."

Like an ear of corn popping in a field fire, the whitened oblong of the flagship began to shiver and shed pieces of itself. Each of the pieces flared to a cinder as it passed through the sphere of superheated plasma sheathing.

"What are those?" Sallee called out.

"Life pods, Your Excellency," the bridge crew

responded. "Unscreened, of course. We don't detect any—"

With a sudden rise in brightness, the warship disintegrated. The blast blew out the enveloping plasma in strands, like a tiny sun going nova. Beneath them, the blackened bones of her steel carcass—actually they would be incandescing at about 2,500 degrees Celsius—stood out.

From that carcass, one last tiny blip darted.

"There's controlled energy readable on that one," the bridge said. "Could just be the automatics, but—"

"Have it picked up, General," Deirdre Sallee ordered. "And if, as I suspect, it contains Governor Spile, I want you to extend to him every courtesy. Make him comfortable in this ship's brig under close personal supervision . . . of the Cernians."

That brought a smile to Follard's lips.

"What about the rest of the fleet, Your Excellency?"

"Have our captains begin taking surrenders. Negotiate where you have to, and *don't* blow up the stragglers. I want those ships intact. This isn't over yet."

Chapter 24

Patty Firkin: UNMASKING

"Forty hours left," Firkin said, retracting her probe from the nested globes of the e-mag antennae. "And that's just holding the field. If these 'trodes have to pass plasma, figure fifteen minutes. She'll fly, but she won't fight. . . . Call it, Tad."

Bertingas sighed, then appeared to make up his mind. "Transport duty. Leave an entry in the active log that the next captain should avoid hostilities if possible; withdraw from fire when necessary."

Firkin made notes. Even though, technically and administratively, a Colonel outranked a Director of Cluster Communications, she let him make the decisions. These ships were to be Aurora's responsibility, let their own representative say how to dispose of them.

"How many does that make?" she asked.

"Saved or shot?"

"Both."

"Fifty-two."

"Just a blur to me now."

For half a solar day, Patty Firkin had stared at

burned insulation and ravaged steel, locked into air-
less hulks, run dummy patterns on AIDs so hysteri-
cal that they tried to tell her about Jesus Xanthus,
tested screen antennas, bounced mass inverters, and
pounded hull plates with the flat of her hand. The
ships that had some life in them she and Bertingas,
working in concert with a dozen other survey teams,
had marked for repair and retrofit. Those that could
still hyperjump and checked out whole, they sent for
transport service—a role many of these hulls had
started in service with the Haiken Maru. Ships so
burned and blasted they could never be made tight
again, the pair wrote down for salvage. The hulls
would be mined for their silicon, titanium, and good
scrap steel. Then the exhausted ceramic shells would
be accelerated on one last, short, looping orbit into
the belly of Kali.

While Firkin and Bertingas processed the captured ships, Halan Follard, Hildred Samwels, and
Mora Koskiusko conducted the fastest prisoner of
war interrogation in Pact history. Follard knew tricks.
He could dope a roomful of squatting men, put just
three electrodes against each sleeping skull, and let a
top-secret AID of his read their blurry dreams. The
Inspector General claimed he could detect intentions, loyalties, even last Tuesday's Lotto pick, from
the mind murk that his electrodes flushed out.

Let him. Central Fleet would be in charge of the
prisoners, and if they got a few dedicated baddies in
among the honest souls Follard recommended for
amnesty, that was their lookout.

The sailors and officers he salvaged from the Arachnid and Haiken Maru fleets would mostly be career
soldiers who had simply followed whatever leader
fate—or the last High Secretary—had put in charge
of them. It was no crime for a good soldier to fight on
the wrong side. Firkin had done it herself a time or
two.

Those who flunked the Follard test would be considered untrustworthy in any regime: gangsters, tribe splitters, hate-filled specists, deviationists, and would-be dictators-in-waiting. Like Aaron Spile. What ultimately would become of them, even Follard would not say. Better not to ask. And Patty Firkin made a note to herself never, not even in a drunken moment of good fellowship, to pump Samwels or Koskiusko for what they had seen. The Kona Tatsu knew ways to make a body disappear, both logically and physically, in datafile and in corpore, that made the Colonel shiver.

All except Spile. He would be kept, like some bacillus in a sealed vial, to be exhibited before the Council of Electors. He was Deirdre Sallee's passport and pledge—which she would need after her failure to return the correct "signals of loyalty," per the Central Center directive she had once received.

Maybe Governor Sallee would even live to deliver Spile.

"Let's get back to the base," Bertingas said. "Neither one of us is likely to be thinking straight after twelve hours of this."

"All right."

They made their way, hand over hand, to the ship's lock. As they gathered up helmets and packjets, Bertingas muttered, "Maybe I'll get a chance to talk to her."

"Who?" Firkin asked.

"Mora."

"Don't. Not yet."

"Well, why not? Mora has a cool head, a sense of humor, and she's good looking to boot. Not to mention, she's full Human, too. For a while there, in the thick of things, Mora and I were practically—"

"Whatever you two were, you aren't now. She's been through a lot. Give her time to adjust."

"You saw how Samwels came up to her," Bertingas

said bitterly. "Like some kind of Central Fleet board-ing party. 'Ho, Mora, my love! You've returned to me! Never be parted from my side again!' Preening like a peacock. Strutting. Pulling her away from me like she was some kind of parcel."

"Yes, Tad. And I saw the look in her eyes as he did it."

"Moonstruck."

"Well, I don't—"

"Aww, what would you know about it?"

"And what is *that* supposed to mean?"

"After all, you're just a—"

"Say it, Tad. Whatever it is. 'Just a meat-brained soldier.' Or 'just a dickie-girl.' Why don't you open your mouth and spit it out." She balled up one square fist. "A few of your teeth would look real pretty floating through here."

"I could punch you out, too, you know."

"No, you couldn't. Not even on your best day as a backwoods boy."

Bertingas looked at her thoughtfully. "I don't sup-pose any Human ever could."

Firkin felt suddenly disoriented. She sagged, drift-ing sideways in the zero gee, and shut her eyes.

"I'm sorry, Patty . . ." He sounded distressed. "I keep forgetting how closely you must identify."

"How—how long have you known?"

"Known? Not until seven seconds ago. But sus-pected? Ever since I saw you in action that day in my apartment. Humans are tough. Even some of our women are tough. They're not tough enough to ride a dragon, on the outside, as it tips for the long slide.

"You're good at what you do, Patty. The make-up and microsurgery help a lot. But you have to learn to give in, flake out, loosen up once in a while. You're too perfect, all the time."

"It's part of our Hive training. Call it a guerrilla tactic for surviving in Human-dominated space."

"I'm sorry," he said, inadequately.

"Can you keep a secret?"

"You mean about—?"

"Yes."

"Only if you'll keep one for me."

"What is it?"

"That—whatever happens, whatever she chooses—I love, have loved, will love Mora Koskiusko until the day I die." He smiled at Firkin sadly, with the forlorn face of a man who was exiling himself to cold space.

"Done." She made a gesture of spitting on her suit glove and stuck it out to him.

Bertingas shook it.

Then, with their helmets sealed on, she punched the lock cycle.

"Don't worry about it," Patty said, after a long pause. "We may none of us live too long."

Outside, in the reflected light of Castor and Pollux, the captured ships moved in slow orbits around the minuscule mass—by planetary standards—of Gemini Base. Cutting her own orbit, at greater distance, was the Governor's flagship, the *Charlotten Broch.*

Firkin and Bertingas took a bearing and then kicked off for the base, thrusting to intercept one of the outside access ports as it came around on the limb of Gemini's metalled surface. They were halfway across to the port when the near space around them, the drifting, wheeling star pattern that swung with Gemini's orbit around the binary planet, suddenly changed.

The points of light flared, expanded, leapt inward. They became hulls locked into a perfect englobement. The strange ships' initial drop out of hyperspace, camouflaged against the stellar background, had probably fooled even Gemini's AID sentries. Twenty ships, and twenty more, and twenty more, they mobbed the Central Fleet base.

If Firkin had thought Spile's warships had executed an orderly englobement, it was for lack of comparison. These ships ordered their interlocking orbits like the wheels and gears in an old-fashioned chronograph. They rode in stately circles like the painted horses of a carousel. Sleek ships, undamaged by war.

"Let's get under cover," Patty said, grabbing Bertingas's forearm and thumping the emergency thrust on her packjet. Moving at seven meters per second, they hit the catchnet over the port. She could feel its cords part under the impact. They clawed their way out of it and cycled through the lock.

"—tingas, report to the Command Center," the all-call annunciator was saying. "By order of Her Excellency the Governor, Taddeuz Bertingas is to report to the—"

Bertingas punched in an acknowledgement and then headed for the drop tube. He was still in his pressure suit, with helmet fittings and packjet straps looped over his shoulders. Firkin followed close behind.

In the Command Center, functionally equivalent to the *Broch*'s operations deck, the brass were gathered: Deirdre Sallee and her consort, that funny man, Regis; Pollonius Dindyma and some of his own Cluster Command colonels; Halan Follard, standing aloof in his role as master of secrets; Admiral Johan Koskiusko, his daughter Mora, and a clutch of his captains, including the beaming Samwels.

Governor Sallee saw Bertingas coming in from the corridor and called out to him.

"Ah! There you are, Counselor. Not a moment too soon." She indicated a patch of floor beside her, facing the comm screen. She placed the Admiral on Tad's other side.

"It's one of your new functions, sir," Sallee explained formally to Bertingas, "to fend off diplomatic overtures to, and enter negotiations for, your Cluster and your Governor. . . . Hmm, you smell of sweat and vacuum. . . . Well, such as you are, you will please perform your function." With that she nodded to the tech at the comm link.

The screen fizzed white and then resolved into a square block of sunburned flesh, topped by a shock of close-cropped white hair. The face was pitted with deep and troubling eyes, cut by a mouth that was accustomed to command.

Bertingas moved forward into the comm focus, so that only his face would be clearly distinguishable to this man. As he did so, the face on the screen darkened. Its shaggy eyebrows came down, and the curve of the mouth deepened.

"I am Anson Merikur," the man said. "General and Acting Governor of Harmony Cluster. Do I have the . . . honor"—and what an ugly twist he put upon that word!—"of addressing Aaron Spile of Arachne Cluster?"

"You do not, General," Bertingas said sharply. "I am Aurora Director of Communications Taddeuz Bertingas.

"Governor Spile's overtures to this cluster have been received in the only manner that loyal citizens of the Pact could find appropriate." The new D.ofC. waited a beat, then raised his voice. "We have defended this base—and Aurora Cluster's loyalty—against the usurper. We have beaten the Spider to his knees and broken his fleet. If you now bring another fleet to his aid, you are too late, sir. We shall—"

Bertingas stopped when Governor Sallee approached and put a hand upon his shoulder. Her face would still be vaguely out of focus to the General.

On the screen, Merikur's rugged face was smiling.

"Counselor Bertingas, you should know," he said, and the voice was not unkind, "that my forces have invested Palaccio and other key planets in your cluster. Your remaining bureau chiefs have told me to find her Excellency here, at Gemini Base. If Deirdre Sallee is still alive, you'd better let me talk to her. . . . It's over now."

Sallee quietly moved Bertingas aside and stepped into the focus. "General?"

"Madam! Are you as loyal to the Pact as that brash fellow has indicated?"

"I am. All of my people are."

"That is well. Know you, then, that I am taking this fleet home, to Earth, to Central Center. There we will defend the claims of Roderick against *all* usurpers. Do you have ships that will jump with me—or may I offer you the hospitality of my own vessel?"

"We have ships, sir. We also take with us the allegiance—after a fashion—of the former Governor Spile and the Arachnids.

"General . . ." Sallee smiled. (Watching her in the monitor, Patty Firkin decided she did not ever want to cross this woman, Human or not.) "You will please disinvest my planets. At once."

"Of course, madam."

"And a parking orbit around this base is all that's necessary."

General Merikur's grin broadened. "It is done . . . Deirdre. Then, shall we arrange with your Protocol Master there, Counselor Bertingas, about docking, personal meetings, and so forth?"

As that final exchange was being made, Firkin noted Mora Koskiusko walking quietly forward, from Samwels's side to just behind Bertingas. Her hand crept into his and closed hard.

Governor Sallee—now confronted with the physical boarding of Gemini Base, the last outpost of Pact loyalty under her actual command—paused. She spun out of the comm focus and searched the faces of

Bertingas, the Admiral, the colonels, captains, and other ranks assembled behind her.

"Can I trust him?" the Governor asked in a low voice that carried only to the back of the room. "I mean, is it *really* over?"

Patty Firkin stepped forward.

"I can vouch for Anson Merikur, ma'am. I have served with the General, once a Central Fleet Commander, for more than twenty years. He's an admirable soldier. I would trust my life to his word. It was he that asked me to come here, to defend the Pact in Aurora Cluster."

Halan Follard also moved to the fore.

"Colonel Firkin's loyalty has been proven to you, ma'am. Where that of others has stood in doubt." Here the Kona Tatsu Inspector General's eyes slid fractionally to the left, toward the Governor's own husband.

"Thank you, Halan," Sallee said, making up her mind.

She turned toward the screen.

"Welcome aboard, Governor."

Have You Missed?

DRAKE, DAVID
At Any Price
Hammer's Slammers are back—and Baen Books has them!
Now the 23rd-century armored division faces its deadliest
enemies ever: aliens who *teleport* into combat.
55978-8 $3.50

DRAKE, DAVID
Hammer's Slammers
A special *expanded* edition of the book that began the
legend of Colonel Alois Hammer. Now the toughest, mean-
est mercs who ever killed for a dollar or wrecked a world
for pay have come home—to Baen Books—and they've
brought a secret weapon: "The Tank Lords," a brand-new
short novel, included in this special Baen edition of *Hammer's Slammers*.
65632-5 $3.50

DRAKE, DAVID
Lacey and His Friends
In Jed Lacey's time the United States computers scan
every citizen, every hour of the day. When crime is detected, it's Lacey's turn. There are a few things worse than
having him come after you, but they're not survivable
either. But things aren't really that bad—not for Lacey and
his friends. By the author of *Hammer's Slammers* and *At
Any Price*.
65593-0 $3.50

**CARD, ORSON SCOTT; DRAKE, DAVID;
& BUJOLD, LOIS MCMASTER**
(edited by Elizabeth Mitchell)
Free Lancers (Alien Stars, Vol. IV)
Three short novels about mercenary soldiers—never be-
fore in print! Card's hero leads a ragtag group of scientific
refugees to sanctuary in Utah; Drake contributes a new
"Hammer's Slammers" story; Bujold tells a new tale of
Miles Vorkosigan, hero of *The Warrior's Apprentice*.
65352-0 $2.95

DRAKE, DAVID
Birds of Prey

The time: 262 A.D. The place: Imperial Rome. There had never been a greater empire, but now it is dying. Everywhere its armies are in retreat, and what had been civilization seethes with riots and bizarre cults. Against the imminent fall of the Long Night stands Aulus Perennius, an Imperial secret agent as tough and ruthless as the age in which he lives. But he stands alone—until a traveller from Earth's far future recruits him for a mission so strange it cannot be disclosed.

55912-5 (trade paper) $7.95
55909-5 (hardcover) $14.95

DRAKE, DAVID
Ranks of Bronze

Disguised alien traders bought captured Roman soldiers on the slave market because they needed troops who could win battles without high-tech weaponry. The leigionaires provided victories, smashing barbarian armies with the swords, javelins, and discipline that had won a world. But the worlds on which they now fought were strange ones, and the spoils of victory did not include freedom. If the legionaires went home, it would be through the use of the beam weapons and force screens of their ruthless alien owners. It's been 2000 years—and now they want to go home.

65568-X $3.50

DRAKE, DAVID, & WAGNER, KARL EDWARD
Killer

Vonones and Lycon capture wild animals to sell for bloodsport in ancient Rome. A vicious animal sold to them by a trader turns out to be more than they bargained for—it is the sole survivor of the crash of an alien spacecraft. Possessed of intelligence nearly human, it has two goals in life: to breed and to kill.

55931-1 $2.95

DAVID DRAKE

"Drake has distinguished himself as the master of the mercenary sf novel."—Rave Reviews